PENGUIN BOOKS

Alecto Gray will Hunt you Down

Alecto Gray will Hunt you Down

LAURE EVE

PENGUIN BOOKS

PENGUIN BOOKS

UK | USA | Canada | Ireland | Australia
India | New Zealand | South Africa

Penguin Books is part of the Penguin Random House group of companies
whose addresses can be found at global.penguinrandomhouse.com

www.penguin.co.uk
www.puffin.co.uk
www.ladybird.co.uk

Penguin
Random House
UK

First published 2026

001

Text copyright © Laure Eve, 2026

The moral right of the author has been asserted

Excerpts on p. 3 are from 'Ac-Cent-Tchu-Ate the Positive'
written by Harold Arlen/Johnny Mercer,
© 1944, © Harwin Music Co.
Excerpts on p. 297 are from 'You Can't Always Get What You Want'
written by Mick Jagger and Keith Richards,
© 1969, © Abkco Music Inc.

The brands mentioned in this book are trademarks belonging to third parties

Set in 11.5/14.95pt Bembo Book MT Pro
Typeset by Six Red Marbles UK, Thetford, Norfolk
Printed and bound in Great Britain by Clays Ltd, Elcograf S.p.A.

The authorized representative in the EEA is Penguin Random House Ireland,
Morrison Chambers, 32 Nassau Street, Dublin D02 YH68

A CIP catalogue record for this book is available from the British Library

ISBN: 978-0-241-72292-3

All correspondence to:
Penguin Books
Penguin Random House Children's
One Embassy Gardens, 8 Viaduct Gardens, London SW11 7BW

MIX
Paper | Supporting
responsible forestry
FSC® C018179

Penguin Random House is committed to a
sustainable future for our business, our readers
and our planet. This book is made from Forest
Stewardship Council® certified paper.

To all the girls in the world who were ever deemed too loud, too difficult, too outspoken, too emotional, too weird, too dark, or too anything that ever made you stand out – this one's for you.

Contents

The Secret Lives of Dentists

Here's a great way to get people's attention: claim you're being stalked by a demon.

The claimant in question is one Justin Gorhammer (age: nineteen; known crimes: none) who despite the brutal surname has the look of a teenager whose future is in suburban dentistry and just hasn't realized it yet. I've only ever seen him in slacks, and he's the one who calls them 'slacks'. Poor guy never had a chance.

I read somewhere that suicide statistics among dentists are curiously high. Maybe they have some peculiar insight into the dark chaos of existence. Something about the effect of gazing into mouths all day long, all those wet, lumpen landscapes prompting a creeping realization that we're little more than meat and teeth. That's enough to send anyone careening over the edge.

Certainly, Justin seems to be cutting a determined path towards the less stable end of his future career because – to circle back to my earlier drop – Gorhammer Junior is apparently on intimate terms with the demonic forces of the world. However, since everyone knows demons don't exist, he's either lying or he's insane, right? And don't you immediately want to find out which one it is?

Well, you do if you're me.

The video starts innocuously enough. A sleepy-eyed and pale-skinned Justin lanks around a cluttered, rather sweetly primary-coloured bedroom. The camera is evidently set up next to his computer, because soon he sits down with his face in close-up, sporting a sleek headset that brings to mind adverts for call-centre jobs filled with suspiciously happy-looking workers, or a heyday Britney Spears.

There is much fiddling and clicking. Then Justin begins droning on in an exceptionally monotonous tone in some archaic dialect. For one excitable moment I assume he's speaking in tongues, before realizing he is in fact narrating the minutiae of playing an inscrutable video game to us, the viewer.

This is what Justin does as a side hustle to help pay off his college tuition debt – records himself playing video games and uploads unfathomable numbers of them to the internet, accruing ad revenue as he goes. My basic research suggests he makes a decent amount from this fabulously anal pastime, too, so frankly All the Points to his entrepreneurial spirit.

Have you ever watched a gamer walkthrough video? These things are *long* – they average out at around one lifetime/two hours per video – so I'm just about getting ready to nod off to Justin's meticulous, soporific stop-start descriptions of his avatar's every move when something changes.

It takes me a second to figure out what has alerted me, and then I have it – his breathing. I can hear it through the tiny microphone hovering around his chin, and it's gotten faster. Pantier.

His eyes cut off to the side, then they flick back to the game screen. Side, then back.

Slowly, haltingly, his voice trembling, Justin starts to sing.

'You gotta'

– pause –

'aaaa-ccent-u-ate the positive'

– pause –

'eeeee-lim-in-ate the negative'

– pause –

'latch on to the affirmative, don't mess with Mister In-Betweeeeen –'

He's singing the perky forties classic like he's learned it as a wellness ritual to ward off negative thinking. He's certainly no barbershop quartet hopeful, but it might be his voice is coming out that way because he's very, very scared. I can see it all over him. His eyes flicker side/back, side/back, and his face has that watery melt of someone close to tears.

With a sudden, violent fumble, his hands reach towards the screen, unhooking the camera from his computer. The view swims drunkenly as the camera gets turned around to point towards the far corner of his room.

'You see it, right?' I hear Justin whisper from behind the camera. 'You fucking *see* that? There's a demon in my bedroom, right? This can't be happening again. Oh god. Oh god. Oh no. Oh don't come closer, don't come –'

The camera tips and rolls and shudders as it is dropped to the floor. In the now-right-angled frame I can just see Justin dancing towards his wardrobe, shrieking incoherently. He opens up the door and pushes himself bodily inwards. The door half closes behind him.

From the wardrobe's depths comes a mindless, bone-chilling moaning.

It goes on for a minute or two more before it is interrupted by a knocking at his bedroom door and a muffled 'Justin? Justin? Is everything OK?'

'Mommy!' screeches the wardrobe. 'Mommy, help me please! Help! It's in here again! It's here – the demon's here.'

There is some more of this before the video cuts out.

'Again' is the word that really catches my attention. Evidently this was not a one-and-done. I wonder if some well-meaning mental health professional taught him that song.

I drag on the video's timer with my finger, back to the moment just before Justin turned the camera to the corner of his room to show us a demon. I play the video back over, then back over, again and again, hungrily searching each frame.

The corner of Justin's room is brightly lit by a standing lamp. No mistakable shadows. No stuffed toys that could conceivably turn menacing on a bad mushroom trip. There's just . . . nothing.

Oh, Justin.

This video is all over socials, sporting half a million views and the usual torrent of comments ranging from rubbernecking concern to outright abuse. He really should have turned off his livestream before getting into the wardrobe.

Poor guy. Seems like he's in a bad way.

Obviously I immediately need to go to his house and interrogate him.

Pleasantville

I'm on my rickety bike and riding through town just as my morning caffeine kicks in.

As soon as I hit Justin's street, cycling through the burbs like a precocious innocent from a Spielberg movie, I notice that I'm starting to cringe at the clicking and clacking noises my bike keeps making. I got it second-hand, and it shows. I feel like I'm vandalizing the quiet.

My research on the Gorhammer family pulled up a complaint from their neighbour two doors down – Keith Harding, unctuous owner of Curl Up and Dye, the trendiest hairdresser on what passes for a high street here (age: forty-three; known crimes: none, unless you count a fondness for frosted tips). Apparently Mr Harding once called the police on Justin for 'hosting a rave' – but alas for our eager best and brightest, when they arrived in furious splendour with sirens a-whirling, all they found was a small knot of sixteen-year-old kids having a *Back to the Future* marathon with a few illicit beers and a party-size bag of peanut butter cups. Justin lives in the kind of neighbourhood that doesn't brook a raised voice.

My bike whirs and groans up the Gorhammer's garden path, passing neatly shaped fuchsia bushes, their lurid

My-Little-Pony-pink-and-purple-coloured flowers shimmying in the breeze. There are two clean steps up to the door, and Roman-style pillars on either side. I lean the bike against one pillar and ring the bell.

Eventually a woman answers the door. She has a neat blonde bob tucked behind her ears, a billowing art-teacher-style shirt and tired, guarded eyes.

'Mrs Gorhammer?' I ask.

She frowns.

'One of you girls again,' she says.

Not quite the greeting I was hoping for. Also – how many 'me girls' does Justin get visiting him?

Maybe she doesn't like my haircut. I was aiming for Angelina Jolie in *Hackers* but since, unlike Angelina, I don't possess the natural beauty more usually found on e.g. an elven huntress forced to depart Rivendell, I've likely bypassed 'sexy pixie cut hacker' and landed square in 'tufty madwoman'.

Or maybe it's the tattoos. My mother would have an aneurysm if they were real so they're only temps, but they are rather confrontationally all over my arms. There's a giant upside-down cross on the underneath of one forearm, because there's nothing a childhood Catholic runs to faster than showboat satanism as soon as she hits pubescence. Then again, the cross is only upside down to me, so I suppose to everyone else it looks like I have a girl hard-on for Jesus.

This is the kind of thing I find funny, just so you know what you're getting into here.

'How can I help you?' says Mrs Gorhammer, with the clear downward inflection that means 'I don't really want to help you.'

'I just came to visit Justin,' I offer. 'You know, see how he's doing.'

A brow raises. 'I had no idea you and Justin were such friends.'

Her surprise is forgivable. Justin went to the kind of school with a PTA that threatens to withhold term fees until the board consents to getting a roof for the Olympic-sized open-air swimming pool. I went to the kind of school where the only way we'd get a swimming pool is if we dug a hole in the parking lot and lined it with trash bags.

'We're not friends, exactly,' I say, cursing my natural obsession with the truth. 'But I just wanted to check on him, after all the hullabaloo over the demon video thing. Offer the old emotional support.'

Charming rarely comes up on the list of Alecto Gray describers. *Smooth* – that's another non-appearer. Mrs Gorhammer hesitates.

'That's very nice of you,' she says, 'but Justin has all the support he needs right now. Perhaps you could send him a message through his social media.'

This woman has the careful grace of a politician's publicist, but also – Justin is still on his social media? That's brave. I stopped checking all mine six months ago, just after *it* happened. Couldn't deal with the sheer volume of horror that digital strangers like to inflict on other digital strangers. If people want to be nice to me, they can do it to my face, where it means more. Also, rarely will anyone have the courage to say the awful things in person that they say on social media without a second's thought, so it cuts out a lot of the nasty.

Speaking of nasty, I play the bad card. The one I'm not supposed to play. My mouth opens and out it comes.

7

'My name is Alecto Gray,' I say. 'Maybe you heard about what happened to my brother, Lucas? And then this thing with Justin pops up on my radar, and, in the words of Alicia Silverstone, I'm totally buggin'. It's been a hard few months, ma'am. Maybe Justin could offer me some insight?'

I see it – the softening, like fridged butter left out in the sun. A tip from me to you: plucking the guilt string works better than a microwave.

Usually.

'I'm sorry,' says Mrs Gorhammer. 'I am. It was terrible, what happened with your brother. But what Justin needs right now to get better is peace and quiet. He doesn't need any more . . . *upsets*. Keep well, won't you?'

Then she shuts the door in my face.

I am an upset, I think.

I feel oddly flattered.

Steering my bike in front of me like a weapon, I make a beeline for the sentried row of pretty pale pink cherry blossoms lining the street and take shelter behind a slender trunk.

Then I deliberately shake out a pre-rolled cigarette from the crumpled packet in my bag and light it. A small, meaningless rebellion, but I'm still waiting for some kind of sky alarm, triggered by my curling cigarette smoke, alerting the neighbourhood to my horrifying transgression.

This burb. This town.

'Can I get some of that?'

The high voice startles me, and I swing around to discover a skinny, coltish girl of maybe fourteen.

'Greetings, young rapscallion,' I say.

The girl scoffs. 'I'm not young.'

'Younger than me. By four or five years, if I'm any judge. Your name?'

She cocks her head like a robin, her bright black eyes daring but unsure.

'You were just at my house,' she says.

Ah. Justin's little sister.

'Amelia, I presume?' I say.

Amelia shrugs.

Amelia Gorhammer. Age: fourteen. Suspected crimes: underage smoking.

I withdraw another cigarette, twirling its liquorice-dark length between my fingers.

'That's a weird colour,' Amelia says suspiciously.

I shrug. 'Don't worry, it won't get you high.'

She eyes it nervously as she takes it. I offer her the lighter. She sparks up and inhales.

(All right, wait a second before you judge me.)

Then she makes a face and sticks out her tongue in comical horror. 'What *is* this stuff?'

'Dried non-toxic, non-mind-altering herbal matter wrapped in clove paper,' I say. 'Dried lemongrass, rose and lettuce leaves, to be more precise. I don't rumba with nicotine. I told you, it won't get you high. The only thing you gotta worry about with these babies is regular old carcinogens.'

(See? I'm not that bad.)

'Normal cigarettes don't get you high,' she says, holding the clove tube cupped to her chest with her back to her house.

'Nicotine? 'Fraid so. It's a stimulant. One of the most addictive on the planet, might I add. It's no fentanyl, but it holds its own.'

'What are you, like a health nut?'

'No, honey, just a life nut.'

Amelia rolls her eyes and takes another drag, and all without even the merest suggestion of hacking up a lung. She's definitely smoked before. Looks like Purgatory Lane boasts a little more rebellion than peanut butter cup binges.

'Tut tut,' I tell her.

'Who's gonna believe *you*?' she mocks.

Gutsy. Suddenly I like her.

'Touché,' I comment. 'My town stock has indeed taken a tumble in recent times.'

She squints at me through smoke curls. 'Why do you talk like you're like Sam Spade crossed with Oscar Wilde?'

'You know who Sam Spade is?' I ask, impressed.

'My grandpa's the biggest Humphrey Bogart fan. He's always got one of his movies on whenever we visit on Sundays.'

'Nice,' I comment. 'Bogart was hot.'

'He was tiny,' she mocks.

I am all of five feet.

'Hey,' I say. 'Tiny people are hot.'

'So you saw the video of my brother, then,' she says, switching back fast. Likes to keep people on their toes, this one.

'I saw it,' I say, more kindly.

Judging by the viewing numbers, I and everyone we know.

Amelia hunches, notices, corrects herself. 'What do you think?'

'What do I think?' I echo.

'He's crazy, right? Just like your brother?'

Right for the jugular, as only fourteen-year-olds know how.

'What do you know about Lucas?' I ask her directly.

She shrinks a little, and then rallies. A challenge. Fine.

'Lucas Gray.' She invokes his name like a curse. 'I mean. It's all anyone around here's talked about for like the last six months. Nothing ever happens in this town, right?'

Seems like even the right side of the tracks heard about my brother. Popular in life, but nowhere near as famous as he is in death.

'And what –' I smile – 'have –' my smile widens – 'you heard?'

Amelia has the nervous-defiant look of the type who suddenly realizes they might have gone too far but will just keep doubling down until someone or something explodes.

'He started going crazy and seeing demons everywhere and then he died by suicide out in the woods,' she says, very fast.

The world holds its breath.

I shrug. 'That's about the size of it.'

Amelia relaxes a little. 'Did he always have a mental illness?'

'I don't even know what that means,' I throw back – a habit of contrariness. 'No, I guess. He was just . . . normal. He was just Lucas. Until a few months ago, that is, and then he wasn't any more.' I sigh. The kid needs honesty. Everyone needs honesty, even if they don't want it. 'The answer is I don't know,' I tell her. 'I have no idea what was wrong with my brother.'

And that, ladies and gentlemen of the jury, is the definition of torture.

'Well, you have to *know*; you've already been *through* it,' Amelia insists. 'Didn't he get like an official diagnosis or anything? They could have fixed it, with the right drugs and therapy or whatever, right?'

What should I say to this wounded girl? Yes, I've already been through it, but it hasn't ended? Can't she see that my sniffing around her own poor brother means I'm *still* going through it? That maybe I always will be? That we mostly still have precious little idea how the human brain functions, or even reality itself, so trying to figure out what might be wrong with someone is a little bit like throwing spears into an indifferent ocean so vast and unknowable it might as well be another planet, and hoping one of our desperately puny weapons eventually hits a fish? That since we first made the terrible mistake of becoming sentient all those thousands of years ago, the greatest minds in each generation take on the question of how and why we work and *we're still no closer to a good answer*?

No, you're right. I shouldn't say any of that.

'Maybe they could have,' I tell her, 'given more time.'

She flicks away the remains of my bequeathed clove beauty and, with trembling fingers, gets out her phone.

'I mean,' she says, bringing up the Justin video with one thumb tap – hoo boy, she must live with it all queued up and ready to relive – 'there's nothing there. There's no demon, no nothing. Did *you* ever see anything? Anything at all? With your . . . with Lucas?'

She holds out the phone like a weapon, or a defence. Showing me the video herself is telling. Wearing it like a badge. Watching me watch it.

This girl already likes to scratch up her wounds. Someone ought to nip that tendency in the bud before it gets to being the only way she knows how to do life. Precociousness with a dash of trauma – it's like looking in a mirror, except mortifyingly she has a better dress sense than me.

'No,' I tell her. 'I never saw a damn thing that he did.'

She stares at me, then snatches the phone back.

'Lucas lost his grip,' I say simply, 'and then we lost him. But you – *you* still have time, OK? Just . . . love your brother, and support him. That's what he needs from you. He's a human being, and all human beings need love. No matter what he says or does. OK?'

Amelia shrugs. Nods. Walks away with the world weighing down her shoulders.

At the time, I really did think this was the best thing to say to her.

No matter what he says or does.

Ah, the desperate lies we tell ourselves.

Stranger Things (Have Happened)

The beginning of the end was nine months ago, at a *Stranger Things*-themed Halloween house party.

The party in question was being hosted by one Devlin Silverberg, son of a prominent local chicken farmer and host to many such a shindig, given the appealingly rambling nature of his family's farmhouse. By the time I arrived it was late enough to be packed to the gills, and early enough to be buzzing hard with the finest in teenage kicks that my small nowhere town had to offer.

I wormed my way into the house and skirted the edges of the kitchen, feeling more than a little anxious, but determined not to have any of Devlin's infamous punch to take the edge off. (The punch was known simply as 'The Dregs'. Devlin's parents enjoyed collecting weird, unpopular tourist alcohol from far-flung places and then leaving them half-drunk and forgotten in the backs of cupboards. One time Devlin mixed a liqueur made from avocados with the remains of a kumquat vodka, resulting in quite the Roman vomitarium on his front lawn.)

I'd always been a loner by trade. I hadn't been invited to a party since I was ten and Deena Lopez's mom had done the mom thing of sending out invites to the entire class, including people Deena hated, without consulting her. I'd played one round of mini golf at the Pitch and Putt paired up with Michael McCallister, an insular boy who had a habit of listing the capabilities of *Star Wars* vehicles, and then spent the rest of the party eating my ice-cream bowl on a bench by myself and passing the time by trying to work out what crimes each of the adult chaperones might have committed. I had Mrs Lopez down for wire fraud, though at the time I had no idea what that was – I'd gotten it from a seventies crime movie and thought it sounded fascinating.

My eventual point: I had no idea what to expect at a regular party, never mind the coolest shindig in town, and Devlin's was the one everyone wanted to be seen at. I looked around. Was this what I'd been missing out on? Sweaty, glazed faces; music where each song sounded exactly like the last and was usually about grinding booties against things; a heavy, acrid smell of weed that thickened the air so much it was hard to breathe, let alone talk.

(My mother once said I'd been born with the soul of a fifty-year-old curmudgeon. I'd blushed and told her to stop complimenting me so much or everyone else in the family would get jealous.)

Well, I wasn't here to have fun. There was only one reason I'd come to this party tonight, and it was not for the all-you-can-slurp vodka jelly shots. It was for –

'Lucas!' came the shout.

My head reared.

'Seriously, man – put it down!'

I saw the shouter first. It was Devlin himself (age: twenty; known crimes: small-time recreational drug dealer to his circle of friends), his anxious tone and the tense set of his body

15

lending him a rare sobriety. One could not say the same re the object of his shout. The tall, golden-haired boy-man standing in front of him gave a booming laugh, twirling something small and fragile-looking in the air above his head.

'It's a fairy statue, Dev,' he said. 'Not one person on this earth will miss it.'

'My mom will miss it,' Devlin hotly replied, making a grab for it and failing.

Even drunk, Lucas Gray could move faster than most jungle cats.

'Your mom believes in fairies,' Lucas hooted. 'I'm doing her a favour, man. I'm saving her from herself.'

The statue in question, on closer inspection, had purple wings and the kind of frozen beatific expression usually found on a Barbie doll. There was no accounting for taste, but given it was equally bad taste to make fun of someone else's bad taste, what we were witnessing here, ladies and gentlemen, was a race to the bottom.

Time for the cavalry.

'Hey!' I called. 'Didn't I catch you with *The Bumper Book of Angels* in the bathroom one time, Sephardic names included?'

'Aaaaaalec,' Lucas drawled. 'Baby sis! Dev, it's my baby sis!'

'Hey, Alec,' Devlin said, relief crossing his face.

'Hi,' I managed to get out before I was forcibly grappled into a bone-crushing Lucas bear hug.

'You came! You never come to parties!' Lucas sing-songed.

'Yeah.' I disentangled myself and gently prised the fairy statue from his distracted grip. 'God knows why.'

I felt Devlin's fingers on mine behind my back as we relayed the statue out of harm's way.

'Thanks,' he muttered to me. 'My mom's weird about her statues; she'd have gone nuclear at me.'

'What happened?' I muttered back.

'I usually lock all the breakables in the basement cabinet, but somehow he got in there.' Dev gestured helplessly. 'He was fine earlier. Then – I don't know what went wrong.'

Story of the last few months.

I took a quick peek at Lucas. He was frowning off to the side, his attention now momentarily caught by something else.

'A book of angels, really?' Devlin asked, trying to lighten the mood.

I shrugged. 'Lesser men make do with porn.'

'You Catholics are messed up.'

'You Jews are scarcely less so.'

'Yeah, but we're the chosen ones. That's bound to mess anybody up.'

We exchanged smiles. Devlin glanced at the frowning Lucas.

'You need help getting him home?' he asked, in the tone of someone offering out of chivalry more than willingness.

'It's fine,' I replied. 'You have to play host, protect the fairies. Besides, I know how to handle him.'

I was lying. I used to know. Now I had no idea. Case in point – when I felt a sudden wrench out of my grip and turned to watch Lucas barrel away from me towards the middle of the room, all I did was stand there stupidly, searching for the thing that had caught his eye.

A blonde, and a tiny one at that. She was a foot shorter than my brother, with a snub nose and her hair in bunches, but despite these intimidation handicaps she was doing an impressive line in 'pissed as hell'.

Was she yelling at him?

I abandoned Devlin and moved in fast.

'She's not interested, OK?' I heard Bunches shout.

'She's here,' Lucas slurred with drunken desperation. 'I saw her, Tippi. I just want to talk to her. I just want a minute of her time —'

'I don't give a shit what you want,' retorted Bunches.

'Just let me, just one *minute. Jesus Christ* —'

I was almost there, hand out to press gently yet firmly on my brother's football-enhanced arm, ready to suggest that he and I round off this excellent evening with a movie back at home and possibly a late-night rendezvous with a toilet bowl. Ready to feel him shake me off, ready to fight —

Lucas's eyes lit up. 'There she is, there she —'

He froze. His mouth dropped open. And then a sound I'd never heard before and never want to hear again came out of him. It was the sound someone made in the throes of a nightmare. A kind of flat, strangled wordless whimpering.

I looked where he was looking. I swear, I scanned that corner. There was Bunches, her anger changing to puzzlement. There was a knot of loud, atonal college kids scream-singing along to Gina G's seminal nineties one-hit wonder 'Ooh, Aah . . . Just A Little Bit'. There was a spartan fireplace, its mantel swept free of mythological statuary. There was a tall girl to one side of it, impossible to see who in the party lighting, but nevertheless reassuringly regular-shaped.

'What's wrong? What are you looking at?' I asked Lucas cautiously.

Lucas grabbed me hard enough to hurt. 'We need to go!'

'What the hell —'

'NOW, Alec!' Lucas bellowed, startling the crowd like a herd of deer.

They watched us owlishly, all those people from the two-years-older-than-me set, aka the most popular people in town who, despite being a curmudgeon, I'd have loved not to be embarrassed in front of.

'We're rehearsing a live theatre piece,' I told them. 'Part Beckett, part Marina Abramović, I'm confident of assuring our place in the contemporary canon, ow, *ow* –'

Lucas burst us both through the front door. Outside, the night sky twinkled and winked at us. The front lawn was mercifully free of audience for our two-man show, so I wrenched my arm from Lucas's manic grip and backed away from him.

'How many jelly shots does it take to become the party asshole?' I hissed.

He wasn't even looking at me. It was like watching someone trapped in a soundproof room inside their head.

'I'm driving you home, right now,' I said. 'The car's over there. Come on, let's go.'

Shockingly, he didn't protest.

Once we were in the car on the road home, belted up (safety first), I finally felt calm enough to broach the subject.

'What did you take?' I asked.

Lucas's face darkened. 'Nothing. You know I don't do drugs.'

'Oh, so you just had the *pamplemousse* soda all night?'

'I didn't take anything!'

'So what was that about?'

'Nothing.'

'*Nothing, nothing, tra la la*, as the Goblin King said?'

Quoting from *Labyrinth*, our favourite childhood movie, was one of our most sacrosanct rituals. Not a flicker.

I tried hard to contain my fury. 'OK, Lux. You get drunk as a skunk over nothing, because that's very like you. Then you nearly come to blows with a Buffy lookalike over nothing, because as everyone knows, that's just how you do. Who were you trying to talk to? Was it the girl you went to the party for? The one you've been chasing? What's her name?'

'Jesus, Alec,' Lucas shouted, 'just leave it alone!'

I drove through the silence, trying to quell my struggling heart.

Lucas never shouted at me. Not like this. We used to be so close. Now there was this invisible wall between us, built without planning permission, and despite investigations both surreptitious and bold, I still hadn't figured out why.

'Something happened a couple of months ago,' I said. 'Why won't you tell me about it?'

Silence.

'You used to tell me everything.'

'Not everything.'

'No,' I replied in my most reasonable tone, 'you once waited a whole two hours to confess that you'd accidentally spilled tomato sauce on my favourite blanket, staining it forever. We don't keep things from each other. From Mom, maybe. *In solidaritum contra parentia*.'

Finally, a soft huff of something that could be called a laugh at invoking our ancient pact.

Encouraged, I glanced at him.

'You can tell me,' I said. 'I promise I won't judge you. I promise, whatever it is, I'll understa–'

That was when my brother gave a wordless shout, reached out and grabbed the wheel.

I felt it wrench under my hands. I heard my own sudden intake of breath, the soft, brief moment of suspense before actions became consequences. A black shape rushed towards us, flipped into white craggy relief from the headlights of my car as it careened and crumpled into it with sprays of glass. The loudest bang I'd ever heard. Pain. Pressure.

We've hit a tree, I remember thinking, *we've hit a tree, we've hit a tree. That's what we've done, we've crashed into a tree*, over and over, as if evoking the simple practical situation we were in would give me back control.

Later, as the hospital staff bandaged up my broken wrist and I sat, dazed, picking the glass out of my hair, Lucas would only say to our scared-furious mother that he saw a coyote in the middle of the road. That at the moment he saw it I was looking at him, and by the time I spotted it I'd already be wrapping the car around it. That he acted on instinct. That he was sorry, so sorry.

When my mother turned to me for confirmation of Lucas's story I agreed with all of it. I didn't tell her what state I found him in at Devlin's house. I said that I was looking at him, just for a split-second, and that I hadn't seen the coyote. I agreed that I absolutely should have my learner's permit taken off me until I could learn to be less reckless. That this was really my fault. I protected him, the way he used to protect me.

In solidaritum contra parentia.

But it was only because I couldn't bear telling her the truth. That her golden-boy son, the one who used to be so obviously sane, had turned to me the moment after we'd crashed, his face drained of blood, his eyes wider than dinner plates, and wildly screamed,

'THERE'S A DEMON IN THE ROAD!'

And that right then I realized I was terrified – not of whatever may or may not be lying in wait for us on the asphalt, but of my own brother, who in his manic insanity looked like a demon himself.

Into the Woods

Quotes about me:

'Far too angry for a pretty teenage girl' – my computer science teacher Mr Forman. Said to me after my fist *very lightly* hammered upon the intermittently working screen of a school laptop so ancient my grandmother would have tossed it in a fire along with her transistor radio, had she indeed been in the habit of burning her stuff and also still alive. Additionally, punchable points awarded for calling me 'a pretty teenage girl' and believing it a compliment. The angry part was more flattering.

'Hyde to my Jekyll' – my brother Lucas. Said to me when he was fifteen, and twelve-year-old me hatched a foolproof plan for him to circumvent a mother-mandated early curfew that seriously interfered with his plans of attending a highfalutin friend's late-night birthday party and therefore crossing paths with his highfalutin friend's 'Uptown Girl'-style sister, who had a penchant for roughing it, if you catch my drift. (The plan involved borrowing the spare mannequin from our school's biology lab, a motion-sensor-activated recording of Lucas snoring, two KitKat Chunkies on ice and *Gilmore Girls* queued up on the living-room TV, but I can't go into details here.)

I think you're getting the picture. I'm the troublemaker in the family, the big mouth, the back-chatter, the upside-down-cross-inking, nefarious-plan-hatching black sheep. I am coriander. Many people are genetically predisposed to disliking my taste.

Lucas was the charming golden boy, the high achiever, the on-to-bigger-and-better, the one all the boys wanted to be and all the girls – plus two boys, memorably – wanted to do.

But he's dead, and I'm not. Ain't life unfair?

Ah, it's one of those days, today. A day for bad thoughts you can't banish, no matter how much meditating you do. The air's torpid, grey, listless and thick, too heavy to allow for hopes or dreams.

I call them weeba days. 'It's a weeba day,' I say to anyone who dares attempt communication, those four words the absolute maximum amount I can muster. Those closest to me, such as they are, know what a weeba day is, even if they don't know exactly what weeba means. But I'll tell you, since we're becoming such good friends now – weeba stands for W.E.B.A., as in Why Even Be Alive.

On weeba days, a child's gleeful shriek is an attack, like throwing a javelin into my ear canal. The din of conversation in the local cafe shreds every last tenuous nerve, a mindless, maddening buzzsaw grinding my soul into chaff. I'd shoot every dog right through the yap. If you can get a full sentence out of me I must want to bone you.

Essentially, weeba days are days I really shouldn't be around people, because it's not their fault that I suddenly want them to crumble into dust; it's mine, all mine. So a weeba day is a good day to take myself off to the woods alone.

An endless summer stretches out before me, filled with egregious nothingness. This was supposed to be an exciting time – the summer before college, the great next step in my life – and until last year I was all on track to immerse myself in philosophy, my second subject choice, because apparently you can't major in 'private detective', so Kant here I come. Except my older brother's recent high dive off the board of life hasn't so much derailed my college plans as caused a ten-car pile-up, so my place is deferred until next year while I tread water, trying to get my muddled head in order. Unlike Lucas, I don't want to be dead, but the alternative seems so damn complicated I don't even know where to begin.

As I leave my house I catch sight of Jeanette Trebar down the way, with her sagging pink tracksuit bottoms and bird's-nest hair and her sweeping broom out as always, moving its stiff bristles in seemingly random patterns across the concrete. Jeanette sweeps the pavement outside and a few feet of extension from her front door every day. No one knows why. No one ever asks. Her husband died ten years ago; apparently there wasn't much sweeping before that. Now sweeping's all she's got, that and reality shows. Her immediate neighbour, Mrs Handsforth, says she plays her reality shows so loud they come right through the wall, as if the Stepford wives and blandly sexed-up younglets and fame-hungry social media stars are standing in her own living room, laughing shrilly over her shoulder like anxious ghosts.

Welcome to Fring. Coastal oasis/backwater of seven thousand and forty-six at the last census. Three thousand of us are trying to leave before it's too late; the rest are the example of what happens when you don't.

We have a sweeping beach made of soft buttermilk sand, gorgeous when it isn't choked with washed-up trash and the roving gangs of criminal anarchists known as seagulls. Inland boasts one of many abandoned mines scattered around the area, holes poked into the hills and left to gape darkly at the sky when the local mining industry went the way of dial-up internet.

My gaze drifts across the peeling boats moored up at the rusting iron posts of the quay that the council has spent at least the entire time I've been alive promising everyone they would renovate. On the warmest summer days the whole town is doubly assaulted by the piercing bloom of seaweed on one side and the thicker throat punch of cabbage fields on the other, our only export these days for a modest profit.

I reach the hill that marks the inland end of town and pass gratefully into the cool rustling green of the woods beyond.

It doesn't take long to find the place. Underneath the canopy of a particularly ancient ash tree, top layer of leaf mould turned crispy from the summer heat, crunching and crumbling under my feet as I squat, rubbing my bare hand over the woodsy floor, breathing in that thick earth smell.

When I was younger, I used to fantasize that I was a hare. I'd leap in my hare body from tree root to tree root, feeling those thick gnarled tangles scratching reassuringly against the soft pads of my feet. Fleet of foot and free of homework. Maybe all I'm doing today is trying to conjure that escape again. Examining my brother's ultimate escape, the Last Escape any of us ever do. I come here to sink into it, turn it over, try to understand it.

This is the spot his body was found. Right here under this tree, wearing a nondescript hoodie and his battered Converse with the hand-Sharpied wings on the side.

'Who are you trying to be, Hermes?' I'd asked as I'd watched him inexpertly but painstakingly draw those black wings on, copying from an image he'd found on a favoured tattoo artist's Instagram.

'Icarus,' he'd replied, and given me his trademark lazy-charming grin.

Only Lucas could get away with something so hammy.

He was found curled on his side around an empty bottle of Old Navy and a pill bottle with the label torn off. *Old Navy*, for Christ's sake. Couldn't even muster up enough pride to go out with a classy liquor. We're not exactly a Cristal family, but he had more than enough of his own money from working private tutoring jobs for local lagging kids to afford something a lot less paper-bag-hobo than that.

There's a proper grave, of course, in a nice and tidy cemetery, with landscaped hedgerows and vases of neat flowers. But he isn't there. I mean, he isn't anywhere, or at least not as the entity that I grew up with, encased in the body shell that I knew. The shell is rotting away in the grand tradition of all organic matter. I'm not going to find anything of him where the dead shell got buried as a worm's all-you-can-eat buffet. This very spot is the last place he was alive. It has more of him than some turfed-over hole in a cemetery ever will.

From out of my bag I draw a black church candle and a lighter, and I set the candle down in front of me, nestling its base into the woodsy dirt.

I know what this looks like. It looks like the actions of someone desperate enough to try raising the dead so they can ask their brother why they chose to exit stage left rather than stick around to see their baby sister graduate.

Trouble is, I don't really believe in this. I might have been raised Catholic, but I've yet to see one good ghost. Lucas isn't hanging out invisibly and watching me rewatch *Brick* for the nineteenth time, repeating Joseph Gordon-Levitt's dialogue into a mirror until I get the voice just right. If nothing else, he'd show up as a ghost just to laugh at me. No. The afterlife is a fairy tale for people who can't hack it in the real version. I once told Lucas that, and he told me that nihilism was for cowards. I say that nihilism is the atheist's version of religious epiphany in times of crisis. In both cases you're left wondering what the hell the plan is, and you either go all in on believing there *is* one and you just don't get it because you're not God, or you end up facing the cold, empty void of no plan, no reason, no rhyme. And neither, frankly, sounds all that appealing, so where does that leave me?

My morose interior monologue is interrupted by the loud snap of a twig. Standing a few feet away is a girl looking down at me currently crouched on the ground like a mouse.

For a moment we just stare at each other, caught in the hypnosis of a sudden encounter.

'I'm sorry,' says the girl. 'I didn't mean to disturb your satanic ritual.'

I look down at the black candle at my feet and the lighter in my hand.

'Ah,' I say. 'After a swift assessment of the visual I can see how you might go that way. But this isn't what it looks like, as the murderer said to the soon-to-be-victim.'

The girl's eyes widen, wary as a rabbit's. 'What?'

At least I always know when I've gone too Alec. I get those eyes a lot. Normally it's hard for me to scrape up any craps to give, but this time I am annoyingly embarrassed.

It's because she's pretty. Like a human Bambi crossed with *Ghostworld*-era Scarlett Johansson. Age: a couple years older than me, at a guess, so that would put her at about twenty. Crimes: unknown, unless you count being attractive to an illegal degree.

'Sorry,' I say hastily. 'It's not anything as fun as Satan worship. I'm just saying a prayer. Or maybe screaming into the void. A black candle just seems more appropriate for that sort of thing, you know?'

'Absolutely,' Bambi Scarlett dubiously replies. 'I do it all the time.'

Weak smiles are exchanged, both of us uncertain on how to proceed. I cast around for something to say that will restore my coolness ratio.

'Your T-shirt is bad,' I venture.

A crushing silence.

'Gosh,' says Bambi Scarlett.

'I mean, bad as in good.' I fumble. Me! Fumbling! 'Do the kids still say that, bad as in good? I'm behind on the current vernacular. Good. It's good. I like that band.'

It's a lurid red shirt, the front splashed with a jagged BOY HARSHER.

She looks down at herself. 'You can see that? I believe the lapels of my oversized blazer only allow for "OY HAR" to shine through.'

'I'm confident I know where it's going.'

Bambi Scarlett laughs and eyes me. 'Are you?'

Am I even more of a fantasist than my mother claims, or was that a tiny flirt?

'So who were you praying to?' Bambi Scarlett asks me. 'God or the trees?'

29

'Whoever's listening.'

'Does anyone ever answer?'

'Too soon to tell,' I say. 'It's only been a few months.'

'Wow. You've been coming out here to pray for months? That's some dedication. Most people just do it the once and hope it's enough.'

'Most people don't have the tenacity required,' I say. 'The really big requests take time.'

'So you're asking for something big?'

'Apparently so, because I haven't gotten it yet.'

'Curiouser and curiouser,' Bambi Scarlett muses.

I can tell she's enjoying my alluring air of mystique.

'Care to venture further down the rabbit hole with me, Alice?' I ask.

She smiles. Her teeth are gently crooked. It's like a perfect slice of lemon to cut the sweet creamy perfection of her looks. (Witness the poetic verbosity of the intellectual with an Insta crush on a stranger.)

'Well,' she says, 'when you put it like that. What happened a few months ago to prompt all this praying?'

Here we go. 'My brother's untimely demise,' I say.

And just as her face changes and the template sorrowful murmurs begin to spill from her mouth, as happens with everyone I tell, I cut in.

'My name's Alec, by the way. Alec Gray.'

There it is.

Gray, the Cursèd Name. Lethally suicidal brother to a coolly rebellious sister. Alcoholic absentee father. Small-time but upstanding lawyer mother who's never been paid enough to get us to the good side of town, and whose prayers could not prevent her family from abandoning her in various embarrassingly public ways. Who'll be next to crack? Popcorn's right here, do you want sweet or salted? Can I supersize that for you? Might as well, it's only a dollar more, and there's always something to see on the *Gray Show*.

'My family's reputation precedes me,' I say. 'I'm jazzed. I've always wanted to be notorious by proxy.'

Bambi Scarlett gives me an uneasy look. 'Sorry.'

'Don't be; you didn't kill him.' I am all nonchalance. 'My turn to be sorry. I've been told my breeziness is a defence mechanism.'

The green around us whispers and rustles, as if the woods are shifting closer to listen in.

'It's OK,' she replies with an awkward 'what does one even say in these situations?' shrug.

'You never went to my school, did you? Fring High.' I shoot for the blandest subject opener to keep her talking to me. Of course she never went to my school; I'd recognize someone like her among its meagre two-hundred-and-something-strong student body.

She shakes her head. 'I'm in second year at Sutherland Hollow.'

A college girl! Darn, the older woman thing makes her even more attractive. Same age as Lucas, too.

'You didn't know my brother, then?'

'Just of him,' she says. 'I never met him.'

That tracks. Sutherland Hollow is the artsy bohemian college in our local area, and it's a good hour's drive from here down the coast. Lucas went to the rather more sciency Brodeman Tech, further inland. They never would have crossed paths.

A new question strikes me.

'What's your name, by the way?' I ask.

'Jesus!' Bambi Scarlett exclaims, pressing a hand to her heart.

I blink. 'No way. Father O'Hallaghan's never going to believe me when I tell him. Can I get your autograph?'

'No,' she murmurs, then points. 'Jesus, I thought that was just a tree, but then it moved.' Her voice lowers further. 'There's someone watching us. Behind you.'

I crane my head over my shoulder.

In the distance, I can make out a faint rectangular shape, like a small house or a cabin. Next to it, details just as obscured, stands a slender figure wearing a baseball cap and giant sunglasses.

I squint. 'It's not moving. Are you sure it's not some kind of art installation – oh!'

The figure, having been dead still, suddenly jerks into life and hares off into the trees, away from us.

'Hey!' Bambi Scarlett shouts – a sharp, angry sound that takes me aback – and then she takes a few steps forward.

'Wait – what are you planning to do, give chase?' I say.

'They were spying on us,' Bambi Scarlett says, glaring after them.

'Who knows what they were doing? Maybe that's their cabin, over there.'

Bambi Scarlett gives me a startled look. 'What?'

I point. 'Cabin. Over there. I wonder who it belongs to.'

'You're very observant, Alec Gray,' says Bambi Scarlett, holding my gaze. 'It's impressive.'

I savagely fight the blush threatening.

Bambi Scarlett shakes her head. 'I'm sorry. I forgot my manners in all the stalking excitement. My name is Megan. Megan Lugner.'

'An entirely forgivable lapse,' I say, and take her hand to shake.

As soon as our fingers touch, I hear a tiny crack. My skin buzzes with a quick sizz of pain. We both flinch back.

'Static electricity,' I say, wringing my hand. 'Ouch. Boy, this is turning into an all-time best "how did you first meet?" anecdote, am I wrong?'

'I actually have to go,' Megan says, rubbing her hand on her jeans. 'Sorry. Nice to meet you, Alec.'

She turns away from me without a pause and lopes off with admirable speed, sending the leaf mould flying.

'Bye,' I say to the empty air.

Necronomicon

There's a resident goth in my town, and I know what you're going to say, but it's not me.

Her name is Lucille Izzard. She wears spiked collars and black lipstick. Ginger roots spider out from the parting of her liquorice-dyed hair sheets.

'Izzard as in Eddie?' I once asked her. Then I launched into a word-perfect skit just as her fingers did a rapid tap-tap-google on her phone to find out who Eddie Izzard was. She seemed displeased with the results. She sneered at me and walked off right in the middle of my superb rendition of 'penne all'arrabbiata from the Death Star Canteen'. I don't think she got that I was trying to pay her a compliment. I don't do Eddie for just anyone.

Anyway, my point is that, growing up, I was nothing like Izzard. I was into aggressively neon colours, sunshine and plastic charms shaped like cherries. My elementary school notebooks were covered in furry Sylvanian Families stickers. Black clothes don't even suit my skin tone; they wash me out. Yet somehow I'm the one unwillingly living the goth life.

Let me show you what I mean.

Underneath my bed is a floorboard possessed of a pleasingly loose set of nails. These nails are loose due to some past negotiation with the business end of a tool or two. Out comes the mini screwdriver I keep in my desk drawer. Up comes the board. And in the dark, cool space underneath, now clean of the dust from a thousand tiny insect carcasses, sits a notebook. It's wrapped in an old Hammer Horror T-shirt, as if the screen-printed power of *Twins of Evil* could keep its contents harmlessly contained.

The notebook is filled with my brother's cramped, crabby handwriting. To the casual observer, indecipherable. But to the little sister who has spent years sneaking peeks into his diaries whenever he was out of the house and forgot to lock his bedroom door? Pie levels of easy.

The subject of his writing is a meandering exploration of demonology. Witchcraft. A general theme of the black arts. Maybe you already guessed that, but it was a shock to me when I first found the notebook in the days after his death. Despite all his talk of demons, I'd had no idea just how far down the rabbit hole he'd gone.

As I'm sitting on my bed flicking through Lucas's notebook, idly wondering if there's anything in here about conjuring up the phone numbers of girls that look a little like Scarlett Johansson, I hear the sound of my bedroom doorknob rattling.

Before there's even time for a proper freak-out to blossom, the door opens wide to reveal my mother.

Now imagine that the shot of her freezes. The whole thing turns sepia, a colour change to signify a shift from the current timeline.

This is how, less than a year ago, the next scene would have played out:

'I'm interrupting Judy Blume time, aren't I?' my mother would say.

According to the commandment of Snoop Dogg I'd drop the notebook like it's hot and give my mother my very best accusatory tone.

'Don't you knock any more? I could have been hosting a sex party in here.'

My mother would lean against the doorframe. 'Well, judging by the lack of noise, I assumed it to be a very boring one, and therefore concluded that my sudden presence might at least serve to enliven proceedings.'

(And now you know where I get it from.)

My mother's voice would lower. Her mouth would tighten into a ready grimace. 'I have a confession. I've known about the hidey-hole since you were six.' Her eyes slide in brief guilt to the loose floorboard under my bed.

I would fake gasp. 'I keep my porn in there!'

'Well, you *used* to keep mouldering Hershey's Kisses and packets of contraband sherbet, if memory serves.'

'Lies,' I would accuse. 'They had far too much sugar in them to ever go mouldy. Anyway, when puberty hit I began to chase harder drugs. Romance novels. Nu metal. The dragon.'

'Well, admittedly, once you hit sixteen I got too scared to keep looking.'

'Thank god. No one should ever have to picture their own daughter in a bright red gimp mask.'

My mother would groan. 'Enough! You win this round.'

And she'd follow it up with a full-throated laugh.

Out of imaginings and back to reality – signalled by the transformation of sepia tones to cold, flat light – my mother makes no jokes. She just watches me, her eyes red.

These days, her eyes are always red.

'What are you doing?' she asks. 'What's that?'

The notebook is still clutched in my hand. *Too slow*, Snoop Dogg admonishes me.

I say nothing, which, as you may be coming to realize, is really unlike me.

'Is that his notebook?' my mother asks, stepping into the room.

Ladies and gentlemen of the jury, the lady can recognize a ubiquitous dollar store notebook with generic cover at ten paces. I put it to you to consider that she has seen it before – maybe even read it herself. (Gasps from members of the jury.)

'Well, you always lauded me for my curiosity,' I reply at last, testing the waters, but she doesn't take up the joke baton – she hasn't for six months – and I feel an incredibly unfair yet unstoppable tidal wave of resentment.

'Alec,' she says wearily, 'you shouldn't have that.'

'You threw out all his books,' I protest.

She hesitates. 'Not all of them.'

'No, not all of them because, see, I have this one. I obviously sanction you getting rid of his collection of Dan Browns for reasons of good taste alone, but surely they weren't *all* blasphemous.'

'Why did you keep the notebook?' she asks me, skilfully avoiding the question.

'His bedroom door's locked. It's been locked since he died,' I reply, skilfully avoiding the question. 'You won't let me near any of his stuff.'

Have you noticed that we don't say his name? I don't even know when that started, but the one time I uttered 'Lucas' out loud I saw my mother physically wince. So I stopped uttering it out loud.

'It's just too soon,' she says to me.

'You haven't gone full shrine in there, have you? Don't leave the burning candles around his Head Boy high school photo unattended; the fire department spent a lot of money on advertising telling us not to do that. Don't let their money be spent in vain.'

'Alec, stop! Just . . . stop.'

I stare at her. She's breathing hard. I've gone too far; somehow I've gone too far, but all I've done is try to make it like it was, try to evoke those old wisecracking days.

She used to love this about me. Black humour is – was – our family's preferred communications device, the way we would overcome the random and careless brutality of an indifferent universe. Lucas had been the best at it – he had a prodigious memory for quotes and lyrics, and could conjure whole skits from shows he'd seen but once, weaving them effortlessly into casual conversation. Catholicism and competitive wit are – were – the twin pillars of our family life.

'I'm sorry,' I say, at a total loss.

It's as though who I am offends her now, but I have no idea how not to be me.

She must regret her outburst, because she comes to sit beside me on my bed, and when she speaks again, her voice is gentle with remorse.

'Why are you reading this? Is it because you want to understand what he was going through?'

'It started out that way,' I cagily reply, 'but now . . . I don't know. I feel like something bigger than him is going on.'

'What do you mean?'

'Have you heard of a kid called Justin Gorhammer?'

She pauses, then asks: 'Is he a friend of yours?'

'Not exactly.'

She listens carefully to my increasingly excitable recitation of recent events, and even, when I show it to her, watches Justin's video all the way through to the end. This – us sitting together, both focused on the same thing that for once is not He Who Shall Not Be Named – has me chasing hope like a kitten chasing a string.

Maybe we can solve this thing together. Maybe this will be what breaks us out of the torpid purgatory that passes for life these days. She's a lawyer, she has contacts, she knows people. I bet she can get the skinny, pull some favours, shake some lowlifes. I bet we both could. GRAY & GRAY, PI AGENCY etched in gold plate on the door of our imaginary possible office.

'Give me the notebook,' she says at last, holding her hand out, and I readily hand it over.

She opens it on the page I was reading. Two sets of eyes fall on the scribbles there – a detailed recipe for a little something called 'Conjuring a Tulpa to Drive an Enemy Mad' – and then she snaps it shut.

'Oh, honey,' she says. 'This is why I don't want you reading his books. It messes with your head.' She pulls in a shaky breath. 'You've been drawn to darkness recently, Alec, and while it's understandable, this is not the right outlet for that famous curiosity of yours. You need to focus on something healthier. Something less dangerous.'

I can't help it. I laugh. I catch a look for it, but come on. These days every fashionista worth their moonlight-infused salt has an altar scattered with amethysts and burns a sage bundle every time they post an Instagram video and is really, really into silver jewellery shaped like crescent moons. An interest in the alt religions is hardly the symptom of chicken-head-biting weirdos it once was. The era of the Satanic Panic, like the femme fatale and low-rise jeans, is one long gone.

But in my very Catholic family? We might indulge in the black humour, but we don't mess with the black arts. 'Darkness attracts darkness,' my father was fond of saying before he skedaddled out of the family unit eight years ago, but it seems like Lucas wasn't listening – or maybe things got so dark for him near the end that adding in a little more darkness felt like no big deal.

Still, I try. 'Mom – it's harmless.'

'Harmless,' she echoes. 'He's dead. He's dead because of it. Does that sound harmless to you?'

My mouth opens and shuts like a surprised fish.

She closes the notebook, holding it tight against her lap.

'I know it's hard,' she says, 'maybe the hardest thing you've ever done, but you have to drop all this.'

'Drop what?' I ask with wide-eyed innocence.

'Alec, listen to me. Just listen. It's just you and me now. We didn't choose this, but that's life.' The way she says this, blunt and bitter, makes me furious and breaks my heart at the same time. 'I'm not having you go down the same road as your brother, OK? You have a future. You deferred college this year, and I accepted that, but you're going next year. You're going, and you'll work this summer, get some money together. Who's that caterer you pulled shifts for in high school? I want you to call her, get as much work as you can, keep yourself busy and focused, focused on your goals. No boys, and no drinking, and no parties –'

'Since when have I been troublesome about any of those things?' I protest.

'Last Halloween? The party you were coming back from where you crashed your car with your brother in the front seat? It's a miracle you weren't killed.'

I grit my teeth, the better to stop the truth spilling out. 'Mom –'

She interrupts me. 'I have to be able to trust you. I can't be around twenty-four seven to make sure that you don't do anything . . . that you're OK. I have to work too, remember?'

'How could I forget? You live at the office these days, because it sure as hell beats living here with me.'

She hesitates. 'I'm sorry. I know I haven't been around much. It's this case. Once this case is over –'

We'll go back to how it was before? Sure.

'I'll be around more,' she finishes. 'I promise I will.'

'Tell me about this case you're so wrapped up in,' I try. 'You've been working on it non-stop for months. I could help –'

'Oh, no,' my mother says firmly. 'This is not one of your crime movies that you sit around watching for days on end. There will be no investigations into what happened to the neighbour's cat, or who stole the lead off the church roof again. Please, Alec. I'm asking you to try. All you need to focus on is your future. Getting into college. Getting out into the world. Living. Exploring. Don't you want to explore?'

Her faraway gaze is fixed on the opposite wall. Even when she's lecturing me, she's barely here. She's always somewhere else now, somewhere I can't reach and I'm not allowed to go.

I get it. I really do. She's already had one kid go mad and die on her, and the last thing she needs is any evidence that the other is keenly gallivanting along the same path. I could wail and gnash my teeth over the injustice of it all, but what would be the point in torturing her more?

So I nod like I mean it. I promise to call up my old boss for catering shifts. I say all the things to make that manic-panic light in her eyes dim with relief. And when she leaves my room with my brother's notebook clutched tightly in her hand, presumably to burn it, I don't utter a word of protest.

I'm on my own in this.

Watching Lucas gradually deteriorate was torture for both of us. Watching all his sunny, beaming zest for life leach away to be replaced by the soul-sucking paranoia, by the constant lying, by the sneaking off in the middle of the night to do god only knew what, by the lying in bed staring up at the ceiling and not moving for hours, by the anger, the sadness.

And the scariest thing of all, the dread. The fear. The day when he swore a demon was following him, dogging him, hounding him, punishing him. A demon no one else could see. Madness up close is never as funny as you think it's going to be.

He used to tell me everything. Then he started keeping secrets. Then he lost his mind. I've since come to really resent feeling like a secret is being kept from me, and that notebook could have given me an insight into his biggest: of all forms his madness could have taken, why a demon?

It could have been passed off as a random obsession – until Justin. That has to mean something. It can't be that two entirely unconnected guys of the same age, in the same town, randomly suffer the same specific delusion.

The slight stumbling block on my quest for answers: there's only one key to Lucas's room, and my mother keeps it in her purse, which these days remains on her person at all times. I'm never going to see that notebook again.

Good job I already took photos of the more interesting pages.

Arachnophobia

Thomas Geist ('Tommy Boy', 'T-Guy' or 'Ghostie' to the nearest and dearest mix of friends he's picked up over the years via his two main loves, football and musical theatre) has his 'Swingin' Summer' birthday beach party every year, without fail, on or around 1 August.

We attended the same Catholic elementary school, and Ghostie used to invite the whole class every year. The nuns all liked Ghostie – well, all of them except Sister Mary Katherine, our maths teacher, but she didn't like any of us on the basic principle that we were a) alive and b) under forty-five years of age – and the fact that Ghostie was a nun favourite should have automatically made him about as palatable to me as watching a Woody Allen movie – but, well, Ghostie is easy to like. The fact that he holds his birthday party on the public beach a hundred feet from his house also means that on a warm summer evening it's the nicest way to see the sun go down you can get around here.

Ghostie's parents knew what they were doing when they scored their place. The beach here edges a small, pretty cove, with plenty of atmosphere to go alongside. At one end, naturally drilled into the dark mass of the cliffs, is a series of dank caves so small even I have to duck my head to walk inside them. The walls are forbiddingly jagged and covered in slippery moss, and even in broad daylight the light hardly penetrates. At night the cave warren is completely black, and you need a flashlight just to take a step without falling on your face. Naturally, it's also one of the most famed hook-up spots in fifty miles.

I haven't officially been invited to Ghostie's beach bash, but no one is — since anyone can walk on to a beach it's an open invite, making it attractive to a broad cross-section of social groups. Which means it's also my best shot at finding someone who knows someone who knows Justin Gorhammer.

I've had to come earlier than could strictly be called cool, since Mom is due back from work at 10 p.m. Her potential fainting fit upon discovering my lack of home presence will only be worth it if I actually find out something useful, so I've put my best game face on and, armed with a confidence so sure it can only be faked, bulldozed my way into a dozen conversations with strangers, asking them about Justin Gorhammer. I've been doing this about an hour, and with zero success, when I finally spot a face I know and out of sheer relief make a hasty beeline for her.

'Hey, Mallory!' I call.

My brother's ex-girlfriend stands tall and elegant, etched against the bonfire flames in an outfit more New York fashion house CEO-in-waiting than beach party attendee. I, in contrast, bear a passing resemblance to an Oklahoma gas station attendant (it's the overalls, and I have yet to accept that the only people who can make overalls work are the kind of people who'd look good draped in a fire blanket).

'Mallory! Hi? Hello?'

I'd swear we just locked eyes, but she's turning her head away. My voice is getting louder and more embarrassing, but when in doubt, double-down.

'Mallory, hey! Excuse me.' I elbow my way directly in front of her.

She hesitates.

If hesitations could talk, this one would say: 'I already saw you, and wanted to ignore you, but your persistence has placed me in the awkward position of not wanting to lie to your face with false body language about having already seen you (admirable) *while simultaneously* not wanting to see you now and be forced to have a conversation (less admirable). This momentary indecision has cost me my higher ground. O, unhappy day.'

Lucas and Mallory broke up last summer, a couple of months before things turned bad for him. He told me at the time it was because he'd confessed to having a crush on someone else. The same someone he'd been trying to talk to at Devlin's *Stranger Things* party a few months later, I'd wager, just before his demonic sighting freak-out that made me crash my car.

I'd felt sad for Mallory when they broke up – I heard she didn't take it well – but these days I'd say she dodged a bullet.

'What's up, Alec?' she says to me.

'Not much,' I brightly reply. 'How's college?'

'Fun,' she nods.

'Good, I'm glad. People should have fun. Be happy and free.'

Mallory gives me an uneasy semi-smile. She has this look on her face. I've come to know the look well over the last few months. It's the 'should you be outside?' look that people get when someone whose brother killed himself shows up to a party like it ain't no thing.

'Well,' I say, 'I don't want to take up a lot of your time, I just wanted to ask you something about Lucas. About his, how shall we put this, troubles, towards the end.'

She visibly stiffens at the casual mention of his name.

'I'm sorry, Alec, I don't know anything. We broke up way before . . . all that.'

'Ah,' I nod. 'So you know the ugly details, then. Earlier eons would have eventually had the town stone him to death for consorting with the Devil. Thank god we're all so tolerant now.'

Mallory just stares at me.

'He never mentioned demons to you, I take it,' I hastily amend.

She shakes her head.

'He wasn't – you guys didn't . . . Mallory, was he using drugs? It's OK if he was. See above re tolerance. I'm just trying to work out what was going on.'

This conversation is upsetting her. I can tell by the way she seems to withdraw into herself, like a turtle into its shell.

'He didn't do anything like that,' she says eventually. 'Never. We didn't do that kind of thing, Alec.'

'No, I'm not suggesting – I'm just asking.' I cast around. 'I'm asking because – do you know a guy called Justin Gorhammer?'

'Who?'

'Justin Gorhammer.'

Her nose wrinkles. 'He's not in bible group.'

'No,' I say patiently, 'he may exist outside of those circles. Actually, that's a good point – is he Catholic? I haven't seen him at church. But if he was, the whole demon thing might make more sense, right? Some religions don't believe in them at all, but you'd have to have at least been brought up within a theological framework that incorporates them, or why would your mind go there without the buried prompt, you know what I'm saying?'

Mallory is staring at me. Next to her, two of her friends are whispering in each other's ears.

I suddenly realize, in that far-too-late way one does, that I've been doing my thinking out loud, where people can hear me. In my defence I haven't exactly been spending a lot of time among fellow humans lately; I've gotten used to talking to myself in the private comfort of my own home.

Judging by the whispering going on around me, this is not a good sign.

'You know what?' I say brightly. 'Forget it. I'm sorry I bothered you.'

One of her friends leans in, talking quietly in Mallory's ear.

'OK!' Mallory says. 'No worries. Take care, Alec.'

Somehow it's that one that really stings. We were never very close, Mallory and I – she's more at the spa days and shopping end of the female spectrum and I'm more of a lady Philip Marlowe, with the world-weary cynicism to match – but we had some good times; laughs over family dinners, clashes over rounds of *Monopoly* and *Cluedo*. She was my brother's girl. She was, for a while, part of the family Gray. Does that not count for anything now? Are my goods too tainted? Is grief catching?

I turn away.

Then I turn back.

'You know,' I say, 'you could have just been normal with me.'

Mallory, midway through walking off, her friend's hand on her arm, looks back.

'I said you could have just been normal with me!' My voice rises. 'Then it wouldn't have been so awkward, would it?'

She looks at me like one might look at a snake.

'Maybe now's not the best time to be out,' she tries. 'You know, at parties. With people.'

'Sheesh, your brother dies and suddenly it's like you have leprosy,' I snap.

The immediate vicinity is noticeably quiet.

'I didn't mean it like that,' Mallory hurries to add. 'I just think you need more time to recover, some quiet time, alone –'

'So you don't have to see me have feelings? You're acting like *I'm* the one who lemminged off the cliffs of sanity. I'm completely fine!'

The shout echoes across the beach. The herd of partygoers freezes like startled deer sensing a threat.

Funny. I've never wanted to be the centre of attention, but you wouldn't know it right now. I can't cry here, not in front of everyone. And not in the middle of an investigation, for Christ's sake; it's unprofessional.

'Well, Mallory,' I say, with radioactive heat emanating from my cheeks, 'it was super seeing you. Cheers for the pep talk. Sorry. I'm just – erm, sorry, I guess. About everything. Have fun at college. Go live life. I hear it's worth it.'

Mallory's mouth falls open, but I don't want to hear whatever well-meaning uselessness she has queued up. I need to get out of here before I make this worse. I need –

– to turn and walk straight into someone else, spilling their drink all over both them and me and upping my humiliation quotient by a factor of at least one hundred.

Oh, good god and a fist shake to an indifferent universe, it's the jumpy girl from the woods. Bambi Scarlett – aka Megan Lugner, aka Pretty College Girl Who Thought I Was a Lunatic – is standing right in front of me, her delicate peach-coloured top soaked in beach party concoction, her eyes wide as if her lunatic suspicions have just been confirmed.

Which, of course, they have.

'I'm so sorry,' I say, aghast.

Wet Megan gathers herself. 'That's OK.'

'No, it's not. Let me help you. Here, I'll clean you up –'

Am I really trying to wipe off her chest with my sleeve right now, you ask yourself? And my reply is yes, yes, I am, and this is what happens when you watch too many romantic comedies. Somehow no one mentions that every character in those things is at best problematic, often teetering on the edge of sanity themselves . . .

Megan's hand covers my own. It is warm and dry, unlike the rest of her.

'Stop,' she says kindly.

I stop.

And then she says: 'Let's go somewhere more private.'

Her hand does not come off mine. It fastens itself around my fingers, tugging them along with it. Megan leads me away through the gawkers and the gawpers, across the beach, plunging us into the cooler air beyond the firelight's reach.

I say nothing all this time. It's for the best.

We tramp silently across the sand, the party music fading, the sound of the waves swelling. When we near the caves at the end of the beach Megan stops, lets go of my hand and peers at me through the bosky dusk.

'How are you doing there?' she asks.

I give her a weak smile. 'Believe it or not, that wasn't my Worst Party Moment Ever.'

'Gosh. I'm impressed.'

'Wait till you hear about the worst one. Then you'll be running.'

Megan laughs. 'I don't scare that easily.'

I'm staring at her, I know it, but I can't help it. The first time we meet, I'm doing a black magic ritual over the spot where my crazy dead brother's body was found. The next time we meet, I drench her in cheap vodka after she witnesses me shouting at my crazy dead brother's poor ex-girl, who must have looked like she was under attack.

'I don't know,' I hedge. 'I suspect you're secretly thinking about beating the speed record of your previous exit from Situation Alec.'

'I'm sorry about the woods,' she says, surprising me even further. 'Not cool of me. I just got a little weirded out.'

'No doubt, no doubt. Well, thanks for not running this time.' I restrain myself from glancing at her chest. 'And for being such a good sport about me ruining your top.'

'It was an accident. Besides, it seemed like you were in kind of an emotional situation with your friend there. I'm glad I could offer an exit scene.'

'And what an exit scene,' I reply, but it's not my finest return serve.

'Friend break-ups are worse than romantic ones,' Megan says, apparently reading my mind. 'So much more of a betrayal.'

I shrug. 'Because they know all your darkest secrets.'

Megan nods. 'And they'll use them against you.'

'M.A.D.'

She looks quizzical, so I go on: 'Mutually Assured Destruction. You have dirt on them, too. Neither of you should detonate, or both sides blow up.'

Megan nods back towards the firelight. 'Betrayal, like I said.'

Her expression is deadly serious. Apparently an ex-friend really did a number on this girl.

'Oh,' I say as revelation hits. 'So *that's* who your stalker was.'

'My . . . what?'

'Your stalker. That day in the woods. The figure watching us over by that cabin. I'm guessing it was your scary ex-bestie, circling her prey with grenades at the ready.' I search Megan's face. 'I'm kidding. It was a joke. A bad one. Terrible. I should be fined. Arrested. Drawn and quartered.'

In the silence that follows, I can hear the gentle roll and pull of the ocean, and ever so faintly, the sound of voices in the caves behind us. Apparently it's never too early to get jiggy. If the talking starts morphing into erotic moans, we're going to have to find another spot.

'Do you . . .' Megan hesitates. 'Do you want to get out of here, maybe? Go get a drink or something?'

Her eyes are on me. By Jove, I think she's serious. With me. A drink. Me. Her. Just the two of us.

I ready an embarrassingly emphatic reply. A shriek interrupts me. At first I think it's a seagull – those rats of the sky – but when it comes again, it has a strange echo to it, a chillingly distorted sound.

'What is that?' Megan has the slow voice of someone trying to ignore their hindbrain. 'Is that a bird?'

'Nope,' I reply, 'that's a human.'

Another piercing yell. I know what pure fear sounds like.

'Wait here just a second, OK?' I tell Megan.

And then I turn and hotfoot it to the caves.

My legs pump. Sand sprays from under my feet. Later there will be time to ask myself why I'm like this. Right now I can hear fear, and panic, and I'm the closest, and that's all that matters.

As I close in on the nearest cave entrance I fumble out my phone to use it as a flashlight – then it thunks into the sand as a tall figure bursts from the cave and collides with me.

Slim and lanky underneath the bulky hoodie. Baseball cap hiding their hair. A snatch of one pale-ringed eye before a gloved hand comes up and slams sunglasses back into place – who the hell wears sunglasses in a pitch-black cave? – and then the tall figure is off, sprinting away from me, away from a stock-still Megan in the distance, sneakers pounding sand, until they're lost in the dunes beyond.

Another shriek dribbles from the cliff hole, snatching me back to business. The sound is weaker, hoarse, losing its strength. Baseball Cap wasn't the screamer, then – but why did they run?

What the hell is in those caves?

No more time-wasting. The flashlight goes on and I plunge into the darkness beyond.

Eyes won't adjust fast enough. I stumble along.

'Hello?' I call out. 'Hello! I'm coming, tell me where you are!'

Silence.

Shit, shit, shit.

Shit, what if it's a serial killer?

Shit, I tell myself again as I shuffle forwards, and only now does it dawn on me that I don't know this cave system at all. I've only been here once when I was fourteen, lured by an inexpertly hormonal Jason Pengrove, and I don't remember how we got in and out –

Relief plus a heart-bursting surge of fear pulls me up short as my phone light picks out a human shape. His eyes are open and, thank god, he's alive. He has his back against the wall, his arms held up in front of his face as if to guard his gaze.

That end scene in *The Blair Witch Project* chooses this most unhelpful of moments to flash through my brain – *thank you, brain!* – and I go against every instinct I have. I move forward to him.

'Hey,' I say. 'Hey! What happened?'

He whimpers. He hasn't even turned around to look at me. His gaze is trained on the far wall. Filled with dread, compelled by that damned curiosity of mine, I turn my phone light to the area he's staring at.

No serial killers. No kraken. Not even a crazed bunny rabbit. There's nothing there. We're alone in the darkness.

'Hey!' I say, relief making me sharp. 'Come on, friend, talk to me! What's going on?'

His mouth opens and closes. He won't take his eyes off the far wall.

'Don't you see it? Don't you *see* it?' he gibbers.

'What? What do you see?'

'Sp-spider. Elephant-sized spi-spider,' the guy mutters.

Then he does the thing people do when they're about to chunk their lunch – mouth open, chin pushing forward, little tremble in the throat. I subtly angle my body away from the potential splash zone and stare where he's staring.

It's not a big cave. I can see every corner of it with one sweep of my phone light, and there is not enough room in here for two teenagers and one elephant-sized anything. It would have to be practically on top of us, for a start –

'Oh god,' the screamer whispers. 'It's *giving birth*.'

Have you ever seen someone faint? It's not a fast, dramatic fall but a slow crumpling, as though their bones are now made of jelly but it's taking a minute for the rest of them to realize.

He's only saved from a concussion because he falls directly on top of me.

The Crucible

I have a scattering of experience with chemically induced altered states.

Everyone does, actually. It's just they somehow tend to forget that human bodies are functionally complex chemical factories and the majority of the good and bad feelings they experience are the result of reactions between various inputs with the stuff they already have inside them. Inputs include, for example, the caffeine in your oat-milk flat white (increased energy and heartbeat, feelings of alertness and focus, anxiety).

I've found that people often view even cautious and informed experimentation with arbitrarily deemed socially unacceptable drugs, e.g. MDMA, over socially acceptable drugs, e.g. alcohol or literally any FDA-approved medication, as reckless or even morally reprehensible.

Obviously, being well informed from multiple sources in both fact and fiction (Sherlock Holmes, every musician I've ever worshipped) that heroin and its derivatives are not experiences worth the consequences, I'm never going to touch that nasty life-ruiner with any kind of pole, barge or otherwise. Much like I don't really need to know what carbon monoxide poisoning feels like just before I expire from it.

But psychedelics? Now, they're staging a major comeback these days. We've come a long way from their demonization in the twentieth century — horror tales of LSD trippers slaughtering their own families because they mistook them for evil leprechauns or sawing off a foot because it started back-chatting them — with middle-class housewives now discussing the benefits of microdosing over their Wednesday jazzercise class.

Anyway, my eventual point: since the housewives have so far said nothing about hallucinating giant spiders giving birth, I suspect that might be the product of something with a little more kick to it than your average magic mushroom.

Our arachnophobe's name is Scott Poltern. He's twenty-one, and back home for the summer after graduating from Harvard in economics. His father is some real estate bigwig who specializes in corporate developments, so it's been a financially comfortable upbringing. He's attractive, popular and well on his way up the ladder of conventional success.

At least, this is what his social media would have us all believe. He certainly doesn't present himself as top contender for 'Most Likely to Be Found Screaming in a Beach Cave', but presentation often doesn't match reality.

And what of Baseball Cap? Were they the cause of Scott's freak-out? I can't see how — they were very definitely human-shaped, just the two legs on them. More likely it was his fooling-around-in-a-cave partner, who got spooked when he started to hallucinate and exited stage left. The whole sunglasses in the dark/head to toe in athleisure combo doesn't do it for me, but whatever floats your boat.

There's just one niggling thing, though. I feel like I've seen Baseball Cap before. Obviously I couldn't see their face, but something about their figure rings a bell – but try as I might, I can't place it.

Probably not important.

My laptop perches open before me, the screen's top line filled with more internet search tabs than the human eye can take in. They include, variously: 'species of spiders as big as humans'; 'what can make you trip balls hard enough to see things that aren't there'; an array of Scott's social media posts; and several of Justin Gorhammer's videos. I've been scrolling through the detritus of their online lives for hours, but the only handily obvious connection I've uncovered so far is that they both nurse long-time crushes on Rachel Weisz. Not exactly damning, however, because who among us does not? (It was *Constantine* for me.)

Is there supernatural evil in the town of Fring? Or is a bad batch of recreational mind-alterers conjuring demons that lurk in the corner of gamers' bedrooms and mutant spiders that like to use beach caves as a birthing suite? I could go railing at the current curriculum that has every malleable young mind in a fifty-mile radius studying *The Crucible* ad nauseam on their way up the matriculation ladder, because maybe this is nothing more than a case of burgeoning mass hysteria. Demonic visions instead of witchcraft running rife through the younger population –

Wait, here's something.

Justin's interminable walkthrough videos have attracted some recent capital-letter comment trolling. A standard internet life annoyance, of course (like seeing the same lip plumper device stalk you across a hundred sites because your eyeballs inadvertently strayed to the damned advert one time, *one* time, for less than ten seconds, and only out of morbid curiosity, I swear), but one comment in particular stands out – and mostly because variations of it appear in the comments section of at least half of his videos:

*U CAN BLOK AND DELETE ME BUT U CANT
DELET THE TRUTH
JUSTICE 4 VIOLA GORDON!*

Now *there's* a name I recognize.

Everyone under the age of thirty around here has heard of Viola Gordon. She's an online influencer with a big following. She's no Kardashian, but she does OK.

At last there's *something* tangible, an actual connection to work with, because not only is Viola Gordon famous but she and Justin Gorhammer go to the same local college. She posts so many live videos from the place, I feel like I go there myself – Sutherland Hollow, my new crush Megan Lugner's very same alma mater. I've even seen Viola in the background of one of Justin's videos – they were both at some influencer convention in the city. They know each other. Coincidence one. They're also both influencers in different ways. Coincidence two.

Influencers attract a fair share of digital crazies to their posts, of course, and the all-caps/seething tone of righteous anger combo is a common enough flag for strangers with nothing better to do – but my gut says the 'JUSTICE 4 VIOLA GORDON' commenter is someone who knows them both.

And I know someone who knows Viola Gordon.

I may never be voted 'Most Likely to Win Prom Queen', but I sure as shit would rank first for 'Most Annoyingly Determined to Discover the Truth at Any Cost'. There is something going on here, and it all began with my brother. Whatever it may be – hysteria, drugs, madness – I just need to pick determinedly and diligently at its threads until the whole thing unravels and reveals itself to me. Whatever it takes to uncover the truth, I have to be ready to do it, no matter the cost to me or anyone else.

That's a healthy response to grief, right?

The Last Seduction

Christien Van Freesburg is an easy guy to get hold of – if you know how to play him.

Christien's father is the Mayor of Fring, and for the apathetically elected official of a one-horse town he pulls a lot of weight across the county. Fring is strategically placed these days, one of the last remaining bastions of what gets diplomatically called 'under-developed'. In other words it hasn't yet succumbed to the relentless march of gentrification – but it won't be long. Mayor Van Freesburg is the driver of the Money Train, and he's tootin' for us all to come aboard.

Christien, in stark contrast, nurses high ambitions of making just enough cash to fund a constant supply of pizza, sex and weed, with the occasional surf trip to Mexico thrown in. A life of politics seems, to him, akin to a daily bathe in a pit of razor blades, but Freesburg Senior has very definite ideas regarding Christien's future, with more than enough ambition to make up for his heir apparent's perceived lack.

Christien compensates for this combative state of affairs in various ways, one of which used to be Viola Gordon. They were, for a hot minute, the ultimate budding power couple. Then, a few weeks before Lucas died, they had the kind of publicly acrimonious split that people film on their camera phones and then post on their socials with captions like 'I feel so bad for both of them! Crazy embarrassing to fight in public!'

There were accusations of infidelity on both sides, apparent indiscretions at wild parties. But they still know each other because in small towns the set they both belong to tends to fit inside a limo. Ever since their break-up last year, Christien has been numbing the pain with an astonishing variety of temporary female companions – including, I have to admit, yours truly.

'That was nice,' I say, nestling into his sheets.

'Nice?' echoes Christien, leaning back against his headboard, the better to display his surfer's torso. 'Well, gosh, I admit I'm more used to rave reviews.'

'Really nice,' I amend. 'Incredible. Consider my mind blown. I just didn't want to gush due to pride.'

Christien gives out a soft laugh. The good thing about him – he takes nothing seriously.

This is also the bad thing about him.

'So how did *I* do?' I ask with a teasing smile.

He considers. 'You're like rhubarb crumble.'

'Er . . . consider me puzzled.'

He waves his hands. 'Sweet and satisfying, right, but also tart.'

'You're calling me a tart?' I riposte with mock outrage.

'In the fruit sense. Wait, listen, this is good.' Christien's eyes are lit up with inspiration. 'So you take a bite of the crumble, right, and you've got all the gooey goodness and the sugary crumbly bit. But then on your next bite there's rhubarb on the spoon, and suddenly you get this spiky sour hit. You're a dessert with an edge, Gray.'

I'm actually flattered.

'What kind of dessert was Viola?' I ask casually.

It is Christien's turn to go spiky sour. He gives me a sharp glance, and then looks away.

'A gentleman never tells. Please say you're not here because you're a Viola Gordon fangirl, Alec.'

'Nope,' I reassure him. 'Just a curious bystander.'

'Well, you'll not get much from me on the subject,' he says.

I can see I've actually scored a hit.

'I'm sorry,' I reply, and I mean it. 'I honestly wasn't planning to open up a wound.'

'There's no wound,' Christien says with a casual shrug. 'It was ages ago. I don't give a crap about ancient history.'

No, Christien, you don't care at *all*.

I change tack.

'I'm not interested in Viola per se, I just came across her while I was looking at Justin's videos, and – you know Justin Gorhammer?'

Christien's torso disappears over the edge of his bed, and then returns with rolling paraphernalia. The unmistakable smell of high-grade weed wafts back along with him.

'Of,' he comments eventually. 'He's that nerdy kid who's gone crazy, right?'

'I mean . . . what even *is* crazy these days?' I hazard.

'I think probably seeing things that aren't there counts,' Christien says with a laugh. 'Guy's a first-rate candidate for the suicide club.'

It takes him a minute to realize what he just said, and how I might reasonably take offence.

His glance at me is the fastest sorry I've ever seen, a blink-and-you'll-miss-it. 'I mean . . . I don't . . .'

'Hey, don't even worry about it,' I cut him off. 'We've all got struggles, right?'

Christien shrugs, intent on his rolling. He's not one for introspection. I've tried to get him to talk about his father before, up the intimacy with a little vulnerable sharing, but he just makes stupid jokes until I give up.

'Even Viola, I'm sure,' I continue. 'She seems like she's going through some stuff right now.'

I'm so good at this, that wasn't an awkward and obvious segue at all – and yet, the bait hooks.

Christien doesn't look at me as he asks, very offhandedly, 'What makes you say that?'

'Her social. It's all . . . you know.'

'I don't, because I don't stalk my exes.'

'Here,' I say, taking my phone and bringing up Viola's main social account. 'Look at these pictures from the last six months.'

Christien gives them a quick once-over. The brief flicker of interest I'd managed to fan snuffs out.

'Same old, same old,' he says. 'Money, pouting and vacuousness.'

I scroll through the photos. Viola on the beach, Viola getting artfully splashed by the tide, Viola on a yacht with her bronzed skin flashing in the sun, Viola in her bathroom with #nomakeup tags even though she is very clearly wearing fake eyelashes. Pouting in sunglasses with captions like 'haters gonna hate but I'm still smokin hot'. The only jewellery she wears is the same vintage-looking necklace with some heavy, esoteric symbol hanging from the chain, flashing gold from its plunged cleavage resting place – a jarring but fashionably pagan touch.

'She's gone from posting a photo once a week, *maybe*, to posting more than once a day,' I tell Christien as I study her. 'Plus the constant live feeds – that's new, too. Shop with Viola. Help Viola pick today's outfit. Watch Viola watch a movie. Watch her take her make-up off. Confessional diary entries before bed. She's live-feeding her entire life, hour by hour, every day.'

'And making a ton with all her paid partnerships,' Christien says with bored contempt.

'Yes, it's a distastefully sad indictment of how our generation has been conditioned to sell a fake version of themselves as the only way to make money and get those juicy dopamine hits of validation; I've read the same opinion pieces in the *Fring Daily News* that you have, Chris. Don't you get it? There's hardly a minute of any day in Viola's life without an accompanying audience.' I glance down at her artfully blurred features. 'It's like she never wants to be alone.'

Christien frowns, his glance dragged back to the Viola video diary entry now playing.

'Do any of you know what it's like to be scared all the time?' she murmurs to the camera – somewhat negating the emotional effect by managing to deliver the line between lips as plumped as two pig flanks.

'So, detective,' Christien says, sparking up his joint. 'What does this mean?'

'I was hoping you could tell me,' I reply. 'She started posting on socials like this just before you guys broke up.'

Christien just shrugs as he inhales. 'So?'

'Maybe she's all heartbroken. You know. Over you.'

Christien nods to a particularly skin-heavy, clothes-light post. 'Does she look heartbroken to you?'

'Who's this?' I indicate a blonde with a cute snub nose who appears often in Viola's photos, wearing an identical pout.

'That's Tippi Pauletti, Viola's bestie,' Christien says.

Tippi. I knew I'd seen her before. It's Buffy/Bunches from the *Stranger Things* party. The one who was yelling at Lucas to stay away – but from who?

Viola?

Another connection to my brother. I feel a stir of nervous excitement. The one I always get when I know I'm on the trail; I just don't yet know where it leads.

'What do you know about Tippi?' I ask.

'She's Viola's partner in crime in the lofty pursuit of social media followers.' Christien shrugs.

Christien, famously, doesn't have any kind of online presence. He says when you have a father in politics, you learn early on to be hard to find. This means he doesn't get the whole social media thing and, like a lot of people who don't get a thing, ends up being dismissive about it.

'You didn't think maybe Viola was going through something?' I persist.

'Viola goes through boyfriends with yachts. That's what she goes through. Anything deeper than that just isn't in her DNA. The Violas of the world are nothing but spoiled divas, going around breaking toys when they get bored of them. That's what I was to her, a toy. You know what it's like to be used?'

'Yes, I do.' And I give him a meaningful look.

Christien catches my drift. His Cheshire Cat grin surfaces, the widest I've ever seen it. 'Oh, come on, Alec. You knew what you were getting into. I told you the score. If you thought anything different, that's on you.'

Example scenario: say you're not as genetically favoured as girls like Viola Gordon. Say your teen hormones seem like they're actively out to make you physically repellent instead of attractive (an utterly counter-intuitive move – isn't the *point* of them to get us all procreating?). Say you desperately spend what little pocket money you make from waitressing shifts on e.g. the latest in expensive hyaluronic acid serums. Say you spend hours and hours a day in front of the mirror, not to enact the myth of Narcissus but to critique every last blotchy curve, pulsating pimple and lank hair strand.

Then one day, someone like Christien starts paying you attention. One of the Blessèd. The flawlessly bronzed skin of a famed Ancient Greek youth, the hawkishly intense eyes of a famed Ancient Greek youth, and the god Pan's hedonistic approach to life. If someone like *him* likes you enough to bed you, you might not be a twenty-first-century Quasimodo after all! Your self-esteem begins to haul itself hopefully out of the mire – only to sink back down further than ever before when you discover that Christien beds girls the way you eat tortilla chips: constantly, mindlessly and without much discrimination on brand.

This happened to someone else, not me.

Fine. It was me.

But I'm absolutely over it. This is about Viola's connection to Justin's connection to Lucas. This is about finding out what happened to my brother.

'Well,' I say, 'maybe you can just get me an intro to Viola.'

Christien's Cheshire Cat grin threatens to cut off the top half of his head. 'You're not her type.'

'I just want to talk to her, gutter mind.'

'Why? You don't strike me as one to play therapist.'

'It's a personal thing. Nothing nefarious, I promise.'

He catches my wheedling look and sighs. 'I can't. I just can't, OK? We're not speaking.' He pauses. 'But I can tell you where she's going to be tomorrow. It's hush hush, otherwise she'd get mobbed by her adoring hordes, but they had to get permission from the mayor's office to shoot at that location. I overheard my dad's PA bitching about it.'

'What location?'

He rolls his eyes at my eager tone. 'The waterfront.'

I give him a sceptical look. 'It's all half torn down and derelict.'

'And ready for primo development,' he nods. 'My dad's next multi-million-dollar deal. I think they're doing post-apocalyptic Gatsby or something, an advertising shoot for some clothing brand starring everybody's favourite influencer. The waterfront is still off-limits to the public, but she raised hell until they made it happen. Naturally someone like Viola Gordon gets her way.'

'Christien,' I say as I hand him my phone to write down the details, 'you're literally the mayor's son.'

'But I don't abuse it,' he grumbles.

I shrug. 'Can't blame someone for exercising a little power. Apparently it's less acceptable when it's a woman doing it.'

'Don't pull the patriarchy card on me,' he protests. 'You just used me to get to my ex.'

'O, sweet recalcitrance, the cornerstone of my personality!'

'Come again?'

'Am I supposed to feel bad, Casanova?' I grin at him. 'Come on, you got something out of it.'

'Wow,' he says with unconvincing outrage. 'Now if *I* did that to a girl, I'd get crucified.'

'You don't strike me as one to play martyr.' I start pulling on my clothes. 'I'll owe you one, if you like.'

'I'll take it.' Christien settles back against his pillows, watching me get dressed. 'Listen, when you talk to Viola, you're not going to do that thing, are you?'

'What thing?' I say as I locate my shoes.

'That . . . *interrogation* thing you do,' Christien says. 'She won't take kindly to it. She can be pretty highly strung. Friendly warning.'

'I'll be nice.' I flash him my most innocent face. 'Promise.'

'Alec.'

'Mmm?'

His silence goes on a little too long, dragging my gaze back to his.

'I don't know how you're doing,' he says. 'I can't even imagine, but if you ever want to talk, you know. About what you've been going through . . .'

I wait, my heart speeding up hopefully.

'. . . I've got this really great therapist,' Christien finishes. 'She's private, and with a hell of a waiting list, but I can get you to the top of the queue, no problem. Just say the word.'

Oh well.

It's comical that he thinks I have the money for that, but everyone's got their blind spots, and I'm not going to make him feel bad for trying to be a friend.

We live in different worlds, Christien and I. His is nice to visit, once in a while – but I don't belong there, and we both know it.

The Great Gatsby

Fring's glorious waterfront is an eerie, tumbledown mess of rusting crab pots and rotting rope coils edging a sludgy brown shoreline. Skulking on the banks of the main tributary, it's inland from the beach and with none of its sandy, windswept charm.

Viola Gordon's shooting crew, down for the day from the city, are hidden from the main road by the crumbling storage warehouses, old fisheries still haunted by the tangy smell of briny blood and rotten scales. As I approach I can see a range of people standing around, holding keep-me coffee cups. One is bent over a monitor. Two more fiddle with lighting rigs. Tripods, ring lights and reflector boards are perched across the waterfront's stained concrete ground. There's even a small trailer.

And, in the midst of them all, easy to spot even if she weren't dripping in full-on twenties flapper regalia, is Viola Gordon. Her hair is beautifully waved and studded with seed pearls that catch the afternoon sun in dots of muted glow.

Everyone around here scores their vintage costumes from the same ancient store in town, which I heard is only still standing in this day and age of declining physical retailers because they get in most of their merchandise from Amazon and resell it for a profit. Though I imagine they got Viola's outfit from somewhere a little more upscale than Patty's Party Pops. It has the heavy drape of actual vintage, for a start.

Viola is poised on a stool with her mouth pursed around a bamboo straw, threatening to smear the precise lines of her pomegranate lips. She is alone, the buzzy man fussing with her outfit having drifted away to join the lighting rig duo.

Now's my chance. No hesitation. Stride as though you're meant to be there.

She spots me on the approach and freezes. Her eyes latch on to mine, wide and wary. I'm not that scary in person, I promise, but from the look on her face you'd think I'd turned up in a killer clown outfit.

'Hi,' I say. 'Your hair is ravishing.'

'You're not on the crew for this,' she says abruptly.

'That's the best thing a girl can be in this world,' I sorrowfully reply, 'a beautiful little fool.'

It was the first thing that came into my head. A heavy silence descends.

'You know,' I encourage. 'From the book. Daisy Buchanan.'

Viola just stares at me. She's intimidatingly tall in person. Aren't famous people always supposed to be smaller than you think?

'Which is who you are being right now,' I addend, a trifle desperately. 'In this photoshoot.'

'Yes, I remember,' she replies.

'OK, you got me. I'm crashing. Sorry. I'm not a crazy fan, I promise. Which obviously is the first thing a crazy fan would say. But nevertheless I maintain my innocence.'

'I thought there was supposed to be security at this thing,' she mutters.

'There was,' I say, 'but I fed him a bone.'

More silence. Tough crowd.

'Listen, I don't want to take up a lot of your time. I just wanted to meet you, and –' don't rat out Christien, he made me promise not to use his name – 'I found out you'd be here today –'

'All right,' Viola interrupts, 'but I'm at work, you know? And we're losing the light, so let's make this quick. Selfies are fifty bucks. You can DoughMe.'

'Doh mee?' I echo stupidly.

'The money transfer app.'

I have to replay the last twenty seconds.

'You . . . charge for selfies?' I ask.

Viola trills a laugh. 'Of course not, that was a joke!'

But something about that too-quick delivery, that mechanical smile, makes me think it's only a joke if the other person doesn't take it seriously.

I wonder how many people take it seriously.

'Come here, girl!' Viola says with a practised smile, holding out her arm. 'Let's do this.'

'I'm not here for a selfie,' I say, stifling the urge to physically back away. People tend to take offence when I do that, and it takes too long to explain it's about my discomfort with unasked-for touch and not, say, a visceral repulsion at their physical presence. 'I just wanted to ask you about something important, if you have a minute?'

Important is always a good word to use, it creates enough curiosity to get a pause, a starter hook. Sure enough, Viola stills. She folds her arms, crinkling the chiffon of her robe into waterfall folds, and studies me.

'My name is Alec Gray,' I say, and I wait for the inevitable wince of recognition.

Nothing.

'You might have heard about my brother, Lucas?'

'Why do you think I'd know who either of you are?' Viola says.

Ouch. Gordon 1, Gray 0.

I change tack. 'But you know Justin Gorhammer, right?'

'No, I do not.'

'Oh,' I nod. 'It's just I saw you in his video? You were both at the convention centre, some sort of influencer gathering?'

Why do even semi-famous people put us on the deference? I've never turned so many sentences into questions in my life before.

'Right,' Viola says impassively. 'The guy who's lost his mind.'

She gives me nothing else, just a blank stare. Waiting.

'OK,' I say slowly, 'what about Scott Poltern?'

Silence.

'What is this important thing you want to ask me?' Viola replies finally, her eyes hard.

'I saw this thing on the internet that suggested maybe something happened to you –'

'Jesus. Who sent you here? Celeb Dirt? Snooper? I don't have any agreements with you guys any more, OK? Are you aware how disgusting it is to follow someone into rehab to try to get a story on them for your shitty little website?'

Her voice rises like a startled bird, attracting attention. A man breaks off from the monitor pack and begins his approach. I've got thirty seconds before I am recognized by virtue of my extreme non-belonging and get booted out of here.

'First of all,' I say with all the dignity I can muster, 'how dare you compare me to a vulture. Second of all, no one *sent* me – I work alone. I'm asking you about Justin and Scott because they're being plagued by the same kind of hallucination. They're seeing demons, for Christ's sake; I mean it's kind of specific, and oh, by the way, that was the exact same thing that my brother was seeing before he took a high dive off the board of life, and apparently I'm the only one in the world who thinks this is kind of a weird coincidence! No one wants to talk about it, and I just –'

Viola reaches out to me, quick and violent, taking me by complete surprise. Her fingers close on my arm hard enough to hurt, her mouth opens –

'Viola, what's going on here?'

The man comes up behind her with his oversized flamingo shirt flapping and his flip-flops flopping. His handlebar moustache drapes handsomely across his small chin. From my contacts over in the cool world, I understand that this nod to the sleazy side of the seventies is bang on current trend.

'Nothing,' Viola says quickly, dropping my arm. 'This is a friend. We're in the middle of a fight, but we'll figure it out later.'

The switcheroo is breathtakingly fast. This Viola is all sweet apology, soft and pleading.

Boogie Nights gives me a once-over.

'Friend, huh?' he says. 'What's your name, my sweet?'

'Your sweet?' I echo, yet too confused to mount a proper defence.

'Shit,' Viola swears. 'Sorry, Neal.' She turns to me. 'You have to go, OK? You can't just turn up like this. I'm at work.'

'What's your name?' Neal asks again.

'Seriously,' Viola cuts in. 'It's not OK, Petra. Just leave.'

My confusion only deepens. 'Petra? What – can we just, can I get your number, or –'

'Look, I wasn't planning to do this in front of other people,' Viola says, 'but I know it was you who stole my necklace.'

'Which the what now?'

'My necklace,' Viola repeats with fervent emphasis. 'You stole it. You know it's my favourite. I wear it in every picture. It's my signature. You're trying to sabotage my look. I need it back, right now!'

Her eyes hold the blank savagery of a goose about to attack.

Neal steps in. 'All right. We're losing the light, and you've lost enough brand partnerships recently, we can't afford for this one to go tits up as well, can we, darling?'

Meek Viola surfaces. 'Sorry, Neal, sorry. I'll nail this one.'

It's Meryl Streep with multiple personality disorder.

Neal steers me away from the scene.

'What is wrong with her?' I ask, astonished.

'She's fragile, Petra. You should know this if you're really her friend.' Neal gives me a searching look. 'You know about the nervous breakdown, right? And the rehab? Right now, what's going to help Viola most is focusing on work. So off you trot, there's a good girl.'

I swear, Boogie Nights, call me 'good girl' again.

Behind me, I hear Viola shouting.

'You'd better find my necklace! You'd better find it and bring it back to me, Petra. I'm not messing around!'

No, I think as I hightail it away from Roaring Twenties Wasteland, *you really aren't.*

The Exorcist

The smell of dense, ponderous incense trickling from a heavy metal ball swung back and forth on the end of a chain. Thick, squat varnished wood, hard and unyielding against the spine. Tough velvet cushions, their plush red faded to the colour of old, dried blood, puffing clouds of dust as your knees plop down on them in ready penance. Bibles with pages as tremblingly thin as moth wings. The particular echo of shoes on flagstones, the hush, every murmured sentence made sonorous. When I think of where I want to turn for solace, I think of church.

Like a Scorsese mafioso, I find comfort here in this dark, cold cavern, its blackness softened by candlelight, sparks of life against the thick surrounding void. It is, despite its hard edges and darkness, my safe space.

If only there weren't all these other people here, spoiling the view.

Still, Sunday Mass at Mary Magdalene Catholic Church is about the only event in town that provides such an equalized cross-section of its inhabitants. José the church gardener sits next to the Mayor of Fring and at the end of their pew is my old elementary school lunch lady, all no doubt wrestling with the same hard-as-rock seat apparently designed to remind the sinner that comfort is a weakness. Behind them I spot –

'Alec,' my mother says next to me out of the corner of her mouth, 'stop watching everyone and trying to figure out what crimes they've committed.'

'I can't help it,' I protest in a whisper.

I once got into trouble at Sunday school because instead of doing the required assignment on Jonah and the Whale I'd stood up in front of the group and expounded upon the nature of sin via a list of my peers' recent examples – I'd even worked out which kid was responsible for writing a bad word on the vestibule wall in thick crayon, something the adults had so far failed to do. I'd thought I was helping, and I'd like to point out that, to make it fair, I'd also included my own sins. That day I learned that no one likes a snitch, even when they snitch on themselves too.

'Alec.'

I glance at my mother. She's hunched, indicating discomfort and tension. It takes me a minute to work out why – today, people are looking at us. It's subtle, but I start catching the pity, the curiosity, in those snatched glances. Vicarious tragedy. Best show on TV.

Still, it stops me looking around.

Mass takes too long, as usual, and I spend most of it daydreaming, as usual, but when things wind up I come to life, ready for the real reason I came today.

'Mom,' I catch her sleeve. 'Let's go see Oh.'

She hesitates. 'Not today, Alec. I've got too much to get done.'

'He's right there; it won't take long. Besides, I haven't seen him in a while.' I fix her with a look. 'Come on. Fine, I'm not allowed to go get soused with a cadre of reckless partying peers, but I need *some* socializing, and who better to keep me on the straight and narrow than a priest?'

'Who indeed?' comes a voice behind us.

I feel a grin threatening. 'Great show, today. One of your best.'

Oh snorts. 'I'd sing a David Bowie song for the next sermon, but I'm not sure the rest of the congregation would respond as well as you, child.'

Father O'Hallaghan is the one human being who gets a lifetime pass on calling me 'child'. For a start, he's known me since I *was* one, and I once read that we tend to hold on to the first version of the people we meet. Secondly, it feels like being given permission to be my boldest, most inquisitive, most truthful self, the one I dimly remember being before life bombarded me with, well, life, and I had to grow some defensive skin.

'In trying to please everyone, you end up pleasing no one,' quoth I.

'Ouch. Well, with friends like you, who needs enemies?' Oh smiles at my mother. 'Hello, Ellie.'

Is it my imagination, or is her nod a touch icy? 'Oh. How are you?'

'Can't complain. How's your big case going?'

'That's probably the last thing we should be discussing right now, don't you think?' my mother frosts.

It is not my imagination.

She shakes her head. 'Listen, I'm sorry, but I have to get going. Alec – call me when you're done? I can come and pick you up.'

I frown. 'I always walk.'

'I know, but I'm offering.'

'That's OK, Mom – you're busy.'

Her mouth opens, as if she has a riposte all queued up, and then closes.

'OK,' she says. 'I'll see you later. I'll be back for dinner.' She nods to Oh. 'It was a good sermon, Father.'

Her shoes clop on the stone, growing fainter.

She called him 'Father'. She hasn't done that in years. It's the equivalent of calling me Alecto, my full name – then I know I'm in trouble.

I round on Oh. 'Are you two in a fight?'

He sighs. 'I shouldn't have needled her.'

'About the case?'

He cocks a surprised eye at me. 'Has she talked to you about it?'

'Not really. She just lives at the office and comes home in moods.'

Oh shakes his head. 'I told her she was neglecting you. That she had more important things to take care of at home than at work.'

'Ouch.' I study him. Can't help feeling some warm and fuzzies knowing he's looking out for me – but guilt soon chases their heels.

'I guess I've been neglecting you a little too,' I admit. 'It's been a while.'

'Has it?' His eyes twinkle, irises so brown they look black. 'I barely noticed you were gone.'

'I deserved that.'

'No one deserves anything,' says Oh, 'except mercy, kindness, compassion, blah blah blah.'

You're probably starting to see why I like him.

'I expect it's common as a cold that people stop coming to church when they're all grieving and blah blah blah,' I say, sinking on to the nearest church pew and feeling it rigid against the backs of my thighs in a deeply familiar, deeply uncomfortable way.

'Common the other way, too,' he comments. 'And in between, as each of us takes to our own way of searching for a rock to hold on to among the waves.'

He glides slowly into place next to me. It's only when he starts folding various bits of his body to sit that the swan illusion is broken.

'Oof,' he explains, 'that click was my knees. Can you believe it?'

'Sounded like Death rattling the dice cup.'

'As witty as ever, young lady. But I'll thank you to keep the mortality reminders to yourself.'

'Sorry.'

He nudges me. 'I'm only joking. When you get to my age you talk about death all the time. It's become a sort of hobby.'

'You're barely seventy.'

'Sixty-eight, thank you. Don't be ageing me two years, that's half a lifetime at this point. It's like dog years.'

Part of Oh's appeal is his massive eyebrows, like two mini badgers in perpetual crawl across his forehead. They lift their snouts or tails, shimmy, rise, gallop towards each other and draw down like shades for his eyes as the emotional occasion demands. They are the most expressive clumps of hair I've ever seen.

'How's the flock?' I ask.

Oh sucks on his teeth. 'Dying, living and everything in between. Diana Roots is getting a divorce, and she's terrified the wingèd demons of shame will cast her into a fiery chasm for it. Poor old Freddie Markham – you know, who runs the grocery store up in Sutherland Hollow – he's estranged from his grown-up son and can't mend the bridge. Lots of cancer, alas.'

We have an understanding. Oh's chief self-admitted sin is gossip, which he declares stems from a brimming attraction to examining the mechanics of human beings – part of the reason we get on so well. I've shown him I'm to be trusted with community secrets, as is he. I'm the only one he tells them to. Hey, even priests need an outlet.

'That all sounds depressing for you,' I say.

He shrugs it off. 'It's a burden of my calling that people tend to come to me in distress, so I get a lopsided view of life. Like counsellors of all kinds, hospital workers, emergency responders. You see people in their worst moments, and you don't often get to see their joy. So I ask for it.'

'You ask for it?'

'Oh yes. Once we're done with the bad stuff, and they're feeling a bit calmer, I ask them for all the nice things that have happened to them recently, large or small. It makes my day, I tell you. People delight in all sorts of wonderful things, and it's wonderful to watch them experience that delight again in their remembrance. A little drop of self-care.'

Oh gives me a happy grin. His teeth are atrocious, discoloured and dotted with dark crowns from a post-war era of dentistry when things got shored up with whatever material was lying around, and the notion of having white, straight teeth was the sole burden of Hollywood stars. It makes me think of dentist-in-training Justin Gorhammer, and the reason I came to see him today.

'Speaking of demons,' I say extremely casually.

One of his badger brows bristles, lifting its curious head. 'Were we?'

'Diana Roots and her wingèd demons of shame.'

'Well remembered.'

'Thank you. Um. Are the Gorhammers in your flock?'

He shakes his head. 'Episcopalian. Those beautiful heretics.'

'Have you heard about Justin's recent . . . problems?'

Oh clasps his hands comfortably in his lap, his robes crumpling and pooling around those gnarled, arthritic fingers. 'The son's been struggling with his mental health, I know that.'

'Yup,' I agree. 'That is one way of putting it. Another way of putting it is that he's been seeing a demon.'

The badgers lift their heads.

'Not seeing as in dating,' I quickly amend. 'An episode of *Buffy the Vampire Slayer* this is not. I think it's safe to say *unwillingly* seeing.'

'Poor tortured soul,' Oh says. 'Does he have someone to talk to?'

'Let's hope so.'

'It's easy to succumb to our demons,' he observes. 'Harder to fight them.'

'We don't actually believe in demons, though, do we?'

'They can be figurative. Whatever way best describes it for you. However it manifests, it's a form of evil. It's hard to be good. You have to remain vigilant. And you don't go around calling out to the dark. It's attracted to the light most of all.'

I stare into the distance.

I should probably wash the upside-down cross tattoo off my arm. I'm partial to long sleeves, so he hasn't seen it yet. He might take offence, think it was meant for him, when really it's meant for everyone else. Its message is clear: *Stay away. Damaged and acting out.*

'What about insanity?' I ask. 'How do you define it?'

'I've only had one coffee, Alec,' he grumbles, but I know this is only his way of buying himself time to consider the question.

'I define it as someone who has lost their ability to make sense of the world,' he says at last.

'So someone who has visions – like Joan of Arc, say, or Moses – has lost their ability to make sense of the world?'

'Ah now.' Oh holds up a finger. 'That's someone trying to make sense of their world, again. The visions are manifestations of their struggle, you could say.'

'Or,' I reason, 'their brain is simply randomly misfiring.'

'Potayto, potahto.'

'Isn't it important how we define things?'

'Of course. It's everything. Your beliefs and your perspectives are your reality. They shape how you think and feel.' Oh contemplates the altar, far ahead of us. 'We are storytellers, at our core. We understand ourselves and our place in things through story. Even if it is the result of a randomly misfiring brain, we still have to make sense of what is happening to us.'

'But,' I persist, 'are demons actually real?'

'According to who?'

'According to some sort of objective judge of reality.'

'So – according to God?' Oh's mouth quirks in a provocative smile.

'Potayto, potahto,' I reply.

Oh spreads his hands. 'It depends on who you ask. That's not the question you should be trying to answer, anyway, because it really doesn't matter if demons are real or not. The question you should be trying to answer is: why are *you* seeing them? What do they mean to *you*?'

'A demon is evil. Isn't it? It's an evil being sent to torment you.'

'It is if it makes you feel that way.'

I think of the despair in Justin's voice on the video. The abject fear of Scott Poltern in the beach cave. The sickened look of dread on my brother's face when he saw whatever he saw in the middle of the road that night.

No. Not dread.

Guilt.

'Maybe they're being punished,' I say.

Oh's glance at me is impressed.

'Father O'Hallaghan?' A new voice echoes behind us. 'Do you have a moment?'

We both turn in our seats.

Standing in the vestibule are two men. One is the mayor himself, having apparently lingered after the service. I can see Christien in him, or him in Christien – either way it's an uncomfortable moment for me, because the state I've mostly seen Christien in is undressed. The man next to him looks familiar too, though I can't quite place him. He's even slicker than the mayor, in a tailored suit and the kind of wristwatch that might secure lesser capitalists a down payment on a house.

Oh hesitates.

'Of course,' he says. 'Give me just a few moments more with the young lady, here.'

'That's OK,' I say. 'Mom's expecting me.'

Besides, I only like talking to Oh when it's just the two of us. I make ready to leave, but then Oh does something odd.

'No, I think you should stay, Alec,' he insists.

I pause, surprised. I don't like the confession box – we always talk out on a pew, so we often get interrupted. It's understood that I get as much of his time as I want, but in return I bow out whenever another shows up needing him. It's Oh's only boundary with me, and neither of us have ever violated it.

'It's, er, it's kind of a private matter, Father,' the mayor says with a fixed smile.

Oh says nothing. Is he going to *refuse*? I've never seen him so rude before. I can't bear it, and I jump up, embarrassed.

'I totally get it,' I say hastily. 'Oh, I'll see you again soon, anyway.'

Oh gives me a curt nod. 'Yes. You will.'

Wow. Oh does not like these guys. Then again, no one likes politicians – what else is new?

'Alec,' I hear Oh call as I turn away. 'The fudge ones, next time.'

I grin. 'You got it.'

I first discovered Oh's Oreo cookie addiction when I caught him huffing three at once in an impromptu post-Mass drive-by. Until that day I didn't even know you could fit that many in a human mouth. Since then I've brought him regular offerings of whichever Oreo flavour he's currently into. It's a call sign between us, an inside joke. Almost like he wants these strangers to know that I'm not just a sheep in his flock, but a friend.

I nod politely to the mayor on my way out, who barely acknowledges me. Slick guy, however, has been watching me the entire time. As I pass him, he gives me a big, big smile.

Diner

In an effort not to look up at the door again, I scan the menu a fifteenth time.

I'm sat at a corner banquette of a new vegan burger joint called Morrissey's, and it is packed out by the college crowd who matriculate but a stone's throw from its doors. Everyone here is two or three years older than me and divertingly attired in various nods to vintage England.

I wish I could get away with clothes like this back in Fring. A guy two banquettes away sports a flat cap. If he wore that on my streets, people would assume he was in a costume parade and mock accordingly – but here, it's cool.

Here is Sutherland Hollow, home to the college of the same name, a campus stuffed with artsy bohemian types who wear neon eyeliner on a Tuesday afternoon if they feel like it. One day I might even be lurking in this joint as a fellow student rather than an anxious interloper, dressed like Jane from *Daria* and having heated debates about Schopenhauer.

My daydreaming is interrupted by an arrival. I assume the heavily pierced waitress, who on her last visit seemed to be tiring of my repeat orders of nothing but oat-milk lattes, is back for another round of 'I recommend today's special, the plant burger/truffle fries combo!'

But it's not her. It's Megan, looking impeccably pretty.

'I'm so sorry I'm late,' she says, her hair blowsy from summer wind. 'Naturally you called out the coastguard.'

I nod. 'They're combing every cove from here to Eureka. I told them you went seal spotting.'

'Oh, I'm not into the seal coves,' Megan replies. 'I'm more of a Cockle Beach kind of girl.'

I can feel a blush playfully stippling my cheekbones.

What can I say about Cockle Beach? If anyone ever developed the area, we'd lose our famed top spot in the state's highest teenage pregnancy per capita rankings. Despite that, I hope it never gets touched. It's one of the few wild places left around here, hard to find and semi-perilous (when the tide comes in, your way off the beach disappears and you drown), which makes it prime real estate for private shenanigans.

I steal a glance at Megan. Her expression is as bland as rice pudding as she sits herself down opposite me. Either she doesn't know the significance of Cockle Beach –

No. She knows. My blush deepens. Tarnation.

'My rehearsal ran over,' she explains as she runs her fingers through her hair. 'I kept giving the director significant looks, but he thinks he's the next Yorgos Lanthimos and everyone has to wait for his genius to peter out before we're allowed to leave – that or he has a caffeine crash and needs to spike up again, whichever happens first. Did you order? I'm thinking the Bananarama Tropicana DeNiro Not Included shake.'

'I got the –' I consult the menu – 'Cruelty-Free Coconut, No Cows Were Juiced in the Making of this Beverage! shake.'

'That one's pretty good,' Megan says. 'My go-to after a stressful day.'

'So,' I ask, 'why did you want to meet with me today?'

Megan pauses with her denim crop jacket half off her shoulders.

'Well,' she says, 'the business plan hasn't quite come together, but I was wondering if we could take a stab at budgets first before that big meeting on the fifth.'

I gape stupidly.

Megan's smile is half-alarm. 'That was a joke. Why did I want to meet up with you, let's see. Curiosity? I think you're fun.'

'One man's fun is another man's Hermann Göring,' I say, while inside my head a voice screams, *Why are you like this, Alec?* 'Fun – like, strange, right?'

'People are strange,' Megan says. 'The Doors wrote a song about it.'

'Yes, but I'm not like "sexy goth Lolita" strange, I'm like "keeping toe clippings in a jar" strange.'

'Why would you do that?' she asks cautiously.

'I wanted to see if they kept growing after they'd been cut.' I pause. 'I was six; my grasp of biology was appropriately rudimentary.'

Megan grins. 'That's actually pretty cute, in a nerdy way.'

My heart speeds up.

'Now who's the strange one?' I say.

'You're right,' she agrees. 'I'm far stranger than you.'

I look her up and down, relishing the chance to look her up and down. 'Please.'

'I might be an axe murderer, for all you know,' she counters.

I shake my head. 'Axe murderers always get found out. You use a showy, messy weapon like that, you want people to *know* what you did.'

Megan bursts out in an enormously loud donkey laugh, drawing stares.

'That's good,' she says. The laugh makes her awkward and fallible, and I start to like her even more.

'Sorry,' I offer. 'I'm suspicious by nature. It annoys everyone around me.'

'But it also keeps you safe,' Megan says. 'Because you can't trust anyone.'

I'm looking for the ironic smile, but her face is set to serious.

'Careful,' I say. 'Between this and the axe murderer comment I'm starting to get my detective out.'

She glances at me.

'Oh,' she says. 'Is that why you said yes to meeting with me? This is work for you? Grilling the suspect?'

'I don't suspect you of anything,' I say with a smile. *Except for breaking into my dreams. Never say that out loud, Alec.*

'Foolish,' Megan comments. 'Remember what I said about not trusting anyone?'

Her drink arrives. She slurps with her mouth puckered voluminously around the straw, and her eyes on me.

'So have you always been a detective?' she asks.

'Solving cases since I could walk. The first was Fargo.'

'The movie?'

'And our dog's name. He went missing once for a week when I was around seven. I suspected kidnapping for ransom, a vengeance prank by one of my brother's doofus friends, or a moment of weakness from my maths teacher – her beloved Misty had died only the month before, and they were a similar breed. Grief can drive you crazy, you know?'

'So which was it?'

'None of them.' I shake my head. 'Fargo had his head turned by a stray from inland who'd come to the coast for the day. I found them shacked up together in the abandoned Burger King out by the highway.'

'Wow. What was the clue that led you there?'

'Oh, I just knew he'd fall prey to a femme fatale; he was the type. Also he was a total sucker for Burger King. I guess he could still smell the ghosts of flame-grilled Whoppers on the premises.'

'Impressive. Was your brother a detective too?'

'Lucas?' I snort. 'Hardly. The boy acted like he'd never heard of guile. He didn't really get why anyone would ever hide anything.'

Until the last few months of his life, that is.

My face must have fallen into my drink thinking about him, because Megan's has gotten watchful. I hastily turn it on her.

'Do you have any siblings?'

'Only child,' Megan replies. 'Now you're going to tell me all about how only children are maladjusted sociopaths.'

'I mean I went to "self-centred princess" rather than "maladjusted sociopath" –'

'That too, obviously.'

'Do you get on with your parents?'

'Talk about sociopaths, talk about my father. College is a relief because I get to spend my days away from him. When it's done, I'm out of here.'

'Wow,' I say. 'We can't both be blunt and spiky; people won't be able to tell us apart.'

Megan fixes me with that watchful stare. 'I grew up alone. No pity – that's just how it was. But I think loners can sense each other.' She pauses. 'I felt a connection with you the first time we met, in the woods.'

'Static shock.' I nod. 'I used to get one from my friend Deena whenever she wore her mohair sweater.'

'No,' Megan pushes, 'I meant a deeper connection than that.'

My heart literally skips a beat.

Megan's eyes lower. 'It's OK if you didn't feel it too.'

'No, I – it's not that.'

'It's just when you cross paths with the most interesting girl in a fifty-mile radius, you'd be an idiot not to follow it up.'

'Fifty miles? That's pretty far,' I manage.

'It is,' Megan agrees.

'Then again, what's fifty miles when you're talking about a desert?'

'How d'you mean?'

'I don't know if you've noticed,' I expand, 'but we live in a cultural wasteland. It made headlines in the local paper when Miriam Kopek scooped top prize at the yearly flower arranging competition, and then it came to light that she was sleeping with half the judging board. She lost the trophy, of course, and people took to screaming "Mata Hari" at her on the street. If only. Apparently there are no worthier causes to put her femme fatale talents to use for than "being best at putting flowers in a vase".'

'I'm willing to bet,' she replies, holding my gaze, 'that Miriam Kopek isn't the only femme fatale in the area.'

My cheeks turn the colour of a clown's nose.

Megan suddenly starts sliding out of the booth.

'Where are you going?' I say with far too much palpable dismay.

'The bathroom,' she says, with a small smile.

'Right. Right. Enjoy!'

Enjoy?

I surreptitiously watch her cross the diner, and I notice how many other patrons are doing the same. I think about signals. Short of lunging across the booth table and then being slapped down for mild sexual assault, how does one clearly signal 'Hey, I like you, but in less of a Jane Austen *let us take a turn about the room and gossip* kind of way and in more of a *Carmilla* kind of way – *can I suck on your neck now*?

A shadow falls across the booth table before I can assemble any kind of action plan.

'That was quick.' I look up, but it's not Megan.

It's Viola Gordon.

'Hey, Alec.' She looms over me. 'How are you doing?'

My mouth opens, but nothing comes out.

'Listen, I'm sorry about the other day. That was really embarrassing. My manager is all about the money.' She fish-hooks her coral-painted top lip in a disdainful 'what can ya do?' move.

'OK,' I manage.

'I was thinking we could get a coffee sometime,' she says to me. 'Somewhere out of town, maybe. I'm just so over being followed around, you know?'

'Totally.' I nod. 'I hate that.'

She pauses – a micro-second.

Then: 'Maybe I could get your number? So we can coordinate?'

'Coordinate?' I flounder.

'Go-innnng forrr ay co-ffeeee,' Viola enunciates for the dunce. 'You said you wanted to talk to me.'

How does one say, *Yes, but preferably in a crowd, from a safe distance* without it sounding bad?

'Don't worry,' she adds, 'I'm not as crazy as I look.'

I gape. 'I didn't believe in telepathy, the headline will read, until the day I met Viola Gordon.'

Viola actually laughs.

'Wait until you see what else I can do,' she replies with a sparkle. 'You free tomorrow?'

'I was gone for two seconds and you're already collecting phone numbers,' says Megan from behind. She's back from the bathroom, and her arms are folded.

Viola whirls around. The two stare at each other like lions over the same prey.

'What the fuck are you doing here?' Viola says, her voice notably higher.

Megan's laugh, by contrast, is easy and relaxed. 'This is my end of town, V, remember?'

'No – what are you *doing*?'

'Meeting my new friend for a drink?' Megan shrugs. Her smile is wide and helpless.

'Your new –' Viola's face turns to me. She's staring at me – presumably, it's hard to tell through the sunglasses – but I've no idea what she's looking for.

'You're friends with her?' she asks me.

'I don't know,' I respond, astonished. 'It's early days, I don't want to put pressure on it, but –'

'She approached *you*?' Viola demands. 'She asked you here?'

'Yes. So?'

Viola turns back to Megan and slaps her across the face.

The sound cracks across the diner, cutting the cheery background noise in two.

'Shame on you,' she hisses.

Megan is hunched, clutching the side of her face. I am frozen, ineffectual.

And then I am a mongoose.

I leap up and place myself bodily between the two, keeping Megan protected at my back.

'What the hell is wrong with you?' I snarl.

'You have no idea –' Viola starts, but my mongoose rage cuts in.

'Touch her again and I'll call the cops on you.'

Beside us materializes a newcomer, a short blonde with a cute snub nose. Her face is familiar, though I can't immediately place her.

'You need to calm down, Viola,' she says in a deadly voice.

Viola looks between the three of us, and then laughs a terrible laugh.

'*Et tu*, Tippi? Unbelievable. Anyone else?'

She looks around, and then seems to clock the size of the audience – and these being the times they are, how many of them have camera phones for hands. Her hands come up instinctively in front of her face, as if by blocking out the scene it doesn't exist.

Then she turns around and walks quickly out of the diner, shouldering her way through the saloon doors and into the hard sunlight beyond.

I turn around to Megan, still clutching at her face.

'Are you OK?' I ask.

Megan gives a weak nod.

'What on earth was that all about?'

Tippi cuts in, looking at Megan. 'You should press charges this time.'

This time? As in: there's been a time before this one?

'The cops don't care about girls bitch-slapping each other, Tippi,' Megan says.

'One of them does.' Tippi's reply is loaded with meaning, and they exchange a glance.

'Hi,' I say, taking Tippi's unresisting hand and giving it a shake, 'good to meet you – Tippi, is it?'

Tippi looks me up and down. Then she pulls her hand out of mine.

'New girlfriend?' she asks Megan drily.

My heart leaps like a gazelle towards a limitless sky.

'Uh, no,' Megan says quickly. 'This is just a friend.'

My heart crashes like a gazelle at the business end of a hunter's gun.

'My name's Alec Gray,' I say, attempting to recover some equilibrium. 'So you're both on intimate terms with Viola Gordon?'

'With her fist, at least,' Megan says. 'How do *you* know her?'

The cold edge to Megan's voice alerts me to tread with care.

'I don't,' I say, 'I just wanted to talk to her.'

'About what?'

'Oh, ya know. Detective stuff.'

Megan looks at me, but I don't want to go into it here, in front of a stranger. I can tell she doesn't like my reticence.

'Alec Gray?' says Tippi in a puzzled voice. She glances at Megan. 'As in, *Gray*, Gray?'

What, am I famous with the influencer jet set? Has Christien been talking me up?

Megan ignores Tippi.

'Don't go near Viola,' she says to me.

I shrug. 'Well, I'm thinking twice about it now –'

Her tone gets sharp enough to cut. 'I mean it, Alec.'

'It's cool, I'll just stay out of slapping distance.'

'Don't fucking talk to her, ever!' Megan snaps.

Now I feel as though I'm the one who's been slapped.

'OK,' I say slowly. 'Clearly I got caught in the middle of something here.'

Megan's face softens instantly. 'I'm sorry. I'm so sorry, Alec.'

'You're riding the adrenaline train,' I murmur. 'It's understandable.'

'Yes, but that's no excuse. It's just – you have to understand about Viola. She told everyone she just got out of rehab, but actually she was sectioned. For . . . attacking me.'

All right. That's a serious accusation. Then again, I've yet to meet Viola Gordon without it ending in some real edgy behaviour.

'Why did she attack you?' I ask.

'It's between me and her,' Megan says.

I hold up my hands. 'Fair enough.'

'Sorry,' Tippi says. 'But Alec Gray, like – the *sister*?'

That's what makes it click - Tippi was the girl I saw arguing with Lucas at the Halloween party last year and Christien identified for me the other day.

'You knew my brother?' I say, trying to keep the eager out of my voice. 'Yes, I'm his sister. Was. Well – I still am. You don't stop being someone's sister just because they're dead, right?'

Tippi glances between Megan and me.

'Um,' she says carefully, 'right.' Then she turns to Megan, her nose screwed up tight like it's trash day in a city's hot summer. 'Are you kidding me?'

Megan's expression darkens. 'If you're implying what I think you're implying –'

Tippi holds her hands up. 'Whatever, sick girl. Your business is none of mine.'

I look between them. 'I'm sorry. Am I missing something? Is it something to do with Lucas?'

Tippi's mouth opens, and then closes. 'You don't know?'

'Do I *look* like I know?'

Her gaze shifts over my shoulder. I turn just in time to catch Megan's deadly stare. No need for subtitles, I recognize a 'don't open your goddamn mouth' look when I see one.

Raise your hand if your reaction to uncomfortable emotional waters is to laugh.

'Gosh,' I say. 'I love it when people keep things from me. Tell you what! I'm going to go. I wouldn't want to stand in the way of all the eyeballing you two are doing at each other.'

I pick up my bag and start off in the direction of the exit.

I feel Megan's hand on my shoulder moments later.

'Hey, Alec, come on,' I hear her say. 'Don't let Viola get to you. She's a crazy bitch. She needs serious help, and she's not getting it. What can you do? Until she recognizes the problem –'

I turn and face her.

'You're real sweet about your friends,' I say.

'Viola is not my friend,' Megan coldly replies.

'Acquaintances don't slap each other in the face, or at least not outside of *Sunset Beach*. You two used to be close, I'm guessing. Something else you conveniently neglected to tell me.'

'What?'

I raise my hands. 'You've been lying to me, Megan. You know a whole lot more about whatever the hell is going on than I do, and yet you sat there and let me prattle on about my brother, and connections, and second-guess myself, and embarrass myself. Is that why I got the friendly diner date treatment today? Is that why you keep coincidentally showing up in my life? Pump the little sister for what she knows, right?'

'There was no pumping!' Megan protests. 'I just –'

'You just,' I supply, 'need to tell me, right now, what you know about Lucas and Viola, and Scott Poltern and Justin Gorhammer. Or forget the whole thing.'

She stands there.

'I don't owe you anything, Alec,' she says finally.

Disappointing. And, boy, do I hate being disappointed.

'Keep your secrets,' I say to her. 'But don't ever fake flirt with me again.'

'Alec,' she says, all sorrowful, but I'm out.

'The shake's on you for my trouble,' I toss over my departing back.

And that, ladies and gentlemen, is how you exit a scene.

Eyes Wide Shut

'Alec, I need you,' Mercy breathes through the phone.

'Not on your life, toots,' I say.

'Come on,' she wheedles seductively. 'You'll be rewarded.'

'That's what you said last time, but all I got was shafted, and not in the fun way.'

'There are no kids at this one, and definitely no all-you-can-eat candyfloss booth. Anyway, I'll put Gail and Elliot on clean-up.'

'Hmm.'

'Plus,' Mercy hurriedly adds, 'since it's last minute, you can do the whole shift on overtime rates.'

A pause.

Then I say, 'How desperate are you?'

It is Mercy's turn to sigh, her voice a breeze down the phone. '*So* desperate. I've had two girls call up sick this morning. Day of. They were both at Surfriders last night. I know they were; Gail saw them doing shots at the bar.'

Gail, Mercy's oldest server – in both age and employment length – hails from a time when the beehive was in vogue. She still bouffants her dishwater-blonde hair ('Sugar paste, doll, monumental amounts of sugar paste'), smokes red

Gauloises – which surely means she no longer has a throat to speak of – and has the tired yet manic air of a decades-long post-rehabber. God knows what she was doing in a club like Surfriders, where the average age hovers over and under legal drinking, but Gail staggers* to the beat of her own drum. (*It's the weight of her hair, she can't keep her balance.)

'Come on,' Mercy wheedles. 'It's a super-fancy gig, you'll make great tips on top.'

My interest is further piqued. 'Where is this *alleged* fancy gig?'

'Mayor Van Freesburg's. He's hosting a fundraiser at his house, last-minute schmoozing for his big campaign to make senator. Everyone with money will be there.'

'I do need money,' I say begrudgingly.

'Who doesn't?' Mercy says, happy now she knows she has me. 'Thanks a million, Alec. See you there at 4 p.m. for prep. I'll text you the address. You've saved my ass. I owe you a favour!'

'I like money more than favours,' I say hurriedly, but she's already put the phone down.

Truth be told, Mercy is the one doing me the favour. A couple of weeks ago I'd made half-hearted overtures to the local franchised restaurant chain, but the only summer job they had left was running their kids parties, which involves slinging paper plates of chicken nuggets at groups of screaming, wiggling children under the age of ten, making balloon animals for their entertainment, and cleaning out the ball pit whenever one of them gifts it with a bodily fluid. Children don't like me (they can sense my fear), I do a passable swan crown but my rabbits always come out deformed, and methodically hosing vomit off a thousand primary-coloured plastic balls is one of the worst things I've ever done in the name of renumeration. Until Mercy called, it was my only option.

Plus, frankly, I could use the distraction. I've hit a dead end in my investigations, and my spat with Megan has been weighing outsize on my mind. I hate liars, and I hate that I got played, and I hate that I'd forgive her completely if she gave me an explanation – but so far not a peep, and right now I've no reason to expect that I'll ever hear from her again.

I was planning to drown my sorrows with an Elmore Leonard marathon and a party-sized bag of Doritos, but I'd rather be paid. Plus, Mom is MIA, holed up at her pro bono firm on the big secret case, as usual, and these days I hate being in this house alone.

So Christien's father is hosting a shindig at his McMansion on the good side of town. I wonder if Freesburg Junior will be making an appearance – then I tell myself not to wonder. Christien is an indulgence, like truffle fries – delicious as a one-off every so often, but they'll make you sick if you start trying to eat them all the time.

Besides, this is a work night, and I am nothing if not professional.

I show up at 4 p.m. on the dot, dressed in my demurest black trousers and white shirt, and head around the house to the kitchen's French doors, currently slung wide open to admit the rest of Mercy's catering crew, who traipse in and out, setting up. Mercy takes one look at me, drags me into a side room, and tugs something off a makeshift clothes rail.

I eye the proffered garment.

'No.'

'Alec,' Mercy says in her 'I am currently walking a tightrope of pre-show nerves, don't mess with me' voice. 'Just put it on, we all have to wear them.'

I look her up and down. 'Where's yours?'

'Well – *you* all have to wear them. I'm back of house; the guests won't see me – but if you're out there serving, it's required.'

I eye the violently luminous shirt and tie she's impatiently waving in my face. 'Is there a squeaky nose to go with it?'

'It's in the mayor's colours, and he favours bright yellow and orange. I think they go with his golf resort tan.'

'Mayors have colours now?'

'This one does. Didn't you see the giant sunflowers rammed into vases all over the place? His wife had to import them at great expense.' Mercy rolls her eyes.

'This is not a uniform, it's a clown suit.'

'You want the job, you wear the clown suit.'

I scowl. 'Mercy by name but not by nature.'

'Stop being a smart Alec and be a dumb, servile Alec.'

'I hate that Alec,' I say as I take the neon clothes off her.

'Well, I love her and I'm sad she's so rare,' Mercy says, whirling out of the room.

I change in the toilet. I can't even look at myself in the mirror for too long, I feel like my eyeballs are burning. If anyone makes a custard-pie-in-the-face joke in my general vicinity, screw the money – I'm out of here.

The guests arrive in trickles until the garden seems full to bursting. Mercy's usual palpitations over the quality of both food and presentation are unnecessary and, despite being several months out of practice, I circulate like a serene swan. All the paddling goes on back in the Freesburgs' vast kitchen, the kind that sports rows of hanging copper pots in descending size, too gleaming to be anything but architecture.

I've actually missed this – work that makes the hours go fast, its requirements amounting to little more than a decent short-term memory and a boatload of stamina. My brain shuts down gratefully, coasting on easy demands for more water, another daiquiri, do you have any of those fois gras thingies left, so sorry seem to have spilled . . . leaving no room for Alec the person, only Alec the server, all notions of dead brothers and demonic visions temporarily banished.

That is, until I see the necklace.

I am waiting with the server's practised neutral patience, having been flagged down by a small knot of animated people. The flagger downer is an elaborately coiffed man in a blue suit I currently have pegged as either a real estate developer, medical sales exec or the fantastically vague-sounding entrepreneur. Welded to his side is a vacant-looking woman three times his junior in a dress that perfectly reveals the lines of her yachting tan.

'Why does no one know about the incredible three-mile-long beach we have?' Coiffed is saying. 'Pure golden sand, perfect surfing at the north end, perfectly family splashy splashy at the southern end with the protected bay. We should be inundated with tourists year-round, but instead this town remains a pit stop for people journeying on to uglier, more crowded beaches. Why?' His eyes widen in readiness to impart. 'No infrastructure. If we build it, they will come.'

Real estate. First thought, best thought.

'Biggest development deal in the town's history,' says another man. 'The whole waterfront, hotels, spas, resort. Maybe even a casino. It's going to be insane. It'll transform the fortunes of every single member of this town, guaranteed.'

'How many millions will this deal net you, Mike?' asks a stately woman with an air of polite amusement.

Mike, aka Coiffed, affects a modest look. 'A lady never tells.'

My bored and wandering eye catches on a shiny object. I am suddenly struck so hard by a case of déjà vu I actually hear myself gasp.

Thankfully the group around me have been trained from birth not to notice the antics of the lower status.

'And Bobby endorses this?' I vaguely hear in the background.

'Bobby *masterminded* it. Once he's in DC . . .'

'If he wins.'

I stare urgently at the shiny object.

'When, Harmony, *when*,' Coiffed says. 'I thought you took that class on manifesting.'

Small laughs ripple through the group.

'Excuse me,' I say, while my heart does strange, sickly loops, 'where did you get that necklace?'

The group pauses, glancing around at each other, and I can see how long it takes before they register that the question came not from one of them, but from their waitress, who just transformed before their eyes from a glorified mobile drinks cabinet into a human being.

The girl on Coiffed's arm finally registers that she is being spoken to. Her brow wrinkles in a pretty frown.

'What?'

'The necklace you're wearing,' I say, a trifle impatiently. 'It's beautiful. I was just wondering where you got it.'

Necklace girl looks hesitantly at Coiffed.

Another man in the group interrupts. 'Could we get some more drinks? I'll have another IPA.'

'I'd love a couple of those cute mini burgers,' Coiffed says. 'You know what? Just bring us a whole platter.'

'Mike,' the stately woman admonishes, 'they have to share them out, they can't just bring you a whole platter.'

'There's a generous tip in it for you.' Mike winks at me. Then he addresses necklace girl. 'Petra? You want another?'

Petra. Petra and a necklace with a pagan-looking symbol hanging heavily from its delicate chain. This is all so familiar. I've heard her name and I've seen that damn necklace, where have I –

And then in a rush it comes to me.

'Viola!' I say. 'You know Viola, right?'

Petra gives me a blank look.

'Viola Gordon, the influencer?'

'No, sorry,' says Petra cautiously.

An image of Viola calling me 'Petra' and shouting at me, 'You stole my necklace, you'd better find it and give it back!' flashes through my head. That wasn't such random crazy after all, because Petra exists, and she's standing in front of me right now, wearing an unusual-looking necklace.

But why would Viola call me by her name?

'So,' I search, 'did you get the necklace at a vintage store, or is it like a family heirloom . . .?'

'Her grandmother gave it to her,' Mike cuts in.

Petra has an uncertain look on her face.

'Oh,' I say. 'Your grandmother has really eclectic taste.'

'Yeah,' Petra vaguely replies.

And that's it. That's all I get.

'She's European,' Mike says smoothly. 'Petra's grandmother. I swear, the things her family brought with them when they fled the Old Country.'

'Totally,' I agree. 'Some weird stuff out there.'

'Absolutely. Petra, did you want another drink . . .?'

'Yeah, that one with the raspberry in it?'

I nod, I smile, I collect everyone's drinks order, I walk away.

Hallmark of a bad liar – vagueness and hesitation. (Petra.)

Hallmark of a good liar – immediate answers with details. (Mike.)

I pick up empties, I glide to the bar, I duck quickly behind it and take out my phone. Mercy would crap a brick if she knew I had it on me while I was working, but I just need to be sure. I open up Viola's socials, scrolling back through her posts, and – there. The same necklace. Go back nearly a year and it's in every photo and video. Then, a few months ago, it disappears from her neck – at least, online.

According to Viola, Petra stole the necklace. But why would she pretend not to know Viola – or, conversely, why would Viola pretend to know her? Secondly, why would anyone bother stealing that thing? It doesn't look expensive, and Petra-with-the-yachting-tan has money, or is at least connected to people with money. You don't get into a Freesburg fundraiser without it.

It's funny – now my attention is on it I know I've seen the symbol on that necklace somewhere before. It's a little on the nose, honestly. The kind of obvious runic thing you'd see in a movie about teenage satanists, where the handsome lead picks up his strange-yet-compelling loner friend's notebook and opens it up and –

Heart in mouth, I flip to the photos on my phone.

Jesus. There it is. It's right there. In the photo I took of Lucas's notebook pages, nestled among his cramped writing – the same symbol.

He *drew* it.

Lucas never mentioned Viola to me before he died, not once, and she said she didn't know him. But right here is proof that they had some kind of connection.

What is it with this necklace? People either have it, want it back or scribble it in their notebooks among a bunch of incomprehensible satanic shorthand.

I zoom in on the drawing. Right underneath it, Lucas wrote a name:

HOFFY MAN

I've never heard of a Hoffy Man – but maybe Petra has.

I return to the bar and put in the drinks orders I've collected up, tapping impatiently as Elliott the bartender gets to work (age: twenty-four; known crimes: can't keep a driver's licence because she thinks speed restrictions are for losers). I have two shift hours left to somehow get Petra on her own so I can –

'Hi there.'

I turn. My heart skips.

Mike, the coiffed real estate developer, is standing next to me, his ridged cockscomb hair gleaming in the stringed lights above us.

'Elliott is making your drinks now,' I say. 'I'm so sorry about the wait, sir, she had a rush on orders.'

'Oh, that's fine,' he replies. 'Actually, it's you I want. Let's have a little chat.'

He moves off towards a dark corner of the patio, beyond the bright lights, where thick hydrangea bushes lurk. I don't have much choice. Dumb, servile Alec follows, with Detective Alec watching warily.

In the shadows, Mike is considerably less smooth and smiley, even with the brightly coloured flower clusters shaped like cheerleader pom-poms nodding over his shoulder.

'So you're friends with Viola Gordon?' he asks without preamble.

What have I stepped into here?

'No,' I reply honestly.

He wasn't expecting that.

'But you think Petra is,' he says. 'Why?'

'I don't know Petra. I just know her necklace.'

'What are you doing here tonight?' Mike asks.

'I'm working, sir,' I say, with a studied touch of bafflement.

'Are you here for Viola?'

'No, I'm here for remuneration.'

He searches my face.

'Great guy, Viola's father,' he says in a serious tone. 'Good friend of mine. Of all of us. Pretty much everyone here, in fact.'

'I don't know him either,' I reply, bafflement growing.

Mike's eyes narrow. He can't make me out.

I make a last grab for dumb, servile Alec. 'I'm so sorry, sir, but I really don't understand what this is about. I didn't mean to offend anyone by asking about the necklace, I just thought it was prett–'

'Please, Miss Gray,' Mike says, holding up a hand. 'Let's just be honest with each other. I'm sure you know all about the incident involving your brother.'

Man, this guy knows how to lob a grenade.

I have two choices. I could continue to protest my innocence and get out of dodge, or I could do the thing I hate doing and swore off a long time ago: lie. Lie to get to the truth.

'He told me everything,' I say.

Mike gives me an indulgent smile. 'Wonderful! Openness in the family is paramount. It strengthens your bonds, don't you think? As secrets do the opposite.'

'I heartily agree with you,' I say grimly.

Mike has the most peculiar laugh – staccato, forced, as if he's doing an imitation of a laugh he once saw online. 'Heartily! What a wonderful vocabulary you have, Miss Gray. And I can see the resemblance to Lucas, by the way. He wasn't as . . . eloquent as you, but such a sweet boy. So eager to please. It's such a shame, what happened. We all miss him very dearly.'

It comes unbidden, as always, and, as always, takes me completely by surprise. My throat closes up with the effort to suppress the tears I can feel pushing urgently at my insides in their quest to be outside. God fucking *damn* it.

'That's not the Lucas I knew,' I force out. 'What happened changed him. I think it broke him.'

Mike's smile drops from his face as though it had never been.

'Mental illness is such a tragedy,' he says. '*Such* a tragedy. It can strike anyone at any time. It can make people say and do the worst things. Take your friend Viola, for example. I've heard she's in a bad way. It's really worrying everyone. No one wants to see her suffer any more. She needs to get well.'

'Maybe she just needs her necklace back,' I suggest.

Mike stares at me.

'Viola was never supposed to have that necklace in the first place,' he says. 'But her father begged. And he's such a good friend of ours. You help friends in a bind, don't you? So her turn came. And what did she do, when her turn came?'

He waits expectantly.

I stand there, brain cogs desperately turning. There is a level of secret knowledge being assumed here, tied into the necklace and its hidden meanings, but the thing about secret knowledge is that people who have it don't like it when people who don't have it try to acquire it – so I'd better tread carefully.

'She slapped someone?' I finally offer up. Seems like a safe bet.

'She *fucked it up*,' Mike pronounces. 'And now everyone is suffering. The entire group. We operate like a family. *You* know that. When one hurts, we all hurt. And we all come together to protect each other from hurt.'

I've only just realized how separate we are here, away from the rest of the revellers spilled out across the lawn. The hydrangeas, those lovable pom-poms, shield us from the noise to such an extent that you can whisper to each other and be heard just fine.

In other words, I could scream, but it would take people a while to find me.

Mike is contemplating me.

'You know,' he muses. 'I'm surprised *you* haven't worn the necklace yet.'

The way he says it sounds like a threat.

'Well –' I bray a laugh – 'I'm no Petra!'

'Au contraire. I can read people like a book, and I've got your number, Miss Gray.'

You've also got a bad case of the mixed metaphors, Mr Mike.

'I'm pretty sure we're unlisted,' I say.

Mike is so close to me now that I can smell his breath, sour with alcohol and fish crudités.

'You're a girl who knows where her loyalties lie. And I really think you'd appreciate the amazing benefits the position brings.'

'Low-cost health insurance? Team-building weekend at Lake Tahoe?' I am trying my damnedest not to edge away. Never show fear to bears. 'I'm so sorry, sir, um, Mike, but I really have to get back to work or I'll get in trouble with my boss –'

'Don't worry,' Mike soothes. 'I'll protect you. What are you getting paid for tonight? I'll double it. And if you lose your job, I can get you one with a snap of my fingers. There are so many people in our network who would be eager, *desperate*, to help you out! In fact, a lot of them are here tonight. I think you should meet a few of them.' He takes hold of my upper arm in one meaty paw. 'Do you have another outfit you can change into? If not, I'm sure we can find you something last minute –'

'Dad, leave her alone.'

Mouth dry and adrenaline surging, I turn in Mike's loosened grip to assess our interrupter.

I know that face.

The last time I saw that face it was shrieking about a giant spider.

Scott Poltern is more upright and less pale than our first ill-fated meet, giving him a new-to-me air of strength and confidence. He's also looking at Mike with an expression of dislike so undisguised that it can only indicate the familiarity of father and son.

'What are you doing here?' Mike seems displeased.

'My name was on the invite,' Scott says. 'Poltern *family*.'

'I don't care. I told you to stay home tonight.'

'Scared I'll embarrass you?'

Mike stares his defiant son down.

'You're ill,' he says. 'Ill people need rest, not parties. Go home.'

Scott has that look on his face that people get when they're trying to decide how far they can push something. The moment grows, let's say, uncomfortable.

And then Scott's gaze flickers to me.

'I will if you leave *her* alone,' he says.

Mike looks at me. I am entirely clueless in the face of his son's unexpected gallantry.

'This is none of your business,' he retorts.

'It is when you're touching my girlfriend!' Scott shouts.

If before I was clueless, consider me upgraded to gobsmacked.

'What?' Mike asks in bewilderment. 'This is your girlfriend?'

'Hell no!' I interject. 'Look, I don't know what's going on here, but –'

'Baby, it's no use,' Scott howls. 'We can't keep it secret any more! I'll just admit it, OK? I came here looking for you; I knew you'd be here tonight. I wanted to tell everyone about us. I want them all to know. And now I find you hiding in a dark corner with my father? What are you *doing* to me?!'

He's all sound and fury, but I keep waiting for a punchline.

'I really don't know,' I say with complete honesty.

Scott rounds on his father.

'If you don't let her go,' he says, 'I will have another *episode*, as you keep lovingly calling them, right here, in front of everybody. And it'll be loud.'

Father and son face off. I try not to breathe.

Mike lets go of my arm.

'We're just having a conversation,' he says. 'What did you think was happening, for Christ's sake?'

'We need to talk about this, babe,' Scott enunciates to me, his eyes aggressively wide. 'Right now, let's go.'

OK. I think, I *think* he's trying to rescue me, but –

Scott takes hold of my other arm and pulls me towards him.

'Hey!' I say.

'Now, young lady,' Scott spits back.

Young lady?! I mouth at him.

He grimaces momentarily, and then rallies. 'I catch you cheating on me with my *dad* and I'm supposed to be cool? No! Let's *go*.'

'Lower your voice,' Mike hisses. 'You'd better find a way to handle your shit, Scott, or you're going to end up just like the other two.' He tosses a look at me. 'The sister? Really?'

I feel Scott's grip tighten on my upper arm.

'Mike?' calls a new voice. 'What's going on? Is everything all right?'

A purple-dressed woman with enormous earrings has arrived on the scene, presumably drawn by Scott's shouts. She looks warily between the three of us. Elliott, the bartender, peeks avidly over her shoulder.

Mike forces a smile, laughs, downplaying the scene. 'Just teenagers, Nora. Apparently they're recreating some silly skit they saw online. When I was their age, I was volunteering with Habitat for Humanity.'

'Scott?' says purple-dress woman in a tremulous voice. 'Is that true? Are you – are you feeling all right tonight?'

'Yeah, Mom,' Scott says quickly. 'Dad's right. It was just a skit we're doing. Don't worry about it. Go back to the party!'

The desperate gentleness in his voice makes me want to wince. I know that voice. Used it on Lucas myself a few times, when things got bad towards the end. It's the one you adopt when you're trying to talk someone off a cliff edge.

Scott's mother holds out a hand to him pleadingly, silver bangles jangling from her thin, bony wrist. 'Come with me. Come and . . . Please? Have a little fun, sweetie! You need it!'

Scott's smile turns pained. If anyone needs a little fun, it's his mother. She wears her fragility on her more obviously than those earrings.

'Coming, Mom,' he says.

'And your friend,' his mother says. She frowns, finally clocking my outfit. 'She's . . . wait staff?'

I pounce on the cue.

'Yes, ma'am,' I say, 'and on that note, please let me get you both a drink! No, I insist, it's my job. What would you like? Another of the mango daiquiris? Wonderful. And a light beer for you, sir? Wonderful. Elliott! Help us out?'

I walk as I talk, but because I'm gabbling it's really more of a semi-sprint, around the corner and back to the bar.

The mother has both males on her arms as she glides, as if they're the only things that can hold her up. I risk a look. Mike is staring straight ahead, ignoring me now – but Scott glances at me as he passes the bar.

Thank you, I mouth.

He gives me a quick nod. His eyes linger on mine a little too long. Then he's pulled away.

Elliott slips back into place behind the bar, a look of absolute delight on her face.

'Dude, did you just get caught with the dad by the mother *and* the son? That is the most telenovela thing I've ever seen.'

I scowl to cover the pound of my heart. 'Just make the drinks, Elliott.'

I give myself a minute more, trying to still my trembling hands, and then I lope quickly up past the revelry, heading back to the kitchen for more food trays. Somebody else can serve them their drinks – I've had enough of chasing down leads tonight. Besides, I can't mess this job up any more than I already have. I need the money. All the great PIs did, too, so I'm in fine company.

Chosen girls who wear necklaces. 'Hoffy Man'. Secrets, lies and networks that are more like families. If the mafia thing weren't enough, the one reveal from this evening spent in the land of *Twin Peaks* that I'm really stuck on? I've never met Mike in my life before, but he already knew exactly who I was. He knew it before he even spoke to me tonight – and he recognized me on sight. I'm not sure why that makes me nervous, but I have a feeling I'll find out soon enough.

'*The sister? Really?*'

Yeah, that's right. *The sister.*

And she's coming for your son like a freight train for a helpless girl tied to the tracks.

The Wicker Man

A manila folder slaps down on the table.

Oh peers up at me over the leaves of his newspaper.

'A rather dramatic entrance,' he says accusingly.

I've found him in the back offices of church, where the stained-glass majesty ends and the beige carpet begins. It was a thrilling behind-the-red-curtain moment for me, the first time I got to step into the inner sanctuary. I don't know what I was expecting but, as it turns out, the place priests go to relax in between flock-shepherding is as banal and comfortable as an old slipper. I've never seen such an array of cracked joke mugs and ancient kettles outside of a teacher's lounge.

I raise my eyebrows.

Oh glances down at the file.

'Uh oh,' sighs he. 'This looks like a case. You and your mother are two of a kind.'

Lawyers are nothing like detectives, thank you, but I can see how an outsider might get confused on distinctions. I definitely stole the manila folder from her.

A pack of golden Oreos lands on top of the manila folder.

'I need your help,' I say.

Oh peers at the shiny pack. 'These are my favourite.'

'Yup.'

'They're hard to get.'

'I hit three Rite Aids and a Walmart before I got lucky.'

'Bribery?'

'Payment.'

'My help is always free.'

'I know,' I assure him. 'But this one's tricky.'

'How so?'

'It's about Lucas.'

Oh's newspaper flops. 'Ah.'

I hesitate. 'You know what? Bad idea. Bad, terrible. I'll go. I'm leaving you the Oreos, though, I just like you that much.'

'Alec,' Oh says calmly. 'Take a deep, slow breath. With me, now.'

I suck in the first one like I'm on a sprint for my life, but by the third I feel calmer.

'I've never talked about him with you,' I say.

'And you never have to, until you want to. And it's OK if that moment never comes.'

'Yes, except – wellll.' I indicate the folder. 'It has.'

Oh precisely and deliberately folds up his newspaper with the air of one who has been waiting for this moment. The knotty hands I love so much reach out, flip open the folder. I watch his eyes focus on the first sheaf of papers inside – on top a printed blow-up photo of Lucas's scribbly drawing of the necklace symbol. The one that found its way first to Viola's neck, then Petra's – and potentially yours truly standing next in line, though I'm still fuzzy on what exactly Mike was offering me.

Oh's finger lands on it.

'So you finally talked,' he says.

'To who?'

Oh looks up at my confused face.

'Where did you see this?' he asks. 'Did someone show it to you?'

'No one showed it to me,' I say. 'That's not my drawing. That's Lucas's. I found it in a notebook of his.'

'Ah.' Oh contemplates. 'Do you know what it is?'

I adopt a peppy cheerleader pose. 'I say "Hoffy", you say "Man"!'

'Oh dear.' He sits back in his threadbare chair and rubs his face.

I know that look. He's trying to decide how much to tell me.

'Oh,' I warn. 'I brought you Oreos, man. Don't hold back, now.'

In a sudden movement Oh stands up from his chair, crosses to the door and closes it, cocooning us in tired beige comfort.

A sense of foreboding begins to stir.

'This isn't one of those "it's time to tell you about your secret birthright" moments, is it?' I say with some alarm. 'I hate fantasy movies.'

'I just don't want any eavesdroppers,' Oh replies. 'It's a bit of a taboo topic. I might get in trouble.'

My brain serves me up a flash of Mike, his sour breath on my face. 'With who? The local mafia?'

'The Church.'

'Ah.' The other mafia. 'Why?'

'Well,' says Oh, 'I take it that means you've heard the name, but you don't know the origin story.'

I indicate my manila folder full of printouts. 'All I've found about them was this article in the local gazette from a few years ago, some puff piece on the "Hoffy Men" raising money for the inaugural Coastal Culture festival. And, by the way, who doesn't hate that thing? It brings in the worst kind of too-much-money-and-no-taste tourists.'

'It's a blight,' Oh agrees. 'Eight dollars for a "sea foam" latte, those festival coffee stands charge.'

'Anyway, that article was useless. It made the Hoffy Men sound like some exclusive and yet very dull social club. Apart from that, there's nothing.' I can hear the frustration in my voice.

'Your generation with your "online",' grumbles Oh. 'If it's not on the internet it doesn't exist, eh?'

'That's right, grandpa. So give me the analogue.'

Oh steeples his fingers and looks at me over the top of them. 'Are you sitting comfortably?'

I take a seat.

'You've been to Gracetown?' Oh asks me.

Sure, I've been to Gracetown. It's only a half-hour drive from here, a small, sleepy place on the coast with a forbiddingly local energy. Surfer's paradise in the summer, empty as a dodo's nest in the winter. Some strange rich family founded it in the sixteen hundred whatevers and named it after themselves, as one does. Their descendants, the Graces, are still around, continuing the tradition of being rich and strange.

'In Gracetown they have carvings of the Hoffy Man up on the walls, around the oldest part of town.' Oh glazes over as his mind's eye goes wandering. 'A face made out of stone, with big glaring eyes and a head of vines and leaves. Sometimes he gets snake hair, like Medusa.'

'I've seen those carvings,' I say, as it dawns on me. 'I thought it was just some New Age-y decorative statement.'

'Alec,' Oh chides, 'the carvings are *old*. Seventeenth century, at least.'

Colour me impressed. The oldest man-made thing around here is the sixties brutalist shopping mall someone in charge back then named 'DISCO MALL', in an apparently unironic invocation of when 'disco' was slang for 'fresh, happening, cool'. Alas, over the years some of its giant neon letters have broken or been stolen and never replaced, so if you ignore the gaps, now it spells 'DISMAL'. It's definitely haunted.

'Who is the Hoffy Man supposed to be?' I ask.

'There's not really a consensus. A spirit of the land. A local nature god. A demon.'

My ears perk on choice number three.

'He's worn a few hats over time,' Oh continues. 'But back in the nineteenth century, I think it was, there were rumours that a few locals had gotten together and begun doing, how can I put it, questionable things in his name. The belief was that if you made some kind of sacrifice to him, he'd bring you wealth and prosperity, and if you didn't, he'd curse you and your life would be blighted. The local Christian leaders at the time were so appalled by the rumours of such behaviour that they cast the Hoffy Man as a demon to frighten people off continuing to worship him.'

'Questionable things? You can't leave me hanging here, Father.'

He shakes his head. 'I forget how bloodthirsty you can be.'

'Please, you set that up.'

'Well,' Oh admits without admitting, 'a few animal deaths at the time were attributed to the cult of the Hoffy Man. Farmers' complaints of missing sheep and horses. People's pets and the like disappearing. They were calling it property theft – until they found all the bones down in the caves.' He clocks my avid expression. 'The Hoffy Man's supposed to live underground, in an old mining complex near Gracetown. A group of people went exploring and found a particular cave with an awful lot of dried blood and bones, some of it fresh. But here's the kicker. It wasn't just animal bones they found down there.'

I blink. 'Oh my god.'

Oh nods. 'No dental records back then, of course, but there were a couple of identifiers. Missing persons going back, ooh, years.'

I remember being made to do a whole semester on local folklore at school, which I found ineffably dull at the time. Tales of local murder cults were completely missed off the curriculum, even though that's exactly the sort of thing that would have kept me awake in history class.

'Where did you get all this from?' I ask.

Oh sucks his teeth – another deliberation – and then points to a shoddy desk in the corner of the room.

'In the desk drawer over there,' he says. 'The key is tacked to the underside.'

I'm over there like a shot. Riddle me this, gentle reader: what would a priest feel necessary to hide in a locked desk drawer? My heart is pounding as I feel around for the key, prise it off and use its tiny iron body to unlock the drawer, pull it out, reach inside –

'A book?' I'm trying not to sound disappointed.

'A *banned* book,' Oh semi-whispers.

It's a slim, inconspicuous brown hardback adorned only with a modestly printed title: *Fring Wars: A Critical Analysis of the Struggles for Religio-Cultural Supremacy 1827–2003*.

'This is a video nasty?' I say dubiously.

Oh snorts. 'You're far too young for that reference. This book has officially and quietly been banned in the five counties surrounding us – neither bookshop nor library is legally allowed to stock it. It talks in great detail about the Hoffy Men, both the original cult and the version of it apparently alive and well today, and its bloody, dirty clashes with the Catholic Church over the last two hundred years. It names names, some of whose descendants are prominent members of society in the area. No one comes out of it well, neither Church nor cult, so it was easy to suppress.'

'Why is it so controversial?'

Oh just nods to the book. 'You should read it.'

I open it at random, scanning as I wander back towards Oh.

'I just tried a sentence and felt my eyes start to close,' I say.

Oh gives a great sigh. 'All right. There are some really graphic parts.'

'Sold.'

'Don't let anyone see you with it, though.'

I can't help the laugh. 'Come on.'

'I'm serious.' He nods. 'I gave it to your brother, a few weeks before he passed.'

The book suddenly seems heavier. 'Lucas read this? Why did you give it to him?'

'He was asking me the same sorts of questions as you.'

I can't deny the thrill that runs down my spine at that. How did he come across all this? Was he running his own investigation? And more importantly – why did he hide it from me?

Which is a good prompt. *He's* not here to answer, but –

'Why didn't you tell me about this?' I ask Oh.

'I'm a confessional professional,' Oh responds, watching me with anxious eyes. 'Lucas wanted our conversation kept private.'

Damn. It makes sense, of course. Oh might tell me bits of town gossip I'll eventually hear about anyway, but he would never violate a real confession. Especially if the confessee had told him not to.

I know my mother often goes to confession with Oh, too. I wonder if one of those sessions was where he told her she was neglecting me for her big case, which she apparently took really well. What an interesting viewpoint this man must have on family Gray. He's got all our secrets, including the ones we keep from each other.

'I know I'm violating his privacy now by telling you,' Oh continues, 'but – he's passed, and you've come asking. And . . . I've a confession of my own. If you'll have it.'

This catches me.

'I sometimes wonder if I shouldn't have given him that book,' Oh says, looking uncharacteristically stricken. 'All that talk about demons in it. Maybe it made everything worse for him. Fuelled his illness.'

Lucas wouldn't have won Best Catholic in any given year, but Oh was as much a part of his life as mine. He altar-boyed for him as a kid. He loved Oh almost as much as I did – and Oh loved him back.

'No,' I reply. 'No *way*, Oh. You can't be held responsible for anything Lucas did. You put that guilt down right now, and tell it to go eff itself.'

It's amazing. Eighteen-year-old rebel, satanic blasphemy inked on her arm – and she still can't say 'fuck' to a priest.

Oh startles at my fierceness, then gives me a sad smile.

'I wish you did not have to bear this weight, child,' he says, honestly and without embarrassment, reaching for my hand and squeezing it.

I want to hug him. I keep telling him he should make a social media account called 'TherapyPriest'. He could be paying for the church's badly needed roof repair job inside of six months, from ad revenue alone. Apparently that's not allowed, or whatever.

After what I deem to be a non-rude amount of time, I gently take my hand from Oh's. Too much concern can make a gal flustered, and I'm on an active investigation. Just like the unbearably kind man before me, I have my own professionalism to maintain.

'So this book posits the Hoffy Man cult is alive and well today, but the only available evidence is a social club that likes to raise money for tasteless tourist festivals and a piece of tacky pagan jewellery.' I pick up the printout of the necklace. 'What the hell even is this symbol, anyway?'

'A unicursal hexagram with an overlaid ankh,' says Oh.

I raise a brow. 'You really have studied this banned book, haven't you?'

Oh contrives to look embarrassed.

'Religions,' I tut, studying the unicursal hexagram with an overlaid ankh. 'Always trying to make the ordinary seem mystical.'

But my heart isn't in the jibe – I'm feeling too uneasy. Because I think I just met a Hoffy Man, and he seemed into the kind of social club that likes giving heavy-handed runic necklaces to 'chosen' girls. If that doesn't scream cult, I don't know what does. Question is, how far down the cult hole do they go? Are they the reason why Viola Gordon lost herself, violently attacked Megan and had to be sectioned?

I wonder what Megan knows about all this Hoffy Man stuff. She had to know something, since she and Viola were apparently such good friends before the Bad Times. (Not that I can find much evidence of it. Megan is one of those Luddites with no social media – always intriguing, people who don't want to be seen – and Viola must have deleted any photos of her after their bestie break-up.)

Maybe I should text Megan –

No. I've still heard nothing from her, which means she doesn't want to talk. Anyway, I'm doing just fine without her insight, and I definitely haven't given her a moment's thought in the last few weeks, so really, who's the winner here? Me. It's me.

'What's your interest in all this, Alec?'

I look up into Oh's face. He doesn't often use my name. His expression is serious.

'Don't worry,' I tell him. 'I'm not planning on following in my brother's footsteps. I'm just trying to understand what happened to him. I need to. Closure, maybe.'

'In peering over the cliff edge, have a care you don't fall off too,' says Oh.

I suddenly have a need for sunlight. Churches are always so damn cold.

'Well,' I say, standing up and breezily dusting myself off, 'you've a Mass to prepare for in an hour. And I've got things to do myself.'

'Then come back and talk with me another time.' Oh cocks a badger brow. 'Not for you, for me. I've missed our conversations. It's a balm to get to talk with an intelligent and energetic human being such as yourself.'

I am touched, and just like every other time in my life that I've been touched, I handle it with both grace and charm.

'You're basically my only friend,' I blurt.

'What about your mom?' Oh gently asks.

I manage to swallow the bitterest of potential retorts before it leaves my mouth.

'Even when she's around, we're just . . . disconnected. It's like we have nothing to talk about any more.'

Oh regards me thoughtfully. 'There's one thing you can talk about.'

'What?'

He nods to the book on the table. 'Your mother's read it too.'

I dubiously pick up the book. My mom's idea of a good time this is not. Her reading trends towards the fantasy-romance end of the literary spectrum. She claims she needs the silliness as a counterpoint to the heavy stuff she has to read all day for her job. An academic tome on local history would bore her to tears.

Still – it seems like Lucas got into it, and a little too seriously, perhaps. I wonder if my mom knew about that. I wonder if this book is not part of the reason she's pissed at Oh.

'How many stars did she give it?' I ask.

Oh just looks at me. 'Show it to your mom. Ask her about it. I think it could bring you two back together.'

Daddy's Home

I don't have the patience of a cat, so before I start for home I take a minute, sitting in my car and flipping through the book.

The controversial magnum opus is too dense to take in all at once, but there's one passage that catches my eye: the author claims that the Hoffy Men was originally a female cult.

Obviously it wouldn't have been called the Hoffy *Men*, though there are no records of what exactly it was called. But there are stories, from as far back as the seventeenth century. Stories of women going down into that cave, existent before it ever became a mine. Women making their way there in the dead of night, clutching offerings. Engaging in secret rituals. Coming out with strange, horrifying powers.

Of course, a lot of people didn't like that too much. The townsfolk claimed it an epidemic of witches, and hanged a lot of them. Drowned some others. Persecution, torture. Once enough of the cult was gone, offering little resistance with most of them dead, the men took it over. The whole thing eventually mutated into sending the bad women, the crazy women, the women who just wouldn't behave the way everybody else behaved, down to the cave to be done away with, so they would no longer cause trouble for the community at large. It was seen as a mercy, by some.

I wonder if that's still the choosing criteria, in today's version of the cult?

When I get home from church, there's a strange car in the driveway.

This used to be the norm. Mom always had friends around, especially after Dad left. Angry, joyful women like her came over at odd times, for coffee and cake or pretzels and wine, and they would hole themselves up in the kitchen, discussing and arguing over anything and everything.

One woman in particular, Juno DiCanso, was the most frequent visitor. Juno and my mother had always been tighter than tight, but ever since Lucas's death she doesn't come round any more, and my mother refuses to say why. I suspect it's to do with the fact that Juno was the one who delivered her the news about Lucas. Juno is a captain in the Fring police force, and she took it upon herself to come to her good friend's doorstep and tell her that her son was gone.

Does it make it easier or harder to hear the news of your son's death from your friend rather than a stranger? I knew, as soon as the front door opened. I knew by the look on Juno's face, a professional mix of kind and grave, a look I'd never seen on her before.

We haven't had anyone around since then. People have tried, but Mom's way of grieving has been to ignore all offers of support and throw herself body and soul into this big case she won't talk about. Now home is as quiet as the grave, pun intended, and though I like to play loner-detective, a little noise and the comfort of other bodies would be nice sometimes, a warm campfire against the dark.

So I admit, my heart does a little leap when I see the car. The tide, I can't help but say to myself, it has turned. I'll open the door and it'll be like the halcyon days, the mythical *back then*, when each member of the perfect American family was happy and laughing and full of zest, when the mother would turn from the stove, her oven-mitted hands full of just-baked apple pie, the brother would bound into the hallway fresh from varsity football practice and the father would play catch with his two perfect kids in early evening's falling light until it was time for dinner –

When I come through the front door and into the hallway, the first thing I see is Lucas's previously perma-locked bedroom door – ajar.

I stare at it, at the inviting sliver of darkness betwixt door and jamb. She must have forgotten to lock it. If I run –

– to see what? What do I expect to find in there? All the Answers? Or worse yet, none at all?

A noise from the kitchen distracts me. A strange noise. Like a gasp.

Visiting friends turns to threatening strangers in my paranoid mind. I barrel towards the kitchen door, burst through it – and they don't even leap apart. They're so involved in trying to swallow each other whole it takes them a minute to register that someone else is now in the room.

They break mouths, their heads turn towards me like startled deer.

I respond with my usual wit.

'Oh my *god*,' I yelp.

My mother pushes the man on her away.

'You're back early,' she says quickly.

I'm nearly an hour later than I said I'd be, actually. On her days off she's a stickler for me returning to the homestead at the mutually agreed-upon time, barring acts of God, and I'd long been expecting a check-up phone call.

I presume this guy is the reason there wasn't a phone call.

I search, trying to think of the worst possible thing I could say to her to communicate how wildly dismaying I find this scene.

'Your neck is all flushed,' I say.

She flushes even more, as intended. Witness my shame-tinted triumph.

'This is . . . a friend,' she says. 'Walter. Walter, this is my daughter, Alec.'

A friend.

Walter.

'Friend Walter' is nicely turned out. He's wearing the muted blue suit of an office worker in the classy, well-paid salary range, and possessed of a hair mane normally found on silver foxes. He's got an uneasy air to him, as if he was just caught doing something he shouldn't be, but he meets my eye steadily enough.

'Hi,' I say, sticking my hand out.

'I've heard so much about you,' says Silver Fox Walter. His grip is warm, firm, reassuring. This man shakes hands for a living.

'I'd love to say the same,' I brightly reply.

'Well, Walter was just leaving, actually,' my mother interjects.

'Oh, no! Stay for dinner, I'm doing homemade tater tots tonight.'

Walter glances at my mother.

'Another time,' she says, too distracted to rise to my tater tot bait.

'It was a brief pleasure,' Walter says to me gravely, before he is forcibly shuffled down the hallway.

'I'll be in my bedroom,' I mutter.

As I close the door and sink on to my bed, I hear them out in the hallway, murmuring to each other as she hustles him out of the door. I can't hear the words but I can hear the tone. His patient, understanding bass, her tight alto. But most of all I can hear the ease, the camaraderie, the intimacy. That's two people in cahoots.

The front door closes.

A few minutes slip by. I stare at my bedroom door, willing it to open.

And it does.

My mother, the composed, self-contained version that I've come to know and resent, is back in the game. Her hands are crossed primly in front of her waist.

'I'm sorry you saw that,' she begins.

A quick pause to explain something to you.

My mother is a catch. All right, so she's a small-time lawyer, which does not, in this town, equal *financial* catch, but she's sharp and funny and incredibly pretty to boot, with that ex-child of nature look – carelessly tousled streaked hair, bronze-sheened skin; raggedy jeans and suede jackets – and if she ever wore make-up I wasn't alive to see it, make-up frankly gilding the lily. Everyone tells her that she does not look her age, and even if she did she'd still look pretty fabulous. I'm fervently hoping it's genetic, because I never, ever want to Sophie's Choice between great skin and peanut butter cups.

Ever since the divorce from my father a few years ago, there have been hopefuls lining up to try their hand. My mother has always maintained an air of polite disinterest over these numerous gentlemen callers. It was a longstanding joke between Lucas and me – what kind of man would it take to finally turn her head? – but she's always made it very clear that there was no point in dating anyone until she found someone she might one day consider marrying.

Now believe me, I'd be the last to begrudge her chasing a little romance – or failing that, a real good tumbling – but she's just not built that way. So –

'Am I getting a new daddy?' I ask in a bemused voice.

'What?' she exclaims. 'No!'

'Well – why don't I know about this guy?'

'I wasn't sure what it was, at first,' she says cautiously.

'And now?'

'I'm still not sure. I wasn't going to introduce him to you until I felt ready.'

'So my first clue would be the save-the-date card in the mailbox?'

Silence befalls us.

My mother stands there, looking small. And it's me who made her so.

'I can see you're angry with me,' she says at last – but suddenly, I'm not.

'Mom,' I say. 'It's OK. It just caught me by surprise, that's all.'

'I bet.' She pauses. 'You really weren't meant to see it.'

Great. I love secrets the most.

'What does he do?' I ask with polite effort.

'He's a lawyer.'

I try to grin. 'So that's the "big case" you've been pulling those late late nights on?'

'That's not what I've been doing,' she protests. 'He works for another law firm, but he and I have joined up to work on this case together, and the, the, er, intimacy thing, that just happened.'

'Mom,' I say, 'did I just walk in on your first kiss with Walter?'

'You really, really did.'

I laugh. 'Holy shit.'

'Blasphemy,' she warns, but there's no heart in it. Her heart's too busy beating for *Walter*.

Here's the obvious truth – that moment there that I intruded on, that I ended for her, was the happiest I've seen her in years. She was lost in that kiss, in that silver fox's arms. She deserves that, that and every moment like it that she's managed to snatch with the guy, no matter how long it lasts.

So I draw her in. I tell her I'm happy for her, really. I ask her to tell me more. She sits down beside me on the bed, and we joke, trading witticisms back and forth. And you know what, ladies and gentlemen? It's almost like the old days. Close enough for government work, as they say.

Maybe that's why I don't tell her about the book Oh gave me, like he said I should. I don't want to spoil the moment, my small way of living that Pleasantville dream. Or maybe it's more selfless than that – maybe it's because I don't want to snuff out that shy glow she's got going on, drag her back down to the pit we've both been living in by talking about Lucas and the investigations I've been doing. Maybe I want to give her some relief. Whatever the real reason, through everything that follows, the book lies fallow in the bottom of my bag, forgotten about.

I'll only remember it later, much later, after the underground nightmare, after the betrayals, after it's all too late, after it couldn't have saved me anyway.

Stalker

I'm in the pantry aisle with my hand on a box of waffle mix when it hits me.

'Oh my god,' I say with glee. 'She's being watched!'

The lady checking out the flours two feet away gives me an odd look.

One of my favourite ways to ruminate is the grocery store. I've solved many a case under the anaemic strip lights at Super Royal ('King of Discounts!'). There's something about having one half of my brain occupied on comparing the price per ounce between brands of canned tomatoes that frees up the other half of my brain to sort through the thing that's really stirring my soup.

I've been thinking about cults, the modern-day version of. Say you were stupid or desperate enough to believe that some nature god, spirit or demon had the power to make your dreams come true – *if* you were willing to make a sacrifice. It's an ancient bargain between mortal and divine. Hitobashira. Agamemnon and Iphigeneia. Jephthah and Seila. How many fathers have given up their daughters to cruel gods for power or protection? If you think about it in that context, the Hoffy Men are simply continuing one of the oldest human traditions of all.

I've also been thinking about Viola Gordon. She might have lost her ability to make sense of the world, according to Oh's definition of madness, but not everything she does is the random firings of a broken brain – she was the one who led me, in a rather oblique way, to Petra and the necklace. I came to her for answers about Lucas, and that was what she gave me.

A sane person would tell me straight out what I wanted to know – unless they had a reason to try to hide it. A sane person would not live their life exclusively for an online audience – unless *they* had an audience. An audience they were scared of.

As I'm leaving the grocery store I'm remembering the video of Viola, staring into the camera with plumped lips, saying:

'*Do you know what it's like to be afraid all the time?*'

'So,' I make a voice note as I drive home, 'Papa Gordon was apparently in a bind, begging his cult friends to let his daughter wear the necklace. Maybe he has gambling debts or what have you, found himself in need of a get-rich-quick scheme and didn't have the patience to learn crypto. So Viola gets chosen, but somehow "*fucks it up*". And when that happened, they all came together "to protect each other from hurt", as Mike so genteelly put it. Viola's wobbling around like an out-of-control spinning top. Keeps talking about being scared to her audience of zillions while she sports the cult's necklace like a trophy. Like evidence. The only concrete evidence she has of what happened to her. So they get someone to steal it back from her. But maybe they're still nervous about what she might spill to the world, so they've got eyes on her. And –'

You know what? Never mind. As I say all this out loud, I start feeling wobbly myself.

Whatever wearing the necklace means, so far I haven't got any evidence that suggests it's anything more than your average religious-tinged ritual, which, when you start examining the ones we just matter-of-factly accept as normal under the lens of logic, all start looking like the actions of a bunch of lunatics. Praying to some poor peace and love hippy from two thousand years ago who once got brutally nailed to a cross to shine down his protection on you is at least as outlandish as praying to some Dionysian offshoot in the hope you'll get blessed with some cold hard cash.

Am I really saying that the businessmen denizens of Fring like to indulge in cave rituals with teenage girls to ensure their latest billion-dollar waterfront development deal nets them even more billions? The only god you can count on for helping you out with that is called Capitalism. That sort of thing just doesn't happen here, or surely someone would have done something about it by now. This is not a big place. If people were being menaced by a pagan cult in suits, we'd know about it. *I* would know about it. I, Alecto Gray, detective and busybody, making it my business to know other people's since I was in diapers . . .

As I glance in my rear-view mirror, I lose my train of thought.

In the classic noirs, the hero is driving along as I am, shooting a glance every so often at the rear-view mirror like I'm doing. His companion talks about something – the narrow escape they just had, the lowdown on how it works in this town or, if it's a woman, how they had no idea that their husband was caught up in such nasty, criminal business – the talk all a distraction from the looming threat, indicated by the tense set of the man's shoulders, his darting eyes and tight mouth.

Finally the companion might, with some exasperation, say, 'Aren't you listening to me? This is life or death!' or similar, to which the terse, chisel-jawed hero will reply –

'I think we're being followed.'

I'd have assumed that in reality most people don't actually have a clue when they're being followed. Unless you're being tracked by a clown car or you're a spotter (like trains but less cool) who takes notes of which unremarkable grey/white/red/blue insert-brand-name-of-car might have taken the same last few turns as you.

I've only noticed it because it's a sleek little Porsche – not that rare on these roads, but more notable than a Ford Focus, nonetheless.

It's probably just going the same way as me.

I slow down. The Porsche slows down.

I take an unnecessary detour off the main road. The Porsche follows.

Huh.

It's all the 'Viola's being watched' talk. My brain is living the experience, making things up out of nothing. No. No, we've just turned into my road and it's right behind me.

Huh.

Maybe it's taking a shortcut through the poor side of town to get back to the highway –

No. No, it's slowing down behind me as we get to my house.

But the fun doesn't stop there. As if to double-down on the weird vibe, when I get within sight of my front lawn I see another stranger's car already waiting for me. A short figure leans against the hood, texting. He looks up as I approach.

It's Scott Poltern.

Well, well, well. Here, alone, to see little old me? Suddenly I feel very popular.

I pull up behind Scott's car. He gives me an awkward little wave. I get out of my car, hold up a finger to pause him, look back – and there's the Porsche, crawling up the street towards us. Its windows are tinted, classic gangster style, and I can't see inside to the driver. Part of me expects it to stop right next to me and for Scott's paterfamilias to step out – the better to trap me in a classic pincer move, stupid Alec; remember your Herodotus – but it doesn't.

As it gets close to us its engine guns and the Porsche roars out of its idle, whoever it is speeding away like a spooked deer. It turns off at the top of my road and disappears from sight.

I turn to Scott. 'Did you see who that was, driving that Porsche?'

Scott seems as startled as me. 'No.' He gives me a hard look. 'Friend of yours?'

'Obviously not,' I counter, 'if I'm asking you who it was. What's wrong?'

He pushes back his floppy, lacrosse-playing hair, scans the street.

'Nothing,' he says finally. 'I just – didn't like that. Feels like I'm being watched.'

Theme of the day.

'Hey, I'm the one who was being followed,' I point out.

'They followed you?'

'I think so.'

We look at each other.

Suddenly this seems unreal, caricatured, a bad high school production of *Tinker Tailor Soldier Spy*.

I shake my head. 'It's probably nothing. Maybe they were coming to see my mom.'

'Is she around?'

I blink. 'Did you want to talk to her?'

'No,' he says, and gives me a shy look. 'I kind of wanted to make sure we were alone.'

Now what the hell does *that* mean?

'How'd you know where I live?' I ask him.

Scott looks taken aback. 'What?'

'How'd you know where I live? This isn't your side of town, and we don't have any friends in common.'

I know that because I've just spent the last few days determinedly trying and failing to find one.

'My side of town?' Scott collects himself. 'Well, I just . . . I don't know, does it matter?'

'Does it matter?' I repeat. 'Honestly, yes, right now it does. I'm not much of a hostess. People don't just drop by for a friendly howdy. I had a sleepover once for my twelfth birthday, but the only girls who showed came because they had a crush on my brother. You on a recruitment drive?'

'Recruitment?' he echoes, bewildered.

'Yes. Your dad send you here to repeat his delightful offer from the other night?'

Scott's face twists in disgust. 'God, no. I don't obey that asshole, thank you.'

'Then why are you here?'

'What?'

'Here,' I repeat impatiently, 'you are, why?'

'Because I like you, Alec!' he shouts. 'OK?' Then, muttering: 'Jesus.'

My mouth hangs open.

Somehow, this one didn't even make it into the top ten of all the explanations for his presence I was hurriedly trying to compute.

'Oh,' I say.

'I mean,' he quickly amends, 'I know I don't know you, but I always wanted to.' A micro-pause. 'Lucas talked about you a lot.'

Points for first blood.

'You were friends with my brother?'

Scott gives me a searching look. 'You didn't know?'

'He never mentioned you. Not once.'

'Ouch.' He considers. 'Not lifelong or anything. It was new. Ish.'

'How long?'

'Last summer.'

Six months before Lucas died. Right around the time he split up with Mallory and started getting all moody and secretive, in fact.

'What did he say about me?' I manage.

I should be asking better questions; I should be asking about secrets and demons. But somehow, right now, all I want is a piece of my brother, from however long ago it might be.

Scott muses. 'He said you were – I think I have this right – "difficult and incredible". He kept calling you Hide.'

I try to laugh, but sudden tears strangle the noise.

'Sorry,' Scott says gently. 'It seemed like a weird nickname to me.'

I shake my head. 'It's a reference to Jekyll and Hyde. His dark half. *I* was the damaged one. Then he went and tried to take my crown, the idiot.'

An awkward silence ensues while I snuffle up my tears before they can leak out and humiliate me.

'I shouldn't have done it like this,' I hear Scott say. 'Shit, I'm so insensitive. I just didn't know how else to run into you. My entire plan was to show up at your house like a stalker, make you talk about your brother like an asshole and then ask you out like a . . . a –'

'Brave little toaster?' I tease.

He laughs. I can't help but notice how nice his smile is, and I can – silently – admit to myself that he is somewhat studly, in an excess calcium, tennis tan kind of way.

Who knew such a smooth, clean stag of a boy would have such darkness as giant pregnant spiders in his head?

I should ask him to come inside. That's the flirty first step, isn't it – 'Let's have a coffee'? An image of my mother and Walter joined at the lips in the kitchen flashes across my mind. It might be funny to play the reverse – let her come home and find me doing the same thing with someone. The someone could be Scott.

In earlier imaginings I had Megan as my kitchen kiss counterpart – but that still stings when I let myself think about it, which is as little as possible. Romance is a bloodsport, someone once said, and I can't help but agree.

'Unorthodox methodology, but not unwelcome,' I say in a rush.

Scott hesitates. 'The what now?'

'Do you want to –' I clear my throat awkwardly – 'talk? More? Now? Just the two of us?'

His face lights up. 'You're free?'

I nod. 'Let's go inside.'

But he doesn't follow. 'Actually, I was hoping we could go somewhere a little more private.' He gives a nervous chuckle. 'That Porsche kind of spooked me, truth be told.'

I consider him. Normally I'd be loath to go anywhere alone with someone I don't know, especially considering the strange circumstances. But, well – he definitely seems in opposition to his father, and anyone who can spill the beans on Mike Poltern has my interest. I'd be an idiot to let this opportunity go to waste. I can play, if it gets me the truth.

'I know somewhere we can go,' I say.

Nancy Drew

Pirate Petey's Pitch and Putt was, in my childhood, *the* premiere birthday party venue.

As a kid I didn't notice the general sad decrepitude of the place, because eight-year-old eyes have only learned to see the bright, loud things. The roaring shark on hole eleven begging you to putt your ball into his wide-open jaws, which would be scary if there weren't four teeth missing. The treasure chest on hole four that used to be filled with giant plastic coins, stolen and replaced so many times that Pirate Petey had finally given up and left the chest empty of treasure. Hole twelve holds the pink castle, its defaced princess Barbie doing her perpetual hang out of the top window (savagely duct-taped in place due to, well, see above, re coins).

Semi-abandoned since the owner fell on hard times and had to foreclose, here is where I like to come when I need to think. After hours it gets a little lively with local peers looking to do a little semi-abandoned partying, but during the day it's deserted, and the sagging fence is easy to defeat.

I lead Scott through the grounds, wondering if he's looking at my legs.

I'm not usually the short plaid skirt and casual tee kind, but I woke up this morning feeling unusually *Clueless* and decided to run with it. Now I'm glad I did. It feels like the sort of thing a gal might wear to land a nervous fish – a sweet, harmless kind of vibe, an outfit to let your guard down around, spill all your juicy secrets to. Besides, it's either that or go full femme fatale, and I left my Jessica Rabbit dress at the cleaners.

Clutching an iced mocha swirl that Scott insisted on buying me from a drive-thru along the way ('A treat for your trouble', he called it, charming me), I lead us to a parental observation bench nailed to the concrete in front of the pink castle at hole twelve. I am more jacked up than a toddler with its fingers stuck in a power socket, and have no business adding a caffeine/sugar speedball into the mix, but it's good to have something to do with my hands.

Together we stare out across plastic crenellations and contemplate sin, guilt and madness. Well – I do. The question that's spinning my dials, now I'm getting within reach of it: do I really want to know what happened with Lucas in the weeks before his death? What if what I discover does not improve my understanding of life, but colours it darker? What about this obsessive need I have to pick up the rock and take a look at the wriggling things underneath?

I've no idea what Scott is thinking.

I fiddle conspicuously with my phone in front of him.

'Just gonna put this baby on airplane or, as I like to call it, undivided attention mode,' I say reassuringly, while I in fact do nothing of the sort, hitting the record button and putting the phone face-down on the bench beside me. Hopefully the microphone picks up our talk.

Scott runs a hand through his hair – a favourite gesture, I'm learning, and it certainly does draw attention to his shiniest attribute. His eyes sweep across the detritus of my childhood.

'This is one creepy place,' he comments.

I shrug. 'People say that, but I find entropy comforting.'

He laughs. 'You like graveyards too?'

'They're quiet. No one's there.'

'So you don't believe in ghosts?'

I shake my head. 'Nope. But I believe you about what you saw in the cave at the beach.'

He looks away.

'I bet you had a bunch of those as a kid,' he says, nodding to poor duct-taped Barbie. 'But you hid them, because you wanted to seem tougher and weirder than the other girls.'

All right, Scott. You wanna play it soft? I can be Ease Girl, as in *put you at your*.

'You're completely wrong,' I smugly reply. 'One hundred per cent. I preferred animals to humans. My number one favourite toy was a farm animal set, with little plastic fencing you could build yourself – you clipped each fence together. Oh, and the light-up hula hoop I had. I used to practise with it out in the garden at night and the first time I did my mother had a heart attack because she thought aliens were landing in our backyard – the strobe effect on it was *quite* strong and she watched far too much *X-Files* before I was born. Probably also, let's see – oh, my father gave me his ancient Gameboy before he skedaddled on us, and I was ob*sessed* with the DuckTales game I had for it. What?'

Scott is giving me a look I can't interpret. He shakes his head.

'I always had a feeling you were super clever. Like a sexy nerd.'

Well, I am wearing a plaid skirt and glasses, like some kind of mid-transformation *She's All That*, so I suppose I only have myself to blame for that interpretation.

'How about you? Favourite toys?' I ask.

He immediately launches into a long reverie about Super Soakers that includes much animated arm waving. It's cute. I slurp at my drink's sugar foam in what I hope is an appealing way as he talks.

'I think I want to be a property developer,' he's saying now, 'but like, with a conscious mindset towards contemporary concerns, you know? My degree specialized in ethical business development. How to build with climate change in mind, how to source materials and resources with the least amount of negative effect on the environment. It's more expensive, but in the long term . . .'

I'm starting to feel like I'm on a getting-to-know-you first date. This isn't really why he wanted to talk to me in private, was it?

'Ethics are hot,' I say. 'Hey, so what happened between you and my brother?'

Scott's demeanour changes fast. Up until now he's been in cruise control, shifting gears with practised ease, flying along familiar roads.

Think of me as a conversational pothole.

'What do you mean?' he says uneasily.

'I just figured, since I'd never heard him mention either you or Justin Gorhammer, you guys had a falling-out?'

Scott gives me a sharp look, and then laughs as if laughing will cancel out his mistake.

'Justin Gorhammer?' he asks, amused. 'You know that gamer nerd?'

'Of him. You're friends, though, right?'

'Nah. He's not my kind of guy.'

'Look,' I say, getting frustrated. 'You, Justin and Lucas – you've all been talking about seeing things. And then I find out there might be this demon-flavoured mafia cult hanging around town, of which your father is apparently a card-carrying member. That's not just coincidence, right?'

He glances at my drink. 'You don't like it?'

'What?'

'The mocha thing I got you. I'm sorry. Too sweet?'

I glance down at my drink in confusion. 'No, it's fine.'

'It's just you're not drinking it.'

'Well, I'm enjoying the talking.'

Scott smirks. 'Yeah. Me too.'

What is going on? Is this guy playing with me? What's his game? I feel like his attention is waning, like I haven't said the right thing yet.

'That night at the mayor's house,' I persist, 'when you rescued me from your dad. Why did you do that?'

'Why do you think?' he says, with a hint of annoyance. 'He was hitting on the girl I have a crush on. It was disgusting.'

'Weird way to hit on me, offering me a necklace.'

'He's always giving women he likes expensive jewellery. And my poor mom has to watch him do it.'

'Look, Scott – it's OK,' I say. 'I know all about the Hoffy Men, OK? You can trust me.'

His eyes narrow. His face turns puzzled. He shakes his head.

'Alec,' he says slowly, 'I'm not sure what's going on, but I swear on my life – I truly have no idea what you're talking about.'

For one eternal, awful second, I believe him. I retrace my memories, my evidence, anxiously looking for my misstep. Is he really not a part of this? Have I been reaching for something that isn't there?

Then Scott does the oddest thing. He leans in close towards me. Too close for mere conversation. If anyone were watching us, they'd think he was trying to kiss me. My heartbeat, the traitor, skips a beat. My cheeks, the turncoats, heat up.

And then, gently, he puts a finger to my lips.

He mouths, *Sshhh*.

He reaches around me, picks up my phone, turns it off and then pockets it.

I rear back. '*Hey!*'

He holds his hands up. 'I'll give it back to you, I swear. We just need to be safe.'

'I feel safer when I have a phone in my hand to call the cops with!'

He leans back from me, his hands go higher.

'Look, I'm sorry,' he says. 'I need to be sure which side you're on.'

His expression is apologetic, but firm.

I'm impressed. I'm anxious to get my phone back. But I'm so, so close. Maybe all it will take to finally get the truth is a little sacrifice of my own.

'OK,' I say slowly. 'How do we establish that?'

'I heard you talked to Viola.' He's watching my expression carefully.

'A little.'

'What did she tell you?'

'Not much. She told me about the necklace. She wouldn't answer anything else.'

He blows out a breath.

'I've been trying to get to her,' he says, 'but they've basically been keeping her hostage. They've got someone around her twenty-four seven, watching her like a hawk. Her parents, her manager when she's out working.'

Boogie Nights. He was listening in, the day I crashed her docklands photoshoot. Was that why she couldn't answer my questions straight out?

'She's not crazy,' Scott says, as if he's reading my mind. 'She's completely faking it.'

'Why?'

'Throw them off the scent, maybe?'

'What scent? Scott – what *happened*?'

Scott watches me carefully. 'Your brother. He unleashed a demon.'

My heart plunges like a rollercoaster drop.

'Lucas wanted to join the Hoffy Men,' he continues. 'There's this . . . initiation ceremony. He was determined. When the higher-ups said no and rejected him, he got really angry. Scary angry. Said he was going to do the initiation anyway. He kept on at Justin and me to help him. It's got to be at least two members initiating someone, right? So he made us do it. And he screwed it up.'

I feel a *little bit* like throwing my iced mocha swirl in his face.

'And here I was, thinking you were a rational human being I could talk to seriously,' I say. 'My mistake.'

'Look, I know how it sounds, OK? But . . . you said you believed what I saw at the beach. You said you believe me, Alec.'

'I believe that *you* saw something. Just because it was real for you, doesn't make it real for me. Look, I'm sorry – I don't have time for this. I'm –'

Scott's hand flashes out, grips mine. His fingers are hard and warm. The sheer audacity – that and the realization that I can't remember the last time I had someone's hand in mine – is enough to stop me.

'I'm not crazy,' he says fiercely. 'And neither was Lucas. If you ever thought he was, I'm telling you, you're wrong.'

That cuts. That cuts really damn deep.

Scott is angry, pleading. 'I can prove it to you. I can show you. I swear. I swear on my *life*, Alec.'

'So far I've been around two of you boys when you've been claiming to see a demon, and all I've seen is a big fat nothing.'

'I'm not saying I can show you a demon. But I can show you the clubhouse.'

'The clubhouse?' I say slowly.

'The cave, near Gracetown. You've heard of it, right? It's headquarters. They've got recordings. Documentation. They record everything that happens down there. Blackmail. Everything.' Scott takes a deep breath. 'I'm a member, right? I can get you in. Then you can see it all for yourself.'

The Descent

The sky has lowered fast. By the time we're in his car and on the road ('I'll drive you back afterwards,' he promises) the light outside has that hazy sleepy gold of pre-dusk.

'How far is it?' I ask.

'Just a little further,' Scott replies, his eyes on the road. 'Hey, you finish your mocha thing yet? Seriously, I'll get you something else. What do you want? We'll stop off.'

'This is fine,' I say hastily, and to prove it I take a big sip. Now I'm close to answers, I don't want to waste any more time.

His car smells of peppermint. The front seat is clean and empty. The back seats are covered with what looks like camping gear.

'I know the Gracetown area pretty well,' he says, catching the direction of my gaze. 'It's my favourite place to go hunting.'

'What do you hunt?'

He smiles, showing off perfectly aligned white incisors. 'Rabbits.'

The drive takes long enough that I've almost finished my drink by the time we're turning off the main road. We follow a country lane that narrows to a car width, hemming us in with tall, thorny hedging on either side. The lane offers up a dirt track with a gate at the end.

'The cave is on someone's farm?' I ask.

'It's just on the border of their property.' Scott parks in front of the gate. 'It's further in, down past the field, but this is the best place to park.'

'Bosky,' I comment. 'Um. Are we going to need a torch on the way?'

Scott holds up his phone in reply.

'Great,' I say. 'Can you give me mine back?'

'I will, once we're in there,' he says, taking my hand and leading me to the side of the gate, where there's enough of a gap between the gate post and the encroaching hedgerow to squeeze through into the field beyond.

The breeze winds a chill around my exposed legs, and I privately curse my choice of outfit. Then again, according to my admittedly limited experience, most first dates don't end in outdoor recreation – or not unless they go *really* well.

All right, I can admit it now. I'm nervous. Is it very, very stupid to be following a guy I barely know into a place I've never been, with no phone and no way to get back-up?

But curiosity, as they say, killed the cat. He says he's got the goods; he says he can get us in there, that no one will know we've ever been – the promise is too tempting to pass up.

I follow Scott along a well-worn track that runs along the side of a vast cornfield. An observation: there is nothing, *nothing*, spookier than walking beside thick, shoulder-height corn in the semi-dark. Every rustle denotes someone or thing about to burst out on to the path. My ridiculous imagination has an animated corn dolly with a loop for a head stalking us among the sheaves, waiting to slip its plaited loop head over ours and strangle us to death. That's what you get for reading Robin Jarvis at a tender age.

'Scott,' I call. 'How much further is it?'

The phone light in front of me stops bobbing, and a shape, black on dark, returns to me, slipping its hand once more in mine, our entwined flesh now pinched and cold.

'Right down here,' Scott reassures me. 'We're nearly there, I promise.'

He leads me on.

'Hey, you know those corn dollies that everyone starts making at the end of summer for Harvest Festival?' I say.

'Mmm,' Scott makes a vague noise, and it's enough to encourage me to launch into a graphic description of what currently lurks in my brain. By the time I'm finished telling him that the only forensic evidence the police would find to explain our deaths would be corn chaff and a plaited rope indentation around our necks, and we'd probably go down in local history as an alluringly gruesome ghost story that subsequent generations would scare each other with at sleepovers, I realize we've reached our destination.

Scott stops us, shining his phone light steadily into a large, black yawn.

'It's a hole,' I say, Captain Obvious riding to my rescue while my hindbrain yowls.

'It's the entrance to an old mine.' His voice sounds reassuringly normal. 'Don't worry, it's fixed up with lights. There's a generator that keeps them running.'

Who runs the generator? I want to ask. Who watches the watchmen?

Scott is tugging me along, plunging us into that dark mouth. As I trot beside him it gets darker and darker until I can't even see him any more, the only indication that he's still there the feel of his hand in mine. I'm feeling oddly weak, and grateful that he's got my hand. As if I might fall over if he weren't holding me up. My heart stops –

And then as either God or the Devil said, let there be light.

The recessed lights stringing along the walls of the cave we stand in are set to dim, I realize a little later, once my eyes have adjusted.

'That was horrifying,' I breathe, and give a great big adrenaline laugh. 'Did you hit a switch? Or is there a motion sensor?'

We are in a disappointingly unspooky rounded space. I spy an ordinary-looking bare cave, maybe a little bigger than my house, low ceiling, packed dirt floor. The lighting reveals a natural protrusion from the cave floor, what I at first took to be a giant boulder – but it has more finesse than that, resembling a shallow carved basin with a lip as high as my hips, and long enough to hold a man lying down. Cut into the lip at several intervals are rough-hewn notches as thick as a finger. All I can think is if you filled the shallow basin with water, it would run rivulets out through the notches before it spilled over the lip.

'Come here,' says Scott, beckoning to me.

I walk towards the giant basin in a strange fug. I feel like I'm a little drunk. The grande mocha swirl has clearly chosen this opportune moment to kick in its queasy sugar overdose phase – but I can't back out now. Not when I'm so close.

I look down into the basin, my breath catching in my throat with sheer anticipation –

'This doesn't *look* like a handy open safe packed with evidence,' I say.

'You sound disappointed,' Scott replies. 'Don't you wonder what it's for?'

I look at its rough surface, its gentle curves, the faint dark smears that stain its centre. Splashes and dribbles of hardened candle wax are visible here and there around the lip.

'My mind goes to bad places,' I say.

'Depends what you mean by bad.'

I look around at him. He is studying me intently.

'Looks like a giant version of the font in church,' I say.

He gives me an eager nod. 'Yes! That's it exactly. Only this isn't a Christian place of worship.'

Candles, caves, basins.

I swallow. I have to ask. 'Scott, are the Hoffy Men satanists?'

Scott snorts. 'Please. The Devil is a Christian construct. This is older than that. A lot older. They've dated this cave as prehistoric.'

Despite my penchant for inking upside-down crosses on to my flesh I don't believe in the Devil, but I do believe in heartless evil, even if it's just in a moment, a split-second's selfish choice. And maybe that is what we call the Devil, because we must name things to understand them. To teach ourselves about them.

To warn ourselves about them.

In other words, right now I'm a little freaked.

'Why are you showing me this?' I ask.

'This is where it happened. This is where Lucas summoned a demon.'

Scott taps his mouth in thought, looking down into the basin. Either: he believes in demons, which bodes ill for his sound judgement, and I don't love the idea of being alone in a cave with people of unsound judgement. Or: demons are real, and I'm about to lose my own mind, because current evidence points to no one coming out of that experience unscathed.

I turn my body very slightly towards the way we came, searching as unobtrusively as I can for the exit. 'So this is where you did the initiation ceremony for my brother?'

Scott nods.

'With Justin Gorhammer,' I venture.

'Yes,' says Scott.

'It involved Viola Gordon, didn't it?'

'Yes,' says Scott again.

A wave of nausea rolls through me.

'Why was Viola chosen?' I ask.

'The initiate chooses.' Scott shrugs. 'Lucas had a big old crush on her, as far as I know. Had done for months.'

Crush. Viola. Lucas had a crush on *Viola*.

That was who he broke up with Mallory for. That was who he was trying to talk to at the *Stranger Things* party.

'What does it involve? The ritual?' I ask.

Scott says, 'Sacrifice.'

Holy Mother of God.

'What kind of sacrifice?'

'Eh, the usual. You know. A tiny amount of blood, some energy raising between the group. Mostly symbolic.'

'Symbolic energy raising?'

Scott casts around for explanations. 'See, the Hoffy Men is a club, right? A network of power and money. And everybody wants power and money. But like all old clubs, it has its traditions. In order to join the club, you have to sacrifice something.'

'What do you sacrifice? Your daughter?'

'It's *symbolic*, Alec. Anyway, that's not – it's all consensual, it's a tradition that stretches back hundreds of years. Everybody knows about it; it's no big deal.' He rolls his eyes. 'Outsiders don't understand.'

'Well,' I say, 'it's hard to get on board with rape.'

I've noticed that some people don't like the official words we use for things. Scott's eyes roll and his mouth downturns with disappointment.

'Come on, Alec,' he says. 'That's not what happens here. I told you – it's all consensual.'

It was a shot in the dark. But seeing how Viola isn't dead and sometimes, just sometimes, my worst thoughts are entirely justified, it was a decent shot.

My stomach churns. I feel sick and strange, my legs all runny like melted candles. Lucas was involved in this? It can't be. It just can't.

I look around. 'Where does the camera go?'

'What?'

'Well,' I say, 'you film all the ceremonies, right? Great for blackmail later, if anyone gets cold feet. Great way to make money too. I suppose it gets filed under "voluntary donations" come tax season.'

Scott is silent.

My heart has abandoned the dancing and is now panic-battering itself against my ribs.

'Cool,' I nod. 'So you filmed yourselves raping Viola?'

Gag. Gag, gag, *gag* –

'Me?' Scott exclaims. 'I didn't do a thing! I didn't do anything wrong, whatever that cancel-culture attention-whore's been squealing. Some people are damaged, they'll say anything to anyone, and that's the sad truth, OK? I'm not the one who touched her! I didn't even *touch* her! That was your brother! *He* was the one who did it!'

'You're a goddamn liar,' I shout – or I try? I really do. I *want* to shout, but I feel like it came out soft and stretchy, like taffy.

Scott is looking at me. 'God isn't here, and in this place I'm the most honest I've ever been. Down here, I *can* be honest. We all can be. You can be, too, Alec. I promise.'

I'm starting to feel weak and rubbery – is this a panic attack? What superlatively bad timing, Alec.

'Where's the evidence you were going to show me?' I manage. Recordings, documents – I don't see anything around here like that. 'What am I doing down here, Scott?'

'Saving my life,' he says with utter seriousness. 'Viola, she totally lost it. Right in the middle of it. I told Lucas she was a bad choice. Didn't matter about her dad being a member, didn't matter that she'd shame him and her whole family by freaking out. Everyone knows you have to be calm. You have to be a hundred per cent all in. See, the Hoffy Man, He can smell fear, He can smell doubt. He does not like doubt.'

I feel hot, shivery. Which doesn't make much sense considering how cold it is down here, and how short my skirt.

'Viola was mistake number one.' Scott stares into the basin. 'Mistake number two was on us, really. I mean, we just read your brother completely wrong. OK, we have to take a scholarship kid every once in a while, right? Poor people, they deserve a shot. But none of us realized He was a complete psycho. When

Viola fucked up the ritual He went absolutely crazy, and Viola escaped – thank god she did, frankly, because I don't know what He would have done to her if she hadn't got out –'

I swear I'm trying to make my legs work, I'm trying to get the hell out of here, but all that happens is that I stumble forward, grappling with the rim of that ancient font to try to keep myself upright, its rough stone scraping the skin of my hands.

'But that's the problem,' I hear Scott say. 'She got out, and she shouldn't have. You're supposed to complete the ritual. If you don't –'

I hear footsteps, scraping. I think he's moving around behind me, but it's taking all I have to keep standing.

'That's on your brother, and He paid the price for his screw-up. But I'm not some try-hard social climber like him, and I'm not some closeted suburban nerd like Justin. I'm the strong one. I'm not going to kill myself no matter how much weird shit I see, and nothing's going to hurt me. This is a test. That's what it is. He's testing us, and they might have failed, but I never fail. All He needs is a proper sacrifice, done the right way. I mean, the sister of the guy who screwed up last time is perfect, don't you think? He'll like that. Just lie down in the basin. It's honestly not a big deal, He just needs a little blood, a little pain. It's over so fast. And we like each other, right? I know you're into me. I've clocked the way you've been looking at me. I always know when girls like me. And I like you, too, Alec; that part wasn't a lie. So that's good, isn't it? We do this together because we *want* to, right?'

Femme fatale. What a joke. I thought I'd led him here, but I was just following his carrot. All his nerves, his hesitation, his wide-eyed 'I'm on your side' routine. This area he knows so well. He had done whatever he could to get me here, charmed and cajoled me, posed as the cute, awkward popular guy, attractive and into nerds, so safe. Conversations about kid's toys.

That crazily sugary mocha swirl that he got me. What a harmless, fun drink. What a –

My legs bow underneath me.

Christ, I'm such a fool.

Scott spins me round, looming in my blurry vision. Our teeth clash. His lips are wet. His tongue is urgent and hungry, probing relentlessly at my mouth.

I've often suspected that you can coast by on being average in every other way if you're physically attractive enough, because no one pushes you to improve. You might never even know that you need to. Clearly none of Scott Poltern's former amours ever, for example, had the courage to mention to him that he's a bad kisser. It's like being caught up in a washing machine.

Then his hands go to his belt, fumbling to undo it.

At this point, what I actually feel is disappointment. This is how it finally happens to me? Really? All those cautionary tales about having your keys between your fingers as you cross a parking lot at night didn't do me a damn bit of good. All my self-defence training, all those half-watched YouTube videos and pamphlets and talks at school – all useless, all gone. The silver screen lies; it has lied to me over and over again – I can't get a thigh in between his to knee him in the balls, I can't turn to get an elbow into his solar plexus, I can't even free one hand to scratch at his face or poke his eyes out. I'm melting from whatever drug he's fed me, melting limp, rag-dolling against the thick stone basin digging painfully into my back.

It's just about then that my brain helpfully serves me up a realization: I've worked out what those dark stained notches carved into the basin are for.

What liquid they might have traditionally let run out.

My body bucks in one last superhuman effort. I feel the body on me slacken – maybe in surprise. I push, I crawl away –

It's pointless. He's on me again. I struggle, I kick, my hip bangs on the ground as he takes me down, jarring through my whole body and shocking me still. He's on top of me, holding me down as easy as you please – strength training, why did I never get into strength training? – and as I look up at him, my brain one big panicked blank, I see that his hair is twitching. No – not his hair. Something on his hair. It haloes his head with spindly, jointed spikes. Then the spikes descend, crawling over his face.

Spider. It's a spider. Its thick, furry tarantula bulk clings to the side of his head like a tumour growth, fleshy legs picking their way down to his mouth.

The cords in Scott's neck pop up from his flesh like he has electrical wires buried under his skin. He chokes out a strangled high-pitched keening, like a dog with its tail trapped under a chair.

I think he's figured out what it is on his face.

He tumbles off me, hands waving frantically around the black spider growth as if he can't bring himself to touch it, but if he doesn't rip it off him it really looks as though it's going to squeeze itself past his lips and down his throat –

Horror freezes you. You're supposed to run when there's something threatening in front of you, but there's a tipping point. If it's somehow too awful for normal parameters, your reasoning cuts out and something darker, and calmer, takes over. Something like acceptance, like giving up.

My vague peripherals tell me, in an absent, dazed kind of way, that my attacker is bailing. Running off up the tunnel in a mad, mindless frenzy.

For a moment I swear I can hear two sets of footsteps – but maybe it's just an echo.

I have time to wonder what spiders taste like before a woozy darkness comes to claim me. In other words, ladies and gentlemen, I do a big old faint, right there in the demon cave.

I know, I know. My timing, as always, excels.

Stand By Me

Picture, if you will, your narrator as a stringy ten-year-old, kicking her legs against the pew in Sunday Mass, looking for all the world like the best little Catholic girl, utterly absorbed in her hymnal, which she has open before her and held up close to her face.

Picture the slim battered paperback volume of a *Nancy Drew* mystery surreptitiously placed on top of the open hymnal, aka the thing she is *actually* reading, the corner of which pokes out beyond the hymnal's edges.

Picture her annoyance at her elder brother sat beside her, who just hit twelve and has, much to the delight of his football coach, been filling out at an alarming rate, and who keeps leaning close to her with his big stupid trunk of a body, his arm occasionally grazing the page edges of her *Nancy Drew*, to the point where she's having trouble concentrating on the mystery.

Picture the moment when his baby sister realizes that he's not being annoying but in fact shielding her from the laser gaze of their mother, who, if he leaned back, would have a direct line of sight to the crime being committed mere feet away by her mildly blasphemous daughter.

Picture every Sunday after church, all throughout their childhoods, long past the point at which it would have been considered cool to hang out with her, Lucas Gray taking his baby sister down to the boardwalk, across the boardwalk to the pier, and along the pier to the arcade, where a dollar went really far on the coin-pusher machines, semi-far on the Skee-Ball, and not far at all on the magical, hallowed *Streetfighter II* game, with all its mysterious buttons and combo special moves and also Chun-Li, the character who would flip on to her hands and deliver deadly spinning helicopter kicks to her opponents.

Picture a ten-year-old girl who loves playing Chun-Li so much that her older brother would spend some of his own pocket money, week after week, to give her the chance to win the game with that spinning kick, which she never, ever did, because she wasn't really very good at fighting games. Too many damn buttons. Picture him doing it anyway because he loves her and the way that he shows love is by doing things for people unasked, and without ever asking for anything back, because then it would become transactional, and it wouldn't be love.

Picture him the day I had played three times in a row and wasted three of his precious dollars and wanted to cry, and him getting out a fourth dollar. Picture the older teenage boys behind us, bored of waiting for the idiot girl-child, jeering and scaring me off the machine so they can take it over for the afternoon. Picture their aggressive faces, their hard mouths opening in shock when Lucas, firm yet courtly, asks them to wait just another turn so that I can get my butt kicked again and he can waste his fourth dollar.

Picture them hating this polite boy, this good boy, looking after his little sister like a loser, picture one of them taking me by the arm, wrenching me off the stool and making me yelp in pain, just like Lucas would do eight years later at a party. Picture another boy getting up in Lucas's face – who knew what triggered this damage bag, who knew how it escalated so fast? – spitting on him, telling him to promise that never again would he be bringing his little sister to *their* arcade, *their* territory, never again would they come in finding that skinny fucking baby on *their* stool, at *their* game, because fucking losers shouldn't be allowed to play.

Picture the boy pulling on my arm so hard I swear I feel like it's coming out of the socket, and I scream. Picture Lucas – completely ignoring the evident leader with the spit and the threats – going up to the boy holding me and asking him to stop touching me, and quoting from Psalms – Psalms, to this jackal pack – some lengthy line about moral behaviour. When nothing happens, Lucas counts to three, slowly, while the boys jeer and bay at him and call him a religious freak. Then Lucas warns the boy again, swings his arm back and punches him in the face.

Picture the boy staggering, relinquishing my arm, keeling over to one side. Bursting into tears. More likely shock at the humiliation of a fifteen-year-old jackal having been sucker punched by a twelve-year-old who talks like Best Boy in Bible Group (a real title that really existed and that a younger Lucas won so frequently that our church's Sunday school stopped bothering to hold the competition).

Picture Lucas walking me calmly and slowly towards the exit. Calmly and slowly and with scrupulous honesty giving a blow-by-blow of the entire affair to our mother, who was back at the church, hanging out with Oh and waiting for us. Unasked, by the way – to this day I swear she would never had found out about it, but Lucas was worried about the bullies' parents somehow impossibly tracking her down, having been given a false version of events. Lucas wanted her to know the truth, and he wanted to say it in front of Oh so that Oh would give him the chance to confess his sin of violence, the proper ritualized way, and be forgiven.

I said if they forgave him I would never forgive them, because in my opinion he acted without fault. From that day on I called him Lucaslot because he was a true Knight of the Realm, a modern-day Lancelot who hated groups of bully boys and could never, ever bring himself to hurt a girl.

But I was wrong.

I was wrong, wasn't I?

Somewhere along the way, he stopped being Lucaslot and became the threat that Lucaslot protected against.

Promising Young Woman

She found me halfway back to Fring.

I'm still a little foggy on the post-cave details, but I know I came round in the cave, somehow made it all the way back up the corn field, over the gate, down the dirt road and hit asphalt before I gave up the ghost.

I sat down on the scrubby verge, dazed and sick. I got out my phone, dialled a number, made some incoherent noises to the person at the other end, and then slumped into a semi-conscious collapse while I waited for rescue.

The person I called was not my mother, or even the police, but Megan.

I know, I know.

It's been weeks since our infamous not-a-date diner clash and, in all that time, we haven't exchanged one text. Yet somehow, when I wake up in a hospital bed and see a familiar mane of hair atop a gazelle-like figure perched on the chair next to me, for one confused moment I think I've somehow woken up in her bed, which makes me cringe and blush at the same time.

Megan's gaze is fastened intently on her phone, but some slight shift of mine catches her attention, and she looks at me.

'You're awake,' she says, immediate and focused. 'How do you feel?'

This is a lot to try to answer immediately. My head is pounding and my mouth is dry, presumably from the drug-laced mocha swirl.

'Weird?' I offer.

'You look more *here*.'

'I do? Where was I before?'

I was half joking, but she sounds serious when she says:

'Somewhere I couldn't go.'

It's the smell that finally identifies the *here*. That faded antiseptic sharpness that immediately suggests the sound of squeaking rubber wheels and bleeping machines.

'Well, this can't be good,' I muse.

'You're fine,' Megan says quickly. 'At least, I think so. They only like to give medical updates to family members, even though I'm the one who brought you in.'

Can I hear a faint tone of somewhat bizarre possessiveness, and do I hate it? Yes, I can, and no, I do not.

Family members – crap.

'My mother –' I say.

'Do you want me to call her?'

'No!' I quickly reply. 'They're not going to, are they? The doctors or whoever.'

'You're eighteen,' Megan says cautiously. 'They're not obliged. You're an adult.'

Relief floods me. 'Good. I will not be the kid who kills her with worry.'

'Do you want to talk about it?'

'About what?' I say, just for the look of the thing.

171

'Whatever it was that happened?'

The official story I now remember giving the ER doctor was that I went exploring in an abandoned mine in the middle of nowhere, got lost, freaked myself out, had a panic attack or something of that ilk and fled to the road, which was where Megan picked me up. So far, so vague.

I shrug. 'I'm an idiot. That's what happened down there.'

She's looking at me, clearly unsatisfied. I hope I didn't babble anything crazy in the car ride to the hospital.

'You kept saying something about tarantulas,' Megan says.

Ah. Hopes dashed.

'Wow.' I nod. 'Hallucinations to boot. That must have been some panic attack.'

'That or you partook of that beach party guy's psychedelics,' I hear her say.

I remember the mocha swirl. I've no idea what Scott dosed me with, but it's a safe bet that it caused the appearance of the tarantula, and is ultimately responsible for the demonic hallucinations of Scott, Justin and Lucas.

But thinking of my brother right now is like a knife in the heart, so I stop.

'What was his name again,' Megan continues, 'the guy that also saw spiders? Scott something?'

I flash her a look. 'You know his name.'

We stare each other out.

I break the stalemate with a theatrical sigh. 'I'll go first, if you like.'

'Go first?'

'With the laying out of our respective cards.'

A pause.

'OK,' Megan says, with the curated blankness I'm coming to recognize as someone holding back an ace or two.

'Pretend you have a bingo card in your hand.' I plough through her confusion. 'Just pretend. Now check off any words or phrases that you recognize on your card.'

I tap my teeth as if I'm thinking, though I already have the first one lined up.

'The Hoffy Men.'

Megan remains blank, and I think I've made a complete error in judgement until her right hand moves, miming scribbling out a word on an invisible card.

As any decent horror movie knows, there are a number of ways to simulate the feel of your hairs standing on end through sound. This moment, if it were in a horror movie, would be accompanied by the slow downtuned slide of violin strings.

'So you know all about what my brother did to Viola,' I say.

Silence.

Her hand mimes scribbling out another hit on her invisible bingo card.

I sit back against the thin hospital pillows. Suddenly I feel drained. I'd love to live in a world where everyone is forced to tell the truth when you ask. People respond best to fear, don't they? Maybe something gruesome should happen every time someone tries to lie, like – oh I don't know, getting choked out by a big fat spider, say.

'Told you I'd find out what happened my own way,' I tell Megan.

'By starring in a re-enactment?' she replies. 'That's what happened down there, isn't it? They attacked you.'

'One of them did,' I admit. 'Spider boy.'

'Where is he?' She looks cold and hard, as though Medusa just stealth swept through the room and gave her a quick stone-turning stare on the flyby.

I shake my head. 'When I woke up in the cave, he was gone.'

'There was no one else involved?'

'Seemed like he was operating alone.'

I say that. But riddle me this, ladies and gentlemen: Scott had my phone before I went into the cave. I had my phone when I came out of the cave. It seems unlikely that Scott paused during his post-attack hallucinatory breakdown escape to considerately put my phone back in my pocket.

So who did?

'You really are an idiot,' Megan says, cutting into my thoughts. 'What the hell possessed you to go down there with him?'

'If you'd been straight with me in the first place, maybe I wouldn't have had to do it,' I riposte.

She keeps that cold, guarded look on for a minute more, and for that minute, I see a future where she walks out of here and we never talk again.

'I didn't want to tell you about Lucas,' she says. 'I couldn't face it. Besides, would you have believed me?'

'About his involvement in a satanic mafia ritual?' I consider. 'Probably not.'

'How long have you known about the Hoffy Men?' Megan asks me.

'Wait, let me get my bingo card out.'

'Alec.'

I cross my arms. All this truth-telling really takes it out of you.

'Not long,' I say.

Megan sighs. 'Maybe I should have said something. But I never thought they'd go after you. Why would they?'

Because I've been romping around asking blithe questions of their members like, 'Boy, that's a pretty necklace, what's it for?' Then again, Scott's luring of me hadn't felt like some clever entrapment by a group of power-hungry demon worshippers so much as the desperate act of a lone, spiralling predator, which makes it even more embarrassing that I didn't see what he was up to – but there seems no point in gnawing at that bone right now.

'Why haven't the police arrested Justin and Scott before now?' I ask her.

'Because the Hoffy Men are in the police. They own this town.'

'Come on.'

'You have no idea,' she says darkly. 'One move against them and your parents lose their jobs. Or you get slapped with some made-up lawsuit to try to bankrupt you. Or you ask for a loan and get denied, even though your credit score's better than good enough and you've never had a debt in your life.'

'Heavies sent round to break your legs?' I guess. 'A quick river dip with weights tied to your feet?'

'You jest, but it's real.'

'Has it happened to you?'

But that's a step too far. She just shrugs.

'They can't be held accountable,' she says simply.

Something tickles at me, some insistence of memory – and then it hits.

'My phone,' I say.

I open it up and flick through my recordings. The last one, there – Scott and I talking at the Pitch and Putt. It's hard to remember what he said now, but surely there's something?

'Listen to this,' I say, and I press play.

Megan listens.

'Wow, your giggle there,' she says, a couple of minutes in.

'Shut up. I was fake flirting.'

'Thank god. If that was real flirting I'd be embarrassed for you.'

Scott's voice is muffled, a word obscured by background noise every so often, but you can hear him. Alas – there will be no pay-off for your narrator. In playing it back, I realize just how little Scott had admitted to or even corroborated – before he took my phone off me, at least. It was all my talk, my conjecture. What, is there mandatory media training when you join the Hoffy Men?

'God, I'm so stupid,' I say aloud.

'You're not,' Megan tells me. 'Trust me, Alec. You can't fight if you don't know what you're fighting.'

I'm wondering, suddenly. Wondering about Megan. Why she came when I called her from the side of the road, some incoherent damaged chick she met in the woods lighting a candle to summon her dead brother. Then again at a beach party with a giant invisible spider as a surprise cameo. Then the ill-fated face-slapping diner fight. When you put it all that way, catch of the day I am not. We've never even had a regular interaction. What must that say about me?

Yet here she is, Florence Nightingaling all over my hospital bedside, sat in that uncomfortable plastic chair as though she's been there for hours and plans to stay for more.

And I'm wondering if it isn't time to scare her away for good.

'Look, Megan,' I say. 'I think I'm probably losing it. Healthy, well-adjusted people don't act the way I act. And you can say everyone gets a grief pass, but the truth is I've always been like this. Grief just gave me the excuse I needed to really let loose. I'm self-destructive, I'm angry, I'm sharp-edged, I can't let things go, I unleash the brimstone for anyone who lies to me, but I'm a hypocrite because I lie all the time.'

I'm staring at the wall as I talk, at that rotten mint shade of green it's been painted with, thinking about what sort of bizarre committee-decision-making came up with that as the perfect shade for sick people to see.

'I wish I was crazy in a sexy, *Donnie Darko* way, you know, a way that signified something interesting, but honestly this might just be an elaborate method that my brain has come up with to torture myself over Lucas. I'm telling you all this because when I needed somebody I called *you*, which I shouldn't have done, because you kept things from me, and we don't even know each other, and no one needs the burden of a drowning stranger, but if it isn't blindingly, glaringly obvious yet I called you because I like you, romantically, in the Virginia Woolf–Vita Sackville-West tradition, just for clarification, and if you don't like me in the same way I absolutely understand, and if you do like me in the same way, god help you, and really either way what I'm saying is I'm a bad prospect, so, you know, you are released from any non-existent obligation. Totally absolved. Be on your way. Go in grace.'

I finally, *finally*, subside.

Why am I not cool?

Why am I

never

cool?

Silence from the plastic chair, excruciating in its longevity. I continue to stare at the wall.

'I just have one question,' Megan says from somewhere beside me.

'Fire away,' I croak.

I can feel her eyes on me.

'Do you think they deserve what's happening to them? Justin, and Scott . . .'

And Lucas. His name is there in the space she leaves.

I think of Scott's desperate, deliberate attack on me. The way my hip still groans from its connection with the cave floor when he brought me down. What he might have done to me if the same drug he had taken hadn't kicked in and gifted him a tarantula hallucination. He must really have a problem with spiders.

The dark part of me hopes that he choked on it. That he hallucinated so hard he convinced his body it was real, and he's lying in a field somewhere for some luckless farmhand to find, having scared himself to death. And right now, I don't care what that makes me. The people who get away with it make me sick. The injustice makes me sick.

'Yes,' I say. 'I think they deserve it. I hope the guilt breaks them.'

The thin sheets tucked around me rustle; I feel a new weight on the rickety bed, a fast second's sensation of hair, warmth, breath – and then Megan is kissing me.

Megan Lugner has her mouth on mine, the softest lips of all time, probably, hot and full, the kind apt to inspire poetry or at least a watercolour.

Megan is kissing me, and it is definitely a *Carmilla* kind of kiss.

Atonement

What do I want to say about guilt?

Do I want to talk about how it poisons you, colours even the small, innocent moments of joy in a day? Guilt does not let you smile. Guilt makes sure to chase up a good feeling with a bad one. Guilt tells you that moments of happiness are self-indulgence. That if you are not suffering, you are selfish. We cannot expect joy, says guilt, and when we get it we should feel bad about having it.

When I wake up in the middle of the night a nightmare is crouched in the corner of my room.

He looks sick. Glutinous and wrong, as though he's been poisoned. He crouches on all fours like a dog, muttering something that resolves, quickly enough in the way of dreams, to something I can't hear but just somehow know.

I tried to make it right, he's saying. *I tried to take it back*.

It's my brother.

I watch the Lucas nightmare from under the false safety of my duvet cover, trying not to breathe. I know it's a nightmare, and I am asleep right now. I know that. It just *feels* like I'm awake. But I will not engage with him as though this is real, because that way madness lies. Instead I will wake up, and he will disappear. Wake up, Alec.

Wake up.

Wake up.

That doesn't seem to work, so I change tactics.

Please, Lucas, go away. I'm begging you.

Dread drips like cold honey down my insides. The only way I can break this is to leap out of bed, fling myself at the door and get through it as fast as humanly possible – but that requires a superhuman level of courage absolutely zero people possess when dressed in nothing but a *Stalker* movie T-shirt and flimsy bed shorts.

Suddenly the hallway light snaps on, alerting me via a thin band of light spidering across my bedroom floor. I hear the creaking grunt of the hallway's loose floorboards, the little click of the bathroom door being shut.

When I re-remember my terror and look back, the figure has gone.

Praise be to my mother's insomnia.

I lie back under clammy sheets, feeling sick and shivery. My spooked brain does its usual thing in moments of high stress, scrambling madly to make sense of what scares it.

It takes a long, sickening moment before reality asserts itself in my brain, assuring me that what I just saw was just a dream, a nightmare – but there's no going back to sleep now.

I lie awake, staring at the glow-in-the-dark stars on my ceiling, and I think about the winter of hell, seven months ago, aka the last time I saw my brother alive.

I slammed his bedroom door closed.

'You can never, ever do that again,' I said.

Lucas looked up from his now-customary thousand-yard stare.

'Do what?'

'Flippantly discuss how you're being hounded by a demon at the dinner table. You can be as crazy and awful as you like in the four walls of your own bedroom, but out there, Lucas, in front of our mother, you will act more dully sober than an accountant who moonlights as a judge. Did you even notice what you're doing to her?'

'What do you want me to do?' he asked me wearily. 'Pretend it's not there?'

'Why not? Give it a whirl. Heaven knows leaning into it hasn't been working out so well for you.'

'I can't ignore what's happening. I have to take it.'

'Why? Explain to me why you have to take it.'

He said nothing. His shoulders hunched. His eyes went down to the floor.

It only made me angrier.

'What is this for, Lucas?' I demanded. 'This endless self-flagellation? What possible mistake could you have made to turn you into this? Did you murder someone?'

He was supposed to snort, roll his eyes. Mutter, 'No, of course not.'

Instead he said, quietly, 'Yes.'

Time itself froze up.

Then he said, 'Myself.'

Then he looked up, startled by my wild laugh.

'Jesus Christ, that's the most pretentiously emo thing I've ever heard,' I replied.

Lucas frowned. 'Don't blaspheme.'

'I'll blaspheme if I goddamn want to!'

He rose from his bed in one swift and sudden bound. 'Don't fucking do that, Alec!'

I shrank, bewildered, from his fire. For one moment, I thought he was going to hit me.

He saw it. He deflated.

'I'm sorry,' he said, quieter. 'I'm really sorry. About all of it.'

'I know you are,' I wearily replied. 'You're the sorriest damn person I've ever seen. But where is all this sorry getting you? What are you doing with it? You're certainly not making *me* feel better. If you say sorry to me one more time, I'm going to scream. Tell you what, here's a suggestion, just wanted to run it by you: don't be sorry. Instead, stop doing the thing that keeps making you say sorry.'

He just shrugged. It was a shrug that meant 'it seems like I'm listening to you but I'm not going to change'.

'I have to see this through to the end,' he said, 'even if it kills me.'

'Well,' I remarked, outwardly calm while my stomach turned over, 'how self-indulgent of you.'

That got him.

'Self-indulgent?' he said.

'Selfish, even,' I retorted.

'What I'm doing now is the opposite of selfish!'

He was angry, but all I felt was savage happiness at provoking him.

'Really? Torturing your family with this penitent suffering bullshit when you could be on medication, you could be seeing a therapist, you could be getting *better* —'

'You think a pill and a chat with some professional about the childhood source of my behavioural patterns will change what's already happened, what's happening now? This isn't a battle for my mental health, Alec! This is a battle for my soul!'

'Well,' I said, 'you're losing.'

'I know.'

He was hopeless. Resigned.

Despair is a kind of evil, and evil feeds on itself. Let despair in and let in a virus that will multiply and multiply, running rampant through your systems until there's nothing left but itself.

This is the moment I've been keeping from you, all along.

My sin that begat a sin.

'So that's what you mean by seeing this through to the end, is it?' I said. 'What's the problem, the whole "suicide is a mortal sin" thing? Hell isn't real.'

'Hell is real. It's here. We carry it with us.'

I wanted to wipe the mournful look off his face. I wanted to shock him out of this state of *melodrama*. I wanted, more than anything, to hurt him the way he was hurting me.

I went to his bedroom door, pausing there. Turning back to him.

'OK,' I said. 'If hell is here, you can't go to it after you die, can you? So don't let that stop you.'

'What do you mean?'

'If this world tortures you so much, Lucas, then leave it. Do us all a favour.'

Then I went through the door and slammed it closed behind me.

Eight hours later, he was dead.

★

I know why the nightmare came tonight, I know why it visits me in the dark sweaty armpit part of the night when the bright, familiar world seems very far away, and the thin line between 'real' and 'not real' seems less of a wall and more of a membrane you can tear open, like the skin on an egg.

Lucas is not the only one who committed an egregious sin. I told my brother to leave, and he did. I killed him. I thought solving this case would somehow absolve me of my own sin, but Lucas was here, and he'll be here again.

Because I know what demons are.

Demons are guilt, and mine just paid me its first visit.

Duel

Two days later, I see the Porsche again.

I eye it in my rear-view. It's the same one that was following me when Scott showed up at my house. He acted nervous of it, as if he recognized it. It's got to be a Hoffy Man. One of his father's lackeys, checking up on me. Trying to scare me into silence.

When I told Megan I wanted to go to the police about Scott, she put me off the idea. Said they were crawling with Hoffy Men. I had no evidence, no witnesses, no one would believe me. Does that mean Scott gets away with it? Does that mean I just have to keep pretending like nothing's happened? She said there was another way, that I had to be patient.

But patience, dear reader, is not your narrator's middle name. (It's Magdalene. Yes, really.) I'm feeling much more like a little confrontation to get me through the day.

Let the games begin.

First move is getting off the main road. Then it's taking a less obvious fork or two. Then it's a sudden diversion down a country lane only wide enough for one car – these properly scare me – towards a barely-a-town surely only populated by members of the family from *The Hills Have Eyes*.

And the Porsche follows me every step of the way.

We crawl through seaside streets, jouncing past thrift stores and diners and crab shacks. We climb up the hill to the tiny local history museum at its rise, idle past retirees braving the summer-storm-coloured skies to take their afternoon constitutional, the seagulls wheeling forlornly above, precious few people around to dive-bomb for any carelessly held food.

I exit slow-death-ville and hit the main road, accelerating as fast as I dare. For several seconds I think I've lost them – but then I see that sleek car bullet emerge, turning on to the road behind me, going my way.

My foot's pounding the gas before my brain can intervene with conscious thought. Not sure I've ever gone this fast. Also I'm trying to outrun a Porsche – it's a house cat up against a panther, but I feel like playing, I feel like screwing with them, maybe somehow getting them to tip their hand –

The siren snaps me out of my vengeance reverie. I glance in my rear-view. A police car! Never have I felt such relief. What beautiful timing, a bone thrown from an otherwise indifferent universe. I slow, pull over to the hard shoulder. The Porsche slows . . . then speeds up, barrelling past me to my jeers.

'That's right, mysterious creep!' I shout. 'Keep rolling!'

Megan's wrong. I need to talk to the cops. I can start with the one thing I do have a witness for – being followed. That cop car must have clocked what was just going on. I'll give them everything I know, and we'll see what happens.

The cop car pulls up behind me. The door creaks open and a man unfolds through it, gesturing at me to step out of my car.

'Am I glad to see you,' I say as I enthusiastically comply.

'Licence,' the cop says.

'Absolutely.' I fumble it out of my wallet. 'Listen, this is going to sound a little paranoid, but that Porsche that just went past? I'm pretty sure they've been following me. I went into Brincombe, you know that little town back there, and the Porsche totally toured the streets with me for literally no reason, and when I came on to the main road it came too, without even stopping anywhere in the town –'

'Eighteen?' the cop says, scouring my licence.

'Er,' I say, momentarily derailed.

'You are eighteen years of age, correct?'

'Oh. Yes. As of two months ago.'

And what a birthday that was. Brother dead. Mother working ridiculously long hours in order to avoid a breakdown. Sat on the sofa with a tub of rocky road ice cream as large as my head, miserably rewatching Lorelai and Emily Gilmore have massive argument number fifteen of seventy-three that season, and thinking that at least they were both alive to fight with each other. Happy eighteenth to me.

'What school?' The cop asks me.

'What do you mean?'

'School,' he repeats, 'that you attend.'

He is stone-faced, his mouth a thin slash, thick fingers still gripped around my licence.

'Um, I don't,' I say. 'I was supposed to be going to college this year, but circumstances have conspired against me. I was planning to study philosophy, which of course should immediately guarantee me a job on graduation and fast track me to becoming a financially productive member of the economy.'

He does not laugh. 'What are you doing out here?'

My goodwill is drying up. 'Driving.'

'You were speeding, is what you were doing.'

'Well . . . yes, but that was because of the Porsche. You know, the one following me.'

'Have you been doing drugs?' the cop asks me in the kind of voice that means he's already made up his mind.

'It's four in the afternoon,' I indignantly reply.

'Answer the question, Miss Gray.'

'Not all philosophers are stoners, sir. And even if I was stoned right now, wouldn't that mean I'd be driving *more* slowly?'

'You're coming down to the station,' he says.

'What? Why?'

'Because you were breaking the law. Stop arguing or I'll book you for worse.'

I gape. 'For worse? You mean, for something you just made up? Fine, I was speeding, but I was being followed! I demand a drug test. All the tests. Breathalyse me. Not only can I walk a straight line, I can probably foxtrot along it!'

'Please get into my car,' he says evenly. 'You will be driven to the police station, where you will answer some questions, and have your fingerprints taken. All the fun stuff you see on the TV, or YouTube, whatever you kids watch these days. Do you understand me?'

I am unprepared for this. Too busy reeling from one threat, I simply did not envisage another one so fast on its heels.

Just then the passenger door of the police car creaks open, and my terror jumps tenfold. Two of them. Two. They'll back each other up, and the next time my mother hears from me it'll be via my one allotted phone call from inside a jail cell; my god, I'm about to cause an aneurysm in my one remaining family member, and when she's lying in the hospital bed and the ER intake doctor asks what happened, I'll have to say, '*I* happened, Doctor. It was me.'

'Hi, Alec,' says a kindly female voice.

My panic semi-deflates out of sheer surprise. 'Juno!'

In all honesty, I don't equate Juno with the police, even though she's been working as an officer now for most of my life. She used to babysit Lucas and me, and she was my absolute favourite due to her habit of sneaking in a pack of double chocolate cookies and letting us have as many as we liked.

As I got older, too, I was allowed to watch the horror movies I wanted to watch but my mother always forbade, albeit under Juno's supervision. I found this the most transgressional thrill until older me realized my mother absolutely knew about it, and tolerated it the way you might tolerate the antics of the 'cool aunt'. Juno's been around since pre-me, and maybe even pre-Lucas, but I haven't laid eyes on her since my brother died.

'What's the word, Officer Graham?' Juno asks her partner.

'We were about to book this young lady for speeding,' he replies.

'Don't forget driving under the influence,' I say, with a boldness I do not feel. 'Still happy to take a breathalyser to prove you wrong, thanks.'

He gives me a sour look.

'Did you realize you were speeding?' Juno asks me.

I shake my head. 'No. I'm sorry. I really, honestly was being followed. It spooked me.'

Policewoman Juno could not be more different than her partner. Statuesque, reasonable, possessed of zero needless aggression.

She frowns. 'Who was following you?'

'Some sexy-looking Porsche with tinted windows. It's the second time I've seen it. I didn't get the licence plate.' Shame plunges me into its thick, humid depths. 'I should have. That's just basic.'

Juno shrugs. 'Barely anyone remembers that kind of thing in flight mode. Don't be hard on yourself. Any idea why you were being followed?'

Not 'why did you *think* you were being followed, you idiot child?' But a genuine attempt at validation, trust building and de-escalation. Juno is good at her job. Also – man, I've missed her.

'I have theories,' I say, 'which I'm keen to discuss.'

Juno regards me thoughtfully. My near future hangs in the balance.

She nods to me. 'Do you want to make an official report?'

'Come on,' Officer Graham moans. 'We're taking weed paranoia seriously, now? Who the hell would be following her? Let's just book her for speeding and get on with our damn day!'

'Listen, *Officer* –'

Juno cuts in. 'Why don't we talk about this another time? Just the two of us? OK?'

I give a sullen nod.

'I think we can let her go with a caution,' Juno says to her partner, who looks intensely put out.

'That's against procedure.'

Juno gives him a patient smile. 'No, it's not.'

A Herculean struggle takes place, the highlights running riot across his face.

'Yes, ma'am,' he finally says.

I am *fascinated*. There's a hierarchy here, one invisible to me but clearly one Officer Graham must submit to. Now he's been power played, I can see just how contrived his attempts to intimidate me were. And I fell for it. I *was* scared of him.

I momentarily despise Officer Graham with the force of a thousand suns.

He trudges angrily back to the police car. Juno takes my arm, and her professional face slips.

'Honey,' she says, 'don't worry about this. I'll make sure it goes away. Just don't do it again, yes?'

I nod with vigorous relief. 'Promise.'

'Do you want me to look into this Porsche?' she quietly asks me.

My earlier certainty drains away. Suddenly I'm tired, and I just want to get away from this. Besides, what's she going to do about it? Go knock on the door of every Porsche owner in Fring and tell them not to follow teenage girls? She has better things to do.

Secondly, if I tell her anything about what happened with Scott, and she talks to my mom about it –

No. That is not happening. I need to protect my mom. I can handle this on my own.

'It's OK.' I shake my head. 'Maybe I was paranoid about the whole thing. If it happens again, though, I'll come running.'

Juno gives me a reassuring smile. 'OK. Get home safe. Drive slowly. I'd give you a hug but I think Officer Graham will squeal favouritism at me all the way back to the station, and I can do without the headache right now.'

'I'll take a deferred hug.' I cut my eyes meaningfully towards the police car. 'Sorry for your troubles.'

Juno rolls her eyes to heaven. 'We all have our crosses to bear.' A pause, a hesitation. 'Tell your mother I said hello, and that I hope she's doing all right.'

She looks, for one moment until all her natural grace and poise wash it away, unutterably sad.

I watch Juno walk back to the police car. I am very aware of the enormous favour she has just done me. It must be so immensely gratifying to have the ability to protect the people you care about, and expose the people who have harmed others to justice for their sins.

In my opinion, there is no greater superpower.

The Invitation

The sunlight is an attack.

The cheeping birds outside the kitchen window are a personal insult.

'Morning!'

My mother's energetic appearance is an offence I immediately take as she sweeps into the kitchen, pinning up her hair with one hand as her other gropes blindly out in the air in front of her, a gesture I've long come to recognize as 'coffee mug claw'.

I sit, scowling against the day and nursing a pint of Tropicana's finest as she bustles around, serving herself the hot go-juice of the Western world. She's got court today, she's wearing one of her suits. It's wrinkled at the back – dry cleaning's an expense she does without – and the grey in her hair is making her look older, more worn, but at least she's bustling.

'You should get a haircut,' she says, her gaze sweeping over me like a prison grounds searchlight.

I grunt. 'Thanks. That will right all the wrongs in my life.'

'You look like you didn't sleep well.'

Oh good. She's in an interrogation mood, and I'm in the mood that lies at the very opposite end of that.

'How can you tell?' I mutter.

'The bags under your eyes have bags.'

I stare into the cheerily coloured orange juice in the glass before me.

It's been five days since the incident in the cave, but you'd be forgiven for thinking I'd made the whole thing up. No one seems to care about it except me. I don't know what I was expecting, but I was expecting something, *something* to happen in response to one of the strangest, scariest events in my life.

Here, instead, is what has gone down: zero, zip, nada. I've texted Scott a dozen times, each more desperately accusatory than the last, now nearing unhinged levels of communication, and not one response have I had. If anything happened to him after that day in the cave, I'd have heard something by now. 'Boy Chokes to Death on Tarantula' would be a pretty grabby headline in any neck of the woods.

Not even the threat of me telling everyone in the land about his attack on me has riled him enough to deign texting back. A cleverer sociopath would respond to my messages, denying everything just to make me look crazy, in case those messages might ever be submitted as evidence – but he hasn't even done that. It's as though what happened just wasn't important enough to have to deal with. It's sweeping under the carpet time. I thought Megan was exaggerating about that, but maybe I'm wrong.

Oh, and Megan – yes, let's talk about her disappearing act too. What kind of a girl kisses someone and then promptly makes herself scarce? I can't even console myself with the excuse that something happened to her because she, unlike Scott, has actually texted me back – vague, non-committal responses that seem designed to make a girl feel like her heart-palpitating crush might be suffering from buyer's remorse. If the kiss has, in the cold light of day, been designated a mistake, just tell me. I can take it; I'm used to devastating news and always handle it so well.

Is this it, now? I discover that my older brother was in a demon-flavoured cult and raped a girl and is now dead and that's . . . it? I just, what, get on with my day?

It isn't fair. It isn't *right*.

I can't stop feeling sickened, violent. A part of me wants to find out where Scott lives, break into his bedroom and put a knife against his throat. I want to see the look in his eyes that he must have seen on my face. I want to be the perpetrator and not the victim. I want –

'Is it a boy?' my mother asks, watching me over the rim of her mug.

My head rears.

'You've been staring at your phone a lot and sighing,' she adds. 'Racing to check every text.'

'No.' I stare carefully at the kitchen table so I won't have to look at her while I lie. 'No boy. No girl, either.'

My mother does not rise to the bait. She bustles around, inhaling coffee, while I take a sip of my juice – and only then do I discover the surprise waiting in the depths of my glass.

Have you ever eaten a wasp?

It's an unpleasant, alien experience. I feel a fizzing on my tongue, and a split-second's horror that I've swallowed a mouthful of juice so out of date that it's come alive – which is not all that far from the truth.

I panic spit up. Most of the juice goes back into the glass, the rest rains down on the breakfast table, aggressively misting its surfaces.

'Alec!'

'A wasp,' I gasp, staring at the floating stripy body in my glass. 'I just nearly swallowed a wasp!'

'Did it sting you?'

I probe cautiously. 'I don't think so.'

'Good.' My mother sounds relieved. 'Keep the window closed when you've got sugary things out on the table.'

I'm too busy scrubbing my tongue with a paper towel to reply.

'There's leftover shepherd's pie for dinner,' my mother casually drops between coffee sips. 'I saved you the crusty corner.'

I stop scrubbing. 'That means you won't be back in time to eat with me?' Yet again.

She clears her throat. 'No. I'm working late.'

The crusty corner is my favourite. A guilt offer if ever I saw one.

'Working late with Wallllterrr?' I drawl.

'That is not how you pronounce his name.'

'What's this case you two are so hot on together? A case of *loooove*?'

'Alec. It's not a date, we have work to do.'

'OK, OK. But seriously, what's the case? You haven't said much about it.'

'Oh, that's because it's boring,' she says dismissively.

'I've never been bored by a case of yours yet.'

'Corporate law? Five-hundred-page contracts to comb through?'

'Ah.' I wave a hand. 'Fine.'

She can sense my disappointment. Amazing that I still am, with every late night of the last few months.

I know, I know. I should be happy for her. I just can't shake the feeling that there's something off with this Walter guy, but then again recent events have surely left me with an excess supply of paranoia. Just please, Walter, don't reveal that you're in a demon cult. That's all I ask, and it's not much, is it, Walter? Knowing our luck, he'll turn out to be the head honcho. That's a good point, actually. Maybe I should look into Walter, just in case . . .

'Ow! Fudge it!' my mother suddenly barks.

She's holding a hand to her mouth.

'Are you OK?' I'm half out of my chair.

'You didn't kill that wasp,' she says through her fingers. 'It just stung me on the lip.'

I stare down at the dead wasp floating in my glass.

There must be two in the room.

'Weird,' I say to myself.

'Let's hope my lip doesn't swell up,' my mother fumes. 'Won't that be a good look for the clients?'

'Even the insects are against us.'

She shakes her head. 'I'll just have to be extra charming. Check the mail for me before I leave, see if there's anything important?'

I sigh, drag myself to the pile of envelopes on the countertop. The last thing I want to do right now is have to look through a pile of depressing bills, late notices and junk flyers trying to sell me area real estate or hot deals on local fast food – hold on, what's this?

From the pile I unearth a plain white envelope, differentiated from the rest of the pile only because it sports nothing but a handwritten name:

ALECTO GRAY

There's no mailing address. It must have been hand delivered. I start to open it up.

'Hey,' I hear my mother say from far away. 'Alec, listen. I know I haven't been around much recently. I know that, and I'm sorry. But I'm here for you right now. You're not alone. You seem like you're struggling a little, and that's completely understandable, and I just want you to know that we can talk, if you want.'

I slide out the envelope's contents and stare at it.

'Alec?'

'Hmm?'

My mother is watching me. She's put down her coffee mug.

'I mean it,' she says earnestly. 'I don't have to go right now. I can push my first meeting back, easy as pie. We can sit, drink coffee. Talk about anything you like.'

'Oh, that's OK,' I say, preoccupied with what I've just seen. 'I know you have to get to work. There's some antihistamine in the cabinet, I think. I'm going to take a shower, start my day. I love you, I'll see you later!'

'Alec!'

I stop in the doorway, the plain envelope and its contents clutched in my hand. 'Yeah?'

She stares at me a little more.

'Nothing,' she says, finally, shaking her head. 'I'll see you later. I love you too.'

I hightail it to my bedroom, the better to get some privacy.

I sit on my bed, waiting until I hear the front door close, a few minutes later.

Finally, eagerly, I turn my attention to the envelope with my name on it.

Watson, the game is afoot.

A Study in Scarlet

The door to the inner sanctum opens.

Oh's head lunges out at me.

'Alec!' he hisses. 'What are you doing back here?'

I blink. 'Nice to see you too.'

'Sorry,' Oh says – and then I see that his hand is pressed over the mouthpiece of a Bakelite phone so ancient I'm surprised the local museum doesn't have it on display. 'I'm just in the middle of –'

'Oh damn,' I say. 'I'll come back later.'

'No, that's OK – no, Alec, don't go,' Oh whisper-hisses. 'Come in while I finish up.' He mouths me in, pointing theatrically to a chair.

I trundle in, clutching my bag, trying not to eavesdrop.

'I know, Nora,' Oh says. 'It's concerning, I agree with you.'

I stare fixedly at the church noticeboard while scanning my memory for knowledge of any Noras.

'Well, how long has he been missing?'

I read a notice for the next fundraiser to fix the church roof: *CRAB POT LUCK – RAFFLE + PRIZES!*

'He's been having problems, recently, hasn't he? No – I just mean, well, he's not been very well, has he? Maybe this is a symptom of that. Well – yes. Yes, of course. And you've done the police report? All right. I'll keep an eye out. Of course. Take care, Nora.'

I hear the phone creak into its cradle, and only then do I turn around.

'Everything OK?' I ask quietly.

Oh is making his way to the rickety table, where a no doubt now tepid cup of tea and several cookies on a plate await him. He sits down with a sigh. 'Oof, my knees.'

'One of the flock gone astray?'

Oh motions me over, takes a sip of his tea, makes a face, takes a cookie.

'Something like that,' he comments.

He seems more preoccupied than usual. It must be serious.

'Someone's missing and there's a police report?' I casually probe.

Oh flaps a hand. 'It's Nora's ancient pet cat. Probably slinked off somewhere to meet its maker, poor creature.'

Ah. Not that serious, then. I watch Oh take a bite of the cookie in his hand – and then immediately and violently choke on it.

He coughs and splutters. I whip out my phone, anxious fingers tapping out 'how to Heimlich manoeuvre', but then he recovers, spitting out into a tissue.

'Oh, are you OK?'

He nods, red in the face, flapping his hand.

'That's what you get for unbridled cookie passion,' I say, relieved. 'Love always equals pain, sooner or later.'

'A fly!' Oh croaks, peering disgustedly into his tissue. 'It flew right into my mouth.'

I'm trying to remember why this is giving me significant déjà vu – and then I have it. The wasps at my kitchen table the other morning. I nearly swallowed one, and the other stung my mother on the mouth.

'The local insects are very orally fixated at the moment,' I comment.

'What's that?'

'It must be because God doesn't want you eating those cookies, Oh.'

Oh gulps a soothing mouthful of tepid tea. 'Then why would He allow their existence?'

'Touché.'

'So how are you, child? What's new?'

'Oh, nothing much. Got an invite in the mail from an anonymous sender a few days ago. The usual.' I fish out the envelope from my bag. 'I've been jonesing all through Mass to show you this.'

The envelope's contents are about as big as a postcard, and printed a classy matte black. On one side is a graphic that, with some imagination, could be the letters K, T and O, fused together.

On the other side is an address, and the following, handwritten in careful block print:

SUNDAY. 8 P.M.
SHOW THIS CARD AT THE DOOR.

Oh examines it.

'Who's it from?' he asks.

I shrug, tracing the K, T, O graphic. 'Kato?'

His brow wrinkles. 'That fellow from *The Green Hornet*?'

'Or maybe it's T, K, O,' I muse.

'Is it some secret birthday party? You young 'uns are brilliant at coming up with elaborate ways to have fun these days. All that immersive theatre.'

'Could be,' I say, but I don't think it is. I don't have any friends left, much less ones who'd invite me to some exclusive thing of theirs.

It's a clever move, this invite. Anyone with an ounce of curiosity and less sense than a lemming – aka yours truly – would be hard put to ignore it.

'What's the verdict, Cagney?' I ask.

'Well, Lacey,' he responds without missing a beat, 'have you googlied the address on the card?'

'Googled. And yes. All that came up was a commercial meat supply company, and that doesn't look like it's in business any more.'

Oh taps the card thoughtfully against himself. The edge bangs repeatedly off the white peekaboo strip of his dog collar.

'You show it to your mother?' he asks.

'Eleanor Gray is Very Busy,' I reply.

'Ah,' says Oh, 'you're going to lie to her.'

I try to look outraged. 'Who says?'

'Well, obviously you're going to go to this meat factory tonight to see what's what, but I'm guessing if she knew about it she might not let you out the door without a fight?'

Darn that spiritual Spidey sense. I blame confession. Listen to enough people pouring their secrets out to you on the regular, and you must get real good at reading human behaviour.

'It's such a *strong* word, "lie",' I say. 'So unnecessarily Teutonic. How about "omit"?'

'Potayto, potahto.'

I give him an anxious look. 'Are you going to make me say a Hail Mary?'

'Oh no. For "omissions" it's at least five.'

His expression is so patient that I can't possibly feel bad, but still a flush of shame threatens.

'Listen,' I say. 'If you tell me not to go, I won't. But I have my things too, Oh. Things that keep me from jumping off my own cliff.'

'Mysterious cases?' he asks.

'Eh, more like disappointments. I'll turn up expecting *Eyes Wide Shut*, but it'll be more like "That must be Nigel with the brie".'

Oh considers this. I wait for his verdict.

'I still think you should talk to your mother about it first,' he says finally.

'Why are you so hot on me discussing every little thing in my life with the person who's barely even in it? She has her own thing going on right now. Which is fine. She should. It's a thing that keeps *her* off the cliff edge, and I'm not going to be the one that pushes her off. Even if he does turn out to be psychotic. Which, so far, pending further investigation, it seems not. A very upstanding fellow is he, according to research. Big-time city lawyer, local boy made good, yada yada. Obviously that makes me deeply suspicious of him, but –'

'Hold up,' Oh says, raising a palm. 'Who are you talking about?'

'Walter.'

'Who's Walter?'

'Eleanor Gray's new beau.'

Oh blinks. 'Your mother has a new beau?'

'Oh boy.' I cannot contain my glee. 'Am I ahead of you in gossip, for once? This minor victory tastes sweet.'

'And he's a lawyer from the city?'

I nod. 'But he's from around here. Walter Kopek.'

Oh sits back.

'What's wrong?' I ask.

'She hasn't mentioned him to me,' Oh says.

'Was she supposed to? I know she comes to confession every once in a while, but –'

Oh nods to the invite. 'I think you should go. Find out what this is all about.'

'Wow.'

'What?'

'Nothing. I thought you were going to try to talk me out of it. Here I was, fully prepared to defend my position, cajole you into my way of thinking, present each of my arguments one by one. You kind of took the wind out of my sails.'

'Well, it's not a Hoffy Man thing,' Oh says dismissively.

'But how can we be sure?' says Alecto Gray, contrarian.

'Didn't you read the book I gave you? TKO – it's not their branding.'

'They could be tricking me.'

'I thought you wanted to go?'

'It probably is just a silly party,' I muse.

'There you go, then! Go out, have some fun.'

I give a theatrical sigh. 'Mom has forbidden fun.'

'Yes, well, Eleanor Gray has been known to make a mistake or two,' Oh snaps.

This is the Oh equivalent of a soap opera face slap.

'What is *up* with you two?' I demand.

'Nothing, nothing.'

'Is it Walter? You disapprove of her having a boyfriend?'

'No, of course not.'

'Then what? Is it because he's a lawyer? No dating in the workplace?'

Oh is uncharacteristically silent.

'You have to tell me, it's my mother!'

'Alec – I can't. I promised.'

'Come on, not another "confessional professional" excuse. I have had it up to here with all the *secrets*, man!'

'I'm sorry,' he says sorrowfully, 'but promises mean something, Alec. They have to. It's your mother's business. I disapprove; she knows it; that's all there is to it. I do what I can from a distance. It's all I can do.' His eyes are crinkled with pleading. 'Please – try to talk to her about it. I'm sure you'd have much to say to each other.'

I sigh. 'I'll try. Tomorrow. I swear, OK? But first, I have an anonymous invite to a meat factory to dress for; the wardrobe choices are endless. I should get home and prep.'

'Wait a minute –'

I raise an admonishing finger. 'You said I should go to the silly party. You can't take it back.'

'And I still think you should,' he patiently replies. 'But just in case it's not what you expect, I think you should tell *someone* where you're going, if you won't tell your mother.'

I give him a meaningful look. 'I just did.'

'Oh, Alec.' He groans, cottoning on quick. 'I hate responsibility.'

'You're the spiritual leader of our community,' I point out.

'Well, I never said I was *bad* at it, just that I don't like *doing* it.'

'If I haven't sent you a text about it by 9 p.m.,' I say, 'call the cops to do a drive-by. Just say you heard someone's hosting an underage rave there tonight. They'll be down there faster than a trip to the Donut Hut.'

Oh's eyes narrow.

'Please?' I wheedle. 'It's a worst-case-scenario, overabundantly cautious ask. Please, friend?'

He sighs. 'Why couldn't you have been more into *The Princess Diaries* or something when you were growing up?'

'Blame my father. He was the one who left his collection of vintage Chandler paperbacks behind when he exited stage left.'

'All right, Alec. But you mark me, now.' Oh fixes me with a serious eye. Even his jowls look stern. 'If I don't get that text by 9 p.m. on the dot, I shall rain down heavenly fire.'

'Roger, wilco.' I give him smile number twelve in my arsenal: 'Innocently Reassuring'.

Oh sighs, but I know I've got him.

I'm not stupid. I'm going in armed for my potential third brush with the Hoffy Men – and with Oh as back-up. If it's Scott Poltern or one of his demonic cronies waiting for me at the other end of this, I have a pocket in my jacket big enough for my Swiss army knife and a travel-sized bottle of hairspray. Hell if a stream of Elnett to the eyes doesn't do the job just as well as mace. And in the other pocket – my Dictaphone. It comes with its own tiny lapel microphone, which I can semi-hide under a cute Peter Pan collar.

This time, I'm getting evidence.

'Do you still have the book?' Oh asks me.

I give him a quizzical look. 'Book – oh! Yes. It's safe, right here in my bag.'

'I'm guessing you didn't talk to your mother about that, either?'

'No,' I admit, 'but I'll bring it up tomorrow too, if you like. Anything else for the agenda?'

Oh studies me. 'Alec – did something happen to you recently?'

My heart jumps. I try to look surprised.

'What do you mean?' I ask.

'You just seem . . . different, at the moment. Isolated.' He gives me a worried smile.

'I'm fine,' I tell him, and curiously, I am. As sick as this may sound, I'm almost hoping that it's Scott I see tonight.

I want to hurt him back.

'Well,' says Oh, going for a jovial tone. 'No more the days of looking into wardrobes on the hunt for Narnia and planning picnics like *The Famous Five*, eh? Where's that sweet little bookish kid gone?'

He means it as a rhetorical question, but I answer anyway.

'I grew up,' I tell him, and out I walk.

The Kindly Ones

From a distance, it definitely looks like an abandoned warehouse.

Closer to, there's the distant, dull thump of cranked-up bassline, felt in the chest rather than heard in the ear. No signage.

Music. Maybe it is just a party, after all.

The only obvious entryway is a very closed-looking steel door, in front of which a large, solid-looking man in a black jacket perches on a stool. Bouncer, security guard, mafioso heavy — whatever he is, he's got the look, and all I got is the best leather jacket of my life that I managed to score for thirty dollars from a shabby downtown thrift store. Sifting out vintage finds is a skill, but maybe instead I should have learned how to throw a decent solar plexus punch. My high school had those free self-defence classes going for a while, why didn't I keep them up?

Courage, Gray.

With one hand shoved in my pocket and ready-wrapped around my mini hairspray, I approach. The heavy, in contrast, keeps his eyes down on his phone, thumbs skating across its screen. Is he texting a warning to someone? A 'she's arrived, boys, sharpen your knives' kind of —

No, he's playing Tetris.

Menacing.

Emboldened, I make my move.

'OK, Knuckles, what's the word on the street?' I say out of the corner of my mouth.

The heavy looks up.

'Excuse me?' he says in a tone that negates any playful follow-ups.

'Um, I'm looking for someone,' I amend. 'I don't know who they are. They told me to meet them here.'

His stony expression becomes positively rocky.

'I'm as baffled as you,' I say, growing desperate, 'but all I got was this card, and it had the address on it –'

His face is a cliff face. He holds his hand out.

I stare down at it.

'Card,' he says.

I proffer the invitation. He glances at it. His eyes roll.

'I thought they'd stopped giving these out; the launch was months ago. All right, in you go. But you don't get a stamp.'

Now I can't have one I want one, even though I don't know what it's for. I try to take the card back, but his fingers flick upwards, withholding. It seems I don't get to hang on to this piece of evidence, curse it all.

Tetris fan nods towards the noisy door. Annoyed but unwilling to push my luck, I mutter a hasty thanks and move, pressing the handle and opening up into an explosion of sound and light.

For a moment I stand on the threshold of a cavernous warehouse space, overwhelmed. It's dark inside, low-lit but strobed in competing bright lights of various neons, like a club or a bar – but instead of quaffing singletons, the entire room is filled with old arcade games, lining every wall and squatting haphazardly across the floor. That's where all the zany *pings* and *beeps* and strobing lights are coming from. Pinball machines. Beat 'em ups. Racing games. There's even an old *Streetfighter II*, bringing back ambivalent childhood memories.

Thumping underneath it all like the Devil's heartbeat is some sort of grinding dark electro, the soundtrack to modern debauchery. It's pretty empty, but then again it is Sunday. Maybe 8 p.m. is squares hour, the real cool kids don't appear until after midnight – by which point I definitely hope to be home, as things will likely have gone quite badly for me otherwise.

I cross the empty space and wander over to the bar. Only one bartender is in evidence, busy wiping up and restocking. She eyes me as I approach, and nods her chin upwards.

'Yo,' she shouts over the noise.

Her bare arms are taut and muscled, and she sports thick eye make-up that makes her gaze stabbier than twin swords.

I am out of my depth. I start to babble something about an invitation, which I remember too late that I no longer possess, but mercifully she cuts me off.

She indicates a vague area near the back. 'Your friends are over there.'

I walk in the general direction indicated, passing two shadowy figures tearing at joysticks and throwing fireballs at each other on screen. Further ahead a girl rides a full-on replica motorbike fixed to the floor, leaning forward with her eyes intent on the giant screen before her, urging her digital counterpart along the death-defying twists and turns of some post-apocalyptic cityscape while zombies lurch into view every so often and try to take chunks out of her pixels.

Gradually, my targets sharpen through the neon gloom. Two figures are lounging around a small table up against the back wall, its surface littered with half-empty glasses. I peer anxiously at them, trying to suss the threat level. There is a glint of long blonde hair pulled into double buns, Chun-Li style, and a pretty, pointy, familiar face in between the buns, currently giving me a real hard going-over.

'Tippi Pauletti,' I say. 'Huh.'

'Hi, Alec,' says another figure, standing quickly and coming towards me. It's hard to tell in the strobing darkness, but she seems shy, coy, and other words indicating non-violent interest. 'I'm really glad you came.'

Megan. It's Megan.

In absence of a more mature response, I burst into a laugh.

'Something funny?' Tippi asks.

Megan reaches out and takes my hand.

'Sit,' she urges.

I take a stool next to her, looking around the room in a desperate bid for nonchalance.

'Cool place,' I say. 'Little hard to find. Thank god I got a mysterious invitation in the mail, huh?'

'That was me,' Tippi replies. 'My older sister owns this bar, she let me have a few of the secret invites they printed up for their test launch.'

Of course. Tippi is the kind of person who would have a sister that owns the coolest and most exclusive bar in town.

'So,' I say. 'What is this, a shakedown? Squeeze the turkey till she squawks?'

Tippi glances at Megan, presumably for a translation, but she just shrugs right back.

'I suggested you,' she says, 'but new members don't get admitted without vetting.'

'New members of what? The Tekken championship team?'

'No,' Megan says. 'We don't play games.'

Arcade games bleep and bloop around us.

'You're going to have to give me more,' I say slowly. 'What is this about?'

'This is about what happened to you,' Tippi says. 'This is about what Scott Poltern did to you. What all of them have done, over and over, to people we know, friends, members of our own families, for hundreds of years. We share a bond over a common purpose that transcends other divides.'

A quick glance at Megan confirms that she's told Tippi all about my cave escapade. And she never even asked permission. There'll be time for recriminations later, when I'm not slap bang in the middle of some bizarre recruitment drive.

'They target the problem girls, Alec.' Megan picks up the baton. 'The women who make trouble. Who say the things no one wants to hear. Who speak up, or won't shut up, or won't behave in the right way. Back in the early days, it was the ones who didn't want to get married, didn't want to have babies. Didn't want to conform. Preferred the company of other women. Bit too handy with the local herbs. Or, you know, had an affair with the wrong husband, and the wife wanted to get rid of her. Or went up against the village priest because he was messing with local kids and no one else would dare speak against a holy man. Or got pregnant out of wedlock and publicly named the married father, who happened to be the mayor. These are all true stories, by the way. Stories told by local women about their ancestors, and gathered by us.'

Her face is calm, but her fists are clenched in her lap.

'You've got a well-established network,' Tippi puts in, 'of men whose fathers were in positions of power before them and have handed those positions of power down. That's how power works around here. Who's going to take it off them? Who has the money, the resources, the allies? They all look out for each other. Don't you get it? It's the first tenet of the Hoffy Men. That's the whole *point* of the club. You stick together. There's nothing the rich and powerful are more afraid of than losing their riches and power. They'll do anything, *anything*, to keep those things. Someone says they got raped down in that cave? Someone says her sister was murdered? They shrug, they laugh. Rape? Murder? Here? By who? Where's the evidence? There is none. Anyone who could corroborate is either one of them or under their thumb. You go to them to get you out of financial ruin, say. You offer up a female family member for the ritual. Maybe someone who's been causing trouble for you. Maybe someone you don't like very much. Or, even better, *they* suggest a woman. Someone who's been causing trouble for *them*. And you agree. Well, after all, it's just a bit of silly tradition, isn't it? Harmless.' She snorts. 'Did it seem harmless to you, when you were down there? Does Viola seem like she got out of it unscathed?'

'She's insane now,' Megan mutters. 'Complete violent breakdown.'

'And if you choose to speak up against them, well. They got you out of financial ruin, and they can put you right back in it. They can ruin you. They film everything that goes on down in that cave.'

I knew it. What I wouldn't give to get my hands on their video library.

'You want to get him back for what he did to you, don't you?' Megan asks me.

Reading my mind. I hate that.

'We can show you the way,' she says.

'And all you need is my credit card number?'

Her brow furrows. 'What?'

I look around. 'Guys, I have to tell you – if this is like a cult type thing, I'm a fully paid up member of the Vatican gang, for better or worse, and they're haemorrhaging members as it is; they'll fight to keep me. It'll be war, and in years to come we'll look back sorrowfully and say that we could have prevented all that bloodshed if only the people involved in this pivotal moment made different choices.'

'We're not a cult,' says Megan. 'It's . . .' She exchanges a glance with Tippi, and some unspoken agreement seems to be confirmed. 'Well, we call it a cabal.'

'Cabaret?'

'Cabal,' says Megan patiently. 'I know you must have been a little apprehensive about coming out here, but the cloak and dagger stuff is necessary.'

'Why?'

'Some of the things we do, they're not completely and utterly and strictly legal. And we have enemies who would love to know exactly who we are.'

I take a look around the futuristic goth techno retro gamer bar.

'Mess with the best, die like the rest,' I say.

'What?' asks Megan.

'Nothing.'

But if Tippi tells me her hacker name is Acid Burn, I'm leaving.

'Enemies are the goal,' Tippi says proudly. 'That's when you know you're doing things right.'

'What enemies?'

'The Man!' Tippi calls, and then, bizarrely, she begins to howl.

Megan joins in, their voices mingling over the thumping music like excited wolves. It's embarrassing. It's sexy. It makes my cheeks flush.

The howls die off. Megan squeezes my hand.

'Welcome to the Kindly Ones,' she says.

T, K, O. Not Kato, after all. Oh will be disappointed.

'She's not a member yet,' Tippi protests.

'The Kindly Ones,' I echo.

'The harpies of vengeance, who punish mortal men for transgressions against –'

'Tippi –' I interrupt her earnest recitation – 'Alec is short for Alecto. You think I haven't read *Baby's First Greek Myths* too?'

Megan snorts a laugh, earning a glare from Tippi.

'So it's a cabal of two?' I ask.

'No, there are a lot more,' Megan replies. 'All ages, all backgrounds. We've got police. Lawyers. Teachers. School board members. Women in local government. Some older members have dedicated their lives to getting into positions of power, in order to counteract the Hoffy Men.'

'Well, hell, like who?' I say, impressed.

Tippi waggles a chiding finger. 'No names.'

Fine. But future me wants to see that membership list – as long as it's not stored in an ancient cave, that is.

'So what's the watchword?' I ask.

'We exist,' says Megan, 'to make sure that people like Scott don't get away with it.'

'I don't need a vigilante superhero team coming to my rescue, thanks.'

'I know you don't. We're asking you if you want to be *on* the team.'

'What are these not completely and utterly and strictly legal things you do?'

'You'll see,' says Tippi. 'Because if you want in, you have to do one of them.'

I look between various face shades of secretive and eager.

'Come on,' I try.

'It's a kind of insurance policy,' says Megan apologetically. 'You can't just sit on the sidelines. You have to be involved. We all do. It's where our strength comes from. It means we're in it together.'

M.A.D. Mutually Assured Destruction. If you've all done something bad, none of you will rat each other out. Isn't that exactly how the Hoffy Men work?

Still. There's something undeniably hot about this whole set-up. A lady vengeance club. All right, there are some shady dynamics I can't quite see, but god knows right now I could use someone checking my six. Besides, it beats sitting at home by yourself feeling scared and angry.

Plus, the clubhouse? I only mock things I like, and this place is something I never thought possible for the landscape of my youth. This place is *cool*.

Something you should know about me that may become relevant information for what unfolds next: I never got picked for team sports. Like all school outsiders I pretended it didn't matter, but that kind of thing leaves a mark.

I should be sensible. I should get up and leave these edgy wolf girls to their vengeance games, go home and live out my thrills in safe, harmless fiction.

'What would I have to do?' I ask.

Sympathy for Lady Vengeance

You know the saying *Her heart was in her mouth*? Mine seems to have gotten stuck in my throat, bulging there uncomfortably and cutting off my air.

The bushes I am crouched in like a scared rabbit scratch at every exposed expanse of my skin, poking me hard in the back of my head and threatening to tangle in my hair like a hand grabbing me still. A cramp flares up in the back of one calf, but I have to ignore it.

I am being watched.

Courage is neither innate nor constant, but made in the moment. Something that Oh told me a while ago, and I was so impressed by this idea that I wore it as a pen tattoo up one leg for a week straight, until my mother caught sight of it and told me to wash it off. If I'm going to get through this I need to look at my leg, metaphorically speaking, and make good on the idea.

Besides, if I have to stay much longer my pulse might reach hummingbird speed, which presumably means either I'll start flying like one or fall down dead, and, with the exception of a commercial dumpster, this has got to be the most humiliating place for my corpse to be found.

With this in mind, here goes nothing. Just do it. *Just do it.* I make a break for the open grass, scuttling across it like an insect, clutching the bulky accoutrements of my nefarious purpose.

Which window did she say again? Second from the left, wasn't it? Shit. Normally I have a good memory, but panic has snatched my faculties from me. Calm down, Alec, it doesn't matter which window, not really, he's still going to see it –

Every clumsy second of movement is accompanied by the dread expectation of floodlights, sirens, signs appearing magically in the air flashing the word 'GUILTY' with an arrow pointing down to my head. How do criminals do this all the time without developing stress angina?

The lawn is mercifully still soft and wet after this morning's bout of summer rain. All it takes is my weight to push the stake in. After that it's quick work to dig in the tripod's feet, steady the camera above it and point its giant lens directly towards the window.

Which is suddenly flooded with light.

I freeze, caught like a cartoon silhouette against a giant rectangle of warm butter yellow. Seconds, years, lifetimes pass – and then I see the curtains twitch, as if about to be pulled open –

I abandon all pretence of cat burglary and run, not caring if I am seen, only caring to get away, leaping over the fence and tripping the anti-theft light that floods the side of the house, my fleeing all caught in a bright, inescapable glare.

But no one shouts, no doors open, no one comes after me.

When those curtains open up, it'll be on to the vista of a large board sign planted right outside the window, printed with the following in large block letters:

WE'RE WATCHING YOU, SCOTT
DON'T RAPE ANYONE ELSE

Next to the board is the camera, pointed directly to the window as if to film everything going on inside, behind closed doors and curtains. Its recording light is on, a steady red, like an unblinking demonic eye.

I make it halfway down the road and keep going without incident, reaching a car parked at its end, idling.

'Genius,' declares Tippi.

I fling myself into the passenger seat, the sound of her giggles in my ears as she drives us away.

Stakeout

The car door opens with a creak and Megan's hair appears first, bouncing impossibly and wafting in a faint scent of jasmine. Then the rest of Megan slides into the driver's seat, laden with snacks and cardboard coffee cups.

'Can't believe I forgot my hot flask,' she grumbles for the umpteenth time in a row. 'I'm normally so on that. Number one item to bring on a stakeout.'

'No,' I say, taking a cup and several snack bags from her, 'the number one item is coffee, no matter the container. Two is toothpicks to keep your eyes open with.'

'I'm just trying to save the planet,' she protests.

'Then let's chain ourselves to a Starbucks and go on hunger strike. It'd have more impact than one person's diligent flask use.'

She makes a face.

I dig through packets. 'Energy bars made from egg whites and raw nut trail mix. My god, Megan, it doesn't even have chocolate drops in it.'

'They are both excellent sources of protein,' she says, 'which is much better than sugar-crashing your way through the hours.'

'This is a stakeout, not a torture session.'

She rolls her eyes at my dismay and then tosses me something she'd been holding back.

'You angel,' I breathe, tearing into the Snickers mini bag.

'If he sees us because you had to get out the car and puke, that's on you.'

'Don't be ridiculous.' The words come out sticky with chocolate. 'I'll puke in the glove box.'

'Oh, I'm the ridiculous one.' She tosses me a look. 'What's our quarry up to?'

'He hasn't come out yet,' I say.

It is the second part of my audition for the Kindly Ones. I aced the first a few nights ago, with even Tippi giving me grudging approval, but now I need to stick the landing.

We are in a familiar part of town, parked a few doors down from a house with a porch held up by Roman-style pillars and a front lawn decorated with fuchsia bushes. I'm almost sure it's the right house, but they all look exactly the same around here, and in the two-plus hours since we arrived no one has come in or out of the house to confirm my guess.

My phone buzzes in my pocket.

'Put that away,' I hear Megan say.

I glance at the notification and freeze.

'One second,' I say slowly.

'Alec, no phones on missions, remember? They can be tracked. You were supposed to leave it at home.' She indicates the old-school handheld Canon squatting on the dashboard. 'We go old school on missions.'

'I know – points for the high paranoia, by the way, that's usually my vibe – but aside from the feeling like I've left one of my limbs behind, I just need to do something real quick.'

'We're on stakeout,' Megan huffs. 'Who could you be talking with right now that can't wait?'

'I'll just be two seconds,' I say, my eyes on the message, typing a fast reply:

> How did u get my number?

Megan turns sharp. 'Is it from one of *them*?'

'No,' I say quickly. 'Not a Hoffy Man.'

'You can't be sure. I might be able to tell you. Show me.'

'Wait – Megan!'

But she already has my phone in her hands.

Oh damn. This won't be good.

Her face turns dark.

'You're texting with Viola?' she says.

'No!' I protest. 'I got her number from a friend, way back, just to – whatever. But I haven't texted her. She texted *me*. I have no idea how she got my number.'

Megan scrolls through Viola's message to me.

'Jesus,' she mutters. 'It's worse than I thought.'

'Well, I only managed to skim it before you snatched my phone off me,' I try to joke.

'How much did you see?' she asks me.

'I managed to catch the word MURDERER in all caps, and I saw your name a couple of times, but it was couched in a veritable essay of rambling – why, what does the rest say?'

I watch Megan's fingers as they delete the message.

'Hey!' I say sharply.

She blocks Viola from my phone. Then she puts my phone in the glove box.

'Megan. Give me my phone back.'

Megan takes a steadying breath. 'You shouldn't have it here. We told you. Let's just keep it in the glove box for now. I won't tell Tippi, OK?'

My temper struggles, demanding to be set free.

'I'm sorry I flouted your club rules or whatever, but that's my phone, Megan. You don't just – Look, just – what did Viola say?'

'It was . . . disturbing. You shouldn't have to see that stuff.'

'Who the hell are you to decide what I should and shouldn't see?!'

'She said you murdered your brother, Alec, OK?' Megan snaps. 'She called you a murderer!'

I blink. My temper slinks away like a kicked dog.

'I'm sorry, Alec. I guess she's still ill. She seems to be getting worse, not better. I'm really sorry.'

Megan looks dismayed, sickened.

I shake my head, trying to get to grips. 'Why are you sorry?'

'It's my fault. It's obvious how much I like you, and she's figured out we're dating. Now she knows there's someone who means something to me in my life, so I guess she's decided to harass you.' Megan sighs. 'I could handle it when the target was just me, but now I've gotten you involved.'

I should care that someone has decided I killed my own brother. That should hurt, and it does, even though I know it's because she's unwell. I should ask what on earth her and Megan's falling-out was about. I should worry that a very unstable person now seems to be focusing their crazy on me.

'So . . . we're dating?' I ask instead.

Megan gives me a cautious glance. 'Oh. No. I mean – only if you . . . I'm sorry, I shouldn't be so presumptuous.'

'And,' I continue, 'you like me, and I mean something to you?'

She hesitates. 'Is that OK?'

My heartbeat does a game impersonation of castanets.

'You're the femme fatale,' I blurt.

She does the look people do around me.

'Of this movie,' I say. 'You swan into the detective's life, blowing his mind and setting him on a single-minded course of sexy doom. From our random meet-cute in the woods to the drama-filled beach party to the face-slapping diner date to the mysterious invite to join a secret cabal. You keep showing up in my life to point me towards another clue. That makes you the femme fatale.'

'I blow your mind?' Megan asks.

I fight a blush. I absolutely won't look at her, because we are on a stakeout, and this is business.

'Logically, then,' Megan murmurs, 'I should be trying to seduce you. Right now, in this very car. Isn't that what femmes fatales do?'

'It's a common theme,' I agree while my temperature rises. 'But, see, I couldn't presume to know what's on your mind.'

'Why don't you come over here and find out?'

Is this heart rate normal for an eighteen-year-old or am I having some kind of episode?

'I was just kidding around,' I feebly protest.

'No, you weren't,' Megan says. 'And neither am I.' Her eyes are hooded with lids of languor. 'I've wanted you from the first moment I saw you.'

That first moment being perched atop the site of my brother's dead body, as I recall. It's every type of wrong.

Must be why it's such a thrill.

She leans in, wraps her palm around the back of my neck, and gently pulls my head towards hers. I feel the insistent press of her mouth. Her wet tongue flickers against mine. We go from zero to eighty-five in 2.4. Never mind crime noir, I should be gunning for a role in *The Fast and the Furious* franchise with this kind of acceleration.

Her hands are all over me. She can do anything she likes, anything. I've stopped being able to think. I am clay, ready to be moulded into tangled shapes more filthy than a group of Ancient Greek statuary. I want, I want, I want. I feel her fingers tugging at the zip of my jeans –

TAP TAP TAP

Holy Mother of God, that's someone knocking on the driver's window. A shape standing there, blurry through the now-foggy glass.

No hard-boiled detective blushes this hard over steaming up a car.

I hastily smooth my hair back from my face and tug my shirt back into a respectable shape as Megan winds down her window, revealing the torso of a girl. The torso quickly backs up, revealing the rest of a girl a little younger than me, lowering her head to peer at us with her arms tightly crossed against her chest.

It takes me a minute, and then I have it. It's Amelia, Justin Gorhammer's little sister. All that's missing is a borrowed clove cigarette dangling from her lips.

'What are you doing?' she demands.

How do I describe making out without actually having to say it?

'Hanging out,' Megan replies. 'What are *you* doing?'

'She lives here,' I put in.

'Ah.' Megan looks her up and down with renewed interest.

'Why are you "hanging out" outside my house?' says Amelia. Her voice trembles with false bravado.

'We're on a mission,' Megan says gravely.

'What's the mission?'

'It's top secret.'

'What kind of mission has you sat in a car for hours sucking each other's faces?'

'The sexy kind.'

She folds her arms. 'You're spying on Justin.'

Megan looks puzzled. 'Who's Justin?'

'My *brother*,' his sister says.

'Nope.' Megan shakes her head. 'No idea.'

'Megan, stop.' I look up at Amelia. 'Look, I'm sorry if we've been freaking you out. We just wanted to talk to your brother, but the last couple times I tried, I've had a door shut in my face.'

'That's because people keep harassing him, but he hasn't done anything wrong.'

'Come on,' I soothe. 'Big online celebrity like Justin? He has to be used to some crap said by crazy strangers in the video comments. Everyone gets that nowadays. It's gross, but that's modern life for you.'

Amelia stares at me. 'Video comments? That's all you're taking responsibility for? How about getting him banned from every social media platform going? How about getting him suspended from college? How about the tyres to his new car being slashed? How about torturing him with *demons* so he loses his mind?'

I glance at Megan.

'Well,' she says with a shrug and a laugh, 'that last part I can't take credit for.'

This is the wrong reaction for Amelia's taste.

'You're laughing?' she says, her voice climbing higher. 'He's losing his mind, and you think it's *funny*?'

I am witness to the smile drop so fast from Megan's face that it's like watching Jekyll turn into Hyde. Her face is carved of stone as she leans out of the window, right into Amelia's space.

'I think it's fucking hilarious,' she says.

'Megan.' I put my hand on her arm.

Amelia backs up, the blood draining from her face.

'It's cruel! You're torturing him! You're torturing my brother!' Her voice is reaching theremin levels.

'Amelia,' Megan says. 'That's your name, right? Well, Amelia, has your poor innocent brother ever told you what he did to warrant such attention?'

'*Megan.*' I nod urgently out of the windshield.

Megan's head snaps around as she spots the new figure.

As if conjured by the conversation, the poor innocent brother himself has arrived on the scene, emerging from his identikit suburban fortress and blinking in the weak pre-storm light.

He looks, no two ways about it, like absolute shit.

Pre-crisis Justin had a pale, sleepy vibe, lit as I always saw him with the sharp, flat wash of a computer screen, but at least he had flesh on the skeleton. This guy's a wasting version of himself – not wasted but clearly wasting still, in process, shuffling along like a dazed George Romero zombie.

'Amy,' he croaks. 'What did they say? Amy. I told you not to talk to any of them.'

Amelia stiffens when she hears her brother's voice, whirling around and running to his side.

'What did they say?' he asks her. 'They're lying. I told you.'

'It's OK,' Amelia soothes. She has the tense, frightened set of someone who has had to learn, very rapidly, how not to set off the human bomb that now lives in her house.

I remember how that feels.

Maybe it's that, or the lying, that gets me going.

I lean over to my door, crank it open. Megan hisses like a goose from the driver's seat, but I disregard the warning.

'Get the camera, put it on him and hit record,' I tell her, and exit the car.

Justin and Amelia watch me like twin hawks.

'Hi, gamer guy,' I say brightly. 'What was that about lying?'

'Stay away from me, you crazy bitch,' Justin says hoarsely.

I blink. 'Escalation! Damn, Gorhammer, who taught you to talk like that to a stranger?'

'I know about you.'

'Sure. I bet Lucas just couldn't stop talking me up, back when you guys were hanging out.'

'Not you.' His gaze flicks to the car. '*Her.*'

Behind the camera, Megan gives a wave.

'She's crazy,' he calls again. 'Her and her whole little club. Stop filming me!'

'Hey,' I say. 'Your club has an extensive video library. We're just playing catch-up.'

'You're all terrorists. That's what you are. It's called domestic terrorism.'

'Actually, I think it's called "Justice for Viola Gordon",' I say. 'After all, no one's been making you pay for what you did to her, have they?'

Justin breaks into a laugh. Hysterical doesn't quite cover it. It starts despairing and climbs all the way up to Pennywise.

'No one's making me pay,' he gasps. 'That's good. That's really good. Yes, I'm getting off light.' His wasted face crumples. 'Fuck *you*. I'm being *haunted*! I can't sleep! It's there all the time! I can't relax! I'm scared out of my mind! Everywhere I go, it follows me! And I never even touched her! I never touched that bitch! I NEVER DID ANYTHING. I NEVER TOUCHED THAT BITCH. SHE'S A LIAR. NOTHING HAPPENED –'

There he is, kicking it up like a steam kettle, his whistling climbing to a scream – and there I stand, dumbstruck by the show, thinking, *Shit, he really might lose it*, and, *what do I do next*, because that's the problem when someone goes for broke: what do the ones who still believe in sanity do in the face of chaos? – when the absolute damnedest thing happens.

There is a jerk of movement, too sudden for eyes to signal to brain in time. Only after it's over can I track the thing that just hit Justin square on the mouth and then bounced off.

Justin's hand jerks to his lips, a *what the fuck* forming there, his eyes screwed up in sudden shock and pain. The thing that hit him now crouches on his shoulder like a tiny nightmare, a sudden wrong note in our human drama. Its body is a fat, dusty-coloured shape, with sharply bent concertina legs and sprouting antennae.

'Cricket,' I say, but before the full word climbs its way out of my mouth the cricket springs again, seemingly trying to climb its way into his.

It hits Justin's pale lips and bounces off again – *Do not open your mouth to scream*, I think suddenly, *it'll climb inside* – and Justin full-body flinches, moving in the fast, jerky motions of animal fear.

'Get it off me, get it off,' he whisper-shrieks, cavorting.

I can only stare, not knowing how to help, watching the cricket cling to his T-shirt neck. Its *weight* – it pulls the flimsy folds of his T-shirt in its tiny clutches, hauling and wrinkling the entire thing across Justin's thin, vulnerable torso.

And then it goes for him again, leaping through the air, tearing at his lips. Amelia and I and presumably Megan, worlds behind me and safe in her metal-and-glass box, just watch, frozen and helpless in the face of the sudden, confounding weird.

My brain tickles at me with insistent déjà vu. Attacking insects. Choking. I've been here before. When? Where? Is now really the time for this, Alec? Then I have it. Oh choking on a fly as he ate a cookie. My mother and I being menaced by wasps. Scott. His weight pinning me down as a tarantula gunned for his mouth.

I'm distracted by a sudden wounded moan from the boy before me. His words tumble out in a torrent.

'OK, OK, OK,' Justin blubbers, the cricket now clinging grimly to his scalp. 'OK, god, please just stop, please stop it, get it off me. I'll tell you, OK, if you promise to stop torturing me; I can't take it any more. Scott, man, I'm sorry but I can't do this any more. Daddy, I'm sorry, it's too scary. OK, we took her down to the cave, we're not supposed to be initiated until we're twenty-one but, Scott and me, we didn't want to wait any more, and Lucas, man, he kept *pushing* for it, so we set it up, we gave in, OK. I'm sorry, Daddy. We broke the rules and we took her down there and we gave her the drink and I was supposed to film, I was the one with the camera, but I didn't, Scott said, I didn't want to go through with it but Scott said to, and so we went through with it but it's not like we were going to kill her or anything, we weren't doing the old ceremony, we don't do that any more they said, not for years, and demons aren't fucking real, Scott said his dad told him the whole thing was just made up anyway and it was just an excuse to have some fun, but then she woke up, she woke up and she *lost it*, she just went crazy, and then she *escaped*, and we're supposed to finish the ritual, if we don't finish it he gets angry and punishes us instead of rewarding us, I know that, I know that, but I thought it was just a story, I swear, but ever since then it's been after me, and it's not fair and Daddy, I'm sorry we messed up and now the Hoffy Man is after us and I don't know what to do, I don't know what to do, I don't want to kill anyone, please, I –'

He's sobbing, on the ground, on his knees, a howling supplicant.

The cricket has disappeared.

Amelia has her hands over her mouth, each eye as big as the moon, looking down at her brother as if she's never seen him before in her life. As if she doesn't know him at all.

Oh, Amelia. I know that sick feeling you have growing inside you right now.

I'm so, so, sorry.

I want to go towards her – but Justin's cricket-induced confession has attracted a crowd. The front doors of houses have opened, and ah, crap – there are his parents, coming towards us full speed ahead.

Megan is leaning out of her window, urging me.

'We've got it on video, we've got it. Let's go. Come on, let's *go*.'

She's right. Nothing I can do to make this situation any better except get out of it and let them deal. Besides, if I got some of Justin's babble right, the 'Daddy' coming towards me right now is a Hoffy Man, and I'm unlikely to enjoy meeting him, even under circumstances that did not involve me scaring a confession out of his broken son.

I look at Amelia square in the face. I give her that much, at least.

'Sorry, kid,' I say. 'Come find me when you need someone who can relate.'

And then we skedaddle.

The Accused

Two nights later, I have a nightmare.

Instead of the same as before, which I'd almost have preferred – there's a modicum of comfort in the familiar – this time I'm not stuck in my bedroom being silently menaced by the corpse/ghost of my satanic-cult-immersed brother.

This time I'm out in my town. I'm running from a serial killer, having escaped by the skin of my teeth, but he's *right behind me*. I keep running up to people on the street, begging them to help me, hide me, do something – but every time I approach I find they can't talk back, they can't help, they can't even see me. Because their heads are covered in crawling insects. Millipedes, moths, bugs with shiny-domed carapaces as big as a fist.

(I'd blame Lucas for secretly showing me *Indiana Jones and the Temple of Doom* when I was far too young if I hadn't been the one to badger him until he caved.)

In the morning I'm dog-tired. My guard is lower than a sewer when I slump into the kitchen, which is maybe why the headline strikes me so hard. It glares from the breakfast table, trumping the usual local exposés on the cow-tipping epidemic or the abject failure of the new crosswalk and traffic light system in slowing down local boy racers attempting doughnuts outside the elementary school.

I stop dead, staring at the paper.

INVESTIGATION LAUNCHED INTO LOCAL TEEN'S CONFESSION OF ASSAULT

'Oh, fuck,' I say.

'Alec!' My mother snaps.

I jump. I didn't even see her standing in the corner.

'Sorry,' I reply, on autopilot, sitting down at the table and grabbing the newspaper.

Video gone viral online . . . the latest in a series of bizarre videos posted by twenty-year-old Justin Gorhammer . . . appears to be a confession of group sexual assault . . . police, bowing to mounting pressure, have announced the launch of an investigation into the video's claims.

Heart pumping hard, I scan the article twice – but there's no mention of Lucas, and I can't help feeling a guilty note of relief. There's also no mention of who actually posted the video online, but my money's on Tippi. Megan had wanted us to wait for a few days, find a time to meet as a cabal and discuss what to do with Justin's confession – but it seems like Tippi went ahead and decided for the group.

Under investigation. He's under investigation. Holy Grail. We've actually gone and done it.

'Is something wrong?' my mother asks.

'Did you read about this?' I point to the headline.

Her lips purse. 'Dreadful affair. If it's true.'

'Oh, it's true.'

'How do you know?'

In my excitement, I completely forget the state of play between us. 'Because I was there.'

Her face changes. 'What?'

'I'm not on the video, but I was there when it was recorded. I've been investigating him for weeks – and, Mom, it's incredible; it's this whole insane conspiracy that no one's been able to crack open, and it was me, I'm the one who finally got him to spill –'

All of a sudden I know: I'm going to tell her everything. I can feel it ready to tumble out of me. *Yes*, I think, *no more secrets*, and I am so eager and so ready to shock and impress her with the truth, the Hoffy Men, all of it.

'Hold on,' my mother says. 'Slow down. You've been *investigating* this boy?'

'Yes,' I say, and I want to laugh with relief, 'and I'm sorry I didn't tell you about it until now, but, well, you'll see why I had to keep things under wraps, because it's not just him, it's an entire network of men who belong to this insane kind of secret club, and there's this other guy, Scott Poltern – they don't mention him in the article but Justin says his name in the video –'

And there I suddenly stop. There's another name in the video too, but I can't talk about Lucas's part in it. Not yet. I can barely acknowledge that he had a part in it. Every time I think of it I feel a sudden, incandescent fury so bright that it scares me, and I have to slam a lid on it.

'Alec,' my mother says in a strange voice. 'No.'

I look up at her. 'No? No what?'

'How did you find out about this boy?'

I search. 'Everyone's seen his videos, he's been going crazy for weeks.'

'So you just took it on yourself to start investigating him? Alone?'

'Oh no, no. Well, at first. But I met this group of badass girls who have been trying to blow the lid on this thing for ages, and we clubbed together because –'

'These girls? What girls? Who are these girls?'

I'm starting to sense by her tone that she's going down the wrong path, and I have to move quickly to nudge her back on to the good one. The 'wow, Alec, this is all amazing' one.

'These girls who know all about what Justin did. But not just him, there's a whole lot of other women –'

'Have you been doing this instead of working? Have you been lying to me?'

'No!' I hesitate – a rookie mistake. 'Not exactly, I mean, I have been working, you can call up Mercy and ask her. I've just been doing this as well.'

'Instead of staying at home, staying out of trouble and working on your college applications like I asked you to? I *asked* you, Alec. I asked you not to fritter away summer "hanging out",' – there's nothing as excruciating as an adult doing air quotes – 'wasting your time running around playing detective! This is not a game, Alec! Life is not a game! You can't do this! I asked you not to do this!' She pauses enough to suck in a little oxygen, presumably for round two.

Eleanor Gray. The one person I most want to impress with my razor-sharp wit. Every good quip, every clever line, every cutting, insightful observation, eighteen years of experience and intelligence, deserts me when we talk now. I end up gormless and silent. I offer all the conversational grace of a toddler in a tantrum. Why is that?

'I don't get it,' I say.

'What don't you get about this, Alec?' she barks.

'I thought you'd approve.'

Her eyes go wide. Her voice climbs even higher. '*Approve?*'

'You're a lawyer,' I shout. 'You have this insanely strong sense of justice, and you always drilled it into us! The world isn't fair, and we have to do what we can to *make* it fair!'

'This?' She points at the newspaper. 'You go after this mentally ill boy, you record him and put it on the internet – presumably without his permission – with your friends, and you think that's justice?'

'No one else was doing anything about it! No one cared about what he'd done! Don't you get it?'

'Oh, I get it,' she says, 'and I'm telling you, this is not about justice.'

'You don't know anything about it!'

'Trust me, I know. You know how I know? By the look of sheer glee on your face when you told me about this poor boy.'

'Poor boy? That *poor boy* is a fucking rapist!'

She draws herself up. Her eyes are furious lasers. 'You moderate your language *right now*, Alecto Gray. *I will not have that language in my house.*'

We both subside.

I can't believe it. I can't be-*fucking*-lieve it. My mother the lawyer, the moralist, the upright citizen who rails against evil. The one person I thought I could count on to be as outraged about something like this as me. I can't believe I trusted her with this. I can't believe I told her. I'm a colossal fool.

Still there's a tiny goblin part of me, hidden down there in the dark, that whispers, '*At least you have her attention now . . .*'

'These girls,' I hear my mother say. 'How did you meet them?'

'Oh come on, Mom,' I wearily reply. 'Now it's the hanging out with a bad crowd tactic? You used to pull this one before, remember, with about the same effect.'

Before has two words after it – before, *with Lucas* – deliberately omitted, but she can hear them just fine.

'Not everyone has your best interests at heart,' she says. She's struggling not to shout.

'I'm tired of doing everything alone. I just want someone batting for me. Someone looking out for me.'

'Alec,' says my mother, as if she's way ahead and has to wait at the ten-mile marker for me to catch up, 'you *have* someone batting for you. You always have. You're my daughter. I'm here to support you and protect you.'

I want to say: 'You protect me by telling me what to do. You protect me by trying to lock me up, away from danger and influence. And I get it. I really do. You don't want to lose me the way you lost Lucas. It's all so obvious. But that doesn't make it fair. That doesn't make it right. And it doesn't make me feel less alone.'

But I know if I say any of this it'll come out wrong, she won't understand what I mean, and suddenly I'm drained. More than being right, more than being understood, I just don't want to keep having this fight.

My mother leans forward. 'I need you to know something. Whatever's happened in the past. Whatever has been happening recently. We're in this together.' Her face is serious, earnest. 'Now tell me. Tell me why you went after this boy. Tell me what's been going on.'

The doorbell rings.

She frowns. 'Did you order something?'

I shake my head, secretly relieved at the shrill interruption.

She sighs, setting out for the front door. I trail her through the hallway, curious to see who might come knocking at seven thirty in the morning.

When I find out who it is, I regret every life choice I've ever made that led me to this precise moment in time, this moment that echoes another from the past, when our front door last opened to the police.

A grim-faced cop and his partner stare back at me.

'Alecto Gray?' says Grim Face, a formality because he already knows.

My full name in his mouth isn't funny at all, so the 'Who's asking' quip stays behind my teeth.

'Yes?' I say instead.

'We need to take you down to the station, please, to answer a few questions.'

'Harry?' my mother says. 'What's going on?'

Relief. She knows the cop. She knows everyone connected to local law enforcement. She'll straighten this out.

'We just need to ask your daughter a few questions,' Harry stubbornly repeats, 'down at the station.'

'About what?' she demands.

She's got that edge going, and Harry seems to know her well enough to know that edge, so he tells her.

'There's a boy been found dead,' he says, 'and your daughter was allegedly the last person to see him alive. Scott Poltern.' His gaze shifts to me. 'Does the name ring any bells?'

Basic Instinct

'Am I under arrest?' I ask.

'No, Miss Gray,' Harry replies.

'Not yet,' the other detective loftily replies.

Guess who it is. I bet you can get it in one.

That's right. Officer Graham, the aggressive jobsworth from a couple of weeks back who wanted to arrest me for a minor speeding infraction. As soon as the door to this wonderfully drab interrogation room down at the local cop shop opened up and I saw the axe grinder's smug mug, I knew exactly what kind of day I was about to have.

'This is just a friendly conversation,' Harry continues.

Or rather, Harry to my mother but Officer Piscowicz to me, expressed in no uncertain terms when I tried to call him by his familiar name.

'Can I have my mother in the room?' I ask.

'Poor widdle girl needs her mommy?' Officer Graham coos, then grins at my expression. 'It was a joke.'

'Actually,' I say, 'poor widdle girl needs her *lawyer* mommy in here, taking notes on everything you say.'

Officer Graham snorts.

'You're not under arrest, you're voluntarily helping us with our inquiries,' Officer Piscowicz says patiently. 'You don't need a lawyer.'

Officer Graham leans in to Officer Piscowicz. 'This generation's seen too many crime shows.'

'Scott Poltern,' Officer Piscowicz says to me, and there is no room for comedy in his face, not with that big serious look filling it from side to side. 'Where did you two first meet?'

The reminder hits: Scott is dead.

My stomach drops to my feet.

'At a beach party,' I say. 'Ghostie has one every year for his birthday.'

'And what was Scott doing there?'

'Hallucinating a giant spider.' I watch the two of them exchange looks. 'He said afterwards that he had a bad mushroom trip.'

'Were you on drugs too, Miss Gray?'

'No,' I say firmly.

'But you drank.'

Saying it as a statement, not a question, so I presume he already knows. Clever.

Don't lie, my mother once told me, when she sat Lucas and I down to drill us in How to Talk to the Police 101. *You can be caught out in a lie as easy as pie. Don't lie and don't embellish.*

'I had one drink,' I say. 'That's all. I'm not much of a partyer, these days.'

'What was your interaction with Scott like?' asks Harry.

'Minimal,' I reply. 'He was pretty out of it. I got him into a taxi home.'

Tell them the true answer to whatever questions they ask, and that's it. No more. Don't fill the silence.

But this one I don't listen to. They want to know about Scott? I'll tell them about Scott. Escalation is the name of the game. We made a little hole with the Justin video, and now I'm going to tear it wide open. I'm going to be goddamn instrumental in nailing every single one of these men.

'The next time I saw Scott,' I say, 'he came to my house. Somehow he knew where I lived, which was pretty creepy, and he asked if he could talk with me somewhere private. And I wanted to talk to him, so I agreed.'

'Why did you want to talk to him?'

'Because I had evidence that he was involved in the group rape of Viola Gordon, together with Justin Gorhammer –'

And. Say it. Say his name. It's on the video. Say it.

'And my brother, Lucas Gray.'

I feel sick. Now it's said, it exists. Now it's made it can't be unmade.

A black hole of silence.

Officer Piscowicz leans back. 'That's quite an accusation, Miss Gray.'

'I'm aware.'

'Did you confront Scott with this accusation?'

I hesitate. Should I have? Was that the correct thing?

Don't lie. You can be caught out in a lie as easy as pie.

'No,' I say. 'I didn't confront him. I wanted to get him to admit it on tape. I was recording him.'

'Did he know you were recording him?'

'Yes. He took my phone off me before he said anything incriminating.'

'Talk me through the sequence of events,' says Officer Piscowicz. 'Where did you go to talk?'

'We went to Petey's Pitch and Putt, on the edge of town. The foreclosed place.'

'What did you two discuss there?'

'Silly things, at first. But I wanted him to tell me about what happened with Viola, so I kept pushing the conversation that way. Or trying. And then he said . . . he wanted to show me something.' Steady, Gray. You can do this. 'And he took me to a cave.'

It could be mistaken, I suppose, for an ordinary pause. Maybe I'm just imagining the weight in the air after I say the word 'cave'.

'Where was this cave?' Officer Piscowicz asks me, his face set to neutral.

Here goes nothing.

I tell him. I tell him all of it. The more people know about the Hoffy Men, the less power they have. Exposure weakens. I want them wounded.

I want them to know that I know, and that I'm coming for them next.

'So Scott attacked you in this cave?' Officer Piscowicz says, scribbling on a pad.

I'd give anything to be able to read handwriting upside down, and I make a mental note to look into learning how.

'Yes,' I say.

'Why didn't you report the attack to the authorities?'

'I didn't have any evidence. It was just my word against his, and I've heard about how that doesn't work so well around these parts. For some of us, anyway.'

Officer Graham, who has so far been completely silent – and taking zero notes, I notice, almost as if none of this matters – shifts in his chair, crossing his arms over his gut.

'Miss Gray, this is a very outlandish conspiracy theory you've laid out here. Are we really supposed to believe that there's some sort of demon-worshipping mafia preying on women, for, what, hundreds of years now, as you say? And no one cares? No one? Not their parents, their friends?'

'People care,' I say. 'They just can't do anything about it.'

'Yes, they can. They bring evidence to the police.'

'I'm sure they've tried, haven't they?'

'It's just so conveniently unprovable,' he muses. 'It's all your word against the words of, according to you, some of the most respected citizens of our fair town. You see that, right?'

I give him a look. 'Yeah? Where's *your* Hoffy Man badge?'

He groans. 'Oh, dear lord.'

'I'm serious. Don't you have to display it at all times, so you can recognize each other? A modest little pin on the lapel? Maybe a Boy Scouts patch sewn on to your uniform?'

'That's enough, Miss Gray,' Officer Piscowicz says. 'Your theories are your theories, you can have as many as you like. What we need from you are facts –'

'I've *given* you the facts. And I think we can both agree that the facts point directly towards the Hoffy Men.'

Officer Piscowicz and Officer Graham exchange looks.

I laugh. 'Well. That's how it is, I guess. And you've got nothing to say about any of it?'

'Actually, Miss Gray,' Officer Piscowicz quietly replies, 'I have plenty to say. It's telling to me, for example, that you haven't once asked how Scott died.'

It isn't the first time I've felt the sting of dread, but it's the first time in a police station, so that's a new experience I'll forever treasure.

'I assumed by suicide,' I say slowly.

Officer Piscowicz just looks at me.

I look back. 'Not suicide.'

'The official determination has not yet been made,' Officer Piscowicz says.

'Well, whatever it is, it had nothing to do with me!'

'Really?' Officer Graham chimes in. 'All right. A few months ago, your older brother Lucas goes nuts and then ends his life. Justin Gorhammer is under suicide watch after you and your friends launch a harassment campaign against him that has pushed him to the brink. And we have questions about who was involved in taking that video of him, serious questions that may have very serious consequences for you. And now, lo! What do we find but our second death, a boy *you* went on a date with? The last person to see him alive? Do you see the common link appearing between all three of these tragedies, Miss Gray? I don't suppose I need to spell it out for you, do I? After all, you're smart. You've had –' a micro-pause, then, witheringly – 'an education.'

'I can't have been the last person to see him alive,' I say. 'What about his parents? There's no way.'

'Their last sight of him is before he left the house to meet you,' Officer Graham replies.

He watches me, enjoying his moment in the sun, while my heart and my brain vie for a new speed record. Where could he have gone when he left the cave? Did he really choke to death on a hallucinatory tarantula? It seems obscenely unlikely, but stranger things have happened. I can't mention it, though, it makes me look even less credible than I already do –

And then I remember.

'Oh my god.' I blink. 'There was someone else down there.'

'Where?' asks Officer Piscowicz.

'In the cave!' I say. 'I remember hearing another set of footsteps! Someone put my phone back in my pocket! Maybe they were after Scott, or . . .' Maybe it was another Hoffy Man. '. . . I don't know, but *they* would have been the last person to see him alive, not me. I was still down in the cave, and they followed him when he left!'

'Did you see this person? Can you describe them?'

'No,' I say, my heart sinking. 'I didn't see them, I just heard their footsteps.'

'Do you think possibly it could have just been echoes from Scott's footsteps?' Officer Graham replies with naked condescension.

I look between them both.

Officer Piscowicz is silent, watching me. Despite knowing my mother, he will not be coming to my rescue on this matter. Whatever his feelings about Officer Graham, he's loyal to the cop clan, or the Hoffy Man clan – right now it doesn't make a difference which clan it is, because it isn't mine.

'So . . . what, you think I'm a serial killer now?' I demand. 'I don't murder people!'

'Calm down,' Officer Graham replies, with the kind of pitying look reserved for Girls Who Are Being Dramatic. 'No one's calling you anything like that. No, you just like a little harassment, don't you? You ruin lives over rumours, rumours started by people like you, without a shred of evidence to support them. You play fire with these poor boys' mental health, until they finally take matters into their own hands. Just to make it stop.'

People like you. Shred of evidence. Matters into their own hands.

There I am, thinking wildly, *You can't say things like that. You're supposed to be all calm and reserved and professional and give nothing away.*

Somewhere out there in the multiverse, there must exist a utopian reflection of ours, where the leaders and keepers of humanity's fair communities are in their positions of power due to an excess of smarts, morals and all-round capability. Alas, it ain't this one. If a lifetime of watching noir has taught me anything, it's that the people in charge can be as dumb as a brick, and just as dangerous when thrown.

'What about the Hoffy Men?' I ask, trying to ignore the sharp claws of my panic. 'Are you seriously telling me that no one has ever, ever mentioned them to you before? That you have no other accusations from other people in the area, ever? They've never come up even once in conversation, not once?'

'Your theory has nothing to do with Scott Poltern's death, Miss Gray.'

'I disagree! I think it has *everything* to do with it! Because if I'm right, if I'm really telling the truth about all this, then they could have killed Scott, couldn't they, for screwing up twice! Once with Viola and once with me! If I'm right –'

'But you're not right!' Officer Graham roars. 'You're just a silly little girl desperately trying to shed responsibility for her actions by blaming a made-up boogeyman! It's embarrassing! You're embarrassing yourself! The Hoffy Men *do not exist*!'

His mouth hangs open in his fury.

Then something flies into it.

I have time to see a small, blurry round shape zipping across his lips before he jerks back violently, his hands coming up to paw at the air either side of his face.

'Paul,' Officer Piscowicz says.

Now he's grasping the table edge with meaty fingers, utterly silent, fighting for breath.

'Paul!' Officer Piscowicz shouts. 'What's happening?'

Heimlich. Someone needs to do the Heimlich, and even though he currently sports the sash proclaiming him my number one nemesis, I'm not going to watch someone die in front of me if I can do something about it, and I'm halfway out of my chair when Officer Graham gives a tortured hacking, the sound of someone trying to cough without drawing breath, and from his purpling visage spits a fat dark ball. It lands wetly on the table in front of him, its legs weakly twitching.

It's a bee.

Under the triple gaze of the room, it shudders once and then stops moving.

'Thucking thing,' Officer Graham blurts, 'thucking thing thtung me on the thongue!'

'You shouldn't have lied, then, should you?' I say.

Both men turn to stare at me.

I have no idea where that came from.

There's a stink outside the door – raised voices, set to the general tone of anger, lifting all our heads in their direction. The door handle rattles, as if someone's trying to break in. I just about have the time for my brain to register my mother's shouty voice when the lady herself shoves open the door.

'– as if you think you have THE RIGHT –' she's saying.

Officer Piscowicz is half rising out of his chair. 'Mrs Gray, we asked you to wait outside while we interviewed your daughter –'

'Yes, *my* daughter, not your murder suspect!' my mother bats right back.

She takes my hand, bodily pulling me from the room and into the corridor.

'Mrs Gray, you need to stop –'

'Harry,' my mother thunders to Officer Piscowicz, 'I haven't been Mrs for nearly eight years! And I've known you and your mother for twice that! And remember that thing I did for you, back when you were sixteen?'

Harry flushes. 'That's . . . that's not pertinent to this situation.'

'It is when you live in a small community,' she counters, 'and everyone knows everyone else's business!'

Harry's mouth opens and closes.

'If Alec leaves now,' he manages, 'it doesn't look good, does it?'

'That depends on who's doing the looking and what absolute bullshit they've come up with!'

I can't help it – a full-on admiring gasp escapes my lips.

'What on earth is going on out here?' rumbles a new voice.

A man with a magnificent moustache that somehow makes me think of a walrus has descended upon the little beige corridor of our dramatic scene.

'Chief Inspector.' The relief in my mother's voice is unmistakable, and my own hope rises in tandem. 'I need to talk to you.'

'You can make an appointment with Officer Piscowicz to address any concerns,' he rumbles.

'No, I need to talk to *you*.'

'Mrs Gray –'

'Ms.'

'– I am in front of you right now because you were having a fit in the corridor outside my office while I was on the phone with the mayor, and it became impossible to hear what he was saying to me. Otherwise we have no occasion to cross paths. Officer Piscowicz is your point of contact. Lower your voice. Good day.'

'Please, wait,' says my mother, and the desperation in her voice chills me. 'You can't possibly think my daughter had anything to do with this boy's death? Please!'

He looks at her – or rather, his moustache does.

Then he looks at Harry.

'Control this situation,' he says.

Harry nods. 'Yes, sir.'

Then he moves back into his office and, without another word, closes the door.

The Break-up

'Bummer on the no-holiday thing,' I comment as we reach fresh air. 'I was going to surprise you with a trip to the Ibiza summer raves.'

I'm still trembling. My mother says nothing, simply heads like a determined arrow towards the car park.

'They can't really stop me from leaving, can they?'

'No,' my mother replies shortly.

'Thank god, because I just booked us Brazilian waxes, and I've been eyeing up this neon green tankini number for you –'

'Jesus, Alec.' My mother whirls on me. 'You can't wisecrack your way out of this one! This is serious. Very, very serious!'

We stand, staring at each other.

'I know,' I say finally.

My mother is tense, tight. The calm before the storm.

'Come on,' she replies, 'we'll talk about this at home. Game plan. I'll get us a good lawyer –'

'A lawyer? What for? You believe me, right? I didn't have anything to do with Scott's death!'

A sudden call makes us both turn back towards the station. Through its front doors Juno has emerged, and my sudden panic flare dims – until I glance at my mother, who, far from being overjoyed at the friendly face, looks even more furious.

'Ellie, wait,' calls Juno.

My mother waits.

Juno reaches us, all tall Amazonian civil authority. Then she sags.

'Why didn't you come to me?' she asks plaintively.

My mother snorts. 'Why do you think?'

'Come on, Ell, we could have put our differences aside for the sake of Alec. I could have been in the room when they questioned her, at least.'

'And what would that have done?'

'We can protect you,' Juno urges.

'I know what your protection looks like, Juno. No thanks, I don't need it.'

'Yes, you do,' Juno insists. 'They're going after you, aren't they? I heard about the lawsuit, they're torpedoing your business. You're going to lose your house, Ell. You're going to lose everything.'

Can I prevent the outraged 'What?!' that escapes my mouth?

Reader, I cannot.

'That's great, Juno,' my mother bitterly replies, with a quick glance at me. 'Thank you.'

Juno is unrepentant. 'She should know what's at stake. She's in the game now, you can't keep hiding this all from her.'

'Oh good, more parenting tips,' my mother shoots back. 'You already did that with my son and look how well that turned out, but by all means!'

'Come back to us,' Juno urges.

'There is no "us". The Kindly Ones split up, from what I heard. You lost control of it, Juno.'

'I'm still in control, and I can *protect* you –'

'No!'

'You don't have a choice. Not unless you want to lose ev–'

'I always, *always*,' my mother replies through gritted teeth, 'have a choice.'

Juno is a statue.

'I know what you're up to,' my mother raises a finger and points it at Juno, 'with your side hustle in recruitment.'

'That was nothing to do with me,' protests Juno, cold in her rising fury. 'Alec found them all by herself, and how dare you –'

'No, how dare *you*. You go back and you tell them, every single one of them, to stay the fuck away from my daughter. I don't care that the group had some big schism, I don't care that you've got rogue members running around. You make them listen to you. You understand me? *They stay the fuck away.*'

I have never, not once in my life, heard Eleanor Gray say the F word.

And it's a shame, because she says it so well. *Fuck* in her mouth is not just a swear word, but an ancient death curse.

I sneak a glance at Juno as I am forcibly moved off. She looks like she's swallowed a wasp.

Seems to be catching.

'Mom,' I say as we reach the car. 'Is Juno in the Kindly Ones?'

I have to hear it from her mouth, because until I do I won't believe it.

Silence.

Silence means yes.

We're at bottom, and I have nothing to lose. 'Are *you* in the Kindly Ones?'

'No,' she replies, and then with heavy, deadly finality, 'and neither are you.'

Stalker II: The Return

Tack.

Wait.

Tack.

Wait.

Tack.

I have the fourth stone in my fingers, ready to launch, when the window opens wide, freezing my hand.

Megan appears, and I breathe out.

'What are you doing?' she calls down to me.

'Trying to get your attention?' I hiss.

'In the toilet?' she continues in normal volume voice. 'This is the upstairs bathroom window.'

'Oh. Sorry. I was hoping it was your bedroom.'

'Why are you whispering?'

'Because I don't want to get you into trouble?'

'No one's home.'

Thank god.

'I'm coming down,' she calls. 'I'll meet you at the front door.'

I wait there, twitching. No one might be home, but I still feel watched, permanently lit with an invisible spotlight.

Megan gave me her address a while ago, but this is the first time I've visited the Lugner family home. It's like a giant dropped a big glass box on to the landscape. The kind of place that gets fledgling architects making orgasmic overtures. A demure, eco, European kind of wealth.

The house sits on the other side of the woods in which Lucas was found, though a good stretch away. It's close to the main road, but obscured by trees, so you'd never know it was there unless you went looking. Like a secret hiding in plain sight. In any case, that explains what Megan was doing in the woods the first day we met. The woods are her territory.

The front door opens wide, the kind of door that would more naturally lead to a drawbridge. Megan stands dwarfed in its vast frame, silk pyjama trousers hanging from her slender hips.

'You were in bed.' I am dismayed.

'No,' she replies, 'just at home.'

Her feet are bare. They are small and perfectly, lightly tanned, feet made to be shown off in pretty sandals.

'I heard,' she says, simply.

My eyes find hers.

Please, I will her, *please take me*.

Her arms open. I stumble gracelessly into them.

'It was crazy,' I murmur into her shoulder. She's warm, soft. Her hair smells woodsy. 'They think I killed him.'

I want to laugh. Even now the whole thing is so unreal to me. I feel like a bad actor delivering a line.

Megan leads me inside, shutting the front door behind us. 'What did they say?'

'That I was the last person to see him alive, and that I've been harassing him, and Justin, and – god – my brother.'

'That's sick,' I hear her murmur. 'But why do they think Scott was murdered? Everyone else is saying it was an accident.'

'You know what happened to him?' I ask, in two minds about actually knowing.

'Just what everyone's been saying. He fell off a cliff edge.'

'He fell off a cliff edge?! Jesus.'

'You didn't know that?' she asks. 'Where have you been?'

I feel like crying, but the world-weary PI never cries. He sometimes looks crushed – especially when alone in his small, shitty apartment nursing a bottle of whisky – but he never cries.

'Prison,' I say. 'My mother's really going for the paranoia high dive. She took my phone off me after our visit with the cops. That's why I couldn't text you about coming over here. She's having the locks changed on the house, for Christ's sake. The only reason I could sneak out is because *she* went out. She said it was a big grocery run, but ten to one she's gone to see Walter. I figured, fair's fair. She checked out to see *her* beau, I can do the same.'

And if she catches me out? I no longer care. She's joined the back of the queue for people just desperate to lock me up and throw away the key. Screw her for dropping bombs about her surprise past life in a cabal, *my* cabal, and then shutting me out and acting like I'm the bad girl for keeping secrets. Screw her for running to her new lover in her time of need, instead of talking to me. Who does that?

All right, so I'm doing it right now. Anything you can do, I can do better.

The hallway is as cavernous as promised. Behind Megan I can see the quiet gleam of expensive appliances. An enormous kitchen island bearing a fluted vase and a tasteful spray of dried flowers. Beyond, a vast open-plan living area. Fireplace. Photo frames on its mantelpiece.

This is someone's home. This is Megan's home. I feel like an intruder.

'Your parents really aren't here?' I ask anxiously.

'They really aren't. They're at some dull fundraiser thing tonight. Usually they drag me along, but I managed to wriggle out of it.'

'Shame. I'd make such a good impression on them right now.'

And I mean it, or at least the first part – I am pretty curious to see the wellsprings from which this gorgeous sprite emerged.

Megan's face turns dark.

'Well, they wouldn't on you,' she says. 'My dad's a Class A prick, and my mom's a meek little hausfrau.'

A nerve has been touched. She's never volunteered much information about her parents, and the freezing cold tone of her voice suggests why. Families. No one's got a perfect thing going, have they?

A pause, too long for comfort.

'I'm going to get you a glass of water,' Megan says, finally. 'Sit over there.'

I head meekly towards the biggest couch I've ever seen, and sit there with my hands pressed between my knees as I watch her flit around the open-plan kitchen, bare feet skimming over the cleanest floor tiles outside of a showroom, fetching a glass, pressing buttons on a gleaming silver double fridge.

I direct my stare towards the shag rug as she approaches.

'I'm sorry,' I say. 'This was inappropriate, coming over like this.'

'Drink the water first.'

I take the proffered glass and gulp. There's nothing worse than being watched as you eat or drink, shame-wise, particularly if the someone doing the watching is hotter than Death Valley in August. Her eyes are agate green. Flecks of gold. How am I only just noticing those flecks?

'Did you know?' I croak, then clear my throat.

She frowns. 'Know what?'

'About my mother. Eleanor Gray. Did you know she was in the Kindly Ones?'

She shakes her head. 'Before my time.'

I try to shake off my roaring disappointment – either because I'd been hoping Megan would be a source of knowledge, or hoping I could be furious at her for keeping such knowledge from me; I'm not sure which right now. I am all feelings, all at once. Rage, frustration, fear. It's a heady cocktail.

'But you knew about Juno,' I say. 'Juno diCanso.'

Megan is quiet. Then: 'I didn't realise you knew each other, honestly.'

'She's the . . . leader, or something?'

'We don't have leaders. We make decisions together.'

'Is that what happened with the Justin video? Group consensus, was it?'

She's quiet again.

'You're angry about that,' she says at last.

Drawing back from me. Not what I wanted.

'No,' I say. 'No. I mean, yes. I'm a lot of things. I'm sorry. I just . . . I feel like I used to swim in shallow waters. I could feel the bottom of the pool with my feet. I knew the parameters. I could see all the sides. It was a pretty small pool. Now it's like . . . I've been swept out to sea, and I'm swimming and I'm swimming, trying to keep afloat above all this deep, dark, bottomless expanse. And I have no idea how deep it goes. And there are things moving down there, underneath my feet, but I don't know how big they are, I just know they're big, and I keep thinking, well, how big? Like Jaws big, or Moby Dick big? Or kraken big? How monstrously huge are we talking, here? I . . . the analogy is getting lost now. Sorry.'

Megan's eyes are round, gazing out at me from the semi-dark of her enormous, alien living room.

'There was a schism,' she says. 'Some members broke away. They felt things were going too far, or not far enough. I'm not sure. Maybe that's when your mother left the group. I'm sorry I can't tell you more.'

Her hand is on my thigh. Those thin silk trousers cling to hers. I'm very aware of her clean, warm smell.

'It will be OK,' Megan says to me softly. 'It will be, Alec. You didn't do anything to Scott.'

'How do you know? I could have pushed him off the cliff. I can't prove I didn't.' I give a weak laugh at her expression. 'Jokes in the wrong moment is a Gray special skill.'

'You're innocent,' says Megan.

Her thumb strokes against the material of my jeans. I am hot. I am cold.

'Why are you so sure of me?' I whisper.

There is a chilling conviction in her voice. 'I know monsters. You're not one of them.'

'I don't know. I feel so desperate. Angry and, and *hungry*. I'm hungry all the time.'

'You can feed on me,' Megan says into my ear.

Then she closes in, and I feel her mouth engulf mine.

Her warm weight is on me, and I can taste the plastic cherry taste of her lip balm, a taste I swear to myself right then and there that I'll never forget as long as I live. The dame has me by the short hairs. I am putty in her hands. Yes.

Oh god, the underwear has been exposed.

Her fingers manage to do the impossible, and quiet my brain. I am losing myself, I am gone, and then a tongue –

Outside, a car alarm starts to blare.

My eyes snap open.

It keeps going. And going. And –

Crap.

'Crap!'

'What?' Megan pants, looking up at me.

'That's my car alarm.'

She cocks her head. 'Are you sure?'

'No other car parked in this neighbourhood could possibly sound as old and tired as that. It's mine.'

'Don't worry about it, it'll shut off in a minute.'

But it does not, in fact, shut off.

'Crap, crap, crap, I'm sorry. I'll take care of it –'

Furiously embarrassed, I pull up my jeans with all the grace of a beetle stuck on its back, then scramble to my feet. Keys, keys . . .

Stupid *junk* heap. Why is something always interrupting just as I'm about to have the time of my life? Does God not want me to get naughty with Megan? My silent ranting distracts me long enough that I don't even look through the glass wall of the Lugner house before busting outside, which in hindsight is reckless, because the reason my car alarm is blaring surely has something to do with the tall figure stood beside it with a can of spray paint in their hand.

They're spraying my car. They're *spraying* –

'Hey!' I shout.

The tall figure looks up. Slender, gender indeterminate due to the baseball cap and giant sunglasses. At night.

You.

You!

The figure watching me in the woods when I first met Megan. The figure who came haring out of the beach caves just before I found a hysterical Scott inside. Watching me. Following me . . .

I do a terrified, furious march towards the figure. 'What the hell are you doing to my car?!'

The tall figure looks at me, looks at the car.

Then bolts.

My legs lock in ready pursuit, propelling me into the run, but the figure doesn't get far. Parked a few metres away is a familiar-looking car. A *bleep bleep* sounds. They throw themselves into the front seat. Turn on the engine. Then there they sit. The windows are tinted, so I can't see them any more.

'That sports car,' I say.

'What the hell?' Megan has run up beside me, her mouth a disbelieving gape.

I point to the idling car. My finger is trembling. Adrenaline, obviously, not fear.

'That sports car,' I repeat, 'has been following me from day one. It nearly got me arrested. And when Scott first approached me to ask me out, it was there. I've seen it everywhere. They've been watching me. It's them.'

Megan says nothing, staring at the car.

'It's *them*,' I repeat, annoyed she isn't filling in her bit. 'It's a Hoffy Man, it's got to be – what? Wait, Megan!'

Megan is not waiting.

Megan is marching towards the idling Porsche.

It all plays out so fast, I've barely gotten my stuck feet off the ground when the Porsche is revving, and then driving, driving *towards* Megan, who stands in the middle of the road, defiant and unmoving.

The car speeds up.

Megan does not move.

I'm just about to scream when the brakes do it for me and the car stops dead, the bonnet inches from shattering Megan's shins.

And still she hasn't moved.

Megan stares into the tinted windscreen, her expression deathly cold.

She reaches out and brings a fist down on to the bonnet with a dull bang.

The car jerks, reversing hot and hard. With a squeal of wheels it turns, roaring off down the quiet road to disappear into the distance.

Only when it is out of sight do I remember to breathe.

'What the hell is wrong with you?' I yell.

Megan's head snaps to me, and for a moment, that cold fury stays in her face as she stares at me.

Then it melts. She actually sags in place.

'My legs are like jelly,' she confesses.

I hurry over to her. 'Why did you do that, crazy girl? You could have been killed!'

She gives a sullen shrug. Then her eyes stray to my car and widen.

Together, we contemplate the giant, jagged word Sunglasses had almost completed across the side before the ancient warning system of my ancient carriage decided, inexplicably, to sound its alarm:

MURDERE

I breathe out a shaky gust of air. 'Quite the set-up.'

Megan is staring at the word in what I'll call a hatred trance.

'What?' she says eventually. 'What do you mean?'

'The Hoffy Men. Obviously they're trying to set me up for Scott's death.' A panicky laugh escapes me. 'Jesus.'

'Alec,' Megan grabs my arm, the grip intense enough to hurt. 'You have to promise me not to pursue this.'

'What? I have to find out who really did it. I have to clear my name!'

'But,' she says desperately, 'that's just what they want!'

'Huh?'

'Listen to me. When I first got you into the Kindly Ones, I had no idea things would get so dangerous for you. I thought we could protect you. And we can, I really believe that. But you can't go after . . .' she hesitates, 'whoever that was in the car. You'll make it worse.'

'He just tried to run you over!'

'Yes, exactly!'

We glare at each other.

'You sound like my mother,' I grumble.

Megan's grip tightens.

'Ow!'

'Sorry.' She lets go. 'I'm sorry. I'm not trying to be your mother, I'm being your girlfriend. And as your girlfriend, allow me a little concern for my honey.' She is pleading. 'Please, promise me you'll drop the whole Scott thing. He killed himself. He walked off a cliff, and nobody can prove otherwise. They'll exonerate you. You just have to be patient, and for the love of god, don't put yourself in the firing line in the meantime. If that car shows up again, do not engage. You can't try to talk to them, or fight them. Call the police, and go somewhere safe. Better yet, come *here*. Come here, to *me*. OK?'

She is so serious, so earnest. She really seems scared.

'You're my girlfriend?' I ask.

Megan blinks, derailed. 'What? No. Yes. Only if you want, I mean. I know we haven't talked about it, but.'

'You're blushing,' I say.

'This is a blush of fire and fury from what just happened to you,' she retaliates, 'the crimson of anger, not the rouge of embarrassment.'

'Now you're starting to sound like me. I think we're spending too much time together, doll.' I give her a big goofy grin. 'I've heard sometimes that happens with couples.'

Megan's blush deepens. Score.

'Promise me,' she insists.

'I promise,' I say, 'I will try to trust in the laughable competency of the local constabulary to figure out what happened to Scott Poltern.'

'Juno is of the local constabulary,' Megan reminds me.

I cant my head in acknowledgement. 'At least one of competence in the mix, then.'

Megan presses into my side. 'Say it out loud, though.'

'Say what out loud?'

'The promise.'

I draw in a steadying breath. 'I promise I will drop all enquiries into satanic mafia cults, anonymous psychos in dark sunglasses who drive Porsches, and guys who may have been murdered.'

I feel a tickling on my lips. I hear Megan gasp as my hand rises and bats away the warm, fluttering body trying to force itself into my mouth.

'It's OK,' Megan soothes. 'It's just a moth.'

I duck and weave, flapping my hands violently in front of my face. The moth flitters and darts, its tiny stick feet and wing-tips brushing my lips and making my skin crawl.

Finally, mercifully, it disappears.

'You looked like the movie poster for *Silence of the Lambs* for a second there,' Megan says uneasily. 'You OK?'

'Yes,' I say, a hand held up in front of my mouth. 'It's just this weird thing that keeps happening.'

'Moths?'

'Let's get inside.' I take her arm and move quickly back towards the house before I can get attacked again.

Megan has no idea what the moth means, but I think I'm starting to.

Every time someone around me – including myself, it seems – tells a lie, something shows up and tries to martyr itself by crawling down their throat. I've heard of cursing someone to choke on their own lies, but I never thought it could be taken so literally.

The moth attacked me because I just flat out lied to Megan. Like hell I'm just going to sit around while I get framed for a murder I didn't commit and my girl gets run over by a Porsche-driving, car-tagging stalker. If they'd left me alone, I'd have left them alone. But they didn't, so here we are.

It's war, fuckoes.

And this time, I got the licence plate.

The Go-between

When I find him he's exactly where I thought he'd be – cosying up to some impossibly cool-looking chick on the low-slung couches of Surfriders.

It is how it sounds – a bar for the surf crowd, or at least those aesthetically aligned, who may not actually surf but love to look like they do. It's a lot of flip-flops, Billabong T-shirts, leather thong bracelets, Chili Peppers blasting from the sound system. They even scatter sand across the beer-stained floor for that authentic underfoot feel, and stunted potted palm trees dot the free corners.

Christien is whispering in the cool chick's ear as I approach, an arm slung casually over the back of the low couch, within skimming distance of her pretty bare shoulders.

I stop in front of him, my arms folded.

'Oh my god,' I say. 'I knew it. I just *knew* it.'

Christien looks away from his target, a lazily charming smile on his face.

'Alec,' he says. 'What's up? This is Taylor.'

Impossibly cool-looking chick gives me a cool nod. 'Hi.'

'Christien,' I say. 'What is this? Are you adding her?'

'Adding her? To what?'

'To *us*, Christien, to *us*. I can't believe it. I just knew if I surprised you in here I'd find someone else.'

I gesture emphatically towards Taylor.

Christien's upside-down frown is slowly turning right side up. 'What are you on about, Gray? You just texted me and asked me if you could come ask me a favour in person, and I told you where I was. It's hardly a surprise.'

'I mean, my sisters warned me,' I say, my voice wobbling. 'When you said you wanted your own harem, I have to admit we weren't sure at first, but honestly none of us have stopped thinking about it since, and if the offer of the new summer house at the bottom of your garden still stands, we're ready to move in, you know, so we're on hand whenever you want, but –' I lean in, the better to emphasis every wounded word – 'honestly Christien, aren't the five of us enough for you?'

'Alrighty, I'm out,' the girl says, standing to leave.

'Taylor, come on. She's just joking around.' Christien is all bemused grin as he watches his prospect prep her exit.

'Just joking around?!' Genuine tears leak from my eyes. 'Oh my *god*. I feel so stupid. Oh god, this is just so humiliating.'

It's the performance of a lifetime. Too bad the Oscar committee aren't here.

'Just ignore her,' Christien says under my wailing.

'Kind of hard to right now, Chris,' Taylor replies with a roll of her eyes. 'Look, this was supposed to be easy, drama-free. That's your rep, isn't it?' She cuts a glance at my brimming, puppy-kicked face. 'So I'm gonna go, and you can deal with . . .whatever *this* is.' She shakes her head. 'I hate those stupid prank shows, dude.'

'I'll text you!' Christien calls after her staunchly departing form.

She doesn't reply.

Christien slumps back, annoyed.

'Your tears dried up fast,' he says sourly, looking me up and down.

It's amazing. He's acting like nothing could possibly be wrong between us.

'I'd have thought you'd be into the harem thing,' I say. 'Seems like your vibe.'

'Jokes like that aren't funny, Alec. A man's reputation is a man's life, especially these days.'

'Then you'd better not cross me.'

'Yeah, I've heard all about what you do to guys who dare.'

'Oh, thank god, because I didn't want to have to pull out the instructional videos.'

He laughs. He shakes his head.

But I see it. He's uneasy. He might even – hot damn – be scared of me. I feel like a hyena who just smelled the fear.

'Shouldn't you be thanking your stars that I'm not nearly as crazy as your last ex?' I ask him. 'Then again, getting gang raped in a cave and then having absolutely zero people, including your own boyfriend, in your corner on it is enough to drive anyone a little mad, wouldn't you agree?'

Christien tosses uneasy glances across the nearest barflies. 'Jesus, not you as well. Who have you been talking to, Tippi? She's insane! All Viola's friends are.'

'Hey, listen,' I say in my friendliest tone, 'I get it. When your daddy's the local cult leader you must get the Kool-Aid in your baby milk, am I right?'

'Alec,' Christien says with sharp impatience, 'what are you talking about?'

'Hoffy Men. You. In the.'

'What?'

'Are you in the Hoffy Men?'

'I don't even know what that is.' Christien delivers this with innocent distaste.

And then he says, 'Ow!'

'The insects this year are really aggressive, have you noticed?' I say cheerfully. 'Tell you what, I'll give you a do-over. Just the one, mind. Are you in the Hoffy Men?'

'It stung my *lip* –'

'You'll be fine, but I wouldn't lie again. Here's the theory I've been chewing on. I came to you. I asked you about Viola, and that strange esoteric necklace she'd been parading in her social media. You told me you had no idea what the necklace was. I went to talk to Viola about it. And ever since then, Christien Van Hoffyman, I've been followed around by this sleek little sports car that very much looks like something *you'd* drive. I'd even go so far as to posit that it *is* your car, mainly because here –' I shove my phone under his nose – 'is a photo of you in the driver's seat on Viola's Instagram! And – well, I'll be damned, what's this? The very same licence plate that I saw, registered in your name?'

Christien's gaze flicks between mine and the screen of my phone. He looks gobsmacked, presumably at my remarkable detecting skills – but he didn't even bother to cover his tracks by getting Viola to take the now-months-old car photo off her socials. It's right there for all to see.

'That's not my car,' he protests, then amends, 'Well . . . it *was* my car, but it's not any more –'

'Convincing,' I cut in with friendly sarcasm. 'Almost enough to let you off the hook – were it not for the rest of the evidence just piling up, e.g. your father's political shindig the other week being packed out with a whole variety of Hoffy Men fat cats, one of whom tried to recruit me as a future victim in your garden. I'm not a huge fan of the company you keep, Christien.'

'That was my dad's party, and you're well aware I have as little to do with his life as possi–'

'But you *know* about it, don't you? You're his only son, you can't help but at least know about it. Logically, at the very least, you've been lying to me. And about my own brother's involvement in your little mafia, too.'

The jackanape can't even meet my eye.

'Here's what I'm thinking,' I say, coasting on furious satisfaction. 'I'm thinking that not only are you the next gen of Hoffy Men, much like your fellow acolytes Scott, Justin and Lucas – two of whom are dead now, doesn't that worry you? – but that your daddy is the chief, or the Head Bastard, or whatever your fellow dicks call the dick in charge. That, or he is, at the very least, rather well connected in the organization. He ordered you to get the "victim necklace" back from Viola, and you did. I'm assuming without her agreement. Was that the beginning of the end for you two?'

Christien just stares at me, tight-lipped.

Shame. I kind of wanted to see him choke on a cockroach.

'I will take your silence as a yes. So here's what I want. I want you to get a message to Mr Head Bastard.' I steady myself. 'I want to parlay.'

'Parlay,' Christien says dumbly.

'Yes. White flag, Christmas Day football match, whole bit.' My eyes roll at his expression. 'Parlay. Didn't you ever see *Pirates of the Caribbean*? We meet. Just head honcho and me, in private. No hangers-on, no recording devices. We meet and we talk. See, I have something I think he wants. And in exchange, I'm willing to bet he can give me what I want.' I smile. 'Humour me. It's fun, I promise.'

'What could you possibly have that he wants, Alec? I'm just *desperate* to know.'

He's trying hard for nonchalant sarcasm, but he keeps missing.

I lean in, the better for us not to be heard.

'I have a video of Scott Poltern before he died, spilling the beans on your little club. Names of members, details of their nefarious crimes against women. He even gave me some keepsakes. I think the forensics guys call it "corroborating evidence".'

I subside, then I clamp a hand over my mouth and nose.

'What . . . the . . . fuck,' says Christien in a dazed voice, staring at me.

I must look a sight. Flies are crawling over my knuckles and battering between my tightly gripped fingers. It's positively demonic. However necessary for my purposes, I am ashamed of the lie I just told, and a little afraid because I have no desire to die choking on flies, but a nice counterpoint is the look on Christien's face, which I'm enjoying very much.

And then he surprises me.

He bolts.

He leaps up from the sofa and races across the half-empty bar. People turn to stare as I hare after him with one hand clamped over my mouth. I finally resemble the predator I long to be.

I catch up with him in the corridor outside. I've never felt this fast, this savage; I'm shocking myself and certainly him as I block his way. One good thing about his escape attempt – we seem to have shaken the flies. For now.

'What the hell is wrong with you?' Christien pants. 'You're acting like a lunatic!'

'Grief pass card?'

'Fuck you!'

'Not this time, Chris.'

People are watching. Christien is very aware of them. His only choice is to try to de-escalate, to humour me – or risk being witnessed assaulting a girl to get away from her.

He sighs. Laughs. Shakes his head. We're going with option number one.

'OK, OK,' he says, still braying, as if this is all some skit, some big joke. 'You could have just called up the mayor's office and left a message, but I'll pass it on for you personally, OK? Is that better?'

'Peachy,' I reply, and I get out my phone. 'I'm sending you a time, a date and a place for the parlay. It's nice and private. Head Hoffy Man honcho won't be seen by anyone. He meets with me, he can have the video. No copies of it stored anywhere, I pinky swear.'

'Someone's seen *Chinatown* too many times,' Christien says. 'You know what happens at this club you're so deranged about? They drink too much whisky, they play billiards, they have an annual picnic for friends and family, for Christ's sake. Everyone's got a brother, or a son, or a father who's in it. Practically every man you know is in it! It's not some big conspiracy, it's a community. It's . . .' He casts around. 'It's just a social club.'

'So's the mafia,' I reply. 'And stop threatening me.'

'*Threatening* you? I –'

'Everyone's in it? Everywhere I turn, there's a Hoffy Man waiting to pounce? That's what you just said, isn't it?'

I want to hit something. I want to point my fingers and disintegrate him, or make him burst into flame with just the power of my terrible thoughts.

'I'm not afraid of you and yours, lackey boy,' I hiss. 'I may only be a girl, but if you *ever* follow me in your little quarter-life crisis Porsche again, or try to run my girlfriend over, or spray-paint my car with any words that aren't "Alec is a goddess", or in any way threaten me or anyone even loosely connected to me, not only will I ruin your precious reputation the way I ruined Justin's, but I'll sure as shit do my level best to permanently break your most favourite body part, so you can never again do the thing you love doing more than anything else in the world. Capisce?'

I've never seen a look like that on a face like his before. I've never seen a man so scared and lost and confused, and all because of little old me.

Gives me the good chills.

'One last parting shot,' I say, putting my phone away. 'You say I'm on the wrong side, but I've seen the same sick look on your face right now that I saw on Scott's, and on Justin's, and I think I know what it means. I think it means you know *you're* on the wrong side, and that it's just a matter of time.' I tut at him. 'You should have believed her when she told you,

Christien. Was it your choice to break up with her, or was it Daddy's orders?'

It's a wild guess, the reason for his break-up with Viola – but what with his high connections to the Hoffy Men, it's a decent one. And judging by the look on his face, it might even be a bull's eye.

As I turn and walk, I hear him give out some final squawks.

'Wait a minute, Alec – I never tried to run your girlfriend over, and I never followed you around, and I never spray-painted your car! I don't even *have* my car any more; it got stolen, OK? It got *stolen*! Are you going around *telling* people that stuff?! Alec, that's crazy, what are you *talking* about, I never tried –'

I don't bother looking back to see which insect got attracted by his lie.

The cowardly stalker can choke on it, for all I care.

Insects and Demons and Curses, Oh My!

Let's take an interlude.

Let our breath catch up.

Just imagine the elevator muzak version of 'The Girl From Ipanema' playing in the background.

So, the mouth-happy bugs thing. Do I really believe that the insect kingdom has banded together, united in their mutual hatred of human lies, to expose our misbehaviour by kamikazeing their way into our throats?

And do I really believe that demons that no one else can see forced a couple of male heirs to the thrones of power to confess their crime and inadvertently expose the dark web of evil ultimately responsible for it and many, many other crimes like it, stretching back hundreds of years?

No?

Yes?

I really don't know. I've never before trucked with so many things that can't be proved.

All I can say with empirical certainty is that something happened when I went down into the dark with Scott that day. When I came back out, I was no longer the Alec Gray of before. My life is now firmly divided into B.C. and

A.C. – Before Cave and After Cave – and never the two Alecs shall meet.

I feel different. There's something inside me now, some new creature. It's been there for weeks, ever since the cave, lurking, growing into and around my guts, becoming part of me, leaching its strange colour into all I do. It's not just a righteous indignation at the secrets that were kept, the damage dealt in the name of power for the few.

It's something darker than that.

A deep, ugly, slow, cold fury, with a mind of its own and an agenda to match. I can't understand it; I can only feel it, stirring like a Ridley Scott alien inside me, ready to burst its way out of my chest.

It wants.

I think it wants death.

I'm not dumb. I know I'm headed somewhere dangerous, stuck on a runaway train, and I know this can't lead anywhere safe or happy. It might even be the death of *me*.

But it's hungry. I'm hungry.

And I feel too good to stop.

A Girl, a Priest and a Hoffy Man
Walk into a Bar

At the top of this Tuesday morning, the day is all set to be delightfully dull.

The muted thud of the front door shutting – the sound of the older and wiser Gray off to her daily grind as legal scourge of petty fraudsters from here to the north coast – wakes me from a harried slumber, as if my dream self knows exactly what life has in store for me in just a few short hours and is feeling pretty damn fretful about it.

As well it should, in hindsight.

The location I suggested for the parlay is the most private and neutral ground I could think of – namely, church. Now, you might be wondering whether a man rumoured to answer to a demon in a cave might be entirely comfortable in what could be described as a rival institution's house of worship, but Christien's message to me earlier today confirmed the meet with a rather terse:

You have your parlay.

So I guess Van Freesburg Senior has no problem with God as a witness.

But the parlay is not for another two days, so I have to find distractions for the next forty-eight hours or I'm going to lose my mind, and those distractions, for the time being, involve (as instructed by both Megan and my mother) Lying Low and Staying Out of Trouble.

I'm halfway through my morning coffee ritual, spinning vague, unpalatable promises in my head to spend the next few hours on my laptop dutifully poking at college applications for next year, when my phone chirrups.

It's a text message from, of all people, Oh.

> Hello Alecto. How are you this mrng? I need to talk to you. Important! Bit of a confession – for ME this time 😂😂😂 I'm @ church, can you come in an hour, maybe before next bible grp @ 11?

And then a quick, puzzling follow-up:

> PLS DON'T BRING OREOS!!!

I check the time. It's eight thirty. Two and a half hours until bible group.

I text back.

> Sure. Be there in 30 mins?

Three dots appear, hovering, tantalizing a reply – and then they disappear.

I watch for a couple of minutes more, but he's apparently decided that all that needs to be said has been said.

Don't bring Oreos? Must be a typo. Oh's approach to texting can best be described as endearingly slapdash. I make a mental note to pick up some Oreos from the corner store on the way to church. He'll have to be cool with the humdrum kind; I'm not a miracle worker under deadline.

Important talks. Confessional talks. Decent bait – especially considering when I, in exchange, confess what I need his church for in two days' time.

To be clear – Oh will let me use it for the parlay. He's always told me to ask him for anything in his power to give. Now, the last thing I want to do is lie to him about what the hell some private church time with the Mayor of Fring at seven o'clock in the morning on a Thursday could possibly be about, but equally, several text message essay attempts later and I'd come no closer to explaining the situation in a way that wouldn't set off his alarm bells.

Especially when I add that I want to come in earlier than the designated time to rig up a couple of strategically hidden cameras and boom mikes that I've borrowed from my ex-high school's audio-visual department. (Miss Varley never did ask for the key to the equipment cupboard back. I'll make it up to you, Miss Varley, I swear.)

But all in all, Oh's message makes for good timing. Now at least is my chance to explain to him what I need and why. God knows I'm so much more eloquent in person.

As I hurriedly get dressed, I text my mother:

> Honouring the promise you extracted from me under pain of death that I would keep you apprised of all my movements henceforth, I am obliged to tell you that I'm off to church.

Why, what have you done?

> It's deeply cynical of you to assume that I'm going in a confessorial capacity. Oh wants to chat.

You know most other people would just text 'gn 2 ⛪ bk soon'

> Aren't you glad I'm not like most other people?

I give thanks every day.
Say hi to Oh for me.

Oreos, and I'll grab a fresh coffee on the way (Oh's preferred caffeine comes freeze-dried, resembling gravel with tasting notes to match). I hop downstairs, pulling on boots, picking up car keys, phone, wallet.

Two pit stops and thirty minutes-ish later and I'm at church, clutching a packet of sandwich cookies to my chest and necking from a takeaway cup.

The front doors are still locked, so I skirt my way through the graveyard to the little hidden side gate. He's left it open, and the back door, which isn't his style. He'd usually meet me here and let me in himself, but he must be busy setting up for bible group.

'Oh?' I call, taking a brisk one through the backstage area.

He's not in the teacher's lounge-alike, nor the little side room where bible group is held. He's not in his tiny office. We're nowhere near Mass prep time, so he can't be out in the –

Voices, of the echoey timbre one might associate with stone walls and a cavernous, brooding space. Voices. Damn, am I late, are people already here? He said eleven, but maybe he got the time wrong. I'll just have to hang out until they're done, and if I eat all the Oreos out of sheer boredom, can I be blamed?

So preoccupied, I head on towards God's playground.

Behind the red curtain and my footsteps tap on bare flagstones, the cool, cavernous darkness beyond a familiar comfort.

'Oh?' I call again – and then I see him, stood before the altar, turned out towards his congregation as if about to forgive them all, except the pews are dark and empty of sinners.

Actually, not quite. It's too dark to make out much – what's all this spooky shadow for? Why hasn't he got the electric chandeliers on? – but there's a big shape in the front pew, facing Oh as if they're about to engage in their own private Mass.

Oh spots me, and his face creases up in annoyance.

'Alec, you bloody idiot, why'd you come here?' he snaps.

I stop short. Never once in our whole friendship has Oh ever displayed such anger towards me.

'Because you texted me saying you wanted to talk?' I reply, my gaze flicking between his tense face and the indistinct person in the front row.

'I was trying to *warn* you,' Oh hisses.

I frown. 'You literally texted "Alec can you come to church now, it's important".'

'That wasn't my doing, was it? I don't normally talk like a robot, do I? *After* that I warned you!'

'Your follow-up text was "DON'T BRING OREOS!!!" In all caps. Forgive me if I'm missing the cue here?'

'Clearly I was telling you to stay away!' Oh throws his hands up.

The shape in the front pew shifts very slightly in response.

Oh notices, and quickly puts his hands back down.

All right, now I get it. Took me a minute to place it because I've never seen it on him before. Oh is not angry.

He's scared.

And only now am I realizing that there are more shapes, lounged against pillars, sentrying the main doors, ringing us, in fact, in a neat little circle – or, in street parlance, a goddamn trap.

'Alecto Gray.' The figure in the front pew speaks in a pleasant male cadence. 'I've been hearing so much about you.'

'Wow, Alec,' I say under my breath. 'He's right. You are a bloody idiot.'

The Devil's Advocate

The drape of the front pew figure's well-tailored suit crinkles as he shifts slightly – likely to ease the buttock sting that comes from sitting on a church pew for more than five minutes straight. A bed of nails is probably worse, but only just.

'Guys,' he says, 'can you – thank you.'

Before I understand Suited and Booted's command I feel the effects of it – literally, as my arm is grabbed by a henchman I hadn't even realized was standing behind me when I walked into the nave. One man holds me in his grip while another approaches and rifles through my pockets. The violation is so quick and so unbelievable I don't even have the wherewithal to yell, or pull away, or do something, anything, to register my affront.

The man rifling through my pockets finds my phone and takes it. My wallet, my house keys. Takes those too. Not even a glance at my face the whole time. I am just something to ransack.

They both step back from me, satisfied.

'My apologies,' says the stranger in the front pew. 'I too am a fan of this talk remaining private, and I've heard that you like to record conversations.'

'Well,' I say, 'it's good to at least try to get your would-be rapist's voice on tape.'

'I must say,' the stranger comments, 'I have a great distaste for your implication. Thank you, Stephen.' This to the henchman who just approached him and handed over my phone, *my* phone, *my* keys, *my* wallet, to him. 'And I've noticed that women are so quick to jump straight to sexual threat these days. It's an unsophisticated weapon.'

'Sometimes a weapon need only be sharp, not sophisticated.'

The stranger laughs. 'And quick, too. You've had a good education. You weren't wrong about her, Peter.'

Peter. Oh's first name.

I risk a glance at him. He looks sick, and he says nothing, as if he's too frightened to talk.

This chills me more than anything else ever could.

'I liked your idea of the private parlay,' the stranger continues, 'so I asked Peter if he wouldn't mind doing me the favour of messaging you.'

It's a smart move. Change the timings, make sure I'd be unprepared and on the back foot. I've got nothing. He just took my only recording device, means of communication, method of escape and call for help. I've no back-up. Only Oh, who's currently about as useful as a dazed rabbit.

I feel like going up to Oh and shaking him. *Why'd you throw me to the wolves, ex-friendo?*

'Too excited to wait until Thursday?' I ask the stranger.

'I have meetings all day,' he replies.

'Even at 7 a.m., which I believe was the time I offered?'

'I'm a busy man.'

He's pleasant-voiced. In his fifties, maybe. Cultured manner. I've seen him before, I know I have. A memory stirs – he was the slick guy who interrupted my conversation with Oh a few weeks ago. He'd come visiting with the mayor.

'Well, you know my name,' I try, 'so how about yours in return?'

'Forgive me. So rude. My name is Martin Lugner.'

For the first time in my life, I understand how the word gobsmacked came to be. I feel like I've been punched in the mouth.

Megan's father. The Class A prick she hates.

That's who this is.

Suddenly, a lot of things start really making sense. The daughter of the head of the Hoffy Men is also a member of an activist group that exists for the sole purpose of raining down vigilante justice on her own father and his cohorts.

Does he know?

We stand there and we watch each other work things out. It's too late to hide my reaction, and his expression shows that he's enjoying it. He's savouring it, in fact, which means he knows everything pertinent about Megan and me, including the fact that never in a million years would she have copped to having Head Bastard of the Hoffy Men as her very own daddy, not even to her very own girlfriend.

'She didn't tell you, I take it,' he says.

'Tell me what?'

He just shakes his head, amused. 'Every parent knows that the time comes when their child is actively embarrassed to be associated with them, but it still stings when it happens to you.'

It costs me to be this civil, but I pay it. 'What do you want?'

Martin Lugner spreads his hands. 'You were the one who called this meeting, Miss Gray. What's the matter? Cold feet? That's not like you, from what I've heard. You asked for me. You have me. The floor is yours. Show me this evidence you have of nefarious deeds and backhand deals done by moonlight. I'll make sure to investigate any serious claims you have.'

This calm, mature adult routine is a neat trick. Now I feel small and stupid and weak, a seven-year-old child putting on a dance show in the living room for the amused, indulgent adults.

Steady, Alec. At times like these, I like to recall a line from *Pride and Prejudice*: 'My courage always rises with every attempt to intimidate me.'

'I don't have any evidence with me,' I say.

Technically not a lie.

'No? I'm guessing it's all at your house, tucked into a hidey-hole somewhere. Loose floorboard under the bed, perhaps. We could go there now, if you like – 25 Cross Street? The one with the little blue gate, and the honeysuckle bushes in the back garden, and – does your mother still have that giant Paula Rego print hanging in the hallway?'

My blood chills.

'How do you know my house?' I say before I can stop myself.

'How do you think?' Martin replies with an eyebrow raise. 'I've been there before. Many times, when you were smaller. You don't remember me?'

'No.'

'Well,' he comments, 'I flatter myself that I'm rather memorable, but you were quite young.'

'Alec,' Oh says suddenly, 'don't listen to him, whatever he tells you; don't listen to a word he says! He's a lying, backstabbing snake; he'll say anything, and he'll –'

'Peter, stop,' Martin cuts in, visibly upset. 'What is this? Look, I know you've been struggling recently, and I've really been trying to support you, we all have. Now, if you're unhappy with my leadership, you can vote for someone else at the next election, you know that. But in the meantime, as long as you're still in the Hoffy Men – this isn't politics, and it isn't organized religion. This is a brotherhood, founded on mutual respect. So be respectful, please.'

Well, this is just a morning of revelations. No wonder Oh knew so much about the Hoffy Men. Was this why he told me their origin story? Did he want me to find out?

Was he trying to confess?

'I left, Alec,' Oh says to me. I hate the pleading I can hear in his voice. 'I left a long time ago.'

Martin laughs. 'That's not what the current membership list says, Peter.'

'That's because you don't let anyone leave even if they want to, you still bloody *lie* about it and inflate the numbers. I wouldn't be surprised if half the names on your lists are in their graves –'

'Shut up, shut up,' I shout. I'm furious, even more so because I know that's what Martin wants. 'I don't care. I don't care who's a Hoffy Man or not right now, all I care about is the deal I offered. I want to know your answer, and then I'm out of here.'

Martin and Oh are both looking at me.

'All right,' says Martin, folding his hands primly in his lap. 'What do you want, Miss Gray?'

'A guarantee of protection. You're going to drop whatever bullshit lawsuit you've made up against my mother, and you're going to leave us alone. Or the evidence I have goes to the police. OK?'

'A guarantee of protection?' Martin says, a frown creasing his tanned forehead. 'Well, you already have that. You've had it since your father joined, just before you were born. And then Lucas, until his tragedy – but he's still an official member, of course, even in death. Just not an active one, ha ha.' He gives me a gentle smile. 'You're part of the family, Alec. You have been your whole life.'

'Oh called it. You *are* a lying snake.'

Martin shrugs. 'Why don't you ask your father about it? He'll tell you.'

'We're not exactly on speaking terms.'

'How convenient. Well, of course your mother knew all about it, too.'

I can't help it. I glance at Oh.

The fact that he's unable to meet my eyes says more than words.

'I don't give a crap,' I blurt. It is not, admittedly, my most eloquent hour. '*I* never joined, did I? I want *nothing* to do with you!'

'You've had a good education, Alec,' says Martin.

This isn't a conversation – it's a game, and I can't shake this feeling that I'm losing.

'You already said that,' I snap.

'Did you enjoy school?'

'Why are you asking me that? What's that got to do with *anything* right now?'

'Plenty.' Martin's smile has faded. 'I bring it up because we – the people you seem so determined to revile for absolutely no good reason I can see – we paid for it. See, when your father skedaddled a few years ago, he left your mother in a bit of a financial pickle. So she came to us. And we helped, without thinking twice, because that is what we do. That is what we're for. We're a safety net. We're your neighbours, your friends. We're a *community*.' He spreads his hands. 'And you're part of it, whether you like it or not.'

I look at Oh. He's looking at the ground. He won't look at me. He won't even *look* at me.

Panic flutters its sickly wings.

'You're lying,' I try again.

But there are no spiders, no cockroaches, no crickets or moths. Not even a measly fly hovering anywhere in the vicinity of his mouth.

Is that God's doing? No demonically inspired insects allowed in His house? Or is it because my entire life has been a lie, and there isn't an insect big enough in the world to cover it?

A relevant character point at this juncture: I'm a sore loser. It was why we had to stop playing board games at Christmas. I'd scream at Lucas and accuse him of cheating if he won, but our parents always took his side. It made me so *mad*.

Anger is an engine. Sometimes you have to let it drive, get you out of a tight spot.

'Megan was right about you,' I say. 'She told me you were a Class A prick.'

A sudden guffaw bursts out of Oh, quickly stifled.

But not quickly enough. Martin rises from his pew, moves forward and cuffs Oh hard across the mouth.

Oh snaps back, stumbling to one knee.

'He's an old man!' I shout.

'Thanks, Alec,' Oh says thickly, his knotted hands clasped against the side of his face.

Martin looks at me. 'My daughter is an evil little cunt. No wonder she likes you.'

Parental love. Nothing like it in the world.

Martin steps away from the downed Oh and slowly massages his fist.

'Well, I tried,' he says with a sigh in his voice. 'No one can say I didn't try. But look at what happens when the rules are broken.' He looks me up and down. 'Monsters are made. And there is no reasoning with monsters. Stephen, would you? Thanks so much.'

I look at Stephen, who comes towards me. The absolute worst thing about this picture is what he's holding in his hand, which is a syringe, half full of some cloudy liquid and ready to rock.

'No way,' I say, backing up. 'No *way* are you —'

But he is.

Fiction lies to you. Fiction tells you that you can escape, even when you're physically weaker than your opponent, even when it's three against one, even when you've been rendered weaponless and deliberately isolated, even when you're terrified, even when everything, *everything* is stacked against you.

It doesn't take them long. I'm prepared to go down screaming; I'm prepared, at any point along the journey I know we're about to make, to look for my chance, knee someone in the balls, headbutt the second, and run for my life — but as it turns out they're prepared for that too, and it's really hard to do anything much when you've just been injected with a boatload of something that feels like being slowly and surely and inescapably wrapped up in comforting, suffocating cotton clouds.

I'm barely aware, by the time we get to the car, of being bundled into it. I'm barely aware of the road bumping underneath my numbed body as I lie in the back seat, barely aware of the ties digging into my wrists.

Soon enough, I can't even feel them at all.

The Hoffy Men

I bet you can guess where we're going.

My legs are like helium balloons, they want to float away, and the hands around my arms the only things keeping me tethered. Stumbling towards a yawning mouth that wants to gobble me up whole.

Down its throat. Into the belly.

On my knees in the packed, ancient dirt of the Hoffy Man's cave.

I never wanted to see this place again, but as the Rolling Stones philosophize, we can't always get what we want. In this situation, though, I highly doubt that if I try sometimes, I just might find, I'll get what I need.

Robed figures loom and shuffle around me. I feel like I'm surrounded by monks. I think of Oh. Priests of various allegiances seem to figure largely in my life. For some reason this strikes me as absolutely hilarious, but my jaw feels numb and I can't tell if I'm laughing.

One of the robed figures turns its head, enough to let me see his face. It's Justin Gorhammer, the dentist-in-waiting.

The scene is so absurd I want to roll on the floor kicking my feet like a cartoon, but my body is having trouble receiving commands from my brain, which is disconcerting, or it would be if I could feel disconcertment. Disconcertation. Disconcersion? I think I swear out loud.

'Something happens to them down here,' another robed man standing next to Justin mutters to him. 'I mean, look at her. Soon she'll be just as deranged as the other one, just as dangerous.'

'She controls insects,' Justin dreamily replies.

'Right,' the other man says, as if they were agreeing on the proper use of mouthwash. 'You're the victim here, Justin. You won't be free of this nightmare until this is done, OK? Trust me. I've seen it all play out before, and it was *messy*.'

'Hey,' I say, 'hey, fuckers, you just let me out of these hand ties and you'll see how deranged I am.'

But neither of them react, and I'm not sure the words made it to my mouth.

I take a bleary look around. I'm ringed by robed men, circling me ponderously. They are, carefully, it seems to me, keeping a good distance – longer than, say, a lashing leg can reach. But mine is not the only ring o' roses. There's another, a few feet away. In between the legs and swirling hems I can see a crumpled shape on the floor.

It's Viola Gordon.

Her eyes are shut and she's not moving. She must be even more out of it than me.

'For hundreds of years,' intones someone, somewhere – and then I see Martin Lugner standing before the big stone bowl, foxy tanned features draped in a hood – 'this has been a sacred space, kept and guarded and made safe. But when it is profaned, punishment ensues. Our poor lost brothers, Lucas Gray and Scott Poltern, have borne the consequences of that profanity.

But we are here to right that wrong, and our chosen are the perfect atonement.'

Shuffling. Swirling. I'm being moved. I register it several seconds after the fact, too late to react. And even if I could, what would I do? There's at least fifteen of them and one of me, and I'm higher than a blimp right now.

Viola is placed carefully beside me by a man grunting with the effort of her weight. Her eyelids don't even flutter.

I look up at Martin, busy with something deep in the bowl that I can't see from my terrible floor-level vantage point.

'Why is it always women?'

I had no idea I'd actually managed to muse that one out loud until Martin glances down at me.

'It's nothing personal,' he says. 'It's not a misogynistic thing. It's just tradition.'

'Oh good,' I nod. 'I feel much better.'

This is not my first time being stuck in a room offering no clear exits with someone who is absolutely, genuinely barking, and it just gets funnier every time. Suddenly, Catholicism doesn't seem so ridiculous (or at least on a par), with the added bonus of not being hazardous to my health (or at least not directly).

Even through the cushiony drug haze, I'm pretty clear on the direction this is going, and I have to tell you, folks, I don't like it, not one bit. Because I think they're going to kill us. Pretty sure that's what 'righting the wrong' means.

What begets evil?

Fear.

That's what this is about. These men are afraid of me. Of us.

I didn't see it coming. I did not truly believe that they were capable of doing this. But in my defence, ladies and gentlemen of the jury, I ask you: who would? A case in point: I found Mulder annoyingly credulous, and couldn't understand why anyone would ever listen to him over Scully. (Bonus points for her being Catholic too, and not weird or fanatical with it. Representation matters, kids!)

The one comfort I can draw from this situation is that my mother is not going to take the death of both her spawn lying down but, I have to admit, it's a cold one. Any sweet vengeance she can muster is hardly going to benefit me when I've already donned my angel wings, with the added calamity of destroying the rest of her life, too.

It's that thought that snaps my disordered thoughts together. The thought of my mother, left behind, all alone and in ruinous pain.

No.

No.

'Viola,' I hiss. 'Wake up.'

But she doesn't stir.

I am hauled off the ground, pressed forward, pinned against the lip of the bowl, its thick, worn stone digging savagely into my hips. I stare down into its stained curve, stare down at the long knife at its bottom. The knife has a pearlescent handle and a wicked point.

Panic, a small voice kept at bay by the drugs, tells me to just charge through them all and run, but my body is made of clouds and my bones are rubber, and I am helplessly pinned by the weight at my back, pressed so hard against the bowl edge that I can barely draw a good breath.

Droning. Chanting. Can't make out what they're saying – too busy panicking. My right arm is freed and held out poker straight across the bowl. Martin has the knife in his hand. He reaches out, slowly strokes my arm, I wonder what he's doing, it seems almost a tender gesture – and then blood, as shiny red as pomegranate seeds, beads along my arm, swells into a river, bursts its banks and drips into the bowl below, plinking into the ancient cracks at its bottom.

And that's when things get, if you can believe it, even stranger.

The shadows in the cave are moving. There, over Martin's shoulder. The walls are crawling, and walls don't normally crawl. The shadows coalesce, gathering like a swarm of bees, locusts, thickening. Tendrils extend, slither over the shoulders and heads of the robed men surrounding me, creeping around their necks, fastening over their skulls. As if each of them wears a squid made of darkness, attached to them, sucking greedily from their marrow.

The drug they gave me – it must be a triple concentration of whatever Scott dosed me with. On that, I saw a tarantula. On this – I see Lovecraft's take on hell.

It isn't real! my brain screams at me. But it doesn't matter. It looks real, so it feels real.

Is this what Lucas was seeing? No wonder he lost his mind. Oh god, Lucas, I'm sorry. Did you deserve this? Did you really?

A commotion behind me. A panicked shout.

I see Martin hesitate, looking up.

Run, Alec!

I feel myself buck reflexively, and the weight pinning me to the bowl is gone in a sudden ecstasy of relief. I fall to my hands and knees amid cacophony, shouts and grunts and shuffles of feet and falling bodies.

I start moving away. Someone kicks me in the side and it momentarily doubles me up, but it doesn't come again – an accidental flail, it seems like, because clearly I'm surrounded by a panic-demic, limbs a-flail as robed men try to get away or fall like me. I crawl, I manage to stagger upright . . .

. . . and then I see Viola.

She's awake.

She stands in the middle of the cave, staring around her balefully. Her face is streaked with tears, her body trembling. Robed men panic and scream around her, but she remains untouched – and I think I can piece together why. Surrounding her is a scene straight out of a Hieronymus Bosch painting.

Demons.

The cave is full of demons.

Distorted, nightmarish forms circle, tug at, crawl on, squeeze and stroke each robed man. Pleading, gibbering, weeping, screaming, or just gaping silently with a mouth like a ragged tear. Justin weeps on his knees in front of a female figure whose features run like tar, her black hands extended towards his face.

If I am hallucinating, so is everyone else. Did they all take the drug?

It's a torture scene, their own horrors and sins made visible, and by god if it doesn't look like Viola is the one doing it to them. She stands, her expression distorted with cold, implacable fury, while the men around her stumble to their knees or press up into corners, writhing, crying, silent with eyes shut as if it'll make their nightmares go away.

A sudden, deafening boom. Viola jerks. Behind her, the wall erupts in a spray of packed dirt.

Martin Lugner is on his knees. Demons claw at his back. One is wrapped like a jellyfish around his head. There are dozens of them, dozens, mewling, pawing, sobbing in his ear, prowling in front of his face. In his hand is a gun.

Of course. He's the kind of man who'd own a gun.

Another deafening shot. Viola is still standing, but the gun in Martin's hands points away from her, wildly swinging this way and that.

He's trying to shoot his demons.

He gets a nearby robed brother in the leg, and the man goes down with a squeal. Men run into each other, trip over each other, push and shove and punch, sudden savage hysteria erupting in front of my eyes. Men take wild swings at each other and at the demons gnawing at their backs and begging at their fronts.

'Let's go,' hisses a voice next to me.

It's Viola. She takes hold of my blood-streaked arm and jerks it. My fascinated anthropological stupor dissipates fast. Feet slipping on hard rock, legs of jelly and a brain of fuzz, I follow her darting form, slipping and sliding and sidestepping dangerous moving obstacles like a real-life Frogger. One robed man makes a grab for me – I feel him clutch the back of my shirt and my brain gives me, for my viewing pleasure, a quick rundown of that heart-freezing scene in *The Texas Chain Saw Massacre* (*thank you, brain!*) – but I wiggle free of his grip and dart up the tunnel, expecting to be grabbed every step of the way.

Outside is sunny and warm and impossibly bright, and on one of the darkest days of my life, too, which just goes to show that the weather doesn't much care what's happening beneath it. Pathetic fallacy be damned.

I stagger after Viola, who seems determined not to stop for anything or anyone. We make it halfway up the cave's surrounding field in total silence, save the rustling of corn all around us.

'Wait,' I gasp. 'Wait, wait.'

Viola turns, chest heaving, staring at me like I've lost my mind. I see her gaze dart anxiously behind me, but for the moment we're not being followed.

'You can see them too, right?' I ask.

'See what?' Viola says, but she knows.

'It's you, isn't it?' I say. 'Justin. Scott. And my brother. You made them see demons. You're the one who's been torturing them.'

Viola says nothing, which says everything.

Looks like I'm not the only one who came out of that cave with a trick. Except, look, that's not possible, is it? It's not possible. It's just really powerful drugs.

So what are the insects about? I haven't been on drugs when I saw them, not once. And they're real to the people around me, too. That's no hallucination.

What's happening to me? Am I losing my mind? Does it run in the family?

A dull boom sounds from underneath our feet – another gunshot – and the ground shivers faintly. Whatever's happening down there, it doesn't sound good.

I can hear shouts rolling out from the tunnel's mouth. The drugs they gave me muffle emotions, but it's as though the memory of fear gets me moving. Viola's already off again, and for the lack of a better plan, I follow.

'I don't have my car,' I pant.

'I have mine,' Viola shoots back. 'Stop talking and keep running!'

I have time to wonder what exact set of circumstances led Viola to willingly drive here and get sacrificed – I remember Martin saying her father has gambling debts, and god knows what else is going on, because there's nowt so queer as folk, nor so secretive, and when you start overturning family rocks some crazy-looking bugs can get exposed, blinking their eyes and waving their feelers in the light – and thus occupied, I come at last to Viola's second great reveal.

Because when we crest the ridge and pass through the field's big gate and wind through a dozen parked cars and I see the one Viola is making for, I stop dead.

She tugs the driver door wide open and looks impatiently up at me.

'Come on!' she hisses.

I take a step back.

'I have no idea what your game is,' I say slowly, 'and I don't care. You need to stay away from me, Viola. You understand? Stay the hell *away*.'

I leave her there open-mouthed and dart away between cars, making for the adjacent field. I'll run across every damn farm in the area if I have to.

Trust No 1. That had been Fox Mulder's watchword, which I had adopted as my security password for years in homage. But I had trusted, and I was a fool.

My mind whirs as I run, as though all the frantic, terrified exercise has cranked up my mental faculties at the same time.

The Porsche that started following me just after I crashed Viola's photoshoot. The same car that was waiting for me at my house, and then drove away when Scott showed up.

It's Viola's car.

Christien wasn't lying about not having his Porsche any more. He must have given it to Viola – or she really did steal it from him. Which means she was the slender figure in baseball cap and sunglasses I've been seeing everywhere – the one who stalked Megan and me in the woods, tortured Scott at the beach party, spray-painted 'MURDERER' across my car and then tried to run over my girlfriend.

It was Viola Gordon. All of it.

This is someone who can conjure men's demons and torture them until they break. Until they can't stand it any more, and take matters into their own hands. I'm almost more afraid of her than I am of the Hoffy Men. At least when they try to kill me they're upfront about it.

But why has she been stalking me? Was Scott's death not enough? Was my *brother's* death not enough? Gotta go after the peripherals too, just to make sure everyone in the family suffers?

I hear cries in the distance. The rats have made it out. I hear car engines. Tyre squeals.

I don't have my phone. I don't have back-up. But I have my legs, and I thank god for them.

And then I hear my name.

'Alec? Alec!'

It's my mother's voice. And then I see her, cresting the ridge like a miracle, with Oh beside her. He must have gone straight to her after they took me, told her what had happened. She's here, she's here and she's looking for me.

I run towards them both.

The Pelican Brief

The three of us sit around the kitchen table.

I have had a shower. Two glasses of water and a mug of rapidly cooling tea sit barely touched before me.

Silence reigns.

'We need to take you to the hospital,' my mother says again.

'I'm fine,' I croak.

'Just to get you checked over prop–'

'I'm *fine*.'

I'm not. Whatever they gave me in that syringe, the fun parts have worn off, leaving behind a streak of fire on my arm from where Martin cut me, plus the bonus of feeling like my insides have been covered in slime. The walls around me don't seem as substantial as they used to, as though at any moment they could melt, dripping on to the floor and revealing the writhing demons that live inside them, always, waiting for sin so they can come out and feed.

I try to shake it off.

Oh's hands are on the table, his knotted fingers playing and twisting with each other, his nervous habit. But he doesn't speak, as though it's not his place to take the lead.

My mother is equally silent, a worried look on her face like I'm a cracked china cup, and if she takes her eye off me for one second I'll shatter. There's nothing like someone constantly acting as though you're about to break to make you feel like you're about to break.

There's only one way out of the deadlock.

'I call Mickey's Donuts,' I say.

My mother frowns.

'One for each right answer,' I insist.

Invoking Mickey's Donuts is serious business. They've been the best in town for twenty years, a true-blue staple of deep-fried comfort and rare reward, and they've seen us through many an emotional low. Mickey's is for when serious shit is on the table.

For a long, terrible moment I think she's going to say no.

'There are three of us,' she points out.

'I'll referee,' Oh offers.

I look at him. 'I've got questions for you too.'

His presses his lips into a guilty line.

'I'll go first.' I wrap my fingers around the mug in front of me. The tea's gone tepid and the mug is cold, but it still helps to have something to hold on to. 'So, Dad was in the Hoffy Men.'

My mother sighs. It is the sigh of ages, of aeons, of pent-up secrets that poison slowly over time, that wither away your tongue until you feel you couldn't even speak them any more, let alone leach yourself of their insidious toxicity.

Something like that, anyway.

'One apple glaze,' she says, invoking a hallowed Mickey's flavour as a yes.

My smile is the bitter kind of triumph. 'And you're in the Kindly Ones.'

'I *was*. Not any more.'

'Still counts.'

Begrudgingly, she replies, 'One maple syrup with pecan topping.'

'A Hoffy Man and a Kindly One. Can't imagine that pairing working out well.' I hesitate. 'Is that why you . . .?'

'There were a lot of reasons for our divorce.' Her turn to hesitate. 'That was one of them. An ongoing point of contention, you might say.'

'Why didn't you tell me?'

'Why didn't you tell *me*, Alec? I had to wait until the police were knocking on our door to find out?'

'Ellie,' Oh says softly.

My mother backs down.

'One apple glaze, one maple pecan.' He nods to me. 'Next question.'

'Is Dad the reason Martin Lugner knows where we live?' I ask.

My mother replies, 'Martin used to come over for dinner, sometimes, when you were a baby.'

I make a face of disgust. 'Oh, *god*.'

'I didn't like it much either,' she admits. 'He wasn't their leader back then, but he was always a slimy toad.'

I study her. The moment you realize that your parents have whole entire lives of their own, decades of memories and choices and mistakes lived before you were ever born, that inside they are filled with landscapes alien to you that you will never walk, is one of the stranger moments of being someone's kid.

'I was trying to protect you,' my mother says, and the failure in her voice cuts me. 'That's why I didn't tell you about any of it. I didn't want you getting sucked in like . . . like Lucas did.'

A jolt runs through me. It's the first time we've spoken his name aloud in months, and I'm dismayed to see that it hurts me to hear her say it about as much as I thought it was hurting her.

'How did he find out about it all?' I ask.

'The Hoffy Men approached him to join. Can you believe it? That's Martin's doing, all over.' She sounds savagely furious. 'When he told Oh, I nearly lost my mind.'

I look up at Oh. At his grave, kindly face. He nods at my expression.

'Confession,' he says. 'Lucas told me at confession.'

'And you told Mom.'

He looks pained, and I get it. That was quite the betrayal of Lucas's trust.

'They get their claws in you, you're cooked,' he says. 'I left years ago, but you never really leave. Not really. They follow you around forever. Tainting everything. I had to tell your mother. I wanted to save him before –'

He stops.

He swallows.

'Before it was too late for him,' he mutters. 'I failed, of course.'

My mother puts her hand on top of his. This simple touch, the sight of her slender fingers on his gnarled, bony knuckles, is somehow the most heart-wrenching thing I've ever seen. It speaks essays, all at once, about compassion, the passage of time, bonds forged over years, help, pity, love.

'We both did, in our different ways,' she says simply.

I want to cry.

'I don't get it,' I mutter. 'I don't get how they turned him.'

'What do you mean?'

I can't say it out loud. I still can't say it.

My mother is staring at me. She can read me like a book. One reason I don't enjoy being around her when I've got a secret to keep.

'Oh, Alec,' she says, 'No. You think he *became* one of them? Is that what you've thought all this time?'

'He did.'

'No.'

'Mom,' I say in my don't-push-this voice, 'trust me. I heard it from the horse's mouth.'

'From who?'

'Scott and Justin. They were there too. The three of them did the ritual down in the cave with this girl, Viola –'

'No,' my mother cuts in, shaking her head like she doesn't want to hear it. 'No, Lucas wasn't like that. He didn't do that.'

'Yes,' I say, my temper making a sudden bolt for it, 'he did. Golden boy was so desperate to join the satanic mafia that he went and roofied a girl and then –'

'No.' Her voice is climbing over mine. 'No, he didn't! Those boys – how would you even know they were telling you the truth?'

'So they're just a couple of evil manipulative liars, and Lucas hauled his halo with him down into that cave?!'

'Yes, Alec, *yes*!'

'How can you possibly think that?'

'Because after Lucas joined the Hoffy Men, he turned on them. He *turned* on them, Alec; he was trying to expose them, and I have the evidence to prove it!'

She's heaving. We both are. I look at Oh.

He gives me a small nod.

'What evidence?' I ask.

There we stand, Mom and I, in front of the locked door. Oh has stayed in the kitchen to give us space.

With trembling fingers, my mother produces a key, turns it in the lock, and opens it up.

It's been more than seven months since I've seen my brother's room, and it does not resemble the memory I have in my head.

Lucas was always aesthetically minded – what kind of teenage jockboy insists on picking out his own laundry hamper so that it matches the duck-egg-blue wall? – and his bed was always made, movie and band posters on the wall each safely ensconced behind glass frames and never askew. Little work desk underneath the window bare of accoutrements save his laptop and a couple of modest-sized speakers. Tasteful. Spartan. Clean.

This bedroom looks like those guys who got obsessed with the Zodiac Killer moved in.

There's an honest-to-god whiteboard, covered in frenetic spider diagrams. Box files and file boxes, folders scattered across the creased bed, piles of newspapers on the floor that just scream hoarder decor. And in the midst of it all, my mother, ladies and gentlemen, standing defiant.

My mouth opens.

Closes.

'Well, he's a very quiet conspiracy theorist, at least,' I say.

'Who?'

'The ex-member of *The Lone Gunmen* that we've apparently rented our spare room to. Mom, what the hell?'

'Language,' says my mother automatically. 'We're building a case. Against the Hoffy Men.'

I digest. I wander over to the whiteboard. I look at the names there. The photographs. The scribbled theories that end in ?!? a lot.

'Silver fox,' I say at last. 'Your boyfriend. When I busted in on you two smooching in the kitchen, Lucas's bedroom door was open.'

'Walter has a big practice in London now, but he grew up around here,' she quietly replies. 'His father was a Hoffy Man, and when his father died, he left behind a small but interesting collection of evidence on the organization. Walter started trying to add to it himself.'

That's why Lucas's room was open that day. He and my mother were in here, working the case.

'*This* is the big secret project you've been obsessing over the last few months,' I say, as it dawns. 'All the time spent at the office. All those late nights. It was about this.'

'I've had to do it on top of my normal job,' she says apologetically. 'It's been overwhelming, to tell the truth. I feel like I haven't had a good night's sleep in a year.'

All this time, we've been working the same damn case. And Oh was the only one who knew it. He knew what I was getting into. He knew Mom was working on the same thing. He knew about the Kindly Ones too, which means he must have had a pretty good idea who sent me the invite, and he told me to go.

He saw the Hoffy Men circling me and sent me to the only protection he could think of.

All his desperate attempts to get Mom and I to talk to each other. If we had . . .

'I should have listened to him,' I say aloud.

'To who?' my mother asks.

I just shake my head. 'Why didn't you tell me about this?'

'I'm sorry,' she replies, still flushed. 'If I'd done that, I'd have had to tell you all of it. Since the beginning. Your dad . . . all of it. I worked very, very hard to keep you out of it. Both of you. And I failed. Twice.'

It's strange being in my brother's room, now. Complex. There are too many feelings, each one nesting in the next like Russian dolls. I try to set them all aside and concentrate on the now.

'So his sudden interest in feverishly collecting books on local folklore and demonology primers was not the product of an addled mind?' I muse. 'Wow. Colour my cheeks red. All this time I thought he was going insane, but now I see he was just really getting into his new studies.'

My mother sighs. Sinks on to a free patch of his bed. She pats the covers, but I stand resolute.

'Lucas was trying to play double agent,' she says. 'He thought if he got in deep with them, he could find concrete evidence he could use to expose them. But they don't keep paper trails and video footage all conveniently locked up in a handy safe somewhere. This isn't a *Mission: Impossible* movie, they're too clever for that. Even Walter's evidence is pretty thin. And Lucas was too junior for them to trust him anyway. But I only know all this from reading his diaries. He wouldn't talk to us about it, and I couldn't keep him from pursuing it. You think I'm this controlling bear, but when either of you set your mind to something, there was nothing I could ever do about it. Especially the last few years, when it's only been me.'

I'd never thought of us like that. I'd always seen me as the loner handful, and Lucas as the compliant golden boy. Them versus me. Perversely it makes me feel closer to him, this assessment of us. This dogged, not-altogether-healthy trait we share.

'I found all this stuff he'd squirrelled away under his bed,' she continues. 'He always cleaned and tidied his room himself, there was never any reason I'd go looking. Anyway, I believed in you having some privacy. Some agency and independence in your lives. Perhaps to a fault.' She eyes me. 'I wish, more than anything, he'd felt like he could tell me. I wish that for you too.'

'Did he . . . did he rape Viola?'

'No!' But she can't maintain it. 'I don't . . . I don't know. Only the people involved know the truth on that, and two of them are dead. Look, Alec. I don't know what was going through your brother's head at the time. All I know is that he turned against it. Maybe he was trying to make amends. I don't know. But they must have found out.'

It's the funny look on her face that triggers it.

'Oh my god.' I blink. 'You don't think it was suicide. You think *they* killed him because he was playing double agent?'

When she says nothing, confirming my ludicrous pronouncement, I can't help it.

'Mom. That's . . .' *Crazy.*

Her smile is bitter. 'Trust me, I know how it sounds. Juno had the same look on her face when I aired my theories to her.'

She throws her hands up. 'I was stupid enough to go to her with all this. I asked her to get another coroner to re-examine Lucas's body. Just see if there was any suggestion of murder. A second opinion. Juno refused point blank. We had a bad fight. Her girlfriend Martha was the coroner who ruled his death a suicide, and I suppose Juno didn't like my implication that Martha had missed something.'

Yowser.

'Juno told me I had to let it go. To move on. All those healthy things.' My mother looks around the room. 'Maybe I should have.'

She looks so frail, sitting there on Lucas's bed with her hands folded in her lap and her shoulders hunched, with her cheap black work shoes and her bargain basement shirt. Suddenly I love her so fiercely that I want to scream and throw knives into the wall.

I go to my mother, sit beside her, take her hand in mine.

Lucas kept his investigations a secret from us. My mother kept her investigations a secret from me. And I kept my investigations a secret from her. Liars all, and all in the name of protection.

My father's favourite saying, the one he would pull out at any given opportunity, was *The road to hell is paved with good intentions*. It was one of his more annoying habits.

Still. Some truth there, I guess.

'What a family,' I say.

My mother gives a shaky laugh. 'Oh, the best. The Notorious Grays.'

'You think *they* have *our* photos up on a wall? Throw darts into them, that sort of thing?'

'I certainly hope so.'

Then, quietly, because I'm afraid of it: 'Are we really going to lose our house?'

She sighs. 'No, we're not.'

'But Juno said they're coming after you with that lawsuit.'

'They're just trying to crash my business with false accusations. It's all completely made up, and it'll be cleared up.'

'But . . . if they succeed.'

'It won't come to that.' She grips my hand. 'We're close, Alec. Walter and I, we really have something here.' Her free hand gestures around the Zodiac Killer room. 'This is how we win. But in the meantime, you have to stay off their radar. Please. We can't afford to get tangled in police investigations. We can't afford to jeopardize any of this. It's why I've kept the door locked, everything secret, no one in on this but Walter and me. They've come after you because of me. They want to hurt you because of me. It was a warning.' I actually feel a tremble run through her, connected by hands as we are. 'I will bury them for all they've done to us. *Bury them*. But the Kindly Ones' way isn't the way. *This* is the way. The right way, through the proper channels. Legitimized. Official. Justice, out where everyone can see it.'

When my father asked me, aged seven, what I thought I wanted to be when I grew up, my primly direct answer had been, 'Anything that isn't a lawyer.' It became a family joke. Now it's not so funny. I can't even get involved, help them out. I was so set on that intellectually alluring but utterly useless philosophy degree that I have amassed zero applicable skills. What am I going to contribute, an interpretive essay on the ethical implications of secret cults? As it stands, at best I'm a clueless nuisance. At worst I'm going to ruin everything with my bull-in-a-china-shop approach to uncovering the truth.

I guess she's right. Now I've done my detective schtick and uncovered everything she already knows, I've got nothing else to offer. The best way I can help right now is to lie low. Which, as we all know, is a well-established Alec Gray approach to life and something I am really good at.

The doorbell rings.

We look at each other, hearts pounding as one.

I hear the scrape of a chair in the kitchen, where Oh has been tactfully waiting all this time. The tread of his footsteps in the hallway.

'Mom,' I say urgently. 'What is he doing? What if it's . . .'

Martin Lugner with a chainsaw, is what I want to say, but there's no need to spell it out – we're both off Lucas's bed and down the hallway in less time than it takes a bull to charge a red rag.

'Oh, don't!' I call, but too late.

'Hello!' I hear Oh saying through the wide-open front door. 'Who are you looking for, then?'

An indistinct reply – but not the sound of a chainsaw revving up, and the voice is too high and soft to be male . . .

I reach Oh and peer over his shoulder.

It's Megan.

She sees me.

'You're safe!' she says. 'God, thank god. I didn't know. You weren't answering your phone. I didn't know what to think. But you're safe.'

She stands on my doorstep, body tense. Her eyes are puffy and rimmed red, her hair an afterthought. She wears dowdy joggers, a shapeless hoodie and an ancient-looking pair of Converse. Her hands clutch tightly at the straps of an enormous backpack, the kind made for high-altitude trekking in Peru. It bulges, stuffed to the brim.

'So are you,' I say.

My mother appears at my side.

'Oh,' I cast around. 'Um, Mom, this is Megan. Megan Lugner.'

I hear my mother's indrawn breath as the name hits. Watch her as she scans the girl before her, taking in the state of her.

'What happened?' I ask.

Megan's hands are so tight around her backpack straps that her knuckles have gone white.

'I left,' she says. 'I left home. Couldn't stay in that house, around *him*.'

'I'm so sorry,' I say.

'No, I am. I am. Sorry for all of it.'

I turn to my mother.

'Megan's my . . . friend,' I say. 'She's in the Kindly Ones.'

My mother's gaze is as penetrative as a searchlight. 'I know.'

'They say they'll protect me,' Megan says. 'Juno says. But . . . I don't have anywhere to stay, right now.'

My mother and I lock eyes, a silent plea in mine.

'You can stay here for a couple of days,' she says to Megan. 'It's safe here.'

I want to tap dance in jubilation.

Relief etched across her face, Megan comes inside.

Picnic at Hanging Rock

It's the kind of bright, clear day that feels freshly washed.

The clouds are occasional white cotton balls scattered across an endless blue sheet. The park the Kindly Ones have chosen for the picnic is a family affair, kids running around, an ice-cream van tinkling cheerfully in the background. We have gathered here today, sisters, to celebrate.

The Hoffy Men's cave, you see, is no more.

It's the talk of the town. The headline: during a 'routine inspection' a group of local businessmen were carrying out of the old mine's viability to be repurposed, that rickety piece of crap started shedding bits of its unsteady walls and damn near buried everyone in it alive.

Luckily – or unluckily, depending on how vicious one is feeling – the businessmen all managed to escape unharmed.

'It's a pity,' Tippi grumbles darkly as she sits cross-legged on a blanket, one hand throwing Ruffles potato chips into her mouth and the other clutching a plastic cup of the most lethal Pimm's ever concocted by woman.

The woman in this case being Juno's coroner girlfriend Martha, who I've never met before today – a curvaceous, warm person with an infectious smile. That she both handles death and can cause it via the strength of her homemade cocktails is all I know of her, but I like her already.

'What's a pity?' I ask Tippi.

'That none of them died in that cave-in,' she replies. 'Problem solved.'

I tut. 'Murder should always be a last resort, Tippi.'

'I don't see why,' she protests. 'Animals kill each other all the time. And some places have the death penalty, besides.'

'We're better than animals,' I say.

'No, we're not.'

'No,' I agree, 'we're not, but we should at least try to be. Otherwise what's the point of all this consciousness stuff? Hell, why even have civilizations? Let's just *Mad Max* it. I'd nail the Thunderdome, and you'd make a fine young cannibal.'

'I'm vegan.'

'The most bloodthirsty vegan I've ever met,' Juno comments as she joins us.

'It's the lack of iron,' I say. 'It makes them irritable.'

Juno clinks her plastic cup against mine.

The Hoffy Men's official version of cave-in events, of course, mentions nothing about the involvement of two kidnapped and drugged young women. I myself remain in utter confusion over what really happened, and Viola, the only person who could help me put the pieces together, has disappeared from my life this past week. No more masked slender figures stalking me, no more Porsche sightings. Even her livestreaming has stopped, though she's still posting online every day, so at least I know she's not dead.

Truthfully, I'm relieved. I don't want another confrontation with her, and I may never know what she got out of stalking me, but I don't think I need to know.

I'll only admit it to you, dear reader, but she scares me.

In the sober light of day, the whole thing in the cave feels like one bad acid trip. My former conviction that Viola's been siccing demons on the boys who attacked her and driving them to suicidal despair now seems blushingly ridiculous. In cases such as these, it is wise to recall Occam's razor. The simplest explanation here being that I had a decent case of drug-induced hallucinatory hysteria, and managed to escape a kidnapping intended to intimidate me – or worse.

The Hoffy Men, for their part, are never going to admit that I was there. And as long as I don't say anything public about it, they may well leave me alone.

May.

May not.

Either way, robust protection in the form of a newly united Kindly Ones seems the way to go, *n'est-ce pas?*

I watch with amusement as Juno quizzes Tippi on her life and Tippi stutters her way through her answers. She seems in awe of Juno, as do the rest of my peers. Some unspoken consensus has her as de facto leader of the older generation of Kindly Ones, as Megan is the ship steerer for the younger ones.

Or rather, was.

'Where's Megan today?' Juno asks Tippi, as if she just read my mind.

Tippi cuts a look at me. 'Uh . . .'

'She didn't come today because she's not feeling too good,' I supply.

Megan has spent the last week at my house, hiding out with my mother and me while she figures out how to extricate herself from under her father's dark shadow. She's old enough for legal emancipation, and apparently it's not that complicated a process. (It's useful having a lawyer in the family.) After some understandable initial wariness, considering her familial connections, my mother has taken to Megan in her plight. Megan, for her part, seems determined to get my mother to like her.

'You're friends with her?' Juno asks me in surprise.

'Rather more than friends.' Tippi leers.

Juno's mouth falls open. 'Megan's your . . . girlfriend?'

'Something like,' I say, knowing I'm blushing and cursing all capillaries.

Juno cocks her head. 'How did that happen?'

'Meet-cute, flirtation, bonding over a succession of traumatic events, the usual.'

'Did she approach you?'

I shrug, puzzled at Juno's sudden intensity. 'Er . . . I don't think so, we just randomly met in the woods one day. Why?'

'Just curious,' Juno says, after a heavy pause.

'Megan was the reason for the recent schism in the group,' Tippi fake-whispers, her eyes wide at me. '*Some* people thought that she was a spy for daddy. Which is obviously ridiculous, considering how much she hates him. How much she risked by turning against him.'

Juno skewers Tippi with a look. 'Her being a Lugner had nothing do to with it, Tippi.'

'Oh no?' Tippi bats back, hostile.

'Come on,' I say quickly, trying to de-escalate, 'if *I* don't hold her father against her, neither should anyone else. She's on the good side.'

A pause. Juno seems to be searching for the right thing to say.

'The Lugners are a damaged family,' she finally replies.

'So are the Grays.' I laugh. 'Don't look so worried! She'll be fine. The sun is shining. We're here. We're alive. It's all good.'

But Juno does not look reassured. Her mouth opens, her frown deepens – and then her gaze sharpens, focusing beyond me.

'What the fu–'

Marching across the lawn like a phalanx of killjoys comes a knot of policemen. They trample through our picnic area, scattering dirt and grass into paper plates of food, knocking over drinks, leaving surprised and angry 'Heys!' in their wake.

Leading them is Officer Harry Piscowicz. Right behind him is Officer 'Alec Gray sucks' Graham. And, my god, bringing up the rear, flanked by two young, silent bobbies, is the chief inspector himself, he of the walrus moustache and cold shark eyes.

Officer Piscowicz stops right in front of us.

Me. In front of me.

I see my future flash before my eyes. They've falsified evidence, finally found a reason to arrest me for Scott's death. Or – hell, why stop there? Why not just pin the entire cave collapse on me? I'd be almost upset if they lowballed the drama. If I'm going down, I want to go down for multiple offences in a blaze of high-achieving glory.

'Juno DiCanso and Martha Watts, you're under arrest,' says Officer Piscowicz, 'for conspiracy to cover up the murders of Lucas Gray and Scott Poltern.'

Picture the scene.

Juno has half turned towards Martha, her mouth open and her face alarmed.

Martha has half turned towards the new arrivals, her wide mouth caught in a grin, mid-laugh at the conversation she's having with two other Kindly Ones.

A tableau of laughing, animated women clutching cups of fresh Pimm's and sagging paper plates loaded with potato salad and quiche, women in various attitudes of startling over the disturbance. All around us – sunshine dappling the grass. Nearby kids and families in mid-cavorting play.

'You have the right to remain silent,' Officer Piscowicz continues in a loud, firm voice. 'Anything you say can and will be used against you in a court of law. You have the right to an attorney. If you cannot afford an attorney, one will be provided for you. Do you understand the rights I have just read to you?'

'Juno?' Martha asks in a small, frightened voice.

Juno swallows.

'Harry,' she says quietly, 'what are you doing?'

'I'm doing my job, ma'am,' Officer Piscowicz replies. His face is steel, and he must have the balls to match.

Around me, the group erupts. Camera phones come out one by one like the stars, recording. Martha clings to Juno's side. Juno takes her hand and glances towards the back of the phalanx. She locks eyes with the chief inspector.

I'm still standing right next to her, so I just about catch the words Juno tosses to him.

'Our deal's off, I take it?' she says.

The chief inspector doesn't even acknowledge her.

Juno snorts while several Kindly Ones swirl and snarl around her. When Officer Piscowicz tries to separate her hand from Martha's to cuff her, she shakes him off.

Her gaze sweeps the camera phones – and then lands on me.

'What's going on, Juno?' I ask, with all the calm a gal can muster.

'Alec –' She shakes her head, but nothing else comes out.

Alec, your brother was murdered.

Alec, I knew about it.

Alec, I lied to your mother.

A howling denial would be favourite, but one of the above would do.

So I ask again. 'What's going on?'

'Captain DiCanso,' Officer Piscowicz calls over the top of the action, 'if you resist arrest –'

'Juno, what do we do?' Martha asks in a frightened hiss. 'What do we do?'

'I'm not resisting arrest,' Juno snaps, 'this will all be sorted out, I promise –'

The Kindly Ones bay and growl – but some stand still, apart. Some whisper behind fingers.

'Juno,' I call. 'Seriously.'

Juno's back is straight and her eyes are on the phones like she's at a press conference.

'This is ridiculous,' she declares to her audience. 'It is not true. No one here is, or has ever been, involved in any conspiracies to cover up murder!'

Juno's eyes don't quite meet mine.

Then she says suddenly, 'Ow!'

Officer Piscowicz is pulling at her wrists, about to cuff her – then he shouts as Juno ducks, jerking away from him.

'Runner!' he calls, and then stops in astonishment. They all do, watching the women around them dance and jerk and squeal.

The reason for that is all the wasps.

They're everywhere. There are clouds of them in the air. It's like a scene from *Candyman*. They crawl all over Juno, all over Martha. They buzz and dive-bomb several other Kindly Ones. Some women stand stock-still, watching the inexplicable chaos open-mouthed (*Don't do that*, I want to advise), while others scream and duck and run. Several peel off from the group and streak across the park. Two police officers break away from their phalanx to give chase. Officer Piscowicz and two more of his helpers finally slap their cuffs on a wriggling Juno and a crying Martha and haul them out of the angry, buzzing cloud.

I step back, carefully, watching the picnic collapse. Paper plates and picnic blankets and wicker hampers and quiche and salad and cups of Pimm's abandoned in the melee.

A hand grabs my upper arm, and I flinch.

'Come away from it, you'll get stung!' Tippi shouts in my face.

'I don't think so,' I reply, but she doesn't hear me, frog-marching me away from the madness.

'Come on, come on,' Tippi says wildly. 'God, that was *crazy*. It was like one of the plagues of Egypt. We'll go in my car.'

'Go where?' I say as I'm pulled along.

'To the station, of course! This is insane! They're innocent! It's the most ridiculous accusation! We'll picket outside and raise the biggest stink until they're released!'

I examine Tippi. No wasps on her. No stings. I don't think she knew.

Then I think of how many women in the group were being pelted by wasps. Plenty of others knew, though, didn't they?

I pull my arm out of Tippi's grip.

'I'll follow you,' I say, 'in my car.'

She nods, grim-faced, and thankfully keeps moving quick enough that she doesn't see me slap a hand over my mouth.

Just in case.

I watch her leave. Look around to make sure no one is watching me. Then, palm stitched to lips and feeling pretty ridiculous about how I must look, I walk quickly away, in the opposite direction from my car.

Into the trees.

The Cabin in the Woods

One must allow that the police can actually get it right, every once in a while. Statistically speaking, it's practically a certainty.

Still. A conspiracy to cover up murder, one involving Juno, her coroner girlfriend Martha, and half the Kindly Ones? Who did the murdering? Who would they risk their careers to protect?

Not a Hoffy Man – no way. But another woman . . . especially one who might have had just cause . . .

What if Viola didn't just punish Lucas and Scott with demonic visitations for their transgression against her? What if she went all the way?

No. Lucas killed himself.

What if he didn't? What if his suicide was staged, just like Mom suspected, and Juno and Martha covered up any telltale evidence that it was murder? Only it wasn't the Hoffy Men who were responsible. It was their victim.

Then why would she spray-paint 'murderer' on your car?

She's in denial? Transference? Crazy people do crazy things?

I'm so preoccupied in arguing with myself and marching among the trees, I don't even notice where I've been heading all this time.

Lucas's grave site. It's right there, up ahead. I've memorized the exact configuration of oak and ash. I know which tree he was found under. Now I know that he must have been placed there after he was killed. Killed. Placed. Staged. Posed. I'll have time to feel sick to my soul later, once the adrenaline has worn off. I guess my mother isn't so paranoid, after all. She'll be able to crow about this forever – god, how annoying.

(Black humour, kids, remember?)

I don't even know what I'm looking for. Any evidence would be long gone. It's pointless being here. It's dark under this canopy of trees, although in a complete lack of deference to current events, beyond the darkness the sun still shines.

Still, I owe the next discovery to summer's full bloom, I suppose, because the thickly leafed branches make enough of a difference that the light catches my eye – a different sort of light to the sun, artificial and shining at eye level through the trees not far away.

That cabin. The one I saw over the ridge, the day I met Megan. The one that had a tall, slender figure in a baseball cap and giant, probably-Prada sunnies obscuring her pretty face next to it, watching us. The figure I now know was Viola. It's that same cabin – only now the lights are on, and lines of light are leaking through the windows like a beacon in the shade.

I don't think. I just approach, crouching low to the ground, trying not to make any noise.

The curtains are drawn, so I can't see inside. Damn it, I'm going to have to get closer. I tiptoe on to the porch, heart so high in my mouth I feel like it's beating on my teeth. No noise. No movement inside.

Well, I've come this far, and I've got nothing to lose.

I reach out and grasp the door handle. I'm no lock-picking Dodger, but I'll smash it in if I have to –

The handle turns easily and the door offers up an open sliver.

I grasp my travel hairspray in my pocket, thumbing off the cap. With my free hand I swing the door open wide. Clamp shut on that ridiculous human urge to announce myself by calling hello. Stand in the doorway, ears pricked harder than a dog waiting for dinner.

All is still, but I give it just one more second. And another. Have you learned nothing from the movies? The minute you start to relax –

– a girl comes barrelling towards the door and knocks you both to the floor, winding the absolute shit out of you. My weaponized hairspray arm is pinned down by her weight and I can't free it. Goddamn it, I will *pull hair* if I have to, and I grab fistfuls of glossy caramel tresses in my fingers.

'Viola!' I wheeze.

The toffee-mopped body on top of me tries to grab for my other wrist and pin it down.

'Viola! You . . . fucking . . . *murderer*!'

Viola freezes, staring down at me as she sits astride my body, panting, eyes wide. Her weight presses me into the cabin porch floorboards. She might be on top, but I could try semi-scalping her, and I bet it would hurt.

We stare at each other, momentarily caught in mutual indecision.

'I'm not a murderer,' she pants.

'If you killed my brother, I'm going to rip off your head and spit in your neck,' I promise.

Convention dictates that she scream astonished protests, but instead she just stares down at me.

'It wasn't me,' she says simply.

I wait. We stare at each other.

Zero wasps. Not even a fly buzzing in the corner.

She's telling the truth. Goddamn it.

'Then who was it?!' I yell.

But she won't answer.

'What are you doing here?' she asks instead.

I consider telling her that a swarm of wasps that can sense lies initiated this current chain of events, but there's only room for one crazy person in the shack.

'I'm not even sure where here is,' I say.

'It's the Lugner family cabin, as if you weren't aware of that,' Viola replies, 'and you came here alone. I heard you approaching with all the quiet finesse of a T-rex crashing through the undergrowth. Besides, I have a GPS app tracking your phone. I knew you were coming.'

The Lugner family cabin thing we'll revisit. In the meantime –

'You put a *GPS tracker* on my phone?' I say, stunned.

'Yes, but –'

'Well, that's OK, because that's a normal thing for someone to do, or at least for someone who wants to hurt me!'

'I haven't been trying to hurt you,' Viola snaps. 'I've been trying to protect you. I only went and rescued you *twice* from the Hoffy Man cave – oh, and no need to thank me or anything.'

'Protect me? From the Hoffy Men?'

'No, from your girlfriend!'

I blink. 'Megan? Why?'

'Haven't you worked it out yet, Nancy Drew? Megan killed your brother! Megan killed Scott! And she's just spent the last few weeks trying to turn *you* into Megan 2.0!'

Congratulations, Viola, you have done what many before you could not.

You have managed to temporarily silence Alec 'the Mouth' Gray.

'Have they made Crazy Barbie yet?' I say, finally. 'You should get your agent to pitch you to Mattel as the model for it if not.'

'A – it's incredibly reductive and narrow-minded to call someone crazy,' Viola hotly replies, 'and B – you're a *lunatic*, Miss Hypocrite!'

'Me?!'

'You crash and totally *ruin* my photoshoot, demanding I spill my guts to *you*, a total stranger, about the traumatic events of my past. Then you join the local chapter of the Ladies Vengeance Club, and next thing you and Super Psycho are dating. What am I supposed to think?'

'And *you* terrorize me by following me around in a tinted sporty number, nearly get me arrested for speeding, destroy my car with "you're a giant murderer" graffiti and then try to run over my girlfriend,' I spit, highly aggrieved, 'and I'm just supposed to lie here and tell you in soothing tones how well balanced you are while you sit on my chest?!'

'I didn't know it was your car, I thought it was Megan's!' Viola shoots back. 'It was parked right outside her house! It was dark, I made a mistake! And I didn't run her over, I may have . . . I may have panicked a bit when I saw her. My foot slipped on to the accelerator. You try driving in Louboutin wedge boots!'

We glare at each other.

I break first. How did I miss that my stalker had been sporting *Louboutin wedge boots* when they were spray-painting my car? Suddenly I'm thinking of Short Round with boxes tied to his feet in the opener to *Indiana Jones and the Temple of Doom*, and before I can shut it down I let out a bray of hysterical laughter.

'What the hell's so funny?' Viola asks in an astonished voice.

'Nothing. Great tension release, though. You should try it sometime, you seem a little wound up.'

'You think *laughing* is the thing to do right now?'

'It beats screaming.'

We eye each other.

'Truce?' I suggest.

'Please,' Viola says with uncertain scorn.

'Come on. Let me up and let's chat like civilized bitches.'

'No.'

'So your alternate plan is to . . . what? Keep sitting on me? We're just going to hang out like this all day?' I consider. 'It's no hardship, actually. Honestly, this is getting kind of hot for me . . .'

'Oh my *god*,' Viola declares with what I take to be a rather insulting level of disgust.

She slithers off me, backing up into the cabin and getting quickly to her feet. Sometimes being inappropriate works where nothing else will.

I elbow myself up.

She points at my pockets. 'Weapons?'

I shrug. Fish out the hairspray can.

Viola nods. 'Nice.' It almost sounds sincere.

'Now you.'

Viola reaches into a bag and extracts a – 'Bowie knife?! Jesus, Viola!'

'It's multi-use,' she defends. 'My dad's passion is game hunting, he gave it to me for my fourteenth.'

She lays it carefully between us, next to my comparatively sad little bottle of hairspray. Both sit equidistant from us. Viola's gaze is suspicious, and her body tense, and she has a giant knife, and she comes from a hunting background.

And I'm alone in the middle of the woods with her.

'So what are you doing at Megan's family cabin?' I ask with the least interrogatory tone I can muster.

'Looking for evidence.'

'Ah yes. Your perfectly reasonable theory that I'm dating a murderer.'

'It's not a theory.'

'Without evidence, Detective Inspector Gordon, that's exactly what it is.' I can't help the laugh. 'You must hear how silly you sound. Apart from the fact that you and Megan seem to have fallen out big time and you both enjoy going around telling people that the other one is nuts, you're presenting nothing that convinces me you're not just having some kind of post-trauma break from reality. Now all the literature tells me I'm not supposed to say that, and I'm supposed to be supportive and on your side lest the accusation of your less-than-sanity antagonizes you into skinning me like a rabbit, but frankly I'm tired of all the bullshit, and at this point I'm running on empty. So unless you offer up some compelling evidence, I'm going to have to –'

'My god, you talk a lot,' Viola says. 'The reason I know your girlfriend murdered your brother is because she told me. That was why we fell out. When I saw you in the diner with her I knew she was deliberately getting close to you, cosying up to the sister of her victim. Frankly, I thought it was in poor taste, so I lost my temper with her. I regret that; I think it made her spend the next few weeks deliberately keeping us apart. I'm sure she painted me as a violent lunatic to you. That was another reason I kept following you – I wanted to talk to you about Megan. But every time I tried, someone else was there that made me think you were working for the other team. First Scott, then the cops. It didn't look good. So I got hold of your number and I tried texting you about Megan, but you never answered. I'm glad I followed you two when Scott took you to the cave, though. I didn't know what he was going to do, but I figured it might not turn out well for you. I got you your phone back from Scott, before he ran from me like his ass was on fire. That was the point when I put a tracker on it. Then you started to wake up. I saw you were OK, and I got nervous about you seeing me there, so I left. Maybe I should have stuck around, but then you called Megan to come get you. I'm a little mistrustful of anyone who hangs around with her, these days. Oh, and by the way, she also murdered Scott. Pushed him off a cliff. After she did it, she texted me saying, "You're welcome." I think that's everything. If you have follow-up questions, by all means, but try not to touch anything. I want to find usable fingerprints.'

She stands up, turns away from me, walks to the back of the cabin, and starts examining the furniture there. I watch her extract a roll of sticky tape from her pocket and carefully press a section of it on to the surface of a cabinet.

'What?' I say stupidly.

Viola doesn't reply. I watch her run her phone light carefully across a bookshelf.

'Maybe the "you're welcome" thing was a joke,' I offer.

'Pretty weird thing to joke about, wouldn't you say?'

'Some humour is ahead of its time,' I argue.

Viola blows out an irritated breath. 'Look, I'm sorry you're having trouble with it. And I completely get it. It is, I grant you, pretty fucked up. But there it is. We live in a dark world, soldier. You think it was fun for me, listening to her? You know how she told me that she killed Lucas?' Her eyes are far away, seeing something I can't. 'You know when a pet cat brings you a dead bird or mouse and lays it on the ground in front of you like a Christmas present? And they're looking at you like they expect you to be happy? And they can't understand why you're disgusted?' A pause. 'It was like that.'

My body didn't get the memo about my brain's resolute commitment to disbelief, so I completely fail at stopping the chill that ripples across my skin like wind through a corn field.

'Why on earth would she expect you to be happy about it?' I ask, for lack of a more incisive response.

Viola flashes me a look that signals supreme irritation at my wilful duncery. 'Obviously she's been offing the guys who attacked me. Justin's next, by the way. It's only a matter of time. Poor boy really needs to get twenty-four-seven security detail.'

I watch her crouch down and pick up something from the floor, holding it up to her phone light to examine it.

'A dust bunny,' I say. 'Compelling. Quick, call the constabulary!'

Viola squints up at me. I wait for another sharp retort, but instead she drops the bunny, wipes her fingers on her jeans and says, simply, 'I'm sorry.'

'Well, gosh, what for?'

'Fair. Look, that was all really insensitive of me. I've had time to sit with this, but you haven't. I understand your scepticism. First denial, then anger, then all the rest, right? I've been through it myself. Lot of people telling me that I'm post-trauma spiralling, telling me how to feel. Truth is, no one gets to tell you how you feel.' She shrugs. 'I'm not proud of the way I act, sometimes. And I've done things I'm ashamed of. But I'm trying to make up for it. You don't have to help me, or believe me. It's your brother we're talking about, and your girlfriend. You have every right to think I've lost it.'

I want to. I really do. The trouble is right now she's proving annoyingly lucid.

'Well, you know what they say,' I counter. 'That Veronica Mars, she's a marshmallow.'

'Do you always funny-quote your way through conversations?' Viola demands.

'With the difficult ones, yes,' I say. 'I use anything fictional, such as movies and song lyrics, to avoid expressing sincere and therefore frightening emotions. You?'

She gives me a considering glance. 'I pretend I'm vapid and shallow to keep people from getting close.'

I nod. 'Makes sense.'

And I join her at the back of the cabin.

'You're helping me?' she says, wary.

I pretend to consider the question, for her benefit. 'Well, I now know my brother didn't die by suicide. You – for whatever reason – think it's Megan, but if I was a betting gal, I'd put one down on Lugner Senior. Either way, we're both in the right spot.'

'Her father? What makes you think it was him?'

I snort. 'You've *met* him, right? Charming fellow. Pillar of the community.'

Later I'll deal with the hows and whys of someone like Juno DiCanso covering up for the head Hoffy Man, but for now I do recall what she said to her police chief about their 'deal' being off.

I can feel Viola watching me as I run my phone light over the floorboards. I'm thinking she might want to go in for round two, but instead she asks,

'What are you looking for?'

'Blood stains,' I reply. 'I'm crouched on the floor of a cabin in the woods owned by the head of a secret demonic mafia cult, looking for evidence that my brother was murdered here, my only companion in this sordid tale a social media influencer who wears platform Louboutins when she's tagging people's cars, presumably to help her in a quick getaway, and says things like "We live in a dark world, soldier." Even David Lynch would have trouble with this storyline.'

'Who?'

'The guy who made *Twin Peaks*,' I say, exasperated. 'Unbelievable. What are they teaching you in school these days?'

'I kind of hate that you're funny,' she says.

'I kind of hate that you're clever,' I retort.

I can hear the smile in her voice. 'Hey, did you ever –'

But I don't get to find out if I ever.

'What's this?' I hear her muse.

I turn away from my fruitless poking to find her crouched down, one slender arm rammed to the hilt underneath a creaky-looking dresser.

'What have you got?' I ask.

'My phone light picked up something shiny when I flashed it underneath the dresser, but it's . . . stuck . . . right at the back . . .' Viola's nose wrinkles in frustration, and curses foul enough to make a sailor blush spill from her coral-painted mouth. 'I keep grazing it with my fingertips, but . . . argh.'

I join her at the dresser, lying down on my stomach and trying to angle my phone to illuminate the sliver of gap between the dresser bottom and the dusty floorboards.

'I can see it, but the dresser's too heavy to lift. Hang on, if I . . . do *this* . . . and you do *that* . . .'

It takes some ungainly scrabbling, but between us we finally manage to wiggle and roll the shiny thing out from under the dresser.

It's a small, transparent glass bottle that fits into a palm. No label. The dregs of a colourless liquid pool at its bottom.

Viola looks at me. She carefully unscrews the top, takes a delicate sniff.

'Can't smell anything,' she says.

I eye her. 'Isn't Rohypnol odourless?'

'Shit,' Viola breathes. 'We need to get this liquid tested. And if it has Megan's fingerprints on it –'

'It also has yours and mine, now,' I point out.

She looks down at the bottle in her hand. '*Shit*. But I think they can separate them out, right?'

I shrug. 'I've seen the same *CSI* shows you have.'

'This could be it,' Viola says excitedly. 'The evidence we need.'

Behind me, a new voice joins in. 'Evidence of what?'

My heart bypasses the obvious routes and leaps straight back into my mouth, which it may as well make its new home.

'Megan!' I exclaim.

The Cabin in the Woods Part II:
The Reckoning

There Megan stands, framed in the cabin doorway.

The expression on her face evokes the husband who comes home early and catches the wife with the pool boy. 'This isn't what it looks like' would just keep playing us into the wrong scene, so instead I hit the concern button.

'Megan, I've been worried about you,' I say. 'You would not believe the crazy hell that went down at the picnic. Juno got *arrested.*'

'So you came . . . here?' she asks.

I consider this. 'Yes?'

'And then you found . . .?' Her gaze strays to Viola.

'She was here when I arrived.'

I glance at Viola, who looks like a cornered cat. There's no sign of the little bottle she found – she must have put it in her pocket.

'Babe,' Megan says calmly, 'can you come over here, to me?'

'Why?' I ask.

'Just come over here, OK?'

'Still peddling the "Viola's a violent crazy bitch" thing to everyone,' Viola says in a trembling voice, 'just to make sure no

342

one could possibly believe me when I tell them the truth about you?'

'Whose knife is that?' Megan says, pointing to the absurdly huge beast glinting dully on the floorboards. It sits, together with my hairspray, between Viola and Megan.

'It's mine,' Viola says. 'Ever since your confession I've been feeling like I need some protection on me.'

'What am I, a bear?' Megan jokes.

'No, you're much more dangerous.'

'Fellas, fellas,' I say, holding my hands up. 'Can we just take a minute here? Step away from the edge? Listen, Megan. Do you know where your dad is right now?'

'No,' she says. And then: 'I'm scared of him.'

Viola snorts. 'Why did you come to his cabin, then, if you're so scared? Why go somewhere he's likely to be?'

I shoot her a look, which she chooses to miss.

'It's not just his,' Megan says, her jaw tight. 'It's mine. I grew up playing in this cabin. Sometimes I'd sleep here overnight if I didn't want to go home. I'd lock the door and stay here and make plans to run away, but I never did. I was always too scared of what he'd do when he found me.'

'That is such crap,' Viola shoots back. 'You read in a book how psychopaths need a harrowing childhood background so people forgive them for the evil they do, so you made up a daddy monster –'

'Jesus, Viola!' I cut in, shocked. 'Stop!'

'It's OK,' Megan says softly to me. 'It's just how she is. I don't let it bother me any more. That's why she's angry with me, because I decided I would stop letting her hurt me.' She stretches her hand out towards me. 'Baby, come here. Just come away from her, and let's get out of here. I don't care what she's doing. She can torch the place if she wants. Let's just go away, together, somewhere safe.'

'Alec, don't!' Viola's voice climbs, urgent and frightened. 'Don't go off with her. I promise you, *I promise you*, I'm telling the truth! Please, don't trust her!'

'OK, OK,' I say with a calmness I absolutely do not feel. 'Look, there's an easy way to resolve things. You just have to trust me.'

'Alec,' Megan urges. 'Let's go, before she picks up that knife and –'

'It'll only take a minute.' I force myself to look at Megan. 'All I need is for you to look me in the face and tell me, out loud, that you didn't kill Lucas.'

Megan's expression goes cold. 'Are you joking?'

'Maybe if Viola hears it out loud from you, it'll help.'

'This is ridiculous, you're just playing into her delusion!'

'No, I'm not,' I say. 'It's quick and easy. Trust me. Just say you didn't have anything to do with Lucas's death, or Scott's for that matter, and we'll leave the cabin together, and we'll go wherever you want.'

Megan looks between us. A disbelieving half-smile plays across her mouth. 'And you'll . . . just . . . believe me?'

'Not if you get a face full of cricket,' I reply.

'What?'

'You don't have to understand it.' I give her a patient smile. 'Just say it.'

Megan laughs. 'Alec, this is so silly. I feel like I'm being punked.'

'Maybe,' I agree. 'Quicker you say it, quicker we can get the hell out of here.'

The moment stretches out. My pulse flutters.

What if she refuses?

Megan laughs again. Her hands throw up in a brief 'what the hell' shrug.

'OK,' she says. 'Alec, I am not responsible for Lucas Gray's death. I am *not* a murderer. There. You happy?'

I wait.

'What are you doing?'

I wait some more.

'Alec? Don't you believe me?'

No cricket. No spider. No wasp. Not even a goddamn fly.

Nothing.

Under the weight of both their puzzled gazes, I turn to Viola.

'You're crazy.' I am all wonderment. 'You've been crazy the whole time.'

'What?!' Viola thunders. 'I'm sorry. Did she just magically hypnotize you?'

'No.'

'So you just take her word over mine?!'

'No. There were no insects.'

'What?'

'No insects for Megan,' I explain patiently, 'but none for you, either. Now either that means the entire *Arthropoda phylum* has decided en masse that humans are allowed to lie again, or you really, truly believe Megan confessed to you that she murdered Lucas. Which, logically, makes you certifiably delusional.'

Viola's gaze swings between Megan's face and mine.

I feel Megan's hand slide into mine, and her subtle tug on my arm, pulling me closer to her.

'Please, Viola, and I mean this in the most compassionate way,' she says softly, earnestly. 'You need to get some help.'

In hindsight, I can absolutely see why that was the moment that pushed Viola over the edge.

A long, low groan interrupts us, stopping my heart. The blackness in the very corner of the cabin, where the electric overhead light doesn't quite reach, shifts like it's alive.

I am not on psychedelics, not this time. No one has drugged me.

Which means the demon I am seeing, crawling on its hands and knees towards us, is not a hallucination.

'Stop,' it says, in a thick, clotted voice. 'Stop, please.'

It is male, human-shaped. Its golden hair is matted dark, its skin is clammy, greasy. It wears battered Converse on its feet with hand-Sharpied wings on the side.

'I'm sorry,' it blubbers. 'I tried . . . to make it right. I tried. To take it back.'

My breathing must have gotten weird, because Megan squeezes my hand, and I hear her say, 'Babe, are you OK?', and I want to reply, 'Of course I'm not OK, my dead brother is in the room, my dead brother is here and he's wearing the clothes he was wearing the day he died and this is not him, it's not him but it is a nightmare of him, I live now in a nightmare.'

But none of that comes out, and the Lucas demon crawls closer towards me.

I can't breathe. I can't breathe.

'Make it stop,' I say in a high voice that sounds nothing like mine.

'I'm sorry,' Viola says. She looks sick and grey. 'Once it's out, I can't put it back in.'

'What? What, Viola?' I am dangerously close to losing whatever self-control remains in my possession. 'Why the *ever-living fuck* would you do this to me?'

'It's not your demon,' she says.

My skin tries to crawl right off my bones.

It's not heading towards me. It's heading towards Megan.

Who tugs on my hand, none too gently.

'What are you two playing at?' she says, sharp and cold.

But not frightened. Irritated, confused. But she's not frightened.

'Can't you *see* that?' I throw my free hand towards the floor.

'I tried,' whispers the Lucas nightmare, 'to make it right. I tried. To take it back.'

The knees of its dirt-covered jeans scrape across the floorboards.

I want to throw up. I want to cry.

'See *what*?' Megan angrily demands.

I search her face.

I glance at Viola, who just shakes her head. She looks like she's close to passing out.

The nightmare stops. There on its hands and knees, it chokes. Gacks.

'I tried,' it says again, 'to make it right. I tried. To take it back.'

It's like a vinyl record stuck on a loop.

You will never unsee this, sings my brain, *never, ever ever unsee —*

'Megan,' I say in a strangled voice, 'we have to run.'

'Run from what? Alec, this isn't funny!'

Holy Mary, Mother of God — *why can't she see it? Why can I?*

'Let's just leave, like you wanted,' I urge her, I beg her. 'Please! Let's go right now!'

'No!' She is suddenly and completely furious. 'What game are you playing with her? Are you on her side, now, is that it? Getting cosy with Killer Candy over there? Breaking into *my* family cabin, by the way, when you're already in trouble with the police? Accusing me of murder! Me! Your girlfriend! The fucking *leader* of the Kindly Ones! You're acting crazy, and it has to stop now!'

The nightmare's outstretching fingers are almost at her shoe.

I push Megan away, and she *actually shoves me back* – but I got her away from the demon, who has stopped in the middle of the floor, its head hanging low like a whipped dog. I don't know what happens if it touches her, and I never want to find out.

If I don't get out of here, I'm going to lose my mind. I can feel it fraying.

'Megan, Jesus God, just move!' I shout. 'Just go outside!'

'I tried to make it right,' I hear Viola murmur, 'I tried to take it back.'

I whip my head around.

'That's what Lucas told you,' Viola continues. She is crouched with her back pressed against the far wall, like it's the only thing holding her up. 'That he tried to make it right. He tried to take it back.'

'Take it back?' Megan sneers. 'No one can take that back.'

'I forgave him,' Viola says. 'I forgave him, and then you killed him anyway.'

'Forgave him?' Megan shouts. 'He *raped* you!'

Viola shakes her head. 'He stopped it. He was the one who stopped the ceremony. He got me out of the cave. I told you that, over and over.'

It's the best news I've ever heard. Even in the midst of this horror, my heart lifts.

He didn't go through with it.

'It doesn't matter!' Megan screams. 'The damage was already done!' Her voice turns bitterly whiny. '*I tried to make it right.* You feel sorry for him, is that it? Sorry for your rapist?'

'He didn't deserve to die,' Viola shouts. 'And neither did Scott!'

'You don't think that *jockstrap* deserved to die? He was never going to change, Viola! He was going to do it again, and again, and again, just like all of them. The world is safer without him in it!'

It's like a bucket of water has just been dumped over my head.

Megan notices.

She leans towards me, trying to take my hand again. 'Baby, it's OK. Don't let her upset you, babe. We make it right when we stick together. They can't stop a whole army of us, can they? We're stronger than them. Anything they do to us, we do it right back, but we do it times five. Whatever it takes. We have to be crueller than them. Deadlier than them. That's how we take back our power from them, right?'

'From who?' I ask in a dazed voice.

'Men, Alec,' Megan insists. 'All the *men*.'

A tremble runs through the demon's clammy body. It coughs, gacks like it's about to vomit.

At the same time, a succession of vignettes run through my mind.

Megan, finding me in the woods that first day. She was on a walk. She was on a walk in *her* woods, making her way to the site where Lucas's body was found, conveniently within dragging distance of her family's cabin.

Oh, god. Was she revisiting the site of his murder when she came across me?

I want to be sick.

That careful, watchful expression on her face every time I talked about Lucas. Asking me in the hospital: 'Do you think they deserve what's happening to them?' Kissing me when I said yes.

Was that when she went off and killed Scott?

Was it because I said yes?

Inviting me into the Kindly Ones. Setting me on my vengeance quest. Encouraging every dark, nasty impulse I had. Trying her damnedest to convince me that Viola is crazy, Viola is not to be trusted, Viola is a compulsive liar, Viola is violent.

All those moments I'm now revisiting, examining each one of her behaviours, her sentences, all the clues that were right there all along, flashing their shiny selves in my face, and I, too doollally over the hot girl to see them. Am I wilfully unable? Deliberately naive?

Or am I just supremely, outrageously, stupendously, prodigiously, monumentally, astoundingly, fantastically, tremendously, unimaginably, wondrously, staggeringly, extraordinarily, spectacularly fucking dumb?

Who would Juno and Martha risk their careers and prison time to protect? Certainly not Martin Lugner, Alec, you idiot. They'd do it for one of their own, though, wouldn't they? They'd close ranks.

Just like the Hoffy Men.

'Huh,' I muse. 'I think I know what that whole schism thing was about, now.' I force myself to look at Megan. 'It was about you.'

Megan laughs, but the expression on my face makes sure it doesn't last long. 'What are you talking about?'

'Here's the problem,' I explain. 'I have this strict policy of not dating murderers, especially, and I can't stress this enough, when they go around killing my family members.'

Megan gives me a look I'll never in my life forget. It is the exact look on my mother's face whenever I've done something wrong and she's counteracted with the 'I'm not angry with you, I'm just really disappointed' line that every child dreads.

For one red-hot second, I think the no-show insects are right, and I am wrong.

Then Megan's face suddenly crumples like a baby's, and her breath hitches dramatically in her chest.

'Oh,' she wails, 'wah, wah, wah.' Her expression clears, and she fixes me with a deeply scornful look. 'It's always the same. Women making excuses for the evil men do. It just about makes me sick, given the world we've grown up in. The stories we've heard. The constant, never-ending litany of things done to us. And no one gives a shit. Another hysterical girl, another sweep under the rug. The atrocities they commit. The daily, hourly *atrocities*. And I'm supposed to feel bad because a rapist got what he deserved? *I'm* supposed to feel *bad*?'

The change in her is astonishing. It's as though she's peeled off the mask that makes her seem normal, chopped through all the ties that keep her real self bound.

'Well,' I say, 'usually one should feel bad about murdering two people.'

Megan looks at me. Her expression is serene.

'Well, I'm sorry, Alec,' she says, 'but I don't.'

That's what makes it click.

The demons manifest for a sin committed to dog their victim through guilt, and the insects come when lies are told, to shame the liar by exposing them. But what if you don't feel any shame? No guilt? No remorse, no compassion, for the harm you've done? Maybe they don't show.

Maybe you can't even see them at all.

'I'm in love with you, Alec,' Megan says. 'I do feel good things. I'm a person, too, and I'm in love with you. I can't help it. I didn't mean to fall in love with you. But I've never felt this way about anyone in my life before.'

Then she extends her hand to me, like it ain't no thang.

Gosh, I'm thinking, *I wish I hadn't heard those magical words for the first time in my life from someone right after they just confessed to killing my brother. It almost seems a tad manipulative.*

She's taken my unresisting hand.

'Let's run away together,' she urges. 'Let's do something crazy, leave all this stupid, meaningless stuff behind. Let's . . . let's go to Scotland . . . to the Highlands, and do mushrooms in the forest, and be in love! Just you and me! No one has to know about anything we don't want them to!'

'It's too late for that,' Viola says, 'everyone already does.'

'What are you babbling about?' Megan snaps.

Viola points upwards, circles her wrist. 'Phone camera, on top of the cabinet. I've been livestreaming this whole time.'

The only sound is the Lucas demon circling like a dying dog around Megan's feet, wheezing and muttering its terrible litany.

'Bullshit,' Megan says in a new, terrible voice.

Viola just shakes her head. I can see the phone. It's the latest model, sat snug on a mini tripod stand that looks expensive, its unblinking camera eye trained towards us.

'You can break the camera, if you like,' says Viola. 'It's too late. I bet this'll be my most watched stream ever. I average around fifteen thousand viewers, even on boring days.'

Viola Gordon.

Louboutin-wearing, Porsche-driving, goddamn *genius*.

'Honey!' I exclaim to Megan. 'Did you hear that? You just confessed to the internet! You're going to be *so* famous!'

Megan is stood rock still. Her gaze flits from us to the camera.

When she moves, she does it with such calm, slow sureness that it takes me by surprise. I don't even react as she crosses back to the door – but Viola does. She jerks into movement, halfway across the room before she realizes that Megan isn't making a run for it.

She's locking us all in together.

I'm dimly aware that my only reaction so far has been to stand with my mouth hanging open.

Megan turns with her back to the locked door. Her hand disappears behind her, underneath her coat.

When it reappears, it's holding a gun.

I recognize it. Last time I saw it was in her father's hand.

'You know, pretending to find all your jokes funny has been the most difficult part of our relationship,' Megan says to me.

Viola barks a laugh, quickly swallowed.

Unbelievable. Everyone's a critic.

Megan points the gun straight at my chest. I want to cry, scream, run.

Instead I panic-babble: 'Megan, don't do this. Don't. We'll go do mushrooms in the forest together. I promise. We'll wear brown suede and have braids in our hair. I'll go sober vegan for you. Baby, please. Let's just go.'

'Well, Viola,' Megan muses, 'your life is a show, isn't it? So let's give your audience a really great finale. It'll have to be over-the-top, though, to compete with the sick shit you can see with the swipe of a finger these days, right? I know! How about a murder-suicide? All three of us going out together in a blaze of snuff drama? People used to have to see death all the time, back before we got all puritan and weird. I mean, I've watched two people die, and I personally don't understand the big deal.'

'Megan –'

My heart is pounding so fast I may puke, and the part of my brain not on overdrive trying to get me out of here intact is thinking about death, my death, and how annoying and disheartening it is that I'm about to find it at the end of a gun. A gun, of all things. I don't like them. I know that makes me a bad noir fan, but I don't. Should I point out the irony of a feminist using such a decidedly phallic symbol to kill us all? Maybe don't antagonize the murderer, Alec. Jesus, Alec, stop thinking about phallic symbols and come up with a way to get you the hell out of here!

But I don't, I can't, and it's the demon who saves us.

I'm pleading with Megan, I'm itching to fling myself bodily at her and risk getting shot, I'm saying things I'll certainly later be embarrassed by, but hey, the chance to be alive and embarrassed is one I'll take right now, when the Lucas demon stops its slow crawling on all fours. It suddenly surges forward and grasps Megan's ankle. It uses this leverage to climb swiftly upwards, clinging on to her like a crab, and then plunges its damp hand into her heart.

'I'm sorry,' it says thickly. 'I tried . . . to make it right. I tried to take it back.'

Megan's horrified eyes find mine. Her mouth pulls into a slow, disbelieving rictus.

The blood drains from her face so fast she seems to turn black and white before my eyes, pulled unceremoniously back into the pre-Technicolor past. Her body sags gently on the spot, as if her knees just lost all their lock. Her hand rises up to her chest and starts to tremble there, rubbing in erratic taps over her breastbone.

She might not be able to see her demon, but it sure as hell looks like she can feel it.

I sense someone standing beside me. It's Viola. She still looks decidedly pale and she's breathing hard, as though she's just about holding back a manic fit of laughter – but the expression on her face is cold, and deadly, and very sure.

Megan makes a funny noise, indescribable other than as a sort of whiffling sigh. Then she slumps to the floor, grey and weak. The gun drops from her slack fingers. I kick it quickly out of the way. As it skids across the floorboards, the demon quietly disappears.

The relief I feel nearly takes out my own knees.

Megan gazes at us both, panting. The hatred on her face is unmistakable. She seems too weak to move, but I'll take no chances. I pick up the gun and aim it at her.

I've never held one before. It's very heavy. Heavy, cold. Megan flinches, mouth moving soundlessly. She looks afraid. I guess that means it's loaded. I guess that means it could kill her.

I lower the gun.

Whatever I am, I am not that.

While I keep a wary eye on my ex, Viola scoops up her phone, and then crouches down to the floorboards for her Bowie knife.

'Do you want to get that coffee now?' I ask her.

'Gladly,' she replies.

We unlock the cabin, stepping out into the rustling trees, leaving Megan on the floor behind us.

Promising Young Women

Something seems to happen to the women who go down into that cave.

Not all of us. There must be women who are compliant, women who don't fight, women who go down, submit to a drug-induced stupor bacchanal, then come out, flush with the victory of securing money or power or favours for their men. Women who drink the Kool-Aid.

But for the women who fight down there? Whatever darkness is already inside us gets cut loose, somehow, and we bring it back up with us to wreak bloody vengeance. Viola with her demons. Me with my insects. No wonder they couldn't let the fighters back out. It's like letting out a monster.

I'll never really know what happened in my brother's version, though I can take an educated guess. Goes something likes this:

Golden boy tapped by popular rich scout for demon mafia talent agency to join ranks.

Golden boy thinks he's hit the jackpot, readily acquiesces to some of the stranger aspects of his new friends' social rituals.

Asked to nominate a ceremonial lady for his initiation, infatuated golden boy chooses his crush, Viola Gordon. Maybe he knew she was unwilling. Maybe he didn't. When he realized is up for debate, according to what you need to believe. But at some point during, confronted with a drugged girl, unconsenting group sex and knife play in a damp cave, he suddenly realizes this is not his idea of a fun night out with the boys, and ruins the show.

Haunted-by-demons downward spiral ensues.

I remember Viola saying in the cabin that once she'd let a demon out, she couldn't put it back in. Even if she forgave Lucas for his part in her ordeal, his guilt lived on to torture him. She may have conjured it, but he kept it alive.

Forgive, says the Church I've grown up in. You have to forgive, and be forgiven.

I've forgiven Lucas. When he finally woke up to what he'd chosen, he did everything he could to right his wrong, and bear the suffering brought on him by his victim.

I tried to take it back.

Yes, Lucas. You did. And you should have been given the chance to see it through.

I hate Megan. I hate her, viscerally, for what she's done to me, and I don't know if I can ever forgive her. I don't know if I can practise the tenets of my family's faith. I might not believe in God, but there are some things I do believe in. Some ways of seeing the world, of moving within it. It's just that not everything that is wrong is always wrong, and not everything that is right is always right. I hate Megan but I also feel sorry for her, trapped in a mind that sees what she did as the only solution. I hate Megan but I also thank her, for giving me back my brother. My Lucas, the one I knew. Lucaslot, Knight of the Round Table.

We all make mistakes. We all are led astray. It is what we do to try to rectify those mistakes that matters. But some people can't even face the fact that they've made a mistake in the first place, because to do so would be their undoing. They would rather live as a monster than ever face what they've done. Evil is easier, much easier, than good.

I could say that Megan is a monster. I could say that I'm nothing like her. But that's not quite true. I may draw the line at murder, but I feel that fury. I feel that darkness stirring inside me, sometimes, and I don't know who to blame for it. Me? Megan? Viola? Whatever it is in that cave?

Maybe we only become monstrous because something monstrous was done to us.

Plus ça change, you could say. Everyone hates a woman with power. But that's not true. Not everyone. Not Oh. Not Walter. And not me.

I confess I rather like it.

Cagney and Lacey

It's the end of summer, and the end of innocence likewise.

The heavy scent of drying seaweed throngs the air. The harsh cries of seagulls mingle with the jagged background hum of sweating tourists as they pull their screaming children around town on one last desperate perambulation before jobs and mortgages for square houses call them reluctantly away.

At one end of the boardwalk, a kid and his laughing parents toss greasy salted fries out of the cardboard cones clutched in their hands to the seagulls flocking in front of them, webbed yellow feet scrabbling for purchase on the ground as they fight each other for the food. At the other end of the boardwalk another child screeches with despair while her parents try in vain to comfort her, the poor tot's first taste of post-trauma shock in the aftermath of having had her ice cream snatched out of her hand by a dive-bombing seagull. Both of these events occur simultaneously, each family standing smack bang in front of a sign that warns every passer-by, in giant red block lettering, of both the short- and long-term consequences of feeding the seagulls.

I desperately want to make an observation about the state of humanity here, but Viola would get annoyed with me.

'A previously undetected heart problem,' she's saying.

Together we sit, perched on rickety chairs under a faded striped awning, sipping at iced caramel lattes and watching the seagull-baiting crowds go by. In deference to her fame, which these days has swollen to comical proportions, Viola is dressed in her now customary baseball cap and cartoonishly large sunglasses. Sculpted leggings, an oversized Marcy Playground T-shirt and designer yet demure sandals complete the 'I'm definitely not that chic celebrity you think I am' look she's going for, but people still recognize her.

'A heart problem?' I repeat. 'That's what they're saying happened to her in the cabin?'

'Officially,' Viola answers.

'Well,' I muse, 'your own invisible sin demon reaching into your chest for a game little fiddle around might well kick-start an issue with your heart.'

'Surprised they found one in there,' Viola mutters.

'Oh come on,' I say brightly, 'only I'm allowed to say mean things about my ex.'

'Sorry.'

I'm pretty sure I'm the only person Viola ever says sorry to and means it. I try not to take advantage of this as much as I can, but it's hard.

She tried to run. Megan. After the cabin.

She got two states away in a beat-up old gas guzzler bought from who knows where before the authorities caught up to her. She did not go lightly, from what I heard. She went kicking and screaming.

'You know,' Viola says in that too-casual voice she uses whenever she talks about the dreaded murder-prone ex-girlfriend to me, 'Megan once told me that when she was younger, she snuck down to the cave by herself. She'd been forbidden from ever seeing the site of "Daddy's little club", of course, but somehow she found out where it was and wanted to take a look. Maybe she came back out with a power of her own. Maybe her power was that she stopped being able to feel remorse.'

We exchange a loaded glance.

'Oh come on,' I goad. 'We're not going to tell each other our moon is rising and then compare notes on the supernatural energies we've totally felt in our lives, are we? *You* can't conjure people's sin demons.'

'And *you* can't pelt liars with insects.' She snorts. 'After everything you've seen, Scully, and you still don't believe?'

I study her. She gazes calmly back.

Instead of coming up with a good reply, I sigh and raise my eyes to the sky.

I don't know what I believe.

I haven't played witness to any more insect attacks, not since the wasps revealed the extent of the Kindly Ones' conspiracy to cover up Megan's murders – from Martha the coroner faking reports on the boys to declare a verdict of suicide, to Juno making a deal with the Hoffy Men via the chief inspector to keep it all quiet, any other evidence of wrongful death suppressed and the boys' families becalmed in whatever manner necessary.

Mutually Assured Destruction, as my mother described it: neither side would expose the other to justice, burying what had happened between Viola, Lucas, Justin, Scott and Megan for the good of their respective sides. No one would investigate or interfere. No damaged girls or boys would be going to jail for rape or murder for the rest of their lives, when their lives had only just begun. Let sleeping dogs lie, especially in an election year, and especially when the town was about to become rich from a billion-dollar real estate deal to develop the docks for high-end tourism, a deal that would fill the coffers of public budgets as well as private ones. Don't interfere with the wheels of money and power, not when everyone benefits.

Of course, then I came along and started interfering.

As much as my ego would love to take all the credit, I was but the latest in a line of women bravely going rogue to try to bring the truth to light. One being Eleanor Gray, mother of yours truly, and another sits before me in her Prada baseball cap. I'm but a lowly third violin to those two symphony soloists. However it happened, between the three of us, we blew the tenuous deal between the Kindly Ones and the Hoffy Men. Juno and Martha are under investigation. I heard the mayor's going to lose his bid for senatorship over the scandal. And last but not least, the high rollers have pulled out of the real estate docks deal, leaving not a few Hoffy Men on the verge of bankruptcy. I guess we'll just have to wait a little longer to be overrun by boutique athleisure stores, eight-dollar coffee shops that look like a Victorian industrialist fat cat's factory with the comfortable seating to match, and resort hotels with infinity pools and a thousand lawns of perfect, lifeless grass that no actual insect would ever touch. I'm not crying into my beer over that loss.

'OK,' I muse. 'Say, just as a thought experiment, what if what we saw – the demons, the insects – were, in some definable way that does not just exist inside of our own heads, real. What does that make us? What does that make whatever is down there? Is it good? Or evil?'

Viola shrugs. 'I don't think it's either, by itself. Is a knife evil? All I know is that it steered me true.'

'You've been torturing boys with it.'

'They tortured themselves,' she snaps.

'Said the Spanish Inquisitor to the dungeon guard.'

'You've been choking everyone around you with spiders and wasps!'

I sidelong her. 'So you believe it's real, then.'

'I don't even know what real means any more.'

'We should tell people.'

'Absolutely,' Viola agrees, 'on our way to the big padded room. Truth is personal. People can believe in things that to another person would sound insane. Belief is the most powerful weapon humans ever made.'

'What does that mean, Viola?' I ask drily.

'It means I have no idea how to describe what we saw and what we did to anyone but you. And even then you'd probably have a different version of it than me.'

'That makes the world a very complicated place,' I mutter.

'Doesn't it?' she says happily.

'Your enthusiasm for challenge is annoying.'

'So is yours.' Viola smiles.

When Viola smiles, she becomes her own sun. Megawatts. Julia Roberts in her heyday couldn't hold a candle. It's a hell of a weapon, and she deploys it ruthlessly.

'What's the word on the livestream, these days?' I venture.

Viola waves a hand. 'The viewing numbers are insane. My new manager called it the most audacious stunt an influencer has ever pulled off. Various true crime podcasts are clamouring for me to guest star. Hollywood producers keep trying to buy the rights to my "awesome meta-fictional web show".' She smirks at me. 'It's not all about me, either. The two biggest crowdfunding campaigns I've seen so far are: one to pay for your legal fees, should you decide to sue Megan Lugner for emotional and physical damages; and the other to pay for Martin Lugner's legal fees, should he decide to sue us for not getting his authorization to film our "cynical money-making stunt" at his cabin. Oh, and the costs he'll need to rebuild the cabin from scratch, after Megan torched the place before skedaddling across state lines.'

In other words, an absolute circus. I'd expect nothing less from our crazy, nightmarish, wonderful species.

'You can have a piece of the action, you know,' Viola says to me.

I shake my head. 'No, thank you. I've told you before. I can admire what you do, but I don't want to be a part of it.'

'You'd make a lot of money.'

And god knows we need it, but I don't want to make money that way. Of course, I'd never actually say this to Viola. Not every truth needs to be told out loud. (Check out the new maturity on Alecto Gray! Proud of me?)

'Maybe I'll write a book about it some day,' I muse.

Viola snorts. 'You'll make literally no money that way.'

My eyes roll.

I finally got around to applying for colleges next year. I've decided to major in journalism. When I told my mother, she laughed and said that it sounded like the perfect fit for me.

I think I could be good at it.

'What about the criminal investigation?' Viola asks me.

'Some people, it seems, actually did take the livestream seriously. Whether there's enough evidence to get it to court . . .' I shrug. 'But it was almost worth it to see the chief inspector's face when he had to announce the investigation into Scott and Lucas's deaths on TV. He looked like he'd been force-fed ground glass. And with all the publicity going on, Walter's managed to persuade his whole swanky city firm to get involved in building the case against the Hoffy Men, so we have you to thank for that powerful new muscle.'

'They'll make sure it goes no further,' Viola says darkly. 'The Hoffy Men. Quietly. Behind closed doors. Anything not to expose themselves.'

'Such a cynic.'

'I've never been proved wrong so far.' She pauses. 'I mean, except for you.'

'Me?'

'I did think you were a stupid lunatic.'

'No way, I thought the same about you!'

'I still think you're a stupid lunatic,' Viola continues, 'but in a sort of admirable way.'

'Why, Miss Gordon, I do declare. Is that a *compliment* I hear issuing from your cherry-coloured lips?'

Viola just shakes her head and sips her latte, the better to hide the smile struggling to the surface. Tippi recently told me that Viola hasn't smiled this much in years. Tippi doesn't seem to care that there's a potential new bestie in town. She's actually a lot of fun, outside of the Kindly Ones.

No, I have not retained my membership to that esteemed organization, and Viola was never, despite their best efforts, part of the club. Solo operators seems safest for now. I've always been highly suspicious of organized groups, and I'm pleased to have an excuse to double-down on this.

'Christien's been in touch,' Viola says.

'Lord,' I snort. 'I hope you gave him a good fuck offing.'

Viola hesitates.

'He's in a complete state,' she replies. 'He says his father's disowned him because he's been talking about the Hoffy Men to the media.'

I blink. 'Wow. Is that true?'

'Little bird told me that he and his mother have applied for witness protection, apparently at Christien's insistence. They're currently hiding out in some cheap motel a hundred miles from here.'

I whistle. Some life change. Still.

'He stole the necklace off you,' I say. 'The only evidence you had of what happened.'

'Well, I did steal it first,' Viola points out. 'And then I kind of stole his car.'

'He was one of *them*.'

'Now you sound like Megan.'

I wince. 'Ouch.'

'Sorry.'

I consider. 'It's OK. Point taken. But, Viola - he's still the mayor's son.'

'And he's got to live with that burden for the rest of his life. He didn't ask for it. He hates it. And he's trying to escape it. He's trying to atone. That's worth something. It has to be. I've seen what happens when you can't forgive someone who asks for it. It destroys both people.'

I think of Lucas. I think of Megan. I think of both sides of the coming war. Hoffy Man v. Kindly Ones. I think of us all, trapped in cycles of vengeance and destruction, both self and other.

'He doesn't deserve that,' Viola continues. 'And neither do I.'

I let this sit a minute.

'You're both braver and wiser than me,' I decide.

She smiles wryly. 'Or maybe I'm just more of a sap.'

I give this the due consideration it needs – at a guess, around four milliseconds.

'No,' I say. 'That is one thing you are not.'

Is that a blush I see stippling her bronzed cheeks?

I sit back in my chair. Cafe buzz swirls agreeably around us. Despite everything, I feel alive. Overwhelmed. And alive.

'We're a decent team, don't you think?' asks Viola.

'We've pulled off a heist together,' I concede.

'We could do more.'

I eye her. 'I said no to the podcasts, Viola.'

'Not that kind of thing.'

'What kind of thing, then?'

'Something like the Kindly Ones, maybe.'

My eyebrows crawl into my hairline. 'You want to do some vigilante vengeance?'

'Not like that,' Viola says. 'I mean . . . all right, yes, kind of like that, but with better intentions. We have . . . *powers*.' She hisses the last like it's a dirty word. 'We should use them. For good.'

'Said every Marvel villain ever.'

'Alec. Come on.' She gives a cross sigh. 'I'm just saying, we could be partners.'

'In what? Crime? Disaster? Nightmares? Listen, honey, I plan to kick back and milk these life scars for all they're worth. I've decided on my first nervous breakdown at the age of twenty-one, and hoo *boy*, it'll be a doozy. I might even buy a motorbike and start doing hard drugs.' I reflect. 'Though by that point they'll probably all be legal, at least in California. Why are the hippies so determined to spoil all the prohibited fun, I ask you?'

'This would be a way to harness our trauma and deal with it proactively,' Viola insists, 'not just sit here and feel like victims. Besides, you don't strike me as the passive type.'

Harness our trauma. God love her.

'Speak for yourself,' I reply. 'I've had enough excitement to last a lifetime.'

Viola scoffs.

'What?'

She shrugs. 'Nothing. I'm surprised a bug didn't just fly into your mouth, that's all.'

My lips tighten. It's a reflex, these days. As a result I talk less than I used to, and everything I say I carefully examine for scrupulous honesty before I say it. Alas, these fabulous probably-not-quantifiably-real powers of ours affect us too. Something about that is monstrously unfair, and also entirely fair, all at once. Whatever might be up there – God, the universe or other – it enjoys a joke.

'Excuse me? Um . . . sorry to interrupt you.'

A girl has arrived at our table. She's perhaps a year or two younger than us, and she has that badly suppressed trembly appearance I've become used to seeing since I started hanging out with a famous person.

'You're not interrupting,' Viola says graciously, her expression unreadable through her sunglasses. 'What's your name?'

'Um,' the girl manages. 'Um, it's Clara.'

'So nice to meet you, Clara. How's your day going?'

I once asked Viola why she had to save all her niceness for her fans, and never gave any to me. She ignored me.

'It's good,' Clara says, sneaking hesitant glances at me. 'You're, you're Alec Gray, right?'

'Me?' I ask, startled. 'Who wants to know?'

'Clara.'

'Right, right.' I search. First time I've had to do this. 'So . . . what's up, Clara?'

Was that a suppressed snort of laughter coming from the chair beside me?

'Um, well,' says Clara. 'I heard.' Her voice lowers to a whisper. 'I heard about what you did. You know. That you guys can, like, find out people's secrets? Like . . . their sins?'

And once again, ladies and gentlemen, Alec Gray finds she has nothing to say.

After all, I can't lie about it, can I?

'I was hoping you could take on my case,' Clara continues nervously.

At this point, I'm floundering. 'Case?'

'Well, your mom's that lawyer that's been in the news, and, with what you can do . . . I just figured. I heard. I mean. You might both be, you know. Helping people, on the down-low. Taking on cases.'

Viola is conspicuously quiet.

Confession: I don't really watch her livestreams. I already have an in on the minutiae of her life these days, and I don't really want to know what she talks about with her fans. I am only now realizing that this choice is to my distinct disadvantage. What has she been saying about me?

About *us*?

'Like some kind of private detective agency?' I suggest, my voice drier than bone dust.

Viola grins. 'Yes! Just like that.'

I cover my eyes.

'Don't worry, I know it's secret,' Clara cuts in. 'Word of mouth only. But . . . see, I'm in trouble. I need to find out if someone's lying about something. It's important. Like life or death. And I don't know who else I can go to.'

She looks, truth be told, a little wretched. Probably *not* a femme fatale, according to story convention, but then again, exactly what about my life has been predictable so far?

'I'm sorry,' I say. 'You heard wrong. We're not doing anything like that. Because if we were,' I turn icy, 'we would both be aware of it. We can't help you. Try the authorities.'

Clara looks crushed.

'The authorities,' she mutters. 'Yeah, right. This is not an *authorities* kind of problem.'

'I'm sorry, Clara. But it's for the best.'

'Well. Thanks anyway.'

'Good luck,' I tell her.

Clara spins on her heel and walks away, shoulders slumped so low they might as well be grazing the ground.

I look at Viola.

'What?' she protests.

'Nothing, PI Gordon.'
Viola just gives me that megawatt smile.
Play me like a violin, why don't you?
I sigh.
Then I call out, 'Clara! Wait a second.'

—FADE TO BLACK—

—CREDITS ROLL—

Acknowledgements

Thank you to Carmen McCullough, Jess Mackay and the whole team at Penguin for your work on this book, and for the Alecto Gray love. I'm glad she found her Marmite fans. A huge tip of the hat as always to Sam Copeland, for being on the ride with me since the beginning.